Redeeming Grace

By Ward Tanneberg

REDEEMING GRACE by Ward Tanneberg
Published by Lighthouse Publishing of the Carolinas
2333 Barton Oaks Dr., Raleigh, NC, 27614

ISBN 978-1-938499-47-0

Cover design by Ken Raney Art and Illustration:
http://kenraneyartandillustration.blogspot.com

Available in print from your local bookstore, online,
or from the publisher at: www.lighthousepublishingofthecarolinas.com

For more information on this book and the author visit: wardtanneberg.com

Library of Congress Cataloging-in-Publication Data Ward Tanneberg.
Redeeming Grace / Ward Tanneberg 1st ed.

Printed in the United States of America

Redeeming Grace uses omniscient point of view.

Lighthouse Publishing
of the Carolinas
www.lighthousepublishingofthecarolinas.com

Acknowledgements

Redeeming Grace is a work of fiction. Grace joined my family of characters over fifteen years ago, remained "in hiding" until now, but never went away. In this inspirational thriller, she has surfaced to tell us her story, about the power of choice and tragic endings and of finding a gift in plain sight, offering courage and freedom and fresh beginnings. She reminds us that grace is forgiving. Grace redeems and empowers when we have lost all hope. Grace exposes the layers of our hidden self. And to the degree and depth with which we open our hearts, God's grace is still a gift in plain sight.

Writers are always indebted to the many people who surround us with interest, supportiveness, patience, professional skills and love. Thanks to my agent and friend, Joyce Hart, and the Hartline Literary Group for the work you do and the encouragement you give; to Special Agent James Tracy, FBI ret., and the FBI Citizens Academy Seattle, for providing valuable insights into the world of counterterrorism; to the business and professional men who make our home a Wednesday morning gathering place in which to share spiritual journeys; to the ministry team, volunteers and the many friends who make up The CASA Network, for allowing me to share in your lives and work; and to the many who over the years have called me "pastor."

Of course, a book is never as good as it should be until it faces the scrutiny and suggestions of the editor. Many thanks to Rowena Kuo, whose suggestions and attention to detail make my work better; to Eddie Jones and Lighthouse Publishing of the Carolinas for your support and participation in turning this writer's idea into a reader's reality; to Bob Burger, who helped shape the Redeeming Grace discussion guide for book club and small group members (available for free download at www.wardtanneberg.com).

Many thanks to Michele for those "first Thursday" 5am coffees at Starbucks with your dad; to Steve, for making your hometown of Savannah come alive for me in this story; to Mark and Nancy for completing the circle of family; to our grandchildren and the "little dude" who never fail to light up our days; and to Dixie, for making every day in life richer for me and for everyone around you in so many ways, just by being in it. I love you, sweetie.

Ward Tanneberg

Ward is a pastor, writer and novelist. He speaks throughout the USA and elsewhere at leadership conferences and spiritual retreats on the high value of men and women "morphing at midlife and beyond in answer to Christ's second half callings." He has served as President & Executive Director of The CASA Network since 2008 (visit www.gocasa.org). Ward and Dixie have two children three grandchildren, four step-grandchildren and a great grandson. Their interests and ministry have taken them to many countries of the world.

For more information about Ward, or to follow his "A Further Journey" blog, visit www.wardtanneberg.com. For speaking engagements or information about The CASA Network, write to: ward@wardtanneberg.com or ward@gocasa.org.

Also by Ward Tanneberg

Fiction:
Without Warning
Vanished
Pursuit

Allegory:
Seasons of the Spirit

Historical:
Let Light Shine Out: a History of
Pentecostalism in the Pacific Northwest

Daufuskie Island, South Carolina

She dropped to her knees, oblivious to the shards of glass scattered about in the dark shadows. Each second passed like the chimes of a clock on the hour.

Unhurried. Sonorous. Deliberate. *Adagio*.

She stared down at her best friend, crumpled grotesquely on the flagstone terrace. Reaching out, she pressed trembling fingers against BJ's throat.

No response. Nothing.

BJ's deep, round eyes, always dancing with fun and laughter—everything in life, a party—stared back at her now.

Interrupted. Empty. Lost. *Caesura*.

Gone.

Beyond her touch.

Death sliced through the sultry night, like an arrow tipped with ice, plunging deep into her soul. Taking her breath away.

She could feel it.

She just couldn't stop it!

Her mind refused to accept whatever was next. There was no next.

Not for BJ.

Not now. Not ever.

Oh my God, what have we done?

A shadowy figure flashed across her peripheral vision and loomed over her.

She looked up at a man she did not recognize. He had a gun.

Where had he come from?

The rancid taste of fish and sweets and too much alcohol exploded without warning. She leaned forward. Hands on flagstone. Gagging. Heaving. Wiping phlegm and saliva with her fingers. The stranger grasped her shoulder with one hand until the nausea passed.

"Stay right here," he ordered, his voice hard and gruff. He turned away and disappeared around the corner of the house, calling to someone as he hurried out of sight.

How many of these people are there anyway?

Then the nausea returned a second time. She spewed another repulsive mixture of food and alcohol onto the flagstones.

Voices filtered through the broken window above her.

Words jarred her back to the moment.

What was it they were saying? She looked up at the window, incredulous.

This cannot be happening! She's still up there. With them!

"Ilene."

No answer.

She cried out again. "Ilene!"

"Go get her, and shut her up!"

Seconds later, she heard a door open and slam shut on the opposite side of the house.

The lump in her throat refused to go away.

He's coming back!

Do something.

I don't know … what can I do?

Save yourself.

Her heart pounded—a wild, erratic staccato, like that of a deer that senses the crosshairs of the hunter's riflescope.

But I can't leave her … Oh, God, how can this be happening?

A last despairing look at BJ's lifeless form. The thought of Ilene … up there alone … with them.

Get away from this place. Run!

Scrambling to her feet, she turned to her left, stumbling as the sole of her high-heeled shoe slipped on broken glass. As soon as her hands and knees hit the flagstones, she was up again, running toward what looked to be a dirt path that led away from the house. With a desperate glance over her shoulder, she plunged headlong into the late night darkness, each step fueled by an incendiary mixture of panic and adrenaline.

Run.

A tsunami wave filled with fear and remorse swept her along the trail. There could be no stopping now. No turning back.

Run!

The path narrowed. Thorny brush stems lashed at her face, scratched her arms and legs, tearing at her dress as she flew past. A canopy of sugar pine closed over the path, making the darkness darker still, slowing her headlong flight. Eyes wide, hands extended in a vain attempt to split the darkness, she pushed deeper into the woods, straining to find her way.

RUN!

A shout from the house. "She's gone!"

"She can't have gotten far. Go after her. Don't let her get away!"

The second voice she recognized instantly.

Brandenbury!

Unnerved, disoriented, she groped her way along the path; her only sense that of heading into the island's interior.

Where am I going?

No matter. Just keep moving.

Away from that nightmarish house!

At last she stopped, bending down to remove her shoes. She clutched them in one hand and pressed the other against her knees, sucking air, heart pounding as she strained to hear the inevitable.

Footsteps!

At the sound, she bolted again, terrified. They were coming. She knew they would be. Getting closer. The words echoed in her ears. "Don't let her get away!"

What's going to happen to me?

Frantic, she didn't see the sharp bend in the trail until it was too late. Her ankle gave way as she plummeted head first off the path, sliding and rolling down a steep slope into a brushy thicket until coming to a sudden stop against the base of a tree. Stunned. Breathless. Unable to move.

Above her, amongst the trees along the trail, a light bobbed back and forth. She could see it. Someone was running. She could hear it. The light drew nearer. She could hear his heavy breathing. The footsteps slowed as they came closer to where she lay. And now she knew. Accepting the inevitable.

They're going to kill me!

1

"Marry me."

The words floated into her ear on his soft and husky whisper. She caught her breath at their sound, fueled by Brad's intensity. Like a match to dry kindling.

"Say yes, Taylor. Please, you have to say yes eventually. I'm not giving up on us."

It was the third time he had coaxed her like this, an ardent proposal of marriage. She turned to face him, gazing into eyes that teemed with adoration.

"You know I love you, darling," she said at last. "More than I can ever say."

"Okay then. So what is keeping you from saying 'yes?'" he asked, gathering her in his arms.

What is it?

A moment in time, that's what. One she could not forget. Not ever. She wanted this man. Wanted so much to say "yes" to him. Wanted to live the rest of her life with him. In this house and in his

1

arms. For years she had steeled herself to the fact that this could never be. Not for her, and certainly not with him. Not with any man. Yet finding Brad, getting to know him and the children these last two years, falling more deeply in love than she could ever have imagined, and right now swimming in that love's reflection as she looked into his eyes … no more hesitation. This was it. The wall was down! Like a huge rush, the suddenness of it left her breathless. And yet …

She leaned her head against his chest for a moment, collecting her runaway emotions, and with a sigh she said, "There is still something I have to work out, Brad … something I need to tell you."

His lips pressed against her hair, the softness of his breath disarming. Irresistible. "I know everything I need to know, Taylor. I know I've loved you for more than a year, almost two. I know my children love you. I know I want to marry you. I know I don't care about anything else." Then he grinned. "Wait a minute. You aren't wanted for bank robbery, are you?"

She poked at his stomach, firm from his daily exercise regimen. "You are crazy sometimes, you know that? No, I'm not wanted for bank robbery."

"And you haven't murdered an ex-lover and hidden his body in a trunk somewhere, have you?"

Taylor felt a sharp pang, avoiding his gaze. "Of course not … but Brad–"

"Then, please. No more 'buts,' my love. If you're so concerned about something from the past, we all have things we're not proud of."

Taylor's vision blurred with tears. "When I was about to graduate … I … something happened …" Her voice choked.

"It's okay." Brad, intent not to listen, brushed his lips against the warmth of her cheek and slipped into his pastor voice, the one filled with Sunday morning understanding and tenderness. "There are things we will both need to share with one another over time. But, sweetheart, the past is the past. You know how we talk about God putting our transgressions in the 'sea of his forgetfulness,' never to be held against us? Well, whatever it is you are so concerned about will never change the way I feel about you. Surely you know that. There will be lots of time later for us to unpack past fears and tears. But this is now. Let's focus on now and the future. There's nothing that's going to keep me from asking until you give me your answer. I love you, Taylor Nicole Carroll. Will you marry me?"

"But ..."

"No more 'buts.' Please. With you there's always something. You're unbelievable. Who do you think I am, the Pope? I've done my share of 'stupid' in the past. None of us qualify when it comes to perfection. It'll never happen. Not in ourselves or in those we love. I've known you long enough to know your heart, to feel your love, to know you're the one I want to spend the rest of my life with, the one I want my children to grow up with. I know they feel the same way, even if they don't always show it. They really do. And I know you love me. I know everything I need to know about you. So let's do it. There's nothing to hold us back. Let's get married!"

As Brad stepped back, the window's half-light held him in its golden glow. His large brown eyes, his sun-bronzed skin, the first gray flecks in his hair, everything about this man reflected the sun, moon, and stars, a universe to be explored. Taylor gazed at him for a long moment.

You don't know the half, my darling.

But her long-drawn-out resistance was melting, like the last ridge of snow in springtime. Brushing aside the troubling shadows she had lived with for so long, she did something she thought she would never do. She let go. Surrendered to her heart. Let caution and worry and vigilance drift away. The answer she'd wanted to give the very first time Brad had asked was on the tip of her tongue.

"Brad, darling," she whispered, "I … I love you so much."

Her words hung between them on the night air.

"You … you're … going to LA on Monday," she stammered, still struggling to collect emotions spinning rapidly as she spoke. "I promised to take care of the children while you're away, right? So, when you come back on Tuesday."

"Tuesday?"

"On Tuesday, I'll give you my answer."

"Not tonight?" His eyes searched hers for some explanation. "You're going to make me wait?"

"Yes," she said. "You've waited this long. Two more days won't kill you."

"Easy for you to say," he said, smiling ruefully. "But why Tuesday?"

"I need the time while you're gone. Time to be sure. Listen, darling, it's not about my love for you. You should know by now there's no question on that score. But I need time to be sure about me."

"I'm sorry. I should have shut up and let you offload whatever your concerns are. I pushed too hard, didn't I? Do you want to talk about it now?"

"Yes and no," Taylor answered. "Yes, sometimes you push too hard and no, I don't want to talk about it now. It's late. On Tuesday."

Brad shook his head. "You're a mystery sometimes, that's for sure, but one I want to spend the rest of my life unraveling. You leave me no choice, conundrum lady. I'll wait until Tuesday. I'll wait however long it takes for you to come to terms with spending the rest of your life with this poor preacher. And just so you know for sure, I'm waiting, but I'm not giving up on asking."

"Thank you," Taylor responded in relief. She threw her arms around him and pressed her face against his chest. "You are the most wonderful man in the world!"

Brad picked her up and whirled her around, kissing her again and again as crickets and cicadas joined in chaotic approval.

"Yes I am," he chuckled, "and don't you forget it between now and Tuesday!"

"Brad," she laughed breathlessly, "be still. You'll wake up the kids."

It was after midnight before Taylor was back in her apartment. Turning out the light, she walked barefoot across the bedroom floor and slipped beneath a single cotton sheet, her movements slow and relaxed. The California desert was like this in June, still warm even at this hour. She stretched languidly, curling around her pillow, relishing the ebullient mood she was in right now. Savoring the ceiling fan's whisper of air over her bed, she thought back on the day, concluding that it had been nearly perfect. As perfect and as wonderful as any she had ever experienced in her thirty-two years on planet earth.

And eventually it surfaced again, as she had known it would.

Yes, it *had* been a nearly perfect day. She saw again the look of love in Brad's eyes, felt their stirring kisses under the stars, the security of her hand in his as he walked her to her car, sensed the promise in their final kiss and the way he stood, hands in his pockets, caught in the headlights as she backed into the street. Closing her eyes she rearranged every mental picture one last time, relishing each one as something extraordinary. Something she had long felt certain would never happen to her. Ever.

At last the night drew her. Taylor smiled again and yawned. Slowly letting go, carried by a current of euphoria that promised a new and wonderful life with a man she deeply loved and two children she adored. Sweet moments. Drifting off, she remembered what Brad had said, the part about none of us qualifying when it comes to perfection. *God does love, doesn't he? I know that. And he forgives. I know that, too.*

Somewhere on the rim between awake and asleep, her thoughts continued drifting in and out. As her prayers and confidence in God had deepened through the years, she'd gathered up forgiveness and opened her heart to God's love, giving hers to him in return. But she tossed restlessly as long ago memories reappeared, hung like unwanted pictures on the walls of her heart. Haunting recollections that served as perpetual reminders of guilt. She was pretty sure God had forgiven her. At least on most days. The problem was not so much with God as it was with herself. That was the real problem, wasn't it? She had never been able to forgive herself. And she never would.

Then there he was! Dark and phantom-like, standing over her. Reaching for her the way he always did. Dread rose like a river at flood stage, sucking breath from her body. Her eyes flew open. She bolted upright, catching her breath, staring into the darkness. But like always, there was no one there. There never was. Slowly she sank back onto the bed and for a long while stared at the shadowy movement of the ceiling fan. And then she wept. Tears of anger, pain, suffering and loss streamed freely, soaking her pillow until at last she lay exhausted, emotionally spent.

The old fears were there again, front and center, as she admitted to herself the truth of it. What her relationship with Brad had been. What it was. It was all a fantasy. None of it was real. Picnics and swimming pools, a summer romance, a September wedding, a happy-ever-after life, her dreams of undying love, all lay scattered in pieces that could never fit together. What had she been thinking? Their whole relationship was built on flights of fancy. It could never be anything else. The Dark-One-Who-Was-Never-There laughed and shook his head, reminding her. She had always known it.

This is your reality, Taylor. Not that!

The growing realization pummeled her. The last twenty-four hours had signaled, not a beginning, but the ending of her desire to ever love or be loved. Warning signs flashed their neon messages on and off everywhere in the dark. They had been there all along. She had just ignored them.

You are a fool. A deceiver and a fool. A Judas!

You have no right to love anyone.

Not when it can place those you say you love in grave danger.

How can it not?

There is only one thing you can do that's right.

There is only one life you can live ... it's not with Brad and the children. It is the one you've been living for the last seven years. A life alone. In a crowd that can never suspect how alone you must remain. Get over it, Taylor. This is your real life. This is your only life!

The Dark-One-Who-Was-Never-There was laughing still. He was the part of her that leveraged guilt, that brought her back to earth in those rare moments she dared to step out from behind her wall and soar on flights of faith and fancy.

She glanced at the nightstand clock's luminous hands before turning onto her side and gradually letting go. Again. Good and bad had a way of meeting in the dark didn't they? Like hungry wolves, ripping and shredding and tearing their prey apart, leaving nothing more than a residue of never-ending guilt and sadness. She knew this. She had been here before. She had confessed to Jesus every sin she could think of many times over. It had been a long-standing struggle, but gradually she had taken his love into her heart and he had given her love in return. But the memories were never far away and like

7

tonight they riddled her soul with doubt. There was no way to erase them, no matter how much she wanted to.

The tenseness, the heartbreak, the lateness of the hour gradually faded as she prayed to be rid of her nightmares, to sleep, and if only for a few hours to dream of an extraordinary life with an amazing man and his two adorable children. Tonight she was free to dream. On Tuesday, she knew what she must do. She had declared her love for another and while doing so had shared with him the story of her life. Just not all of it.

That would happen on Tuesday.

Seven years had been a long time to remain alert. Too long. The protective guard she had so carefully built up and maintained over time was eroding, eaten away by the one luxury it seemed everyone else possessed and she could only wish for.

The feeling of being safe.

She was certain they had given up. Nevertheless she could not take the chance. They had stopped looking years ago. To them, she was unimportant by now. Forgotten. Already dead. At least that was what she wanted to believe.

She had run before. She could do it again. She *would* do it again. But the survival instincts she had at one time honed with an animal's sixth sense, had been overcome by a higher need.

The need to love. To be loved.

Only none of this made any difference now.

Not for survival.

Not for love.

It was already too late for that.

2

Shandrel Davis was there with his mom and dad and his little sister, Shona. They had been out of town the last two weekends, and he was glad to be back. He had missed singing along with the grownups and children who gathered here each Sunday evening.

It was a joyous song, and these were his people. The voices of men and women and children blended as one on the rhythmic lilt of a guitar, soft, enchanting, endearing. Hardworking folk, like his parents, mostly poor but proud in a good way. A handful of the 200,000 souls that lived here, two hours drive west of New Orleans on I-10. A good town and a good place to worship God with family and friends on a sultry Sunday night.

Holy, Holy, Holy—bringing to life words sometimes lost amid the rafters, the overpowering beam and glass and stone of grand cathedrals elsewhere in the world.

Lord God Almighty—but here tonight, in this humble setting an old hymn newly defined, made warm and beautiful by a roomful of believers.

9

All thy works shall praise thy name—The small children down front, lined up on the tile floor with Shandrel and Shona, their bodies gently moving from one side to another, embracing the easy tempo of the hymn.

In earth and sky and sea—The men and women stood shoulder to shoulder between rows of wooden chairs, their backs to the doorway of this makeshift little church, some with hands raised, others with eyes closed, hearts lifted in worship.

Holy, Holy, Holy—Out of the corner of his eye, Shandrel saw something roll beneath the third row of chairs. It bumped against the heel of an elderly lady's sandaled foot. She looked down.

Merciful and Mighty—Shona had turned and was looking back toward the door. Shandrel followed her gaze as a second object, shaped almost like a ball, came bouncing toward him along the narrow aisle between the chairs.

God in Three Persons—He raised his head and stared at the man who stood in the doorway. In the next instant, the man vanished. Shandrel glanced back at the worship leader, who had stopped singing, eyes tracking the bouncing object.

Blessed—the worship leader's look of split-second surprise turned to alarm, and then to overwhelming dread, as a sudden knowing filled his eyes—*Trinity!*

Startled worshippers stopped singing as the guitar dropped from his hands. Those along the aisle followed his line of sight, struck silent as the object bounced past.

Shona reached for it.

The old woman's warning cry was lost as the first grenade exploded directly between her and the man standing next to her, tearing apart her frail body.

An instant later, a second explosion rocked the building.

The melodic strains of their beloved hymn were transformed into a requiem of horror and pain. And dying. Dust and smoke, the smell of burnt flesh seared Shandrel's lungs. Bodies were flung in every direction with the deadly force of close-quarter explosions. Stunned, dazed, Shandrel could not hear at first. The sounds of crying and pain seemed far off, not close at hand. Around him those still standing began pushing and shoving and stumbling blindly toward the solitary exit.

He struggled to his feet, reaching for his sister. She wasn't there! Dad? Mom? Others propelled him forward now, pushing, shoving, desperate to reach the exit.

Bursting through the screened door, they tumbled onto the landing in a mad rush for the stairway where they were met by a hail of bullets. Pandemonium swept over the scene as defenseless worshippers became helpless targets. Round after merciless round tore into unprotected bodies. Some tried to turn back. Parents threw themselves over children. A young mother, baby in arms stumbled over the first stairway victims. Bullets tore into her flesh as she and her infant child plunged headlong down the steps.

Panic turned into hopeless chaos with people pushing to get out of the room while others tried desperately to get back. Shandrel's face and hands were crushed against the belt of the man in front of him. There was no place to run, no cover to hide behind. The first bullet went straight through his shoulder. Men, women, children fell indiscriminately as the merciless rattle of automatic weapons continued, offering a demonic benediction to what only moments before had been an innocent, peaceful gathering of Christian believers. And then a second round tore into his abdomen, driving Shandrel backward onto the staircase.

Seven heavily armed men continued firing round after round into

11

the crowd, pausing mere seconds to reload before resuming the deadly crossfire, until finally no bodies were left moving on the staircase.

With a sharp command from the leader, all firing stopped. As quickly as they had come, the killers vanished. Moments later the sound of vehicles roared away from the village center into the night.

An eerie stillness followed the cacophonous rattle of gunfire, broken only by the sound of rainwater running off metal rooftops into the gutter. The smell of cordite and gunpowder hung like incense over the dead and dying as the night air tightened its sultry grip. Rainwater formed crystal beads on windshields and engine hoods. The dim glow of a streetlamp at the corner spread slivers of light and shadow over cars and pickup trucks, a jeep, and an old panel van parked in front of meters with red flags. It was Sunday night. Past the time that coins were required. Until early tomorrow morning parking was free.

At the bottom of the stairs a baby's cry broke the deadly silence. Bleeding from bullet wounds and bruised from pitching and tumbling down the steps, Shandrel reached out to grasp a tiny hand.

"Shona?"

But it wasn't Shona.

What's happening? Why are they shooting us? Where is everybody?

His eyes closed.

The sound of sirens pierced the darkness.

§

Subject: Fwd: Reuters: Massacre in Lafayette LA
Date: Sunday, 06 June 06—11:00 p.m.
At approximately 8:00 p.m., tragedy struck in Lafayette, Louisiana, when at least forty-three worshippers, including fourteen children, at a Christian church gathering were brutally murdered in an attack that one survivor said lasted for five terrifying minutes. Authorities indicated that fourteen survived and were rushed to nearby hospitals, all but two wounded seriously in the firestorm of bullets and hand grenades.

No one has stepped forward to claim responsibility for the attack on this defenseless group of innocents. Reports are that the church group had been meeting on Sundays in a room directly above the store for about a year. Still, the question on the minds of the citizens of Lafayette and those charged with keeping the laws of the land is — why? Why this seemingly random act of terror on a group of innocent men, women, and children?

3

"That went quite well."

The voice was disguised, using new encrypted cell phone technology with a signal that bounced from tower to tower, country to country, virtually untraceable by even the world's best trackers, arriving seconds later in a cell phone pressed to the ear of a nondescript-looking man in jeans and a tan golf shirt, his only extraordinary feature a scar on his right cheek that ran through his beard almost to his ear. He stood near the entrance of Bloomingdales in McLean, Virginia's busy Tysons Corner Center, his eyes moving constantly as shoppers strolled past. But just as it had been since his arrival at the Tysons Corner Marriott the evening before, all conveniently ignored him as though he did not exist. And in many ways, he did not.

"It sends a clear message," the voice continued, a Swiss-German accent clipping the consonants. "I like that."

"Yes," replied the man. "It will keep things unsettled for the foreseeable future. Long enough at least."

"Are you prepared to concentrate on additional targets?"

"Yes."

"It has taken us longer to arrive at this point than I had hoped."

"I agree. But we are ready now."

"Our candidate. Is he still unaware?"

"Totally."

"And his backer?"

"The same. The backer is fixated on his own self-importance. Thinks he knows all and is in complete control. He's a cold one all right, ruthless, but clueless. Obsessed with dreams of power and glory, but useful for our purposes."

"All right then. It is time."

"As I said, we are ready."

There was a long pause. The sound of breathing. A sigh. Then a sudden change of subject. "I understand you have located the woman."

"We have. We were unsure she was still alive until recently. That we found her at all was Allah's gift."

"Of course," said the voice dismissively. "So, now that you've found her, make her disappear!"

"We must be careful until we know with whom she may have confided. A net has been thrown around her even as we speak. She is ours, there is no doubt."

"Good. It is important that you succeed this time." The voice paused, then, "Do you understand?"

The man's gaze followed a passing shopper pushing a stroller with twins. There was the briefest of wavering as he swallowed the angry response resting on the tip of his tongue. But he knew better.

"Yes," he said at last.

"This will be our greatest coup," the voice said, conviction punctuating each word. "Our enemies have been sleeping while our long-term investments have been put in place. It has taken years. This will be the tipping point. With this we will pierce the eagle's heart and bring the world to its knees. It is a great responsibility you have been given, one that has not always gone well for us in the past, as you know. You are certain that everything is in readiness?"

Another brief pause as the point pressed its way home. The man closed his eyes, quelling the rising animus aimed at the voice and the implied censure. Then once more came his one-word answer, "Yes."

"When we awaken our warriors it must result in a total victory that will be seen as our finest hour."

"I understand," the man repeated solemnly as people moved past in increasing numbers, unaware that the world as they knew it was about to change and that they had been chosen to help make it happen.

"Then let us go forward. *Allahu Akbar*."

"*Allahu Akbar*," the man murmured as he had done in so many places and at so many times before. Slipping the cell phone back into his pocket, he walked away and was soon lost among unsuspecting shoppers whose primary focus was centered on the latest fashions in myriad beautifully appointed window displays.

Not on the future of the world.

4

During the last five minutes, Calle Bodega, *street of the wineshop,* had lapsed into an exceptional serenity. There were few sounds. The muffled dissonance of morning traffic in the suburbs. A nearby bird song. Soft breezes stirring the pliant branches and lace-like leaves of a mesquite tree opposite the sidewalk, just beyond the driver's rolled-down window. That was about it.

From seven until seven-twenty, "going to work" activity had now and then broken the morning calm of this modestly middle-class stretch of four-year-old houses. Automobiles with lone occupants backed out of cement-covered driveways and onto the asphalt street, each one turning toward him, picking up speed, and then braking a short distance past his parked car at the stop sign on the corner. As they did, he wrote down the addresses, the license plate numbers, and the times of their departures on the small yellow pad resting on his ample lap. No particular reason. Just something to do while he waited. Anyway, it was habit. One never knew when little things like this might turn out to be important later on. In his business, detail was everything.

In the rear-view mirror, he watched as each driver slowed or came to a complete stop at the corner. Without exception, every car turned left instead of right before disappearing from view. He expected that. The main thoroughfare, East Palm Canyon Drive, was to the left, only three blocks away.

A few of the locals glanced at him as they drove by, passively curious at the presence of this stranger on their street. He busied himself with a manila file folder, holding it up high enough to be seen by oncoming drivers, careful not to reveal the fact that the folder was empty.

The *Sunland Realty* emblem, on the side of his silver Dodge Avenger, coupled with the *Century 21 For Sale* sign on the adjacent property, legitimized his being here. Everyone on this street knew the house was for sale. The owners had moved north last month. Job transfer. All the elements for his cover were in place. The leap in logic for passing motorists was not difficult. He was simply an agent waiting for a client who wanted an early morning showing.

He had noticed the *For Sale* sign in front of the house the day before on his initial "drive-by." A stroke of luck, actually. A quick Internet search and the rest was easy. The fact that *Sunland Realty* did not exist was lost on passersby. He was just another guy trying to make a buck, like them. Some smiled, one even waved while others looked away, preoccupied with more important things.

He stared down the two-block long, palm-lined street to where it curved right. From his reconnaissance visit the day before, he knew that Calle Bodega continued in a U-shape until it opened farther down onto the same cross-street that he could see a half-block behind his car.

As a matter of fact, it was situated in the midst of an older section of Palm Springs. One street over was a mobile home park, populated mostly by retired seniors who had made this locale their permanent homesite years ago, and by "snowbirds," who savored the temperate winter clime of the Coachella Valley for five or six months each year before returning to homesites in northern and Midwestern states and Canada. To the south and west, behind the row of single-story, tile-roofed residences and the nearby mobile park, Mount San Jacinto rose abruptly, towering more than ten thousand feet above the sandy valley floor.

From the listing description and visitor comments, he had learned that Calle Bodega had been the site of a small, turn-of-the-century winepress, operated by an elderly Indian who had lived out his simple existence here in a shanty under a palm tree. At least that's what real estate people said in romanticizing this come-lately development tucked into an otherwise worn and unassuming neighborhood. The fact that grapes grown in this region were generally considered suitable for table use only, and that this Spanish word also meant *small market* was not lost on those who came to live on this street. One website visitor had joked that the street name more aptly depicted the decidedly unromantic and characterless quick-stop market and service station down on the East Palm Canyon corner.

Through the open car windows, he picked up the faint sounds of voices coming from behind the house next to the one for sale. Laughter, as two female neighbors commiserated over some indecipherable exasperation foisted on them by their children the night before. Sounds of a baby crying.

His oversized frame slouched behind the steering wheel, lifting and falling with a heavy sigh of boredom as he glanced again at his watch. Seven thirty-seven. A lad, about twelve or thirteen, with a pack strapped on his back, swung around the street corner, looking to his right and waving at someone the man couldn't see. With long, steady strokes, he rollerbladed along the street. As the young skater flashed by, the man gave him a quick look in the mirror, then turned his attention back to the house situated across the street two doors down. His hand fondled the camera lying in the passenger seat beside him. He was ready.

Glancing at his watch every minute or so now, he licked his lips, grunting and belching sourly, his stomach reminding him of the several bottles of beer and large greasy pizza he'd consumed the night before. His gaze returned to the white stucco house across the way.

It wouldn't be much longer now.

5

Brad ran water over the last of the cereal bowls, placed it in the dishwasher, then downed a final swallow of coffee before setting his cup on the washer tray.

"Hurry up, guys."

The children were still at the breakfast table, dawdling over glasses of juice and partially eaten toast, spread thick with peanut butter and jam. The Children's Bible, from which they had just taken turns reading out loud, was pushed to one side.

"Come on," Brad urged again. "Taylor will be here any minute, and you're going to be late."

Eight-year-old Nancy was first away from the table, a half step ahead of her older brother who was still busy cramming a last oversized piece of bread into his mouth. They raced each other, Nancy arriving at the bathroom door first. With a mischievous giggle she ran inside, pushing the door shut in David's face.

"Dad!" complained David, wiping peanut butter from the edges of his mouth with his fingers. He shifted from one foot to the other in front of the door, casting a doleful look across the room at Brad.

21

"Patience, son," Brad encouraged, and with a louder voice he called, "don't waste time in there, honey. We've got to go."

Moments later the impish-looking eight-year-old, sparkling brown eyes and long auburn hair, opened the door and absorbed her brother's glare as he pushed past her and slammed it shut behind him.

"Save the door, David," Brad called out, his eyes following his daughter, watching as she tossed her head in the same familiar way as her mother, causing her hair to fall delicately over the blue blouse of her school uniform. Her mannerisms. Her whimsicalness. The soft curve of her cheeks and nose.

You are so much like your mother.

David opened the bathroom door and came out, offering Nancy a sheepish grin as they stood together by the front door.

"Are you two ready for school?" Brad asked.

"Yes," they chimed with one voice, their sibling contentiousness already forgotten in the enchanting manner of children whose relationship is healthy, if not always tranquil. Brad often wished for this trait not to be lost on the adults he worked with on a daily basis.

"Don't forget your lunch money, kids. What's on the menu today? Do you know?"

"I think it's spaghetti and hot-dogs, or something," answered David, pushing his book bag against the wall with his foot.

"Now there's a balanced diet for you," Brad said with a grimace.

"But, Dad, the neat thing is there's only four more days of school lunches—and then we're free for the summer!"

"Well, hopefully you won't be eating hotdogs and spaghetti tonight."

"Where will you eat tonight, Daddy?" asked Nancy, with another swing of her hair.

"Probably at the hotel," he replied. "I'm not sure at this point.

And you guys are going to have fun with Taylor tonight. Right?"

"Yes," Nancy declared. "Taylor is always fun."

"I guess," was David's noncommittal reply.

Brad tousled David's hair. "You are such an enthusiast. I left the hotel phone number on the dresser in the bedroom. I'll call you tonight. Okay?"

"Okay," David answered, a trace of moodiness in his voice.

Just then the doorbell rang. Nancy ran to open it.

"Hi, sweetie," Taylor greeted her with a hug, dropping her overnight bag on the floor.

"Taylor!" Nancy's arms went around Taylor's waist and held her tight.

"Hello, David."

"Hi."

Brad waited for Nancy to turn loose and then gave Taylor a hug of his own.

"Hi. How are you doing this morning?"

Taylor's eyes sparkled. "What do you expect? It's a great day. Sorry to be late, but traffic is a bear this morning."

"It's okay. The guys are ready."

Taylor smiled at the children, then back at Brad.

"I hope you enjoy your day at the studio. You love shedding your pastor role and doing this gig, don't you?"

"I do. And I intend to enjoy, given how I feel about things right now. Especially today."

Taylor jabbed him, wrinkling her nose, an indication she knew what he was thinking. "Are you still worried about Howie and—what's his name again?"

"Gary. I'm okay with it. Howie's bringing Gary by the hotel. We got on really well when he was younger, but a lot can happen in a kid's

23

life in five years without a mom." Brad glanced at Nancy and David. "I'm sorry this turned out to be happening today. As much as I like getting together with these guys … " his voice lowered as he grinned, "I would much rather stay home and … well, anyway, Gary and I will get reacquainted tonight, and then maybe I can find out what's eating on him. I'll take him to breakfast before he goes to school. Then I'll head home."

"Do you know what has Howie so concerned?"

"Not really. I just know he is. I'll find out."

"Well, have some fun while you're at it. Take a real day off from being a pastor, okay? And don't worry. We'll be fine. Won't we, guys?"

Nancy grinned and nodded enthusiastically. David shuffled his feet.

"Okay," Brad echoed with a slow smile. He took her in his arms, and they kissed.

"O-o-o-o," both of the children intoned together, giggling as they watched. Brad chuckled as he glanced down at them standing by the door, backpacks strapped over their shoulders. Even David seemed to be enjoying their affectionate display. He kissed Taylor again.

"Oh, yuk," sputtered David, wrinkling his face. "Come on, Dad. We'll really be late for school if you guys don't stop kissing. Let's go."

"And I'll be late for work," declared Taylor, easing herself out of Brad's embrace and opening the door.

Nancy and David ran out to the driveway and climbed into the car.

"Don't sit on my clothes," Brad cautioned as David plopped himself down in the backseat. Brad had taken his carryon case and garment bag to the car earlier in hopes of finding the newspaper while he was outside. But the delivery person had been late. Now he spied it at the edge of the driveway, but before he could pick it up, Taylor had it in her hand.

"Sorry, darling," she said, opening the door to her smaller, ten-year-old Mazda and tossing it inside. "I'm taking it with me to enjoy at lunchtime."

"But it's my paper," Brad feigned his protest.

"Mmm. Deal with it," laughed Taylor. "You're out of luck."

They kissed again, and she lingered in his arms before gently pushing him away.

"Thanks, sailor," she said in her most sultry voice, smiling as she wiped lipstick from his lips with her fingertips. "But you still don't get the paper."

"A cruel and heartless damsel," he growled, opening the car door and sliding in behind the steering wheel. "What am I letting myself in for? Anyway, 'bye for now. Have a good day, and I'll see you tomorrow. Let's all of us have dinner together tomorrow night. It will give us some special time. All right?"

"Sounds great."

"Come on, Dad," David urged from the rear seat.

"Be careful," Taylor called after them as Brad backed out of the driveway. "Kids, I'll pick you up between four-thirty and five. Okay?"

Taylor watched and waved as they drove away. Nancy waved back through the rear window. She stood in the driveway until they reached the corner. A glance at her watch said it was nearly eight o'clock. Broadmores of Palm Desert didn't open until ten. Today, however, there was a department training meeting scheduled at nine. On top of that she was this week's designated "opener," which meant arriving a half hour early each day. She went back into the house, hung her dress for tomorrow in the closet, set out the rest of her personal things, then walked to the door, shutting and locking it behind her.

Seconds later, she dropped into the driver's seat, adjusted her skirt, and fastened the safety belt. Turning the ignition key, she glanced over her shoulder to check the sidewalk, put the car in reverse, and rolled back into the street. That's when she noticed the car parked in front of Louis and Emily's house.

The house had been for sale since Louis transferred with his company to Las Vegas. There was a man standing on the sidewalk, taking pictures. As she drove past, the man's back was turned. He seemed focused on the house. She decided it must be a realtor or someone interested in buying. Checking her rear view mirror, she slowed to a stop at the corner. The car had not moved. The man was still standing on the sidewalk.

If he did have a buyer, Taylor wondered if they would have children David and Nancy's ages. That would be nice.

He dropped the camera through the open window onto the passenger seat, swearing under his breath.

She'd seen him.

He would have preferred otherwise, but through the telephoto lens he sensed that she'd noticed him as she backed out onto the street. He should have quit taking pictures when she first got back in the car. Did it matter? He didn't think so. She couldn't have recognized him. Pretending to photograph the house for sale had been cover enough. Besides, there was no reason for her to be suspicious. Not after this much time had gone by.

He came around to the driver's side and got in. It was definitely her, all right. The hair color was different. And it was cut short. But there was no mistaking her face. And that figure. She still looked as great as the first day he had laid eyes on her. Exactly seven years ago.

Reaching into his shirt pocket, he pulled out a cigarette, lit it, and drew deeply. Exhaling out the open window, he started the car and released the brake, deciding to take the long way around the U-shaped street back to the other corner. As the car rolled out onto the street, he punched a series of numbers into a cellular phone.

6

Broadmores' summer sale training session ended with coffee, rolls, and conversation as coworkers from other departments visited with one another, catching up on the latest. Taylor made her way to the home furnishings showroom floor, sat down at the nearest station, and began the customary routine that officially opened the day's business.

Jim Flessing and Kaylin Martin, the other two salespersons on duty this morning, offered to open the other stations themselves. Taylor handed them the moneybags she had retrieved earlier and returned to her task.

It was a familiar routine. A menu appeared on the screen. *Open register.* Push the *Enter* key. Give the computer the last four digits of your social security number. This was security's way of double-checking any person who dared enter the hallowed repositories of Broadmores' cash funds. Once the drawer opened, she counted the pennies, nickels, dimes, quarters and the currency that had been left from the night before. It totaled exactly $300, as it was supposed to. Noting this amount on the appropriate data sheet she placed the form in the media drawer where, by the end of the day, all the store copies of sales receipts would also be stacked.

Then Taylor turned back to her computer and logged on, checking first for email messages from various buying officers, operations and store managers, as well as other company officials. She checked the last minute information on special closeout items and noted a problem with a particular manufacturer's delivery date on one of her earlier sales. No surprise there. *Carolina Desks* was notorious when it came to on-time deliveries, but the price and quality of their product made them one of the most popular manufacturers among her customers.

She glanced up at the clock above the storeroom doors. It was already five after ten. Taylor left the desk and made her way around the showroom, dusting lamps, fluffing pillows, cleaning fingerprints off glass table tops, and returning a special order fabric swatch book to the rack where it belonged before stopping by her IN basket for memos or phone messages. A pleasant rarity. It was empty.

Her mind wandered, as though thumbing through a stack of random, out of order photographs, scenes of what seemed to be her random, disconnected life. Brad. Nancy. David. The church. Herself as a pastor's wife—*what is that about?* Her job at Broadmores. Back and forth. Was it all finally coming together for her at last? Or was her dream closing out? Last night, after David and Nancy were in bed, she had even asked Brad if he wanted another child.

What was I thinking? I'm losing focus. I know it. I'm still trying to figure out what instant motherhood is all about, and I'm asking if he wants more? Taking on two young children would be such a major challenge. I don't know. It's hard to imagine being a mother. I'd given this whole idea up years ago. Even last night. I knew. But today, seeing Brad, feeling his kisses, touching the children, I want this life with them. I want it so much! I just don't know if I can go through with it. With everything ...

Putting on her name tag, she checked to be sure she had enough business cards to hand out, then returned to her desk and started thumbing through customer files. *Maybe I should say goodbye to my job. Brad encouraged me to do it. The church is growing. His salary is adequate for us to get by. So what's holding me to this place? Has Broadmores become my refuge from reality? Am I too frightened to give up what I know to tackle what I might never do well?*

For a brief instant, Taylor closed her eyes. *What am I afraid of, Lord? You are my refuge now. You are my strength. Aren't you?* She opened her eyes. *Well, aren't you? You brought us together. Didn't you?* The nagging thoughts were still there. Her fears refused to let go. Last night, she thought she had made the decision to explain to Brad and then leave. But had she expected her fears and her longings to simply disappear? She felt torn. And deep, deep down, Taylor knew the reason why.

At ten twenty-five the telephone rang. Her first call-in customer. As they conversed, Taylor spied Barbara Riley, a well-to-do widow from a posh La Quinta country club with whom she had done business before, stepping off the escalator. She waved as Mrs. Riley headed in her direction. Then another couple came into view. She remembered them from last week. They had been looking for a dining room suite.

Taylor, one of the most popular sales representatives in the store, sighed as she put the phone down. This was going to be a busy day, but that was okay. Staying busy was exactly what she needed to do.

7

It was one-fifteen before Taylor managed to retrieve her sack lunch and newspaper, making her way off the floor, down the escalator, and through the store's main exit. She crossed the street to her usual spot a block away, a bench on the promenade situated along the edge of a tiny park. After the initial lull, it had been nonstop customers.

What a morning! Good for commissions. Bad for my back and feet.

She looked around for Fred, the businessman from across the way who'd joined her on the bench with his book during lunch the past three days. Every day the same. Small rye bread sandwich and mineral water. That was it. Trying to lose some extra pounds, he said.

Fred was an executive transfer from Phoenix with a company just moving into the Palm Desert area. Their specialty was alternative fuel research and development, a welcome addition to the Coachella Valley's environmentally sensitive communities. His wife would be joining him when their house in Phoenix sold. Nice guy. Taylor enjoyed talking to him. No sign of Fred today, though. Probably already come and gone.

Today's brown bag lunch consisted of a lettuce, tomato, cucumber

30

and cheese slice sandwich. Dill pickle, whole. Small bag of chips. A Perrier that she'd kept cold in the employees' refrigerator. She watched as afternoon shoppers strolled past, her thoughts returning to Brad and her dilemma. For a long moment she closed her eyes. Then with a shake of her head, she unwrapped the sandwich and arranged the other items beside her on the bench.

It was warm today, even here in the shade. Not many lunchtimes left on this bench before saying, "Adios" until October. Summer temperatures in the desert usually ranged from 105 to 115 degrees, with occasional rare days that staggered past the 120F mark. That's when she condescended to eat in the second-floor employees' room. It was not an attractive place, and she avoided it as much as possible. But it was air-conditioned, and that was the deciding factor when it came to summer in the desert.

Taking a bite of her sandwich, she picked up the morning paper and glanced at the front-page color photo. She caught her breath, her eyes riveted on the face smiling back at her.

"What in the … Oh, my—"

She swallowed the bite, almost choking, and she chased it down with water from her bottle. She could not stop staring at the photograph. And the emblazoned headline directly above it:

SENATOR PARKER THROWS HAT IN RING!

Her hands shook as she dropped the remainder of her sandwich on the bench, next to the pickle and unopened chips. Taking a deep breath, her eyes remained locked on the laughing face of Noah Parker, United States Senator from South Carolina. And there was Parker's wife, Billie Lee, standing at his left, smiling and waving to the camera.

No. Oh, please, no!

The words slipped from her mouth, more like the whimper of

a terrified child than a prayer. She stared at the picture. There were three other men standing a step behind the Senator and his wife. Two of them she didn't recognize. But the one to Parker's right—she would never forget his face! Her eyes scanned the brief story capsule beneath the photo. It promised a more extended biographical feature about the Senator on page 2:

Beneath ancient live oaks garnished with Spanish moss and lining the sidewalk embankment facing Fort Sumter, forty-nine-year-old Senator Noah Parker made it official last evening in his hometown of Charleston, South Carolina. On the site at which the first shots of the Civil War were fired, Senator Parker fired off his own volley, an emotional speech announcing his candidacy for President of the United States to a crowd of over a thousand cheering well-wishers and media representatives.

Parker vowed that he would assume the place recently left vacant by the untimely death of his colleague and close friend from Ohio, Senator Elwood Burton. While campaigning in Alabama for the presidential nomination, Senator Burton was killed in the tragic crash of his private airplane on May 20.

In one of American politics' more unique twists of fate, Parker, who had been on Burton's short list of vice-presidential candidates, now seems on the verge of inheriting the Senator's campaign chairman and most of his staff. In declaring his candidacy, he pledged to "follow in the footsteps of the man I have admired more than any other modern American leader, carrying on the fight for the heart and soul of our party and our nation."

Some view his candidacy as a long shot underdog presidential fantasy this late in the campaign with the nomination only weeks away. But with adequate financing and a political machine that is already well oiled and in place, political pundits admit that anything is possible. The charismatic and popular Parker is the fourth candidate in his party to officially declare for the coming election in November.

Seen with him are his wife, Billie Lee; South Carolina Congressman Lucas Austin; former Burton campaign chairman, Donald "the kingmaker" King; and business tycoon, Charles Brandenbury, a close friend and long-time supporter of Senator Parker. Brandenbury is thought by many to be among those certain to make Parker's own list of vice-presidential possibilities should the Senator be nominated at the forthcoming convention. [See PARKER, page 2.]

Taylor felt herself drifting, cutting loose from the world as she knew it. A world she had created to take the place of one in which she no longer existed. The surrounding buildings and people felt freakish and dreamlike, twisting in slow motion. She was nauseous. She was sure she was going to faint. Her sandwich forgotten, she fumbled again for the bottle of mineral water and pressed it to her lips, sipping this time, praying that the emotional tide threatening to drown her senses would recede.

The morning paper lay crumpled in her lap.

8

Back on the floor again, still reeling from the shock of the newspaper story, she spent more time than she should have with Mrs. Carrington, who was "almost ready" for the second, or was it the third time now? She just wanted to confirm the price she had been quoted on her last visit. There was still one other place she intended to look before making her decision. Taylor shook her head knowingly as Mrs. Carrington disappeared down the escalator. The woman was fishing for a further reduction in price. Oh well, that was part of the sales game, wasn't it?

A steady stream of customers wandered onto the floor during the remaining hours of Taylor's shift: a newlywed couple "just looking" for their first sofa; two gay men checking out the prices and styles of top-of-the-line entertainment centers; an elderly woman who kept insisting on seeing a specific brand of floor lamps that had not been manufactured in years. Kaylin had been tending the woman, but eventually brought her to Taylor for help.

At ten after four, Taylor began closing out her station. At four-thirty, she gathered up her purse and headed for the employees' exit. The afternoon heat wrapped around her like an invisible blanket. The desert had to have topped 100 degrees today. It felt closer to 110.

Unlocking the car door, she dropped her purse and the newspaper on the seat beside her, rolled down the windows, folded the windshield sun reflector, and stuffed it in the pocket behind the passenger's seat. The car was an oven. Summer was definitely showing up early this year. She wondered, what did people do around here before air-conditioning? It was a question she'd asked herself a hundred times since moving to Palm Springs and the Coachella Valley. Backing the car away from the curb, she eased out onto the street, thankful that she didn't have to find out the answer firsthand.

David and Nancy's school was located two miles from Broadmores. By the time she turned into the parking lot, the interior of the car had begun to cool down. Taylor parked in the shade of a lone Washingtonian palm, not that it would help all that much in this kind of heat. Inside the after school care center, she scribbled her name and the time in the parents' book at the door.

"Hi, Ms. Carroll." One of Nancy's young friends greeted her. At the sound of her name, Nancy looked up from the book she'd been reading and waved, then ran outside to call her brother. Through the window, Taylor could see David hanging upside down on the parallel bars.

"Hello, Taylor," the daycare supervisor called out from across the room. "How are you today?"

"I'm good, Mrs. Fernandez," Taylor lied as convincingly as possible. "Thanks for asking. Looks like they're keeping you on your toes around here as usual."

"I swear, these kids are wired to go on forever," the supervisor answered, smiling as she approached. "If we could just harness all this energy and plug it into that wall over there, we'd lower our electricity rates."

Taylor smiled. She liked Mrs. Fernandez. Slim, Hispanic, always a happy face, even at the end of a long day. The right woman in the right place. Working with kids like this, day in and day out, was a gift Taylor knew she didn't possess.

"Nancy tells me you're doing an overnight together."

"That's right. Brad's in LA, so I've been elected."

"Good luck with that," Mrs. Fernandez laughed.

"Hi." David's matter-of-fact greeting broke into their friendly banter as he and Nancy gathered up their book packs. "What's for dinner?"

"David—it's not even five yet. Dinner won't be for another hour."

"I'm hungry."

"So what would you like?" asked Taylor as they walked to the car.

"Dad's not home. Let's go to McDonald's!"

"If you're not careful, you'll turn into a Big Mac some day."

Once inside the car, Nancy spoke up. "I don't want a hamburger."

Taylor eased out into the late afternoon traffic.

"What would you like, sweetheart?"

"I want the 'Colonel.'"

"Ah, a more discriminating palate than your brother, I see."

"What's a palate?"

"That's something an artist mixes his paint on, stupid," David answered.

"Please don't call your sister 'stupid,' David. Besides, an artist's palette is not the same as a person's palate."

"Yeah." Nancy grinned, arms folded, triumphant. "And it's not polite to call people 'stupid,' stupid!"

"Okay, okay, you two, knock it off. How's the homework situation for tonight?"

"Done!" both shouted in unison.

"Are you sure?"

"Done!" they declared again, laughing, poking at one another playfully while Taylor fell silent as she drove.

"So how about Angelo's for pizza?" asked Taylor as they rounded the corner and started down Calle Bodega.

"Yea!" Nancy clapped her hands at Taylor's suggestion. "The world's best pizza!"

"It's okay," said David, "but my favorite is Round Table."

Taylor rolled her eyes as they came to a stop in front of the house.

"David, would you get the mail, please? Both of you guys go to the bathroom, and I'll be ready in ten minutes, okay?"

"Okay."

The car door slammed as David ran to the mailbox. Taylor followed Nancy up the sidewalk, unlocked the front door and entered, turning down the hall and into Brad's bedroom. Dropping her purse and the newspaper on the bed, she stood in front of the window, rubbing at the tension in her shoulders and neck. The brilliant pink and red bougainvillea that spread across the block fence beyond the small patio and the grassy backyard always lifted her spirits. Her thoughts turned to a day soon when she and Brad could have been here together in this room, in this bed, husband and wife. But what she had seen in the newspaper had rocked her to the core. Shadows. Memories. Why now? Had her visit last night from the Dark-One-Who-Was-Never-There been more than a nightmare? A premonition? Maybe a warning?

She heard Nancy flushing and washing in the bathroom down the hall. The front door slammed behind David as Taylor slipped out of her dress, and in its place, donned a loose-fitting blouse and walking shorts, the garb she normally referred to as her "desert uniform." She was tying the laces of her tennis shoes when David called from the kitchen.

"Taylor?"

*If I do marry Brad, will there ever be a day w*hen he calls me Mom? Taylor felt more nanny-like than mother-like. Particularly where David was concerned. Nancy would be easy, but David—well, it was different with David.

"Yes? What is it?"

"There's a letter here for somebody. No address. It must have been put in our box by mistake."

Taylor walked into the kitchen and took the envelope from David. Turning it over, she looked at the name typed across the front in stunned disbelief. Familiar. Terrifying. Sucking her breath away as if struck by an invisible blow.

"What is it?" David asked, watching her as concern all at once crowded past the usual non-committal tone he reserved just for Taylor. "Is something wrong?"

She caught herself against one of the breakfast chairs.

"Taylor?"

Dropping onto the chair, she stared dumbstruck at the words on the envelope. Familiar words. A name. A name that for seven years she had made herself believe no longer existed. Until now.

Grace N. Grafton. Personal.

With a finger she slid open the flap and withdrew a single sheet of paper. Her hands shook as she unfolded it. There were two lines, typewritten. Nine words. Each word hit her like a fist:

Hello, Grace.

Did you think we wouldn't find you?

Taylor sat frozen in disbelief as something else fell out of the envelope onto the floor. David bent over and picked it up.

"Hey," he exclaimed in surprise, holding it up so that she could see. "It's a picture of you. In your car!"

9

" ... you are right, absolutely. As I said a moment ago, my first priority will be jobs and the economy. We intend to give America back to the people. And, as I said, I'll make the elimination of influence-buying in Washington one of my first priorities when my new administration takes over the White House in January."

Noah Parker's nonstop smile seemed tireless, his salt and pepper hair glistening under the television lights while cameras gathered up his good looks. Reporters busily scratched notes on paper pads, and staff members feigned importance as they swished back and forth along the sides of the small conference room adjacent to the Senate Chamber. Their leader was in the spotlight, and they were eager to grasp this moment of glory with him.

"You can count on it, ladies and gentlemen. You have my word!"

"And how much southern-fried chicken do you suppose that will buy?" muttered Sandra Cole, who had arrived late and was leaning against the wall in the standing room only gathering of reporters and camera crews. One of PSBNC's finest, she was used to covering the

Capital beat and listening to political rhetoric pile up like humus in the back of a barn.

Next to her, Lora Hardin of CCN murmured, "You're a born cynic, Sandra. You've been in this business too long."

"What is your position going to be on public education, Senator?" shouted another reporter as hands shot into the air and voices clamored in hopes that their question would be the next one responded to by this, the nation's newest, and for all intents and purposes, the hottest presidential candidate.

"The percentage of students that don't finish high school continues to rise at alarming rates," Parker shot back with a disarming smile. "We all know this. And higher education is beyond the reach of many others who are deserving students. We know this, too. Great teachers can make a tremendous difference for students of every background. All children deserve great teachers. Every family should be able to choose an excellent school.

"If I become my party's nominee and am chosen by the voters in November, a focus on public education will be one of my top priorities, I can assure you of that. Furthermore, deserving students shouldn't need luck to get a good college education. The spike in higher education costs is disturbing. Public dollars belong where they can make the biggest difference. I will fight ineffective programs and bureaucracy and will do my best to see that the entire nation is engaged in the effort to improve our schools. You wait and see."

More hands shot up and voices rose in a discordant, but attention-demanding chorus.

"Senator, what about the tragedy that took place yesterday in Louisiana? It seems to have been a terrorist attack on a group of defenseless men, women, and children worshipping in a Christian gathering. Do you have any information that this might have been an

Islamic terrorist group? And do you think we're involved in, not just a political, but a religious war with these people?"

Parker's countenance changed, taking on an air of sympathy and grief; his tone, one of compassion. "I was truly heartsick when I received the news. It is a huge tragedy. Our office has been in touch with my Louisiana colleagues, and we're ready in South Carolina to do all we can to assist there. There is still too little information as to the perpetrators of this atrocity, but I'm sure state authorities and the FBI will get to the bottom of it soon. And to answer your question about a religious war, my answer is, no. We are a nation in which the right to worship God, however we choose, is paramount. For example, here on Capital hill, we open sessions with prayers from all major faiths, Protestant, Catholic, Jewish, Muslim, and Hindu, and will continue to do so. People will continue to worship God in America in various ways on their personal journeys of faith. We must preserve that right for all our citizens, and we will. That's all I can say about that at the moment."

"What about the entitlements issues like Medicare and Medicaid?"

"Health care entitlements are major issues, no doubt about it. We've got to take care of our seniors, and the time has come for Congress to nail down the kinds of adjustments and reforms that are necessary to rein in the costs while preserving the programs. I'm committed to help lead in that task."

"Senator," a familiar network news voice called out from the front row, "another major issue facing us these days is personal privacy and identity theft. Hackers are tearing us up at will. What can the government do to help in this regard?"

"A good question, Dan. It's a huge problem. The Information Age continues to take us by surprise, no doubt about it. Standards of personal privacy that we assume to be our right as citizens appear to be inadequate with all that the rapid changes in technology are forcing on us. We've become dependent on an infrastructure that is no longer dependable. Philip Zimmerman, the guy who created the most widely used email encryption software in the world, summed it up pretty well, I think. He says that 'when making public policy decisions about new technologies for the Government, one should ask which technologies would best strengthen the hand of a police state. Then, don't allow the Government to deploy those technologies.' He calls it a matter of 'civic hygiene.'

"Of course, I can't speak for the President," he continued evenly, "but I can assure you that, if I am elected, protecting personal privacy on the one hand while maintaining a government that is as open as possible on the other will be a high priority. It's the right of every American citizen.

"You all are bringing up some of our nation's most important issues. Next week I will present a ten-point plan for dealing with each of these. Our team is working on this even as we speak, so get ready."

Some heads nodded in appreciative agreement. This was what they wanted to hear. Others glanced at their colleagues and grinned with a slight shake of the head. Most of those present in Parker's press conference audience were veterans of the Hill. They had heard it before, all in one form or another. But they had to admit the guy was smooth, charismatic, and filled a camera lens as well as any movie star. And after all, that's what really won people's hearts and votes these days, not the issues. The cameras moved in on Noah Parker's smiling face, soaking up the appeal of the man's dancing blue-green eyes and relaxed countenance like a collection of illicit afternoon lovers.

"I can tell you this for absolute certain," Parker went on. "If we all pull together around this great country of ours, the job will get done. You can count on it. You have my word!"

"What's that supposed to mean—'you have my word?'" Lora had been standing along the back wall next to Sandra throughout the press conference.

Sandra smirked. "I think it means wear your hip boots," she said, kicking off her heels for some orthopedic relief while Parker fielded a question on the merits of the flat tax. Having heard the Senator before on this subject, she knew this one would take a while.

"How much stock can we put in the rumor mill?" whispered Lora. "I hear the Senator is quite a ladies' man."

"Well, take a look. What's not to like? I mean, the guy's a hunk, isn't he? He's better looking than John, Jr. ever was in his best days, and that's saying something."

"You really think so?"

"Come on. He's Camelot revisited, sweetie. A Kennedy do-over with a Carolina accent. Personally, I'd stand in line to audition for the part of Guinevere!"

"So, is our presidential 'wannabe' King Arthur or Sir Lancelot?"

"He wants to be both," Sandra laughed quietly.

"From what I hear, you might have to wait your turn for a night with whichever one he turns out to be."

"Yeah, I'll bet you're right on that. Speaking of Guinevere, I wonder what the Mrs. is like?" Sandra mused, glancing around the room.

"Devoted to her family and determined to redecorate the White House in all her favorite colors," replied Lora. "A combination of Michelle and Laura in St. John's knits … with a mint julep accent and in total denial where the Senator's wandering eye is concerned. She's sitting over there against the wall. Next to that guy, Brandenbury, the one with all the bucks. Can you see her?"

Sandra caught a glimpse of her just before Charles Brandenbury, seemingly absorbed in watching the senator's performance, leaned forward and blocked her view. In that brief instant, she was surprised to see Billie Lee Parker appearing crestfallen, the opposite of what Sandra had expected.

"Maybe I'll try for an interview later," she said thoughtfully.

"Lots of luck. I gather she's a pretty private person. Wait. Money Bags is moving. You can see her better now."

Brandenbury was leaning back in his chair, apparently satisfied with Parker's performance. Sandra looked at the candidate's wife with renewed interest. Whatever had prompted the dejected look on her face just seconds before was over. Billie Lee Parker once again appeared poised and lovely, arms folded over her navy blue suit jacket, eyes fastened on her husband as he answered a final question on campaign ethics. Was that thin smile camouflaging tenseness in the set of her jaw? Or was the woman simply uncomfortable with this kind of media circus?

"What do you think?" asked Lora.

"I think Lady Parker could probably give a seminar on the subject of 'The Relativity of Political Ethics and the Bedroom,' Sandra answered dryly. "She doesn't appear to be stupid. Who knows? Maybe she's got a few keys that fit doors around town herself."

At last Noah Parker had finished and was moving away from the podium, late for a dinner being held in his honor, he said. Reporters pressed forward, trying to get one more quotable comment for the upcoming news hour.

Lora glanced up as Sandra squeezed swollen feet back into her shoes. "Do you really think sexual morality matters to the voters anymore? I mean, to anybody but the religious right?"

"Are you kidding?" Sandra replied, incredulous. "Presidents have been doing the bimbo thing for decades, Lora. Look at the sleazy stories we've been covering lately. Nobody cares anymore. Not really. Just so long as it looks like the guy is taking good care of John Q. Public and has a knack for flexing the country's muscles in front of the world's mirror without getting us into any more really nasty wars. Just a little of that 'my old man is stronger than yours' thing, you know? The sort of stuff that all little boys have to do once in a while. If he makes sure Social Security and Medicare stay afloat for us, what does it matter if he makes a few 'indecent proposals' along the way?"

"I suppose you're right. The main thing people look for in presidential ratings is the guy's competency as a leader."

"That's the way the public sees it," Sandra agreed, gathering up her things. "At least it's what they want to see. You know the criterion we've all grown up with—'as long as nobody gets hurt, then anything's okay?' Well, that's the way it works here in Washington. We're not living in the Old Testament, girl, in spite of what some may say. It's the 21st Century. We took the Ten Commandments off schoolroom walls years ago and replaced them with condom machines for thirteen-year-olds, so we can't condemn a few dalliances on the way to the White House, now can we? Anyway, professional and personal ethics are two different stone tablets these days."

"Maybe," said Lora, sounding unconvinced as they headed for the exit, "but you really believe the decisions someone makes in their private life don't affect the kind of decisions they ultimately make in public life?"

"What say you, oh wise one?"

"I guess I'm not sure. That's why I'm asking. I think it could, though. Maybe it should. But, then again, you're probably right."

"I'm glad you finally recognize real reporter genius." Sandra chuckled under her breath. "Nothing is ever as simple as black and white anymore, girl. Life is too complicated. Besides, look what we've lived through already. The average voter is used to not expecting much by way of character from their Great Leader. In fact, it's what most people want."

"Why would you say a thing like that?"

"Hey, if the guy at the top is morally superior to the rest of us, we'll be even more nervous than we already are about him. It's kind of reassuring to know when the leader appreciates true beauty. You know what I mean? It gives all us girls equal opportunity."

"Sandra, that's sick. You're so bad!"

Sandra patted Lora's arm. "Gotta run, girl. See you on the tube."

"All right," Lora said.

"Hey, want to catch a late night snack somewhere?"

"I could do that."

The two reporters entered the hallway, joining other media members walking rapidly along the marble hall in the direction of the exit. From a reporter's viewpoint, the timing of the press conference couldn't have been worse. A key legislative vote had kept the Senate in session until after seven, forcing Parker to miss prime time for the evening news, except for the West Coast. No matter. Their respective bureaus were waiting. It was time to wrap up the story and catch a late dinner.

Camera crews were busy setting up by the time they reached the Capitol steps. Both women were on cellular phones to their studio counterparts, outlining their commentary. Moments later, while standing just a few feet from each other, their respective images flashed to New York and Atlanta as they highlighted details of the first Washington press conference of the nation's newest presidential candidate.

47

—ɯ— **10** —ɯ—

On the opposite coast, at that exact moment, a very different group of Parker's potential constituents were standing before microphones of their own in a Burbank, California, recording studio, creating commercial radio station jingles. They were tired, but still having a good time as they always did whenever they got together.

Brad looked around at the others while they waited for the sound engineer's signal that he was ready to continue. They were definitely a motley collection with, for the most part, one primary thing in common. They loved to sing, and that love had turned this diverse group into more than just a good sound. They had become good friends.

Missy's long hair, with a kind of 'blond-for-now' look about it, ranged loosely over the shoulders of her pink blouse, a blouse that had hung half-in, half-out of her unbelted jeans all day long. It was hard to imagine her as the superintendent of one of the largest Southern California school districts, which in fact she was. She had once told Brad this was her idea of recreation, something that gave her white space in an otherwise margin-less lifestyle.

On the other hand, Joan's Korean-American extraction was very evident in her smooth ivory complexion, offset by jet-black hair that brushed the collar of an equally black blouse tucked neatly into the waistband of her pinstriped slacks.

Elizabeth's blond curls hearkened back to another era of Hollywood glamour, somehow softening the not-so-becoming look of a long blue dress. She kept glancing at her wristwatch. They were already overtime by thirty minutes and Elizabeth, a single parent with two school-age children, seemed anxious to leave.

Next to Elizabeth stood Fernando, a heavyset Hispanic man, wearing an orange T-shirt stuffed into green shorts.

Completing the cast of characters was Howie, balding and as black as an eight ball, with a shirt that sported a "WWJD?" logo across his thick chest. Obviously a body-builder, everything below his narrow waist had been stuffed into a tight-fitting pair of blue jeans.

Brad felt relaxed in his open-collared sport shirt, casual slacks, and tennis shoes. He couldn't help grinning as he brushed back an obstinate strand of hair. He loved this—being here with these people. These were his friends away from church. They asked nothing of him except to blend in and do his best as one of the best. Standing in front of a mike. Singing with the pros. It was great fun. Singing had been a big part of his life, ever since college days when he had worked his way through school as a singing waiter in a local Italian restaurant. Besides, he made a few extra bucks doing this, and every little bit helped on a minister's salary. But truthfully, he would gladly have done it for free.

"Okay, gang," said John Carey, the director. "I know we've gone over, but we're nearly there, so let's nail down this WCBB ditty and go home."

Each of the singers shuffled the pages of words and musical notes that their director had just identified as the "WCBB ditty." Missy cleared her throat. She'd been fighting a summer cold all day. Howie adjusted his mike. All eyes were on the man.

Carey turned to squint through a glass window into the semi-darkened control room. "You ready yet, Andy?"

The sound engineer's voice boomed over the speaker. "Sorry, John. All right, I'm ready. We'll over dub this one twice."

"Okay. Here we go. One-two-three-four—" John gave the down beat and six pairs of eyes somehow managed to follow his lead along with the words and notes spread out before them on their music stands. Their vocal blend was impeccable, each person possessing the kind of voice that, when put together with the others, became a perfectly balanced chord.

The thick purple carpet and specially engineered sound walls gathered up each word—

"oldies in the morning"—

poured them through six microphones—

"oh, what a thrill"—

carried them along invisible wires and imprinted every subtlety on audio tape—

"oldies radio ninety-six!"

In the next room, Andy tweaked one of the controls on the fully automated 48-channel recording console. He gave a hand signal. "Sounded better, except for 'six,' guys. Do over."

They repeated the process.

"Still not good, John. Sorry. Do over."

"Take one."

"We're fighting 'oldies' now, guys."

"The 'six' sounded okay, but the 't' in 'ninety' didn't align."

"Oh, shoot," Howie voiced his frustration, suddenly backing away from his mike as they broke off another take. "Sorry, John. It was like an involuntary muscle. I said 'seven' that time instead of 'six.'"

"That's all right, we'll get it. We need to make the solo sound slightly vocally and musically impaired. See it there? On measure five?"

"Got it."

"Here we go."

The six singers blended their voices, their eyes on John, striving to finish well.

"Great!" Through the control window they saw Andy's hand lifted in a thumb up gesture this time.

"All right, everybody, wait a sec. Are you sure we're okay, Andy?"

"Yep. It's a wrap."

"Terrific. Hey, thanks again, guys," said John, wiping at his forehead with the back of his hand. "You were great today. Just like always. Does everybody want to be called next time around? I'd sure like to have you, but I'm not certain when the next one will happen. The way things are going though, it could be as early as next month."

Everybody nodded, murmuring a confirming "yes'" and "sure, John," as they gathered up purses and music and miscellaneous stuff that had been dropped here and there during the last four plus hours.

Hugs, quick air pecks on cheeks and hurried farewells were passed around as one by one they moved through the studio doorway and down the hall toward the main exit. The "work" was over, though Brad's view of it was more of a day spent relaxing. A change of pace. He shook hands with John, said good-bye, and headed for the exit behind Fernando.

11

They had been seated around the table for five minutes; time enough to dig into a bowlful of chips and salsa before ordering the main entree. Iced tea all around, except Missy, who ordered a Margarita. Elizabeth and Joan had gone home immediately following the session while John had wanted to stay behind to listen to some tape playbacks. The others had decided to eat. Everyone was hungry.

La Fiesta was close by the studio and only two blocks from the hotel where Brad was staying overnight. Howie's son, Gary, had joined them for dinner, a good-looking lad of fourteen, but quiet and seemingly a little uneasy around his father's friends. Brad made sure he sat next to Gary and tried to engage him in small talk. It was not as easy as he had hoped.

At the far end of the dining area a trio of guitars and a pan flautist played and sang "south of the border" favorites while servers, carrying food and drink, expertly worked their way around tables at which diners in casual dress relaxed and conversed about their day. The place was noisy, with more customers waiting near the hostess desk and in the bar for a table to open up.

"It's a good sign," Fernando commented.

"What's that?" asked Brad.

"The place is full. People are waiting. The rule is never eat at a restaurant that has a near-empty parking lot."

"That's the rule, eh," Brad and the others chuckled.

"That's one rule. The other one is, never eat anywhere that doesn't have a Mexican cook!"

Fernando Ravez, husband and father of three and a successful insurance broker, was also the lead singer in a popular San Diego Latino group that worked one of the better nightclubs in that city on Friday and Saturday nights.

Howie White sat to the left of Brad. The senior member of the group, he facetiously called himself the "blackest White" in southern California. For the past eight years, Howie had turned the African American absentee father statistic upside down by single-handedly raising his only son, following his wife's death. An outspoken Christian believer, he made a modest living doing what he enjoyed, singing as a regular with the Los Angeles Opera Company and as a guest soloist at various churches throughout the Greater LA Basin. Kadisha had been gone five years now. Howie had never remarried.

The fourth member of the table group was Dr. Melissa "Missy" Brace, Riverside Public School District Superintendent, and a fine soprano vocalist. She frowned, her attention focused on the large menu. "How am I supposed to pick one thing out of a hundred that all look delicious?"

"What are the rest of you guys eating?" asked Howie. "Do yourself proud now, and next time I'll take you to the best 'soul food' shack in the Valley."

"Soul food?" Brad gave Howie a concerned glance over the top of the menu he was holding.

"You got it, bro," Howie smiled back, his big voice booming. "Sticks to your ribs, man, and fills your mind with fine thoughts."

"I can't wait," Missy retorted unenthusiastically, her face twisted

53

in feigned distaste.

"Ah, you highbrow *ejucators*," Howie responded by accentuating the word. "You just got to come on down the food chain a little ways and get it on once in awhile, that's all. It'll do your stomach *and* your soul some good now, and that's the truth!"

There was laughter all around. Even Gary smiled and shook his head, grinning at his dad.

Just then, the hostess who had seated them reappeared at their table. "Is one of you Reverend Bradley Weston?"

"I am," Brad replied, looking up in surprise.

"There are two policemen at the door who would like to speak with you."

Brad and the others glanced toward the entrance, but it was behind a wall and hidden from view.

"Well now, what's the good reverend gone and done this time?" Howie chided good-naturedly.

"Hey, man, you park in a handicap zone again?" asked Fernando.

"They probably want to show me your pictures to see if I recognize any of you," Brad retorted, pushing away from the table. "I'll be back in a minute. If the waiter shows, order me one chicken and one cheese enchilada a la carte. Okay?"

He followed the young woman across the room to the hostess table. Beyond the table, near the entrance, stood two uniformed highway patrolmen. The woman paused in front of the officers.

"This is Reverend Weston," she said, pointing to Brad. Then she turned away, directing her attention to a group of waiting patrons.

"Reverend Weston?" the nearest officer repeated his name.

"Yes."

"You reside in Palm Springs. Is that correct?"

"That's right. Is something the matter?"

It was such a short distance from the hotel to the restaurant that he had not driven his car and his first thought was about where he had parked, wondering if something was wrong. But that didn't make any sense. His car was in the hotel parking lot. Besides these were highway patrolmen, not local police. Then a feeling of apprehension swept over him.

"Wait a minute. Has something happened?"

"Please step outside for a moment, sir," the officer responded, turning to open the door. Just then three more people entered, and the officer stepped to one side, waiting. After they passed, he proceeded through the doorway, continuing until he was well away from the entrance. Brad and the other officer followed him outside.

"Reverend Weston," the second officer began as they paused near the edge of the driveway, "we're sorry to have to interrupt your evening with bad news ... "

"What's happened?" asked Brad again, steeling himself for what he suddenly sensed was coming.

"You are acquainted with a Ms. Taylor Carroll?"

"Yes."

"You have two children?"

"Yes, David and Nancy. What's wrong?"

"Reverend Weston, I'm sorry to tell you but Ms. Carroll and your children were involved in a serious accident about three hours ago on Interstate 10, east of Palm Springs. Actually, the accident took place near Rancho Mirage. Apparently Ms. Carroll's car swerved into a left hand lane and was hit by a tanker truck. CHP dispatched us to find you."

Brad felt himself go numb.

"Are they ... ?"

"Your daughter has a broken arm, but your son is in critical

55

condition. So is Ms. Carroll. We're here to take you to them."

Brad's knees suddenly felt weak and rubbery. He wondered for one crazy second if he was going to pass out. Taking a deep breath, he willed himself to pull it together. "Wait here. I'll run in and tell the others what's happened and ... "

"There's no time, Reverend," the first officer said gently, placing a restraining hand on his arm. "We'll call the restaurant and leave word from the car. It's already taken us a while to find you. If you want to see Ms. Carroll ... and your children, I'd suggest we leave right away."

Brad hesitated for an instant as the implied gravity of the officer's words set in. "Okay. Let's go."

"We're parked around the side," the first officer indicated, leading the way at a brisk pace. The second officer walked beside Brad. As they rounded the corner of the building, Brad glanced about for a patrol car. The patrolmen continued walking.

"Where's your car?" he asked, looking again at the dozen or so vehicles parked in front of him.

"Right over there," replied the first officer. "We're in an unmarked car."

Brad pulled up abruptly.

"Wait a second." Tentativeness now adding to his mix of shock and grief. *What's wrong with this picture? Two uniforms but an unmarked patrol car?* "How did you guys know where I was having dinner?"

The first officer returned his gaze but made no effort to respond. Brad felt a sharp prick in his left arm, halfway between the elbow and shoulder. Wincing in surprise, he turned to the patrolman standing beside him.

"What was that?" he asked, rubbing his arm with his hand. "What are you doing?" Again no answer. "Hey, what's going on here?"

He stepped back but, for some inexplicable reason, the pavement was not where it should have been. Instead, the parking lot was starting to spin, slow at first, unsteady, then with increasingly sickening revolutions. He felt nauseous as he stumbled, knew he was falling, but couldn't stop. He tried moving his feet again—demanding that they take him away from these two—only to sag against the nearest officer and watch helplessly as the parking lot opened up and swallowed him.

Half-dragging, half-carrying Brad, the two officers were only steps away from a dark blue sedan when another car turned into the parking lot and came to a stop three cars away.

"Look, something's going down, Jackie." Mark Hollis pointed as he opened the car door.

"Leave it alone, Mark." Jackie put a hand on his arm. "Don't get involved, okay? I'm hungry."

"Hey, you guys need help?" he called out, ignoring her urging. "I'm a police officer, off duty."

The two dressed as patrolmen hesitated, then continued to shove the limp form into their car. "It's all right. This guy's just passed out."

"Is he okay?"

"Yeah, too much alcohol."

The young off-duty policeman came around to his companion, who by this time had let herself out of the passenger side and was standing near the front of the car, waiting.

"Where are you taking him?"

There was no response.

The car door slammed shut and both patrolmen turned toward the off-duty cop. Hollis took a step toward them and then hesitated. Something was not right.

"Hey, where are you guys from?"

It was only a split-second, but it was long enough. With no

warning the nearest patrolman drew a handgun and leveled it at the off-duty cop.

Hollis' eyes widened at the sight of the weapon, at the same time taking in the significance of the extra long barrel pointed at him. Definitely not standard police issue. He gestured protectively toward the woman, moving between her and the man with the gun.

"Run, Jackie—"

Phfft. A deadly pop, partially muted by the attached silencer. The young man's knees buckled. *Phfft.* With the second shot he was all the way down, one leg twitching helplessly. Then nothing.

Jackie stood frozen.

She didn't scream.

It was more of a whimper, like a frightened animal.

And she didn't run. She wanted to, but she couldn't.

She stared in disbelief at Mark, sprawled on the asphalt surface in front of the car. Her mouth worked at forming a cry for help, but the word stuck in her throat, and her feet remained fixed to the pavement.

She saw the shooter's hand move ever-so-slightly in her direction. *Phfft.* In a split-second the bullet tore into her chest.

With a groan she staggered back, clumsily reaching out to break her fall, sliding down in an awkward position against the front bumper of Mark's car. Her left hand reached up in a futile attempt to stop the unstoppable. The man moved quickly. A half-dozen steps. The barrel of the gun loomed large in his hand. She knew then. Her eyes closed. *Phfft.*

Back to their car. Seconds later they were headed east away from the parking lot.

A full five minutes went by before another car turned into the restaurant, wheeling into the first available space next to a brown Honda. The driver skidded to a halt, narrowly missing the prone form of a man laying face down in the parking stall. His date grabbed his arm, crying out in shock as she caught sight of a woman slumped nearby in front of the vehicle.

La Fiesta's early evening diners were jarred from their casual camaraderie as the driver and his companion pushed through the entrance, yelling excitedly for someone to call 911. Soon, Ravez and the others were standing with a growing knot of onlookers, shocked, mesmerized by what they saw. But Howie was looking past the two bodies, his eyes scanning the gathering crowd.

"Where is he, guys?" he asked quietly.

"Where's who?" Missy responded, still overwhelmed by the sight of the two young murder victims mercilessly gunned down just two stalls from where her car was parked.

"Brad. Where is he? I don't see him anywhere."

At that, the others looked around as well.

"Maybe he's in the restroom," Missy suggested.

"I'll go check," Ravez offered, turning back to retrace their steps. A few minutes later, he returned, shaking his head. "I looked in the restroom. I even went back through the dining area again. He's not there."

As the trio stared at the bodies in the parking lot and then at one another, a police car, siren blaring and lights flashing, wheeled into the restaurant driveway. Their voiceless concern continued to mount as their gaze returned to the two lifeless young people in front of them.

12

The two "patrolmen" turned onto a nondescript side street less than a mile from the restaurant, changing into slacks and sport shirts while Brad lay drugged and unconscious, slumped against a door in the rear seat. Wearing latex gloves, they worked swiftly without conversation, stuffing the police uniforms into a cardboard box and sealing it with tape.

A few doors away the street opened onto a main avenue with several small businesses facing out. Making certain no one was around, one of the men tossed the box into a garbage bin behind a neighborhood electronics fix-it store. Back in the car, they drove onto the avenue and headed for the freeway.

Two hours later, having given careful attention to the speed limit signs all along the way, they took the Gene Autry Trail exit and made their way to the Palm Springs International Airport. Instead of returning the car to the rental area, however, they found a stall in long-term parking not far from where they had earlier left a second car. The car they were driving was rented for five days, so no one would be looking for it, at least not for a while, and especially not here. When it was discovered, the information recorded earlier on the rental contract would lead investigators nowhere. With soft cloths, they wiped off any surfaces in the car that might have accidentally been touched with bare hands. They had been as careful as possible, wearing gloves most of the time. Still, they were professionals and understood the problem that even one incriminating print could produce.

It took less than three minutes to recover the second car, transfer Brad into it, and begin making their way to the exit. Back on the freeway they continued east for another twenty minutes to Exit 139 for Indio Boulevard, following the signs to Jefferson Street, then right on Country Club and left at Avenue 42. The Bermuda Dunes Airport was only a quarter of a mile off the freeway. Here, an all-white Learjet 60 stood ready and waiting.

The driver came to a stop, popped the trunk lid open, removed a collapsed wheelchair, unfolded it, and brought it around to the rear door. At the same time, the other man lifted Brad out of the back seat. Together they strapped him in the chair and covered him with a light cloth, making sure all the while that no passersby or any airport employee was near enough to observe anything out of the ordinary.

Brad's head drooped onto his chest as they wheeled him from the parking area, across the street and through the terminal entry. Once inside, two more men met them, one dressed casually, the other wearing a pilot's uniform with hat, white shirt and tie, dark slacks. The man pushing the wheelchair unobtrusively passed a small object to the man in the sport shirt who, without breaking stride, slipped it into his pocket and headed for an exit. The others kept moving through the checkpoint toward a side door beyond the counter area. Another reason this airport had been chosen. No tedious security lines.

Twenty minutes later the airplane, carrying two crewmen and three passengers, was given final clearance for takeoff. Flashing along the five thousand foot asphalt runway 10/28, the jet soared into the air, and with the grace of a white swan, banked gently over Indian Ridge and Palm Valley Country Clubs, turning eastward across houses and hills and away from the setting sun.

13

Charles Brandenbury pushed his way past several people who were waiting to speak with the senator. He grasped Parker's arm and drew him to one side.

"Where do you go from here?" he asked.

The dinner had started forty-five minutes late with Parker arriving even later, due to the press conference that had followed the Senate's narrow passage of a controversial environmental bill. The room was still bursting with excitement. There was glad-handing and posturing among the party faithful who felt they deserved a piece of tonight's limelight, and congratulations all around, though no one seemed sure of what part they might play after tonight. To top it off, Brandenbury's veal marsala entree had proven even tougher to stomach than Parker's distasteful pandering to the press. It seemed as though there would never be a suitable ending in sight, and he was ready for it to end.

This had been a *power room* tonight, the kind Brandenbury soaked up incessantly, even though he himself had not been on tap for any speeches. He preferred it this way actually, nights like this when the focus was on someone other than himself. He knew he was not what this night was about. What it *was* about had been carefully scripted and was being carried out meticulously. No, this was not his night. Not yet. He and Noah had agreed that he would keep a low profile until a week from today. Next Monday, on the steps of the nation's Capital, Parker would announce his choice for a running mate, this time early enough to make the evening news. Brandenbury intended to be certain of that.

Such a brief interlude between Parker's hat-in-the-ring announcement and the selection of his running mate was sure to evoke cries of protest. Especially among party leaders who would no doubt feel slighted at the lack of opportunity for input and, equally important, for consideration of their own worthiness.

The planned-for rejoinder to critics would be that Parker's late entry into the field required fast and daring action. Parker would, in fact, be the first of the candidates to name his running mate. This would free both men to campaign with high visibility in the few weeks remaining before the formal nominating process began.

Brandenbury was confident that most, if not all, of the delegates committed to the late Senator Elwood Burton would swing to Parker if they moved swiftly, before the other candidates saw what was happening and began making inroads. When time was taken to reflect on it, the pundits and politicians would interpret it as "decisive leadership," a harbinger of greater things in store for America, with Noah Parker as the bright, shining new president beating out a beleaguered incumbent for the nation's helm. In any event, it was what Brandenbury wanted, and Parker knew he had little choice but to accede.

"I'm in Dallas for a breakfast speech in the morning at eight, Charlie. Then on to Florida. We've got a rally in Orlando tomorrow, and before that I'm meeting with Dwight Horn and Lee Decker."

Brandenbury's eyebrows lifted in surprise as Parker continued. "King arranged it. Those two are major north Florida movers and shakers. They were real tight with Burton's camp."

"I know who they are," Brandenbury purred. "I just didn't know *you* knew who they were."

Parker let the remark pass as he continued, "They've got the votes, Charlie, and their hands are in some deep pockets for TV ads."

"Good. But keep in touch. Stay flexible. I have someone coming in that I want you to meet."

"When?"

"Thursday will be soon enough."

"What time?"

"I'll let you know."

"Thursday's going to be tight. I'm supposed to speak at a dinner in Cincinnati. They're holding a memorial for Senator Burton. His wife and family will be there, and I need to show up, too."

"Noah, hear me on this." Brandenbury leaned closer and whispered through clenched teeth. "I'm talking about what could well be the most important meeting of your—*our* campaign. So, when I call, you come. And come alone. No security people. Leave everyone else at home. You got that?"

"Yeah, sure, Charlie." Parker flushed angrily at Brandenbury's unmistakable lack of respect for the man of the hour, the man about to become president. "But that may not be easy. Who am I meeting?"

"An old acquaintance. Someone who has decided to be a donor."

"Oh, yeah? Who is it?"

"A surprise, Noah."

"How much is he pledging?"

"It's not a 'he.' It's a 'she.'"

"Really? Well, then, how much is *she* pledging?" Parker's curiosity was aroused even more.

"Everything she's got," was the terse reply.

14

Taylor's mouth went dry, her heart pounding.

That man in the car this morning! It had to be him. He must have been taking pictures of me!

She took the photograph from David. By this time Nancy had returned.

"Let me see, let me see," she cried, her hands reaching out in childlike impatience. "What is it?"

"A picture of Taylor in her car," David announced importantly.

Taylor fought to regain her composure.

Deep breaths. Keep your hands from shaking!

"It's only a picture, Nancy. That's all. Here."

She handed it over. David moved closer to his sister for another look.

"What does the letter say?" he asked. "And who's Grace N. Grafton anyway?"

"It's just someone's idea of a practical joke," Taylor answered, fumbling for an explanation that would seem logical to this keen-minded ten-year-old. "Wait. There was a man parked in front of the Schuster's house this morning. He was taking pictures as I drove past.

I think he might have been a real estate agent."

"I saw him, too," remembered Nancy as she handed the photo back to Taylor. "But he was just standing there."

"Why would he take pictures of you?" David persisted.

"It was probably just a mistake. He saw me back out of the driveway. When he realized what he'd done, he put it in your mailbox."

"But who's Grace Grafton?" David asked again.

"Whoever put this in the box must have put the wrong name on the envelope." Her mind was racing for anything that sounded logical. "Or maybe it was already on the envelope, and he just didn't take time to change it. That's probably what happened. He was in a hurry when he dropped it off. Anyway, it doesn't matter. Let's go eat, what do you say?"

"Yea," Nancy squealed. "I'm starving!"

"That'll be the day," snorted David. "Nobody has that kind of luck."

"David!" Taylor and Nancy exclaimed in unison.

"That's not at all nice, David," Taylor added. "Please don't taunt your sister like that."

"Okay, I'm sorry," he said with only the faintest touch of conviction in his voice. Under his breath he whispered, "but it's still a good idea."

Nancy didn't hear it. She was already out the door and halfway to the car. David followed after her while Taylor paused to lock the door. Turning toward the car, her eyes swept the street and the surrounding houses for any sign of the man who'd been taking pictures this morning.

I remember there was a name on his car door. Something-or-other-Real Estate. Was it "Desert?" No. Sunrise. Was that it? One word or two?

She couldn't pull it up.

Think, Taylor. Think!

The blur of disconnected thoughts swirled as she got into the car.

15

"Wait." Taylor suddenly turned and nodded to the children. "Let's go back inside."

They stared at her, open-mouthed. "Why?" they asked in unison.

"Because I said so," Taylor snapped, motioning to them again.

David shook his head, saying something unintelligible as he nudged Nancy. Opening the car door, Nancy jumped out, followed by David. Nancy ran around to Taylor. "What's the matter?"

"Maybe it would be better if we ordered pizza in tonight."

"But why?" Nancy persisted, accenting her disappointed tone with her tested and tried pouting look, the look she always defaulted to when attempting to weasel something out of her father. "I want to go to Angelo's."

"You guys have homework," Taylor offered lamely.

"It's done," David declared. "I told you, I did mine after school while we were waiting for you."

"Yeah, me too," Nancy chimed in. "It's finished. So let's go to Angelo's."

"Listen. I'm not feeling so good right now," Taylor said truthfully. "I could use a break here. I know you're disappointed, but I need for us to order in. Tell you what. If your homework's done, you can watch television until the pizza gets here even though it's a school night. Okay? I just need to rest for a little while."

"Okay." David shrugged his shoulders, the look on his face implying he still wasn't convinced. Back inside, the children made their pizza requests known, and Nancy went to turn the television on. But Taylor could feel David watching her as she searched the telephone book for the number. When the two had settled themselves in front of the TV, Taylor walked through the house, double-checking the alarm and the locks on the doors, and making certain all the windows were closed, latched, and secure.

Taylor returned to find David, remote in hand, flipping from one channel to the next while Nancy sat beside him on the floor, hands folded, looking on. *Is flipping channels somehow built into the male DNA?* "Come on, guys, find something and stick with it," ordered Taylor. As she turned to go, she glimpsed a fleeting image. "Wait. David, go back one channel."

David glanced at her, the "why" forming on his lips. But instead, he shrugged and pressed the channel-selector button again. A man's face reappeared. He was smiling into the camera, his deep southern accent pleasing and commanding, filling the room. "I can assure you that, if I am elected, the White House will once again be the house of the people. Every American citizen, not just the rich, the powerful, and the famous."

Taylor couldn't break away, unwilling to believe what was happening as the sound byte concluded, and the image was replaced by that of an attractive redheaded reporter declaring, "That's all the excitement here in Washington, Paula. This is Lora Hardin reporting from the nation's capital." Her eyes remained fixed on the screen as the scene cut away to CCN as an announcer promised more details ahead.

"Can we change it now?" asked David, waving the remote at her, his patience at an end.

Taylor didn't speak.

"Taylor?"

"Yes," she answered at last, her voice strained as her mind spiraled back into the room from the world of Washington and a politician's television pledge that "if I am elected, the White House will once again be the house of the people."

She looked in silent desperation at the two innocent children she had just locked up in their middle-class American house, aware of how pathetic her attempts were at protecting them against the powers represented by that Other House and by the man whose face she had just seen. The one she'd hoped never ever to see again. "Change it."

She turned and hurried down the hallway into the bedroom.

Letting out a ragged sigh, she dropped face down onto the bed and closed her eyes, willing the tension to leave her body.

Breathe deeply.

Release slowly.

It wasn't working.

Get hold of yourself, Taylor.

Try again.

Breathe deeply ...

Gradually her breathing returned to almost normal, and she thought again of the crumpled note in her pocket. Rolling over, she took it out and unfolded it. She stared at it before letting it drop beside her on the bed. Her hand brushed across the newspaper she'd gathered up from the driveway that morning. Was it only this morning? It felt like an eon ago!

Unfolding it, her heart skipped a beat before resuming its fierce, pounding rhythm as her eyes fixed on the man laughing at her from the front page. It was the same face that had startled her moments ago on the television.

The all too familiar headline burned like a searing iron: SENATOR PARKER THROWS HAT IN RING! Once more she glanced over the brief story caption beneath the photo. Then she turned to the biographical feature on page two, replete with yet another picture of Parker, this one posed in front of the Capitol Building in Washington D.C. It was all there. Born in the hills of east Tennessee, he had moved with his parents to Charleston when he was eleven. After high school Parker received a degree in Humanities and Social Sciences at the College of Charleston before pursuing a law degree at Tulane University in New Orleans. But she knew all that. He had told her himself!

Parker's vow that he would assume the vacancy left by the untimely death of his Senate colleague and close friend from Ohio contained more threat than promise to Taylor. His pledge to "follow in the footsteps of Senator Burton, the man I have admired more than any other modern American leader," and the assurance that he would "continue the fight he had begun for the heart and soul of our party and our nation," was a farce. A bold-faced lie. The Noah Parker she knew admired only one person. She was looking at him.

Washington pundits and so-called experts seemed to be all over the map, viewing Parker's late entry into the presidential race as anything from a "long shot upstart candidacy" to a "very strong and charismatic leader, perfect for the times we are in." The idea of Parker ensconced at a desk in the Oval Office turned her stomach. But with adequate financing and a robust political machine behind him, she knew instinctively that anything was possible. The public persona of a charmingly southern Noah Parker just very well might gather enough votes to win the nomination and, if he did, nothing would stop him after that. His next residence would indeed be the White House.

Yet as much as she despised Parker, he wasn't the one Taylor feared the most. She swallowed the sick feeling in her stomach, clenched her eyes shut, and tried curbing her emotions. It wasn't working.

Her mind drifted.

She felt numb.

The morning paper lay crumpled at her side.

Memories swept over her like an incoming tide.

Breathe, Taylor, breathe ...

She had worked so hard to gather those memories into one place ... then hide them in the darkest closet of her psyche, behind walls constructed with great care, taking years to build. In the end they had remained hidden, yes, but *definitely* not forgotten. And now ...

"Oh, God." Her lips shaped a silent desperate plea as she lay staring at the rotating ceiling fan, the jabberwocky voices of television cartoon characters drifting in from the other room. Her fingertips swiped at the tears she could no longer hold back. "What am I going to do?"

An upsetting blur of disconnected images swirled through her mind; all the "could haves" and "should haves" assaulted her like enemy fire on *Private Ryan*'s beaches. She had crept through this minefield many times, so carefully and for so long. Now it had all exploded without warning and in ruthless cruelty, like a roadside bomb laying bare the futility of her meticulous efforts at cover-up. So much time had come and gone. She'd let herself become a believer. But no more. Not now. Not ever again.

In spite of everything she had done to disappear from the minds of the others, they had found her. She had been discovered, her secret a secret no longer. It had just been ripped open with coldhearted vindictiveness by the only people who could possibly do this to her. People she hated. Evil people whose sudden recall numbed her with fear. More tears leaked onto her cheeks. She should have told Brad before now, should have made him listen. Soon he would know everything, and David and Nancy, too. But there was no one else to blame. She should have done it when she had the chance. A wave of shame washed over her, mingling with her tears. What will people say at work? At church?

What will Maggie say when she finds out? Will she think I've betrayed her, too? Of course she will, because that's what I've done, isn't it? There's no getting around it. I've done what I set out to do. I've deceived everybody, including myself.

They would all soon know she'd been living a lie. She'd tried hard to make a new life. She believed that God had helped her become a different person, but the note beside her on the bed confirmed her darkest fears. Nothing had changed. Not really. In spite of everything, the truth was in. She was not a different person after all. Taylor Nicole Carroll was still *Grace Nicole Grafton!*

Her secret was over.

She was sure of it.

Her life would soon be over as well.

She was sure of that, too!

Like Jericho of old, the walls behind which she had hidden her terrible secret and her darkest terrors for seven years were tumbling down around her.

16

Taylor's eyes flew open as she caught her breath.

What was that?

She lay motionless, listening for any unusual sound. But there was nothing. She sat up then, fingers rubbing her eyes and face. How could she have fallen sleep? Sleep was inexcusable. She had to stay awake. But a hoarded store of physical and emotional exhaustion, mingled with the euphoria of the weekend was like a drug, drawing off what little remaining energy she possessed.

She shook her head, clearing out a mental path littered with foreboding, like fallen leaves and broken limbs after a storm. The nightmare she'd managed to briefly hold in check came back with numbing force. All evening she'd felt its crushing weight, at times so much that even breathing was hard.

Long and slow. And deep.

Get hold of yourself, Taylor ... Grace ... whoever you are!

Staring across the darkened room, her despair deepened, burning in her gut like stinging sand in a desert storm. *I really don't believe this.*

Tomorrow was a school day. David and Nancy would be up early.

They had had more than enough television time for a school night. At eight-thirty, she had tucked them in their beds with kisses and hugs and goodnight prayers, sans their usual bedtime story. That was Daddy's domain. She knew David, in particular, would not take kindly to her presuming on his dad's place as an impromptu storyteller. Besides, she was not in the storytelling mood. Foremost in her mind right now was a story not befitting their tender years.

As soon as the doors to their rooms were closed Taylor had set about wandering through the house again, lights out, careful to recheck the alarm system, along with every window and each one of the doors that she'd inspected twice already since reading the note. Drawn blinds closed out the world beyond the windows. But even as she went through the motions of securing the house, she accepted with deadening resignation the futility of her efforts. If they wanted in, there was nothing she could do to stop them.

What are they up to? And what are they waiting for? After they found me, why didn't they just ... get it over with? She trembled at the thought. It was hard to give up on her quest for survival after all this time. Hard to accept that her long run was finally over.

Taylor wondered if the children had noticed her preoccupation during dinner, knowing the answer before finishing the thought. Smart kids, of course they did. She had hardly touched the pizza. She'd tried coming off as calm and normal for them, even though she felt anything but. She'd barely been able to hold it together for their sake. The note and picture had been forgotten, put aside in their young minds as unimportant, at least for the moment. They hadn't mentioned it again.

Taylor was certain, though, that it was not over. It would come up again. David's brain worked that way, cataloging every aberration in a day or a week or even a month, and then with an uncanny knack for saying the unexpected, rehearsing them during a dinner conversation or on the way to church. At the thought of church, her mind turned to the strong, desirable man who, only yesterday, had stood in the pulpit, preaching. Yesterday? Yesterday seemed long ago now.

Oh, Brad ...

Her eyes filled with tears as she pictured the man she loved. Hair with its first flecks of gray. Eyes like deep brown pools she could swim in and often did. Smile so warm and inviting. Deep-throated laughter, engaging with anyone but especially with the children. Touch, disarming and tender when he whispered words of love to her. He had broken through the wall at last. And left her more vulnerable than she had ever been since ... since *it* had happened.

What will I do about you? What can I do? The irony is I was going to tell you everything tomorrow when you came home. Is it too late for that now? Of course it is. They'll never let it happen. Will I ever even see you again?

Taylor felt her panic level rising.

I'm not even sure who they are now. Or what they look like. But I know the one who's behind them, controlling them. Controlling everything. I know what he looks like. And he scares me to death!

She was certain she was near losing it altogether. Even Brad was becoming a fearful reality. What will he think, what will he do when he finds out the truth?

When I knew we were getting serious, I should have left then. I think somewhere down deep inside I knew we were impossible. I just love you so much I wanted us to be together forever. The Prince and Cinderella. It was only a fairy tale after all. But I wanted it to be real. I hope someday you will believe that.

Taylor went to the refrigerator. Her hand shook as she poured a ginger ale on ice and wished for something stronger. Even before becoming a Christian she'd never been much of a drinker, for the most part limiting herself to an occasional glass of wine at dinner. Only twice had a room turned unsteady beneath her feet. Once in college. She had panicked that time at the thought of losing control and vowed never to let it happen again. But it had happened again, one last horrific night. And ever since that night, self-control had been the driving core of her life. It had to be. She would never survive without it.

And now she'd lost it. Maybe she'd never really had it in the first place. Maybe she had been kidding herself all along. Truth be known, her life had been out of control for years, hadn't it? It was still out of control. Of all the people she knew, she'd deceived herself most of all. One thing was for sure. She was not just frightened right now. She was terrified! Dark, odious reminders of the past tumbled through her thoughts, grotesque and out of sequence, paralyzing her ability to see her circumstances clearly. Total panic was only a short breath away.

Oh, Jesus, what am I going to do? Now ... now I've led them here ... and the children. Her hands were cold and clammy. *I've put the children in danger, too! Brad will never forgive me for this. How could he when I can't begin to forgive myself?*

Barefoot, she stepped beneath the kitchen arch and made her way down the hall, checking the children to be certain they were safe and asleep. Returning to the darkened living room, she pulled her blouse free of the waistband before dropping onto one of the old sofa's familiar indentations, her fingers moving across the fabric, feeling its frayed texture. This was where she and Brad sat most often, where she cuddled close to him, drawing strength from his presence and warmth from his body.

One area along the cushion's front edge was so frayed it had begun to unravel. Her fingers twisted at one of the loose threads as her thoughts turned to Brad's first wife, Helen. Her forerunner had no doubt spent many an intimate evening lounging on this very sofa with her husband. Had she felt the same vigor and passion emanating from him as Taylor did? Had they shared moments of intimacy together on these old cushions, whispered secret words and shared the touches of love that bound them together until "death do us part?" Had they made love here? Of course they had.

Yet she felt no resentment, no jealousy or insecurity. If anything, it was just the opposite. There was a kind of awe or envy, a mystical connectedness she felt with Helen, though she had not known her in life. It was as though in some mysterious, inexplicable way she had been chosen to complete the unfinished tasks of loving and caring for this family that Helen had, way too early, left behind; a kind of covenant relationship with someone she had never known or loved and yet knew and loved full-well. The silent esteem she felt for Helen was mixed with genuine sadness over the fact that one so young, so beautiful, and so loved had been taken before her time.

Why Helen? Why not me, God? Why didn't you take me? I don't belong here. She does. What were you thinking?

Taylor experienced a quiet wonder whenever she thought about how she and Brad had first met and then fallen in love. Until now, she had thought it providential, something divine, as though at long last God had looked on her tortured soul with the kind of favor and blessing she had only dreamed about. Only now she knew she had conjured the whole thing up on her own. God hadn't really been the author of any of it. And now the devil had come for his due.

Beneath the wonder she'd felt in those early months of courtship there had always been a convergent inability to acknowledge her own self-worth. In another life, Taylor had been filled with a sense of hard-earned value and competence. She'd been ready to tackle a world she'd been sure she was good enough to tame. All that had changed in one terrible night. A night of terror that had left a bottomless well of condemnation and shame. So much so that, try as she might, she could mask but never overcome her lack of self-worth on almost every level. It was an insufferable reality, one she'd finally learned to live with and keep well-hidden long before she met Brad.

Of course that had not made accepting the idea of Brad's vocation and what it would mean to her life in marriage any easier. In spite of everything Brad said to reassure and encourage her, she knew deep down that she was not qualified for the role of pastor's wife. She was not worthy. Helen had been. The many 'Helen' stories she'd been told by the congregants at Desert Community Church confirmed this.

It was the same with motherhood. Taylor loved with such passion and wanted to be loved by the two children fast asleep down the hall. But they were not hers either, were they? They were Helen's. *Never mind what you were thinking, God. What was I thinking? Even this sofa belongs to Helen, not to me.*

Her quiet battle with depression had done its reprehensible work, decimating her once-upon-a-time poised and self-assured spirit. Even on the best of days, insecurity, suspicion and distrust lurked over her like a dark cloud. And while these had become all-too-familiar feelings, tonight they were overpowering. She was tearing apart, crumbling inside.

She didn't belong here. Not really. And yet she wanted to belong here. She wanted more than anything to be Brad's wife and lover and best friend and mother to these two beautiful children. And to have more. She wanted to be the person God wanted her to be. But she wasn't, was she? Not even close. She would never be. Tonight her eyes were *so* open to all that she really *wasn't!*

What hope is there for me? I've repented, Lord, again and again.

79

I've asked you to live in my heart. To make me what you want me to be. I have truly tried. So what is the matter with my prayers? Why don't you answer me? I never intended for this to happen.

This morning she'd been a man's choice to love and to cherish. Tonight she was an intruder, a trespasser, an alien. Worse. Oh, yes, *much* worse. A deceiver! *That's it isn't it? I've been dishonest—to Brad, to David and Nancy. Oh God, I've been dishonest with everyone.*

Taylor felt a sudden surge of clarity, a kind of epiphany. It wasn't anything she'd said or done. No. It was what she had *not* said and done. It wasn't a sin of *commission* that stank like fetid marsh water in her soul. It was the sin of *omission*, a disturbing awareness accompanied by a rush of guilt. And by a realization that Helen would never have let things get so out of control.

She's the one who belongs here, Lord, the one who deserves to be here. And I am not Helen. You got this all wrong!

Her head dropped as she fought back the tears. But it was no use. Huge drops ran down onto her cheeks, unrestrained, as if to further confirm that nothing in her life was in control.

Oh, Jesus, please. I know I'm not Helen. I wanted to be, but I can't. God, I'm not even Taylor. I am so lost. Brad deserves more than this. You know that, don't you? And the children? They deserve so much more than someone who is forever trapped inside this terrible lie.

She yanked the thread from the sofa fabric, rolling it between her fingers. Brad had promised to buy a new one when the summer sales got under way. Taylor had been looking forward to its replacement. A new place to sit, to cuddle. Their place. Now the thought of new furniture or anything else new was inconsequential. It no longer mattered. It was over. She was over. The future was something she no longer possessed.

Tears continued unchecked as she poured out her heart to God.

Sobbing, asking for forgiveness, as she had done so many times before, for courage to overcome the terrible 'sin living in me.' The dishonesty. The deception. All the lying, even if she thought she had done it for all the right reasons. Forgiveness for letting so many people down. On and on she sobbed and prayed as though a dam had burst and the rush of all that had been held back for so long pounded against the walls that had contained her secret. Finally, they too, crumbled and fell away.

At last the tears subsided and she was silent, exhausted, stripped bare of pretense, of the forgery she had lived for so long. But there was something else, too. Something that was … unfamiliar. A different kind of feeling than she ever remembered having in prayer. What was it? What had just happened?

She waited. It returned. The Soul Whisperer, a holy Breath.

Nothing held back. You've come to the end at last, Grace. You've nothing to fear now because you've nothing left to hold onto. No more secrets. No pretense. There is only my perfect love for you. And perfect love casts out all fear.

She sat in silence.

Alone, yet knowing she was not alone.

The fragrance of Love.

The touch of Understanding.

The release of Forgiveness.

The genuineness of Acceptance.

Then, as quickly as it had come, it was gone.

She rubbed her eyes and leaned into the sofa, exhausted. Trying to think ahead as far as tomorrow left her head pounding. What was going to happen? What should she do? What *could* she do? She jumped involuntarily as the grandfather clock struck its familiar Westminster cadence, royally calling out the eleventh hour.

She felt drained, empty. Yet the thought of going to bed was out of the question. Something had just happened here. Something different. Something holy. *I've prayed so many times before, but this ... this was ... incredible.*

She looked up.

Helen, I don't know if it works this way or not, but maybe ... maybe you were praying for me just now? For Brad and the children? If you were, please don't stop. We need all the help we can get here. And I still haven't a clue as to what to do. I'm honestly scared out of my wits. Only I'm not just afraid for me anymore, as if that helps anything. I'm so afraid for your children, for Brad, for America ... and the world.

Taylor's thoughts suddenly shifted, and her prayer stalled out.

America ... and the world?

The enormity of what had just crossed her lips washed over her like the first wave of a tsunami. Its implication was staggering. A revelation.

It's not just about me any more, is it, Lord?

All at once, the woman known for seven years as Taylor Nicole Carroll experienced something she had thought would never be possible. She was more frightened, one hundred percent more terrified than she had ever been in her entire life!

Oh God, please help me. I need to talk to Brad. But I can't tell him about this over the phone. He would never understand. Who else is there? Who will ever believe me?

For several minutes she sat perfectly still in the darkness. At last she reached for the phone on the table beside her and touch-dialed seven numbers she knew by heart. She had done this so often before. Holding the receiver to her ear she waited, fingers drumming nervously on the sofa cushion.

One ring ... two ... three ... four ...

"Hello, you've reached Maggie. Sorry to have missed you. Please leave your number and a brief message. I'll get back to you."

Taylor waited for the beep, and then spoke in low tones so as not to disturb David or Nancy, whose bedroom doors remained cracked open.

"Maggie? It's Taylor. Please call me when you get home. I know it's late but it's important. Thanks."

Taylor returned the phone to the end table, her nerves taut. Memories pushed their way into the corners of the room like unwelcome guests.

Seven years.

I was so sure it had been long enough …

She folded her legs beneath her.

What can I possibly say to Brad when he calls?

She set her glass down next to the phone. The house was still enough for her to hear her breathing mingled with the ticking of the grandfather clock.

I thought it was over.

The words repeated again and again in her mind. She clenched both fists and rubbed her eyes.

And now it's finally here. It's happening, God, but why? Why now, after so long? What reason could there possibly be?

A way of life honed and perfected to ensure sanity and survival. She had done it for a long time, but no longer. She was crumbling. Steadying her hand, she reached for the glass, then drew back empty-handed.

Taylor trembled as tears once again ran down her cheeks onto her blouse.

"Dear God," she whispered, staring up at the darkened ceiling. "How many times have I asked? Please help me. Tell me. What am I going to do?"

Leaning back against the sofa, she all at once felt cold. Her whole body shook. It was just like before. No matter how often she prayed, no matter how many times she asked the question, no answer was forthcoming. There never had been. She understood now. There was never going to be. Only the repetitive jumble of more frightening questions.

And the memories.

— Part Two —

In the path where I walk

men have hidden a snare for me.

— Psalm 142:3

Written in Chinese, the word "crisis" is composed
of two characters – one represents danger and the
other represents opportunity.

— John F. Kennedy

We all like sheep have gone astray. . .

—Isaiah 53:6

17

The bricks in the sidewalk were warm beneath their feet as the three young women dodged in and out of quaint little shops huddled in weathered old buildings along the cobblestone street across from the river. The feeling on River Street this muggy June afternoon was that of sluggish listlessness.

With vigilant demeanor, ice cream vendors and candy makers, shopkeepers and barmaids, all waited in readiness for the afternoon crowd that was sure to come. Infrequent 'locals,' stopping by for a drink or a last minute birthday gift for an out-of-towner, would soon be supplemented by busloads of tourists rolling in. It was the same every day this time of year as sightseeing seniors and vacationers of all ages checked into the Hyatt and other nearby hotels for the night before continuing on to, or returning from, Orlando and the Florida Peninsula the next day. Then River Street would bustle.

Grace took refuge from the muggy heat in Jezebel's dress shop, admiring some of the unusual styles. She caught up with Bonnie Jo and Ilene again at the Regatta Sportswear. In and out of shops they went, looking without buying, exclaiming over novelties and clothing, laughing at humorous and often suggestive quotations stamped on T-shirts hung in windows to entice tourists into contributing to the Savannah economy.

In front of the River Street Sweets Candy Store, they asked a stranger to take their picture with Bonnie Jo's camera. Then they went inside to sample taffy, fresh from the taffy-puller, and gaze longingly at the huge squares of dark, mouth-watering fudge.

The routine was familiar. Georgia State University students, in general, looked upon Savannah as their 'party town' and River Street as the place to begin the party. But while the street was familiar, it was also different. Today, it was memory lane, a right of passage for three young graduate students who, in the process of completing their education, had become the closest of friends.

Earlier in the day, they had arrived in Savannah's historic district, parking Ilene's car beneath a row of trees spreading leaves and branches in canopy-like fashion over Jones Street. Then they ran to join the line of customers on the sidewalk in front of Mrs. Wilkes' landmark restaurant. Once inside, they were seated at a large table with a couple from Florida celebrating their engagement, a husband and wife from San Francisco, and two elderly men who lived within walking distance and declared themselves to be "Mrs. Wilkes' regulars."

By the time breakfast was over, they had broken every dietary rule known to man, gorging on a cholesterol-lover's fantasy that ranged from bacon and sausage to biscuits, grits and gravy, and every breakfast goodie imaginable in between.

Standing in line to pay, they checked out Mrs. Wilkes' memory board, covered with pictures of people from who-knows-where, pinned side-by-side with distinguished news anchor, the late Walter Cronkite, and other celebrity guests. President Obama had eaten here "with the folks" during his re-election campaign. Above the enamel wainscoting, Mrs. Wilkes' brick-walled eatery was lined with articles from *The Washington Post*, *Time*, *Esquire*, *Southern Living*, and *People*, telling stories of "this charming place with its legendary hostess who had first started providing meals for hungry Savannah souls during the '40s."

Next they drove to the City Market, parked under cover, and proceeded to head for the shops. Three hours later as they emerged from the candy shop, Bonnie Jo moaned and stopped to rub one of her feet.

"Y'all, I didn't think I'd ever say this again after this morning, but I'm hot and thirsty and beginnin' to 'glow.' Can we get somethin' to drink? I'll buy."

"Good idea, BJ. I always hate it when you start glowing," Ilene agreed, wiping at a thin line of perspiration on her face. "But you don't have to buy."

"That's okay. I want to. It'll be my treat. Okay?"

"Okay, big spender. There's a place over there."

They stepped off the sidewalk and started across a cobblestone alley that dead-ended on their left along the base of a steep rocky incline.

"Not outside," Bonnie Jo protested as soon as she saw Ilene heading for the Warehouse's *alfresco* sidewalk setup. "It's too hot and humid to sit out here. Let's go up to the hotel."

"Dressed like this?" Grace asked uneasily.

"So what's the problem?" asked Ilene. All three had driven down from Statesboro that morning dressed in shorts and cotton tees, sandals and sunglasses. "Just think of yourself as a tourist in town for the day. Everyone on the street looks skuzzy to me. You'll fit right in."

"Thanks. Back to you."

"Come on, Grace." Bonnie Jo tugged at her arm. "You look fine. Besides, it'll be air-conditioned."

"But—"

"Don't be a party pooper," begged Bonnie Jo.

"Okay, okay," Grace agreed as the others took her arms and pulled her along.

They pushed past the hotel's heavy glass doors and into a small, plain-looking lobby where an elevator awaited. No one else was around. Taking the elevator up one floor from River Street onto the hotel's Bay Street level, they stepped into a corridor adjacent to the main lobby.

"Thank God for air-conditioning," exclaimed Bonnie Jo. The others agreed as they paused to look around. Grace had never been in the hotel before.

The lobby itself boasted a high-vaulted ceiling and seven stories of rooms opening onto indoor balconies festooned with hanging flowers. An escalator angled upward, away from a raised sitting area, toward the first balcony. At the registration desk, a travel-bedraggled family of four waited for a clerk to finish checking them in.

After a stop in the ladies room, they checked out the menu posted outside Windows, the hotel's main restaurant. Then they went next door to the bar. MD's was quiet, and for the most part, vacant. An older man and woman occupied a corner table. At the bar two men perched on stools, swapping stories and drinking beer. A third sat alone, talking to the bartender.

They seated themselves at a table directly in front of the windows looking over the riverfront.

"Now that's a view," said Ilene appreciatively. "Look how the bridge sparkles in the sunlight."

To their left, the twin spires of Talmadge Memorial Bridge stood laced together by steel cables covered with white, erosion-protecting PVC, spanning the river with the intricacy of a spider's web. Highway 17's endless flow of traffic moved over the Savannah River on this engineering marvel from Georgia to South Carolina and back again.

Bonnie Jo ordered a Sam Adams from the bartender while Ilene asked for a Chardonnay and Grace, an iced sweet tea.

Below their window, the Savannah River Queen dinner cruise boat, bedecked in red, white and blue, lay moored among several smaller pleasure craft and a couple of yachts tied up along the promenade that extended away from the hotel. A tugboat chugged its way into the river panorama, headed at an angle toward Hutchinson Island and the Westin Hotel and Convention Center, directly opposite the Hyatt, adding to the pleasure of the spectacle spread out before them.

"Everything seems to be in slow motion today," said Grace, peeling the protective cover away from her straw.

The others nodded, staring out onto the river, its seductiveness working into their over-heated bodies and tired feet. It appeared as though the harbor understood that spring was about to offer the white flag of surrender to the suffocating heat and humidity of summer in the Savannah lowlands.

The conversation turned to Ilene's newly acquired post as an English teacher and assistant principal in a small town high school in the northern part of the state. They reminisced about their lives, promising one another that wherever they each decided to settle, they would stay in touch with Facebook, Twitter and telephone calls at least once a month. No matter what.

They were relaxed, savoring this season of closure on a time in life they instinctively knew would never repeat itself when an unexpected voice intruded from behind them. "Excuse me, ladies."

Grace looked up to see the man she remembered sitting alone at the bar when they walked in. She guessed him to be in his thirties. He was dressed stylishly in a pinstriped shirt, blue and burgundy striped tie, navy blue jacket and white slacks, his dark shoes gleaming with fresh polish.

"Pardon me for interruptin', but I couldn't help overhearin' some o' your conversation. Enough, at least, to know you're celebratin' the 'Great Graduation Day.'" His smile was broad and engaging. Though trim and athletic in build, his gravely voice signaled the effects of a long-term smoking habit.

"So?" Ilene's curtness made clear her irritation at this stranger's effrontery in breaking into their privacy. "What business is it of yours?"

"Please." He held up his hands to signal an immediate surrender. "I'm not tryin' to hustle you. I just wanted to congratulate you on your achievements. Are y'all from Savannah State or SCAD?"

"Neither one," said Bonnie Jo, spreading out her hands to reveal the "Eagle" team logo on her shirt. "You must not be from around here if you don't recognize this. We're from Georgia Southern. Can't you tell by the way we've dressed up for the occasion?"

Everyone laughed at that.

"Well now, I'm truly sorry to have bothered you ladies. I just thought that y'all might be from this area an' could help me." The man turned and started to leave.

"Help you with what?" asked Grace, biting her lip the second the words slipped out, wishing she'd left well-enough alone. But helping people was the polite thing. It was the way she'd been brought up.

"That's all right," he apologized. Then pausing, he turned back to their table.

"My name is Reynolds. Terry Reynolds. I work for Charles Brandenbury of CB Enterprises." His announcement ended with his voice modulating upward, as though having just asked a question instead of making a statement.

The girls blinked in surprise. They had all heard of CB Enterprises. The company was a household word in the South and throughout much of the United States. And Charles Brandenbury *was* CB Enterprises. He had quite a reputation. The word was that he didn't make or sell anything. He just bought up everything.

"Sure you do." Ilene grinned skeptically, still suspicious of the suave-looking character standing by their table.

"Here's my card," he assured them, extracting it from his wallet and handing it to Ilene. Her eyebrows went up as she passed it on to Grace.

Charles Brandenbury's story had been well-rehearsed in recent years by all the major media outlets and retold on the lips of every young Southerner who entertained dreams of one day "making it big." Grace had heard the name bandied about often in GSU's business department. The man was an absolute investment genius. The book, *Buy Low And Watch It Grow: The Charles Brandenbury Story*, had remained on the New York Times' Non-Fiction Best-Seller List for more than a year, inspiring covetous dreams of profit and avarice in thousands of "wannabe" investors.

Before the Civil War, the South was reputed to be full of "old money" families whose wealth passed from generation to generation. Following World War II, however, attention had focused on a new breed of young and exciting cutting-edge entrepreneurs springing up from Birmingham to Atlanta. And leading the pack was Charles Brandenbury.

A hint of scandal had surfaced briefly when Barbara Brandenbury died from a mysterious fall in their exclusive Biltmore Forest mansion in Asheville, North Carolina. Autopsy reports had confirmed the strong presence of alcohol, and a reluctant Brandenbury revealed that his wife had been undergoing private treatment for acute alcoholism for some time. Her death was ruled an accident.

Two years later, he married the plain-appearing but very wealthy Claudia Jerson, only child of widower J. R. Jerson, communications magnate and majority stockholder at IBC Computers and The Jerson House, one of America's largest publishing firms. When Jerson succumbed to lung cancer, his entire estate passed to Claudia, thus merging the two families' assets in the time-honored fashion of aristocratic connubiality. Those who spent their time doing such things estimated the combined fortune to be well in excess of twenty, and more likely approaching, thirty-five or forty billion dollars.

The Brandenbury name had been fixed at the top of Asheville society's most discriminating guest lists for years. A major donor to several of the South's higher educational institutions and medical research centers, and the South's genteel answer to Donald Trump and Bill Gates, his ever-expanding list of financial investments and properties placed him among the richest of the rich.

"So what's your problem, Mr. Reynolds?" Ilene asked, interested now as she leaned forward with hands folded beneath her chin. "We may not be from Savannah, but we are from the greatest little schoolhouse in Georgia and are about as enterprising as three girls can get."

"Ilene ... " Grace threw her a look of caution.

"That's okay," the man said again. "It's just that Mr. Brandenbury is in town on business and headin' over to his Daufuskie Island estate shortly to host a little party honorin' Senator Noah Parker. Talal Itana is comin' with them. You've heard of him? No, I didn't think so. He's a United Nations diplomat an' a very powerful man, believe me. Some predict he'll be the next UN Secretary. Anyway, at the last minute, Mr. Brandenbury asked me to try an' find a couple o' local ladies who'd be free to join the three of them at his li'l party. I was just hopin' ... but then y'all are not any more acquainted 'round here than I am ... that is unless, o' course, y'all were free for the evenin' yourselves."

The three women stared at the stranger, then at each other, as they burst out laughing.

"Let me get this straight," Ilene repeated. "You're asking *us* if we'd escort Senator Parker and this Itana UN guy to a party at Charles Brandenbury's estate?"

"Well, that's about what I'm sayin', an' since there are three o' you, one could be Mr. Brandenbury's escort as well."

"Where are these guys' wives, Mr. Reynolds?" asked Grace, her query edged with skepticism. "I don't know about your UN diplomat, but I know Brandenbury and the Senator are married. Why aren't they going? Just to set the record straight, Mr. Reynolds, we're not hookers. And we're certainly not empty-headed bimbos willing to spend an evening amusing the rich and powerful with interesting table conversation and whatever else might be on their minds."

"Of course you're not. Please. Ladies, that never occurred to me, even for a moment. You're much too beautiful and intelligent for that. But to answer your question, Mrs. Brandenbury is in Europe and unable to join her husband until later this week. The Senator's family is in Washington an' his wife is unavailable as well. Mr. Itana isn't married. The problem is, Mr. Brandenbury's kinda fussy 'bout some things. A little eccentric you might say. An' one of his eccentricities is eatin' alone. He hates it. He always has someone with him at mealtime. He hates even worse when he's attendin' a male-only function of any kind. Especially dinners like this evenin'. He believes a feminine presence is important when hostin' a dinner party. You know, Southern hospitality an' all. Besides, he says men can't carry on an intelligent conversation by themselves past baseball and politics."

"Can't argue with him on that," Ilene agreed.

"Your invitation to hobnob with the rich and the powerful is very kind, Mr. Reynolds," said Grace. "We're flattered, to say the least, but what you see is what we've got. It sounds exciting, but we came in our 'fast-food' attire and what we're wearing is all we brought with us. It's okay for McDonalds, but hardly suitable for a dinner party."

"You mean you'd actually consider helpin' me out?" the man said in undisguised delight, a look of relief transforming his face.

"No, that's not ... I meant ... I was just pointing out one more reason why we *can't* accept your very gracious, albeit highly unusual, offer. So, thank you, but the answer is no."

"Pardon me, ladies, but may I have the pleasure o' sittin' with you for a few moments?" Reynolds asked.

Before Grace could verbalize a second "no" perched on the tip of her tongue, Ilene motioned to an empty chair. Reynolds pulled it toward the table and sat down.

"If y'all would consider doin' this li'l thing, it'd get me out of a real jam. Fact is, I just don't know where else to turn this late in the day. Tell you what. I know Mr. Brandenbury wouldn't mind. I'll take y'all out to one o' the stores around here. Each o' you buys a complete new outfit—your choice. Everything you need. Dresses, shoes, whatever. 'Course you'll be paid for your time, too. I didn't think to mention that before. There's a thousand dollars in it for each o' you. Cash, paid in advance."

"Double wow," exclaimed Bonnie Jo, looking at the others. "Let's do it!"

"Wait a minute." Grace pushed back from the table. "This is crazy. Mr. Reynolds, you're not giving away a thousand dollars for nothing. What exactly would be expected of us as escorts? If these men are looking for sex, we're not handing it out. I think we've made that plain enough. We didn't come planning to stay the night. Not here and certainly not with three men we don't know."

"Please." Reynolds leaned forward with an embarrassed grin. "I can imagine what y'all are thinkin'," but, rest assured that this evenin' is just a li'l ol' party with some o' Mr. Brandenbury's close an' *very* powerful friends. If Mr. Brandenbury wasn't enough, I mean, we're talkin' 'bout a United States Senator here. A leader o' this great country of ours. You'll go over to the island on Mr. Brandenbury's yacht, have dinner, mingle a bit—I guess I didn't mention but there'll be three or four other business associates and their wives comin' over from Charleston. Maybe that'll ease your minds a bit. You offer the occasion a li'l 'Southern belle' beauty, charm and stimulatin' conversation an' be back by, oh say, one o'clock. I'll even reserve a room here at the hotel for the night for you an' y'all can go on back home tomorrow. Now how's that sound?"

"No." Grace could feel enthusiasm building around the table. "I don't think so. I can't believe anyone wants to spend that kind of money just to have three women go to dinner with them. There's got to be more to it."

"Listen, this is small change to a man who's worth—well, a *lot* o' money. You have my word, ladies. I know it sounds strange, but you just have to know Mr. Brandenbury."

"And this is our chance to do just that," Billie Jo interrupted excitedly. "Come on, Grace, you're such a mother!"

"A *mother?*"

"Yes, a mother. Let loose. Let's have some fun. This sounds like a great evenin'. Who knows, maybe they'll like us so much that they'll want us to go to work for them."

"That's what I'm afraid of," Grace countered, careful not to mention how tempted she herself was by Reynolds' offer and the near

96

empty condition of her own bank account. Bonnie Jo giggled like a child at a birthday party, her face animated by their unexpected good fortune.

"I say let's do it," Ilene joined in. "I can use the thousand bucks. Wining and dining with the rich and famous sounds like an adventure. Lots better than taking in a dumb movie and driving home in the dark. Besides, girls—it means new graduation outfits!"

"Yes!" Bonnie Jo waved her hands in eager anticipation. "I'm in. Come on, Grace—say, yes!"

Ilene nodded, raising her hand as she looked at Grace. "Okay?"

Bonnie Jo's eyes were dancing. "Grace?"

Grace felt her reluctance crumbling. Ilene reached across the table and took her hand. "What can possibly go wrong? We'll be chaperoned by one of the wealthiest guys in America and a United States Senator, for goodness sake."

"All right." Grace heaved a reluctant sigh, setting aside the last of her misgivings. "I guess I'm in."

"Good. We'll draw straws," Ilene said, taking three wooden toothpicks out of her bag and breaking off part of the first one.

"You always carry 'straws' around for occasions like this?" Grace asked.

"These are from Mrs. Wilkes'. First short pick gets to choose who she wants to escort. Second short pick decides between the two remaining. Okay, here we go. By the way, Mr. Reynolds, I'm Ilene Randle. This is Bonnie Jo Senter and that's Grace Grafton."

"My pleasure, ladies," Mr. Reynolds murmured, leaning back to watch as lines of amusement crinkled around his eyes.

Ilene moved the toothpicks around until only an inch remained showing above her fingertips. Bonnie Jo drew first. Long. Grace pulled the next— "It's short," Ilene declared. "You get first dibs."

"Guys, I don't know ... I'm not really into this ... why don't you two choose, and I'll take what's left."

"Because those are the rules," Ilene shot back with a grin. "Choose."

"All right, I guess I'll take the Senator."

"Good choice," Ilene said, rolling the long and short toothpicks between her thumb and forefinger once again. "Okay, BJ. It's you and me. Choose."

Bonnie Jo reached over, closed her eyes, and drew—the short pick! Ilene sat back, resigned to her fate. "Which one are you taking?"

"You're sure you don't care?" Bonnie Jo asked.

"We play by the rules. Choose."

"I choose—Mr. Brandenbury! Oh, my goodness," she squealed, pressing her hands together. "I'm goin' out to dinner with a gazzillionaire!"

"And I'm spending the evening talking to some guy from the UN with a name I'll probably forget a dozen times at dinner," Ilene concluded. "Oh well, live by the toothpick and die by the toothpick, I always say."

18

As the three women stood to shake hands with Reynolds, Bonnie Jo was still giggling excitedly over her good fortune at having drawn the escort assignment with *the one and only Mr. Charles Brandenbury.* Out of an inside pocket, Reynolds withdrew a handful of $100 bills held together with a very expensive-looking money clip. Their eyes widened as he held it out for them to see. Then he unfastened the clip and started counting.

"This is yours, ladies, an' I thank you very much. You've taken a really big load off my mind. A thousand dollars each. This'll give you somethin' to shop with now, won't it? Just bring back whatever's left. I'll need all your receipts, too. An' I'll have your personal thousand cash ready when you're done shoppin'. Y'all know where you want to go?"

They watched Reynolds count out one hundred dollar bills, placing them in three small piles on the table. Grace picked hers up and spread them like cards in her hand. She looked across the table at the others and shook her head. "I don't believe this."

"I know an exclusive li'l shop on Liberty Street," said Reynolds. "I'm sure y'all can find somethin' there if you don't have any better ideas."

"Sounds fine to me," said Bonnie Jo enthusiastically.

"Well, then, shall we go?" Reynolds got to his feet. "My car is out front unless yours is closer."

Ilene shook her head. "It's at City Market. We'd better go with you." "This is great." Bonnie Jo's eyes sparkled with a mix of incredulity and enthusiasm. "A real shoppin' excursion. And there's no price limit?"

"If it's your size an' you like it," Reynolds answered, "that's the only limit. Up to a thousand dollars. Listen, y'all wait here, an' I'll reserve a room. Then, we'll run out an' get your shoppin' done, an' you can spiffy up for dinner. Leave your things, and the room will be waitin' for you when you get back later. Oh, an' I'd appreciate it if y'all didn't mention to the store clerk or anyone who it is you'll be escortin' tonight. Mr. Brandenbury's always bein' hounded by the press, if you know what I mean. Sometimes it's a sight. He's hopin' to slip into town this afternoon with his friends an' without a lot o' folderol. O' course, you do understand?"

They nodded, though none of them could really comprehend such a problem ever occurring in the life of anyone with whom they were acquainted. "Let's get on with it then," urged Reynolds. "Time's awastin'."

The drive was only a few blocks. As the three young women in shorts entered the shop, a fashionably-dressed older woman greeted them with a polite, but reserved, "May I help you?"

From the look on her face, Grace was certain that she'd waited on college students before, an exercise that in most cases had probably turned out to be long on effort and short on sales. An hour later, however, one *very* pleased clerk smiled profusely as she handed each of her three young customers from Georgia Southern their remaining change and purchase receipts. Grace glanced over her shoulder as they exited from the shop and walked to where Reynolds was waiting in his car. The clerk stood in the entrance watching them. *I'll bet she's thinking, "Oh, to be young again."* Grace was confident that when they first entered her shop, she had never dreamed it would be her biggest sale of the week. Minutes later they were crossing the hotel lobby again, this time in the direction of the elevator, carrying their purchases and talking excitedly among themselves, more like high school girls than university graduates. Grace looked up in time to see Reynolds' dark blue jacket disappear around the corner ahead of the package-laden trio. They hurried after him, Bonnie Jo still chattering away as they rounded the corner and stepped into the elevator.

The door opened onto the seventh floor. They followed after Reynolds to the end of the hall, turned right and continued down the passageway until he paused, slipped a key card into the door lock and pushed it open. Room 722. Stepping back, he motioned them inside.

"Whoa—get a load of this, ladies," Bonnie Jo exclaimed as she led the way. "This is not just a room. It is a suite!"

Once inside, they exclaimed over the view of the river and Hutchinson Island and the Westin Resort on the opposite side of the river. "Better even than downstairs at MD's."

A sofa faced opposite a fireplace and to the right and left of the sofa were love seats done in matching floral patterns. *Very* elegant. There were additional chairs, a full-size dining room table and two more chairs situated behind the sofa. On the wall opposite the table, a matching chest. To the right of the entry a wet bar, surrounded by mirrors. Doors opened on opposite ends of the room into bedrooms, one containing two double beds and the other a king-size. Each bedroom was equipped with a private bath, vanity area and television.

"Will this be satisfactory for the night?" he asked with a knowing look that anticipated the answer.

"I think it will do," Ilene responded dryly looking into the bathroom. "It's not up to our usual standards, you understand, but we'll manage." The bathroom was done in an elegant blue and burgundy tile. The room itself contained an enormous tub with whirlpool jets and a separate, glassed-in shower with three shower nozzles protruding at different levels and angles. To one side were twin sinks and a vanity table in front of a large mirror surrounded by makeup lights. "This place is bigger than our apartment!" Bonnie Jo exclaimed as she peered into a similar bath off the other bedroom. "Our whole living room would fit in here. And look, a king bed!"

"Forget it, BJ," said Ilene, walking across the sitting area to join her at the door to the other bedroom. "You two have the billionaire and the senator. The king is mine."

"I can leave if you like," offered Reynolds, smiling at their effusiveness as they dropped their packages onto the beds. He glanced at his watch. "But, if you don't mind, I've no place to go until y'all are ready. May I just sit out here and watch a little TV?"

"Sure, no problem," Ilene responded quickly. "You're paying the tab." The others nodded their agreement. Reynolds made himself comfortable on one of the love seats. Moments later, he was engrossed in the fifth inning of an afternoon baseball game between the Braves and the Mets.

"What's the score?" Bonnie Jo called out through the bedroom door as she hung her new dress in the closet.

"Mets by two," answered Reynolds.

"Are they playing in Atlanta?"

"New York."

"When do we need to be ready?" Grace inquired, wanting to be sure they were all on the same page when it came to using the bathrooms.

"We'll leave here at five-thirty," said Reynolds. "You've got a little

102

less than ninety minutes to freshen up."

"Where to from here?"

"To Mr. Brandenbury's yacht. It's tied up alongside the promenade. You probably passed it earlier."

Grace thought back on their afternoon stroll. "There was one big one—all white with a cabin and everything."

"That's the one," Reynolds declared absently, his eyes not leaving the game. "Sleeps eight."

"Holy cow," Grace muttered under her breath. Closing the door and grabbing a towel, she headed for the shower. "I really don't believe this!"

19

Exactly one hour and fifteen minutes later, Ilene was first to emerge from her room, wearing a silk, lemon-colored top and a flared skirt. Through the open door, Grace could see Reynolds give Ilene an approving nod as she walked barefoot to a full-length mirror on the far wall, her new leather pumps in hand. Setting them on a tabletop, she fussed for a moment with an uncooperative strand of blond shoulder-length hair.

"Well, what do you think?" she asked, giving up and turning toward Reynolds. Ilene's face was a trifle long to be considered beautiful, and her lips a bit too thin, accenting an initial impression of severity. But today the flecks of yellow in her eyes were highlighted by the color of her dress. And the gold-colored bracelet and matching earrings completed her transformation.

"I think you are a lovely young lady," he answered with polite indulgence, "an' I'm sure you'll be a welcome addition to the evenin's festivities."

Ilene checked her wristwatch. "Ten minutes, girls,"

"I'm comin'," Bonnie Jo answered. A moment later she stepped through the opposite doorway into the center of the room with the confident stride of a model on a fashion house runway, pirouetting saucily in front of the other two. "Ta-da!"

Her reputation as the most daring of the three was confirmed by the animal print, silk column sleeveless dress, with a cutout back and deep front slit showing off her shapely legs and olive-tone skin. A black rope belt circled her waist, complementing a pair of black, double-banded heels.

"Will this get Mr. Brandenbury's attention?" she asked, one hand resting on her hip and the other completing her pose as she touched a matching silk cocktail hat perched on the side of her head.

Ilene whistled. "If it doesn't, the man is already dead."

"I'm sure that he'll be fascinated an' truly delighted to have such a dazzlin' companion as his escort for the evenin'," Reynolds added with an appreciative stare as Bonnie Jo sat down opposite him, crossing her legs as she leaned back in the chair.

Finally it was Grace's turn. She checked herself one last time, slipping her lipstick into an unobtrusive zipper pocket she'd found in the waist of her dress. She entered wearing double-banded, three-inch heel sandals and a black tank dress with a sheer double flounce that ended mid thigh. For a long moment, no one said anything. She extended her hands, rotating gracefully in a slow complete circle, allowing the soft blackness to glide sinuously with each move of her body. The cream-color of her skin and long straw-blond hair emphasized the elegant simplicity of the dress.

"Well?" she asked finally. "Say something."

"Double-wow, Grace," Bonnie Jo exclaimed, getting up from her chair. "You are 'drop dead' gorgeous, girl. That dress looks wonderful on you! Hey, look at you. I didn't see these at the store." She ran her fingers over Grace's white chain link necklace and bracelet, at the same time eyeing the white stud earrings, giving her that familiar once-over look women often give one another.

"Can you believe this?" she glanced over at Ilene. "These things are plastic. And look how perfectly they set off her dress."

Ilene and Reynolds were both on their feet now.

"You do look beautiful," Ilene murmured softly, pecking at Grace's cheek with a kiss. In her ear she murmured, "Are you okay now?"

Grace shrugged. "I'm okay. A little nervous, but okay."

"I'm tellin' y'all, I couldn't have found three more charmin' and dazzlin' damsels in the entire South," Reynolds declared with obvious relish. "An' graduatin' next week with degrees an' everything. Beauty *an'* brains! Y'all are really somethin' now, that's for sure. An' don't you worry yourselves even a little now, you hear? Mr. Brandenbury is goin' to be so pleased when he an' his guests meet up with y'all. Speakin' o' the Devil ladies, your gentlemen friends are most likely on the boat by now. We'd best be on our way."

Reynolds flicked off the television and moved to the door, holding it open as the three exited into the hallway. Making sure it was closed and locked, he slipped past Grace and walked on ahead to push the elevator button.

"Did you leave your money in the room?" Grace whispered to the others as they followed a short distance behind him.

"Do you see a place on me that would hide a thousand dollars?" giggled Bonnie Jo. "The only thing I brought is my camera in this little purse. I'm going to get my picture taken with Mr. Charles Brandenbury!"

"As a matter of fact, I did leave it," answered Ilene. They arrived at the three elevators just as the middle door slid open.

"After y'all," said Reynolds, holding the door back with his hand. They were silent on the way down, lost in thought and gazing on the scene below through the elevator's glass wall. Entering the lobby, Reynolds motioned to them. "Wait here. I'll leave your key at the desk. You can pick it up later, all right?"

They nodded and he walked briskly across the lobby.

"Where'd you hide it?" Bonnie Jo asked Ilene, resuming their whispered conversation. "I just left mine in my shorts in the closet."

"In my bathroom there was a loose tile in the corner behind the stool."

The others looked at her.

"Well, that's the place."

"Do you think I should run back up?" asked Bonnie Jo, concerned over having left her money in her clothes. "I never thought about hiding it."

"There's no time," Ilene said, her voice low as she glanced in Reynolds direction. "He's coming back right now. Where'd you put yours, Grace?"

"I'm wearing it," she whispered, touching the bodice of her dress.

Ilene grinned knowingly. "I thought about that, but isn't it uncomfortable?"

"When was the last time a thousand dollars made you uncomfortable?" Grace chuckled, though her voice carried with it an edge of tension.

"All right, ladies, here we go," announced Reynolds, punching the River Street elevator button. A minute later they emerged into the muggy, late afternoon heat, eyes adjusting to the sunlight. They paused beneath a portion of the hotel extending over the cobblestone street to a banquet facility opposite and forming a covered passageway for cars and pedestrians. As they looked about, it was easy to see that River Street was waking up.

20

Automobiles were plentiful now on the cobblestones, most of them filled with teenagers and college students cruising the waterfront. Stereos blared as boys hung out of car windows shouting and waving and "high-fiving" one another as they passed, welcoming the beginning of a summer sans stuffy classrooms and demanding teachers.

A gray-haired African-American stood in the sweltering shade beneath the hotel overhang playing a melancholy *Amazing Grace* on an old, worn-smooth trumpet that had seen better days. The shape of each note was remarkable in its clarity and suggested talent that belied his present status as a street performer. Grace's passing thought was that, like his trumpet, the chances were he'd seen better days himself.

An open instrument case at his feet served as a makeshift offering plate, its shabby velvet lining saving the occasional coins dropped in by passersby from bouncing out onto the pavement. There was a lone crumpled dollar bill there, too. Reynolds paused, reached into his pocket and pulled out a twenty, dropping it into the case. The musician smiled and nodded his appreciation, his eyes remaining all the while on the three beauties trailing after his benefactor. For a split second, Grace met his gaze, lifted her hand in acknowledgment, and smiled as she hurried past.

Somewhere along the street in the direction they were headed, a small jazz combo could be heard doing warm-up scales. The girls looked at one another and giggled with excitement. This was the Savannah they knew and loved.

Reynolds walked several steps on ahead of them, crossing over to the red brick promenade along the water's edge. They followed, dodging between two carloads of teenage boys leaning out of their cars, whistling and hooting as they passed.

"Hey, beautiful ladies, wherever y'all are goin', we'll be glad to take you there!" one of the boys called out.

Grace smiled as they reached the other side realizing how overdressed they must look for this time of day on River Street.

"Cobblestones and high heels do *not* go together," declared Bonnie Jo in exasperation, halting briefly to readjust a shoe. Reynolds paused and looked their way, waiting for them to catch up. A short distance beyond him was the sleekest, most beautiful vessel that any of them had ever seen.

"Would you look at that boat?" exclaimed Bonnie Jo. "Is that what we're goin' on?"

"That's no boat, BJ," Ilene corrected her with an appreciative gaze. "That's a yacht!"

As they approached, the low rumble of its twin diesel engines could be heard idling and ready, stirring the murky waters of the Savannah. Their steps slowed as they took in the vessel's graceful lines, its all-white finish accented with rich-looking teakwood decks and rails. A sudden realization hit Grace. They were only steps away from entering a world that none of them had ever experienced before, a world of mega-riches and power.

"Hey, stand right there," ordered Bonnie Jo. She zipped open the small leather case she had been carrying and withdrew her digital camera. "Let me get one of you guys in front of this thing." She snapped off a couple of quick shots. "Now take one of me, okay?"

Grace took Bonnie Jo's camera and held it to her eye. There were two men leaning against the deck rail, watching as they approached. She snapped a picture of Bonnie Jo with the yacht in the background. At that precise moment another man stepped out of the cabin, arms folded, and paused on the narrow deck. Grace snapped two more with Bonnie Jo and Ilene together.

"Your film card is full, BJ. It won't take anymore."

"I knew it! Wait. I have a spare." She took the camera and released the card, handing it to Grace. "Here, hold this a sec." She fished the spare from the leather pouch and inserted it into the camera.

"Wait, wait, stay there," Bonnie Jo said, lifting her camera once again, snapping two more quick pictures of the girls with the yacht in the background. Reynolds, who had continued walking toward the yacht, looked up to see the man on board making protesting motions with his hands. Turning back he noticed Bonnie Jo and the camera for the first time and shouted, "Stop!"

The three looked up, surprised at the sound of his voice.

"I'm sorry," Reynolds exclaimed as he hurried toward them, holding up his hands. "Mr. Brandenbury doesn't permit cameras. I didn't notice that you had one with you, or I'd have told you to leave it in the room."

He took it from Bonnie Jo and examined it, his tone casual once again. "It's so small. No wonder I didn't see it."

"But I wanted to get some pictures of this evening," Bonnie Jo pouted.

"Sorry," Reynolds said again. "It's the same rule for everybody. Tell you what. Give it to me. I'll take it back to the hotel for you and leave it at the desk. You can pick it up later. No one else has a camera with them, do they?"

Grace hesitated as Bonnie Jo sent her a knowing glance. Grace shook her head, feigning innocence; a loose fist cradled Bonnie Jo's filmcard against her thigh, hidden by the flounce of her skirt.

Reynolds moved between them, stuffing Bonnie Jo's camera in his pocket as he took Bonnie Jo by the arm. "Okay then, come on. Let's not keep the man waiting."

As Reynolds turned and started toward the yacht, Grace unobtrusively slipped the filmcard into the pocket that held her lipstick. There was nothing to give it away short of a pat down. It was a stupid rule anyway. What could a few pictures hurt? These guys probably got their pictures taken every day. This was too good an opportunity to pass up. At least BJ would have these to download and share with them later.

One of the men they had seen on the deck walked out onto a gangplank inlaid with non-skid material, sporting chrome handrails on either side that gleamed in the late afternoon sun. He stood on a small platform with three narrow steps leading down to the brick sidewalk.

"Good evening, Terry."

His voice boomed out in greeting. Grace guessed him to be about six feet, maybe a little taller, and a bit overweight. He wore a dark, double-breasted jacket buttoned at the waist, gray slacks, white shirt and tie. What likely at one time had been a full complement of dark wavy hair was receding, exposing a high forehead and a deeply tanned face, eyes behind glasses that automatically darkened for the sun. Grace let out a quiet sigh of relief. He looked … well, normal. Ordinary, even if the man was neck-deep in money. Perhaps the evening was not going to be so difficult after all.

The late afternoon air was sultry on this warmest part of the day.

Grace's dress was already beginning to cling, but she noted their host didn't appear at all uncomfortable, even with jacket and tie. She hoped it was because he'd just stepped out of an air-conditioned cabin that would soon give them all some relief.

"And who have we here?" he smiled, unfolding his arms and stuffing both hands into his pockets. "My, my, my, Terry. You certainly exceeded my expectations after being given such a last minute request. Come, ladies. Welcome aboard the *Brandenbury*."

He reached for Bonnie Jo's hand first as she walked up the steps. Soon they were all crowded together on the small platform, too close really for comfort. Grace eased back as far as she could against the rail, continuing to size up their host as Reynolds carried on the introductions.

"Mr. Brandenbury, this is Bonnie Jo Senter, who's agreed to be your escort this evenin'."

Brandenbury lifted her hand and touched it lightly to his lips, radiating gracious old South charm. "I'm pleased that one as lovely as you are, my dear, would consent to being my guest for the evening." He released her hand and, with a smile that seemed genuine and appreciative, said, "Welcome aboard."

"Why thank you, Mr. Brandenbury," Bonnie Jo gushed with a suitable amount of shyness, though her dress and demeanor intimated anything but. "It's a pleasure."

"Go on ahead into the cabin and get out of this heat, Ms. Senter," Brandenbury said, guiding her toward the gangplank, his eyes following her as she moved past. "I'll be along in a moment."

"And this is Ilene Randle," continued Reynolds. "She's plannin' on joinin' Mr. Itana."

"How do you do, Ms. Randle? Now be careful as you step up on deck, all right?" Brandenbury continued to receive his guests with all the warmth and poise of a polished Southern gentleman. Grace was beginning to relax.

"And last, but certainly not least, let me introduce you to Senator Parker's dinner guest, Ms. Grace Grafton. These are all Georgia 'peaches,' Mr. Brandenbury, an' they're graduatin' from Georgia Southern next week, all of 'em with Masters Degrees."

"Well, well. You've honored us with charm, beauty and intelligence as well. Wonderful. Thank you, Terry. By the way, will you be joining us for the evening?"

"Thank you, no sir," Reynolds replied. "You've got me much too busy. I've another appointment this evenin' and a full day tomorrow. Oh, and I've reserved the suite at the Hyatt for these ladies upon their return later this evenin', just like you requested."

"Good. One of my men will bring them back in the speedboat."

Grace felt Brandenbury's eyes follow her as he spoke. She crossed over to the vessel, accepting the hand of a swarthy, unsmiling man whom she surmised to be the captain by virtue of the nautical hat he wore.

Stepping onto the narrow deck, she turned to see if Brandenbury was close behind. In fact, he was not. He and Reynolds were still on the platform, their voices low and unintelligible. She turned back just as Brandenbury's sonorous voice resonated across the narrow span of water from shore to yacht, "You'll handle everything here then, correct?"

It wasn't so much what the man said, as it was the tone in his voice that caused her to tense up again. There was an edge to it, an unexpected hardness, not the warm, convivial air of moments before. Grace looked his way again. She was being silly, of course. They could be talking about anything. Reynolds looked up and saw her watching them.

"It's all under control," he called out, snapping off a perfunctory smile in her direction. Shuffling his feet, he turned his back to her, but she still made out his next words. "Everything's taken care of, Mr. Brandenbury. Have a good time."

Grace hesitated, feeling a renewed uneasiness. Then the Captain's hand was on her arm, guiding her toward the cabin door. "Right through there, Miss." She moved forward, ducking her head as she entered.

What was that about?

Probably nothing, she told herself, just her own jitters over being here on this incredible yacht, in the company of one of the world's richest men and his powerful friends. Yet she couldn't help thinking of Reynolds' uneasy glance … and the tone of the other man's voice.

21

Inside the cabin, people greeted each other with genial bonhomie, though Grace's thoughts remained on the two men outside. She watched through the window as Reynolds pulled each of the mooring lines free and tossed them onto the deck. The increased rumbling of the engines signaled the yacht's movement away from the dock, causing some of those standing to put out a hand and adjust their footing.

That's probably it. He was just telling Reynolds to release the lines. Yet as the vessel came about and headed out onto the river in an easterly direction, something inside her said it was more than that. It was strange.

"Good evening, Ms. Grafton."

Grace turned to see an extraordinarily handsome man whom she guessed to be in his early forties, standing a head taller than she in her heels and wearing a light gray suit and dark tie. He held a glass of champagne in each hand and smiled as he extended one to her. "I thought you might like a little bubbly."

"Thank you," she said, taking the glass. He shifted his drink and held out a hand.

"I'm Noah Parker. Your friend over there tells me you're to be my escort for the evening."

"The name is Grace, Mr. Parker ... I'm sorry," she said, accepting his hand. "*Senator* Parker. Please forgive me."

"That's quite all right, Grace. And I'd prefer that you call me Noah."

At that moment, the cabin door opened and one of the world's richest men stepped through. "All right, friends, welcome once again to the *Brandenbury*."

His voice was deep, resonating throughout the cabin though he made no attempt to amplify. The confidence with which he carried himself and the way he spoke reminded Grace of Anthony Hopkins, one of her favorite Hollywood actors. She wondered if at some time or other he might have taken voice lessons or maybe even some stage training.

"Apparently you've all introduced yourselves to one another. That's wonderful. Now there's plenty to drink at the bar, so help yourselves to whatever you like. You're welcome to go out on deck, though with the humidity like it is, I'd have to say it's much more comfortable in here. But whatever. It's up to you. Relax and enjoy the scenery. Enjoy each other. We'll be arriving at the island in about an hour."

"I suppose the other guests are coming by boat from Charleston?" Grace queried the Senator. "There didn't seem to be anyone else leaving from Savannah."

"I'm not sure," Parker answered, hesitating. Grace registered his quizzical glance at Brandenbury. "Charlie would be the one who'd know about that. He's made all the arrangements."

They moved to a window through which they could observe Savannah's skyline, gradually receding in the distance. The conversation turned to the Senator's wife and two sons. Mrs. Parker and the boys were in Washington, Parker said, though they came back home to Charleston as often as possible. They talked about the Senator's rapid, hard-fought journey up South Carolina's political ladder to the United

States Senate. He had been elected Lieutenant Governor and was serving out his first term when South Carolina's incumbent Senator died following a sudden, massive heart attack. Parker was appointed to be his successor. It had been an opportunity from which he'd never looked back. He'd served the people in Washington for almost two years now and it was quite obvious that he enjoyed the power and status of his office.

Grace recalled having heard or read bits of his story, though she had never followed South Carolina politics. Her nervousness dissipated after finding the Senator surprisingly easy to talk to, especially when she guided the conversation into trivia pertaining to himself and his accomplishments. On the other hand, she offered up few details of her own life, not out of an unwillingness, but simply because she wasn't asked. This was no mutual exchange. From the start, it became an exercise in one-way listening. Well, she'd been out with guys before who were full of themselves. Why should she expect any less of a United States Senator? It no doubt required a mile-high ego to arrive at the station he'd already attained.

Time passed quickly with everyone engaging in lively banter. Talal Itana was the quietest of the three men. At first Grace thought he was simply uncomfortable with himself or his surroundings; she wasn't sure which. She caught snatches of Ilene's attempts at conversation and sensed she had to work at it a whole lot more than either she or Bonnie Jo. Grace maneuvered the Senator until they were standing next to the UN diplomat who hailed from Beirut. Ilene looked relieved, smiling her appreciation at Grace as the Senator went off on some Washington inanity that neither of the girls understood or cared about. But Mr. Itana didn't really seem to be listening. He gave an impression of being rather bored with the entire scene. Like he had better things to do and wished the evening's vanities would soon be over.

Bonnie Jo and her consort, on the other hand, appeared to be having little trouble getting acquainted. She was perched happily on a bar stool, holding a glass in one hand while waving the other as she talked. Meanwhile Brandenbury leaned into her much closer than necessary, Grace thought, as he pointed out passing landmarks through the window.

The most one could see was marsh and swampland thick with trees, reeds and tall grass, a veritable sea of green along the shores of the opaque Savannah River. Although she knew little about this part of Georgia, she understood that whether or not portions of the flat coastal lowlands were visible depended largely on where the tide was on its twice a day, back-and-forth cycle.

Her conversation with the Senator continued to require little more than an occasional "yes," "really?" or "how wonderful, Noah," as Noah went on about himself and his grand deeds. While at first she'd been unsure of how to act in the presence of so public a figure as Senator Parker, now she was growing bored and wishing she had gotten the Lebanese guy. Uncomfortable as a conversationalist, but at least he seemed nice enough.

She peered over the Senator's shoulder out the windows and into the growing dusk as the vessel turned northward, away from Bird Island's shoreline visible off the starboard side. Brandenbury announced to his guests that they were now cruising the Intracoastal Waterway in a locale known as Fields Cut. That was Jones Island off the starboard bow. Grace thought the "sameness" of this low country terrain to be confusing. She didn't really care though, so long as the captain knew where they were.

While the Senator expounded on how well it was working to have a party majority in both the House and the Senate, a random thought suddenly pushed its way to the surface of her mind.

Mom's birthday! Oh, no. I was going to call her earlier, and in all the excitement I forgot! She swore under her breath, feeling sudden guilt over having been so thoughtless. *What should I do? I know she expects to hear from me. Maybe I could call from the island. No, that probably wouldn't do. After all, I'm being paid to give my undivided attention to the Senator here. Even if he understood, I have a feeling Mr. Brandenbury wouldn't.*

Grace closed her eyes for an instant, opening them again as Parker continued regaling her with tales of politics and power in Washington, oblivious to her preoccupation.

A few minutes later, Brandenbury moved to the front of the cabin and pointed off in the distance. "Daufuskie Island is a short way ahead now." They were plying the New River at the moment, he said, while the last vestiges of a beautiful sunset cast an impressive orange glow over the coastal lowlands of Georgia and South Carolina.

"The only way to get to Daufuskie is on the water," Brandenbury intoned to no one in particular. "Used to be the population out here was almost entirely black folk. There are even some wild horses on the island. If we were staying longer, we'd have a look at them tomorrow in the daylight."

The way he said it, Grace was left wondering if he meant the horses or the "black folk." She watched as their course altered several degrees to starboard.

"Mr. Brandenbury," she called out, taking the opportunity for a momentary diversion from her loquacious political friend. "Where is your house?"

"That's the dock up ahead at one o'clock, my dear. You can see it out that window." He pointed again, this time a little to the right of the yacht's bow.

"Oh yes, I see it. Some boats are there already. They must have brought your other guests for the evening."

119

Brandenbury's hesitation was brief, hardly the blink of an eye as he cleared his throat, but she caught it nonetheless. "Ah, there's been a last minute change of plans, Ms. Grafton. I thought you all knew."

"Knew what?" Grace felt herself tense as she studied the man's face, the lines around his eyes. Always the eyes. *You can tell a lot about a person by watching their eyes.* That's what her father used to say when he was alive. Grace decided she didn't like this man's eyes, watching as they tightened almost imperceptibly. She glanced over at Ilene and Bonnie Jo. They had turned to listen, surprise written on their faces as well. Parker and Itana remained quiet, waiting to see what Brandenbury would say next.

"I'm sorry. I thought Terry had told you," Brandenbury continued smoothly. "I was expecting some friends to join us, but they were detained in Charleston this afternoon. Noah and Talal were still in the area, so I decided to go ahead with dinner plans. Harold—that's one of my men in Charleston—was supposed to have contacted Terry to let him know. Didn't he say anything about it?"

"No, actually he didn't," she replied. Grace fell silent, weighing her thoughts with renewed cautiousness. Could what he was saying really be true? Had there ever been anybody else coming? What was the matter with this picture? Why was she continuing to have misgivings about this evening's adventure? She didn't have any real reason. Everything seemed fine.

"I'm truly embarrassed and apologetic, Ms. Grafton. I do hope you don't mind."

Brandenbury's tone sounded sincere enough, but it seemed to Grace that for an instant the lines in his face stiffened, his eyes, cold; then, just as quickly, they twinkled again, though this time it seemed more with amusement than regret, as though he were laughing at her. She glanced over at Ilene. Her face was expressionless at first, and then she shrugged.

Bonnie Jo remained blasé to it all, sipping from her wine glass and gazing out the window as Brandenbury turned away from Grace and leaned forward to whisper something in Bonnie Jo's ear. Her sudden laughter seemed to indicate an acceptance of their host's apology and a readiness to go on as though nothing was amiss.

Happy-go-lucky BJ. If spontaneity and whimsicalness could be packaged, BJ would doubtless be the wrapping. It was one of the reasons Grace loved her so much. The look on Ilene's face, however, was more subdued. Grace knew her well enough to sense that Ilene's discomfort from their situation had all at once become more in sync with her own.

The yacht was slowing, and she turned back to the window. A long wooden dock extended well out into the water, perhaps forty meters, maybe even longer, its length no doubt a necessity for coping with the tide's fickle behavior. She watched as the yacht was brought alongside where a man dressed in jeans and a sleeveless black and gray striped shirt waited to catch the lines and wrap them expertly over large hooks.

"All right, everybody, we've arrived." Brandenbury's voice broke through Grace's tension, and the cabin conversation quieted. He looked pointedly at Grace for a split-second before turning to the others. "Ms. Grafton, it's unfortunate that my man in Charleston somehow missed being in touch with Terry, but let's not let it ruin our evening. Come on, everyone. Let's head on up to the house. Dinner should be ready, and I'm famished. I hope you all are as well."

There was a murmur of concurrence as the door opened, and before she had time to concern herself further, Brandenbury had once more become the consummate Southern gentleman. First onto the dock, he stood by, hands extended, helping Bonnie Jo debark, then

Ilene with Mr. Itana, and finally Grace and the Senator bringing up the rear. His smile was as disarming as the island surroundings were lovely.

With the freedom that came from moving out of the cabin and onto the dock, the pall that Brandenbury's unexpected announcement had cast began to dissipate. The evening air was muggy still, but it felt good to Grace to be back on solid footing.

22

The dock and its railings were constructed from redwood that humidity, salt water, and coastal storms had weathered and darkened over time. Two speedboats bobbed and pulled against lines tied to a boat hoist that rose from the opposite side of the dock. An ornately-carved gazebo at the water's end of the dock afforded anyone who lingered unrestricted views of sunsets over the South Carolina and Georgia lowlands.

Moments ago, the sun had disappeared below the horizon, and dusk was settling as the guests walked along the dock toward the land's end. Somewhere a hidden timer clicked on automatically, and low voltage lighting appeared around them, illuminating the dock and walkway beyond with a soft radiant glow.

Grace reached for Ilene's hand. Ilene squeezed it and offered a brief reassuring smile. Or was she merely fortifying her own courage for the evening ahead? Grace wasn't sure. Stepping off the dock, they continued toward the house along a variegated, gray brick walkway edged with flowers and decorative shrubs. Innocuous comments were punctuated with numerous oohs and aahs as they passed through the Savannah tree-lined path with its colorful floral displays and surroundings of natural beauty accented by subtle lighting. Every so often they came to a step up, marked with a white safety stripe and illuminated by low light.

The small lawns and colorful flowerbeds along the walkway gave the manicured appearance of having been cared for by professional groundskeepers. Every shrub and each grassy area had been trimmed with a perfectionist's eye. Even the Spanish moss hanging from twisted, curving branches of trees looked as though an artist had placed it there to create the sensuous feeling of lace and shadow over the path.

Grace's tension dissipated. In spite of the sticky heat, everyone seemed moved by the idyllic beauty of the surroundings. The chitchat and laughter inside the yacht's cabin and on the dock had been replaced by a subdued, almost tactile feeling of quiet awe along the path. She tried to drink in all of it for storytelling later on. It was a fairyland of light and shadows and solitude, in every way removed from the familiar sounds of neighborhood traffic that they tolerated near their apartment.

Well-lit, high-arched windows greeted them and their male companions as they mounted the last steps that opened onto a wide terrace, gleaming with imported Italian stone tile. They entered the house through a massive mahogany door. Grace stood speechless as her eyes gathered in what copious amounts of money could buy. It had to be the most beautiful home interior she had ever seen.

The entry was inlaid with marble squares, its moldings and baseboards trimmed in solid cherry millwork. Beyond was a large living room, its primary feature an extraordinary pecan floor accentuated by a few well-placed Persian and Oriental rugs and some very expensive-looking furniture. And slightly off to one side, a curved staircase offered access to whatever was on the next level.

"Oh, it's ... it's so beautiful!" Bonnie Jo exclaimed, walking to the middle of the room, turning around slowly, gathering in all its charm and beauty. The others hung back, enjoying her whimsical spontaneity. Grace smiled at how her lithesome form and natural grace seemed to complete the loveliness that surrounded her.

To their right a lighted glassed-in sun porch opened out onto another terrace. And to one side in the room immediately ahead, a large dining table appeared ready to be encircled by its guests. A Waterford crystal chandelier hung from the high-beamed ceiling, its light dancing playfully across the table, creating a subtle glow of light and shadow.

"What a grand old house," Bonnie Jo declared. "I'll bet tons of restorative work has gone on in this place. Right, Mr. Brandenbury?"

"Right you are, BJ," he declared, joining her at the center of the room. Grace noted that their host had already passed beyond the initial "Ms. Senter" phase to the more intimate and personal use of Bonnie Jo's initials; a privilege she as a rule allowed only her closest friends. But she didn't seem at all bothered. She was clearly absorbed in the moment. If she had entertained any earlier concerns, and that was doubtful, they had been set aside. That Bonnie Jo had decided to enjoy herself to the full at this one opportunity in life to be the dinner guest of a "gazillionaire" was incontrovertible. It was Bonnie Jo at her best. Grace envied her ability to throw herself into any situation with such complete spontaneity. As the others gathered in the room, she glanced at her watch. It was seven thirty-five.

At that precise moment a man, with distinctive Asian features and wearing a chef's white jacket, entered through a swinging door at the far end of the dining room and pausing, stood a distance away from the table, waiting for their host to acknowledge his presence. The man's air was aloof and impassive. Without smiling, he nodded to his employer but said nothing.

Brandenbury turned to the others. "Are you ready to eat?" His voice boomed out the question. Grace thought of the announcer on Monday Night Football. It was like that. The group voted enthusiastically in favor of the idea.

"Ho San here is one of the greatest chefs on the face of the earth," Brandenbury emphasized with a flourish. "He's prepared a wonderful meal, and he is ready to serve, so let's be seated. Everyone dig in and enjoy."

At this a second man appeared, deftly carrying at shoulder level a tray loaded with salad plates. Though he was now dressed in dark pants, white shirt and bow tie, Grace recognized him as the one who had met them at the dock and tied up the yacht when they first arrived. How had he managed to change so quickly?

Brandenbury seated himself at the head of the table with Bonnie Jo on his right. Next to her sat the Senator, then Grace at the end, opposite Brandenbury. Talal Itana was seated to her right with Ilene between the diplomat and their host. The table had been set with fine china featuring an exquisite, hand-painted likeness of the mansion. The silverware and cloth napkins were monogrammed with the initials CB. Grace unfolded the napkin and placed it in her lap. *Very nice. So this is how the upper one-hundredth of one percent lives. I guess anything worth doing is worth overdoing.*

"Have some more wine, Grace," ordered Brandenbury. At least that's the way his tone sounded to her, more an order than an invitation. On the yacht coming over, she had seen him put away at least two, maybe three glasses. She wondered if he had a limit.

A delicious Caesar salad was followed with generous portions of Charleston she-crab soup, then small cups of sherbet for "cleansing the palate." Needless to say, no expense had been spared. Grace was certain of that. She wondered if their host dined this way all the time. She knew that she didn't, but what did it matter? The moment was the only thing that really mattered. Hadn't she been told all through her young adult life to live in the now? This was a once-in-a-lifetime evening, something to recount someday while warming herself by a fireplace with her grandchildren. She smiled at the thought of wide-eyed little ones listening to the adventurous tales of their legendary grandmother.

The main course consisted of a crispy flounder that Ho San had first quick-fried and then baked. Its accompaniments included red rice, a green vegetable, and apricot chutney on the side. When the final bite of apple pastry dessert had been consumed and several more bottles of wine were drained dry, Grace touched her lips with her napkin and thought to herself that this had to be the very best dinner she had ever eaten. At last, as Brandenbury busied himself with pouring everyone generous snifters of cognac, they pushed back from the table and made their way back to the main living area.

23

Though she had tried to go easy on the evening's alcoholic libations, Grace knew she was already well past her limit and concentrated on dismissing a feeling of lightheadedness. Bonnie Jo and her "gazillionaire" had moved to the chairs nearest the French doors opening onto the sun porch. She glanced at Ilene sitting at the opposite side of the room sipping her drink and conversing with Talal Itana in front of the unlit fireplace.

She had to admit that Noah Parker had proven to be an interesting and entertaining dinner partner, even if his conversational prowess was in general used up on himself. He had traveled a great deal in America as well as in Europe, Africa, Asia, and the Middle East. Places that Grace dreamed of going to one day. And while he asked very few questions about her background and life, it was no trouble at all getting him to talk about the subject he was most fond of.

It was easy to start him off on another travelogue or coax him into waxing eloquently on the new Senate majority leader's lack of political skills or the reasons why the current Speaker of the House was doomed to failure. Even though they were members of the same party, she could see there was no love lost between the two. The "waxing" continued to flow with increasing ease as night closed in on them, and generous amounts of alcohol loosened not only the

Senator's tie, but his tongue as well. Grace thought to herself it was a good thing she was not a foreign agent. Noah Parker would be easy pickings.

Wait.

Her eye had caught Brandenbury and Bonnie Jo leaning over the small end table between their two chairs, their heads only inches apart.

What's going on with those two?

Bonnie Jo clearly had had more than enough to drink. Her infectious laugh, so delightful and familiar to Grace, had become brassy and uncontrolled.

Noah Parker was oblivious to anything going on elsewhere in the room, fully absorbed in describing his most recent Southeast Asian trip to exotic Bangkok. Grace tried keeping one ear tuned to his running travelogue, nodding and smiling appropriately, while glancing back again at Bonnie Jo. Brandenbury lifted something in his hand as Bonnie Jo leaned forward. They were partially turned away from her line of vision so she couldn't see everything, but ...

Grace swore under her breath.

While she had never experimented beyond a brief flirtation with marijuana on the night of her high school prom, she'd been around the college scene long enough to have seen this before. And it frightened her.

Cocaine! It has to be. Oh, BJ. Please, not again!

Grace felt her skin crawl. Bonnie Jo had done enough alcohol and drugs in her high school and early college years to land her in a rehab center to get clean. When she first approached Ilene and Grace about the apartment, they had made her promise never to bring in drugs if they agreed to accept her as a roommate. She'd kept her promise.

Until now.

Grace was struck once again with the fact that they were quite alone with these three men. On an island no less. What had happened to the supposed cream of America's business and political leadership? She cursed again, this time out loud, positive that one of these elite gods of politics and commerce had just given her roommate a friendly little snort of cocaine. What a nightmare! Was it the first, or had there already been others?

She watched the small white envelope disappear from the lamp table into Brandenbury's pocket as he stood to his feet. Extending his hand, he helped Bonnie Jo from her chair. She closed her eyes, swaying. Brandenbury placed an arm around her waist, pulling her against him. At that moment, Parker realized that something was diverting Grace's attention away from him, and he followed her gaze across the room. Brandenbury and Bonnie Jo were headed toward the spiral staircase.

"BJ!" Grace called out after them. "What are you doing?"

Bonnie Jo's foot slipped on the first stair step as she turned to look at her. Everyone's attention had been captured by the sharpness in Grace's voice. Bonnie Jo leaned back against Brandenbury allowing him to balance her with his arm.

"I'm going ... up," she giggled, pointing an unsteady finger, "with Mr. B to see the second floor of this ... gor-gee-ous house!" Her words slurred together as she waved and started up the steps.

Grace was on her feet now, throwing a look of concern at Ilene, then back at Bonnie Jo. Her own lightheadedness surprised her, forcing her to close her eyes for an instant, her hand reaching for Parker's shoulder as she steadied herself. A dull throb pounded in her head as images swirled, blurred by too much alcohol. The alcohol had not been enough, however, to curtail the apprehension she'd felt from the very beginning. It was back again, big time, turning into fear mixed with anger and washing over her like a returning tide.

Brandenbury was at the top of the staircase now, laughing as Bonnie Jo waved again to the others. "Don't worry, folks. She'll be fine. BJ's just had a little too much that's all. I want her to see my collection of paintings."

Your paintings? I'll bet! How original can you get?

"BJ ... " Grace started toward her when she felt Noah Parker's restraining hand on her shoulder.

"Hey, Grace, don't worry. She'll be all right. Besides, it's getting late. I was thinking maybe we could go upstairs, too."

Grace turned to stare at the Senator from South Carolina in disbelief.

"You ... what do you mean ... go upstairs?" The evening had suddenly turned upside down! "I suppose you have some paintings up there you want to show me, too, Senator?"

From the look on Parker's face, she was certain that art was the last thing on his mind. More apprehension rolled in, this time bringing with it a crushing misgiving about their being here at all. This fantasy courting of the rich and the powerful had suddenly turned sour.

"Hey, it's okay," the Senator put his arm around her waist, pulling her against him. "After all, it's what we came for, right? I'm sure Charlie has paid you well. He always does at these little parties. So let's go upstairs. I promise you won't be disappointed." A crooked grin spread across his face as his hand brushed upward through her hair.

Grace shivered. She and the others had been paid well, she thought, but for what? She could feel perspiration breaking out along the lower part of her spine. It always did when she was nervous. She pushed Parker's hand away. Her mind carved a path through the alcohol.

"I'm already disappointed, Senator. More than you can know. What is this anyway? Did you think we were hookers or something?

131

Mr. Reynolds told us there would be a dinner party with several other guests present. That man upstairs paid us to come here because he wanted some additional female presence at the dinner. That's all. There were no other expectations. At least none of which *we* were informed. I'm beginning to think we were just three naïve little girls from Georgia. But I did not hire out to spend the night in bed with a stranger. A married stranger, I might add, just in case you have forgotten that little detail. None of us did. This was a spur of the moment adventure—an opportunity to meet and hobnob with three powerful and respectable men. Leaders that the rest of the country looks up to."

Grace checked her watch again.

"In case you didn't know, we're booked at the Savannah Hyatt tonight and if we're going to get there on time we need to start back now. Sorry to disappoint you, Senator, but I've no intention of spending the night here with you."

Parker stared at her in disbelief, his eyes flashing at first a mix of surprise, then embarrassment, and finally anger. He obviously was not used to being talked to like this. "Look, Grace, you've got this all wrong. It doesn't mean anything. No offense, but we're just looking for a little relaxation and a good time."

"Then go home to your wife, Noah!" she exclaimed, surprised at her use of his given name. She had been using it all evening, so what was different? She was blood-boiling mad, that was the difference. "Look at you. You're a United States Senator, for goodness sake. Don't you have any respect for yourself? Or your family? How about your office and all those American people you supposedly work for? Have you forgotten about them, too?"

Grace spat the words out, all at once fired up; enraged as much at the greed and stupidity that had contributed to their being here as she was incensed by one of America's political icons standing there, expecting to have a casual night of sex with her. She should have known. Perhaps if she'd been honest with herself down deep, she had known it might come to this. But the adventure of it all had arrived out of nowhere and had sounded so thrilling back at the hotel that she'd buried her instincts—laid her judgment aside. Had this been what was eating at her from the start?

One thing was certain. Whatever else she'd thought might come out of this evening she was not expecting what happened next.

24

"Don't. That hurts!" There were muffled sounds of scuffling, then Bonnie Jo again. "Stop. Please. Stop it. You're hurting me!"

Brandenbury's voice was raised in anger, his tone ominous, his words thick and harsh. "Who do you think you are?"

Then a dull thud. Something had slammed against a wall. *Or someone.*

"Get your hands off me!" BJ's sharp scream raged through the house.

Then everything went silent.

Grace stared at the others. They stood frozen in place.

"BJ?" Grace took an uncertain step toward the staircase, her voice shaking as she called out.

Parker started toward the staircase and then stopped. The Senator from South Carolina was obviously as indecisive as the rest about what to do next. *So much for taking care of the world.* She caught Parker's glance at Itana. The look on his face left no doubt that he was shaken. It seemed to Grace as though everything had suddenly shifted, continuing on in slow motion. In reality, mere seconds had passed. Ilene was the first to break away.

"BJ!" she shouted, dropping her wine glass. By the time its monogrammed shards had scattered across the stone fireplace hearth, she had bounded across the room and headed up the stairs taking them two at a time, stumbling at the chilling sound of breaking glass somewhere above and to the left, beyond the staircase landing.

Regaining her balance she scrambled up the steps. By the time she reached the top, Grace was running after her with Itana and Parker close behind.

"BJ," Ilene called out again, "are you all right?"

Ilene reached the end of the hall just as Brandenbury came out of a doorway to her left. His hair was disheveled and his dress shirt torn away from the top buttons. He was pressing his hand against his cheek. He was bleeding. She ran at him, pushing past into the room.

As Grace rushed down the hallway after Ilene, Brandenbury moved in front of the door to stop her. She could smell the man's sweat, feel his chest heaving as she tried to push past. He grabbed her shoulder, digging powerful fingers into her flesh. In moments, Ilene was back again. She ducked under Brandenbury's outstretched arm and stood in the man's face, screaming, "What happened here? Where's BJ?"

Grace glimpsed a look of wildness in the man's eyes—and something else. *Excitement?* Brandenbury took a half-step back, distracted for an instant by Ilene's angry cries. As he did, Grace twisted away from his grip and slipped behind them both through the doorway.

Her eyes swept across the room, its furnishings outlined in shadowy darkness from the light through the open door behind her.

Where is she?

There was nothing.

"BJ?"

Grace felt along the wall until her fingers brushed against a light switch. She flipped it on. An old-fashioned floor lamp near a chair opposite the door cast a soft yellow glow throughout the room. She

135

caught her breath as she stared at the window on the opposite wall from where she was standing.

Jagged edges of broken glass were caught in the frame.

The sound of glass breaking. It rang in her ears. But ... there's no glass here. No glass on the carpet ...

Instinctively she began backing out of the room, her eyes riveted on the window, horror mounting as she bumped against Ilene standing in the doorway behind her. Ilene had seen the broken window, too, and the magnitude of what it meant had etched itself with ghost-like panic on her face.

"What have you done?" Ilene, out of control, spun around to face Brandenbury, her eyes ablaze, screaming, cursing, and pounding clenched fists against his chest.

"Shut up!" Brandenbury snarled, and with a vicious slap, drove her back against the wall. Her ankle twisted beneath her as she fell to the floor. Brandenbury's face was flushed, his eyes malevolent slits that gleamed with feverish exhilaration when he turned to face Grace. In that moment, she experienced a new kind of fear. She saw there were fresh scratches on his chest where his shirt was torn. *BJ must have done that!*

Ilene continued spewing out curses. In a blind rage she scrambled to her feet and faced the other men. Pointing at Brandenbury, she shouted, "The window in there is broken. He pushed her. This stupid moron pushed BJ through the window. Get out of my way!"

They were all crowded together in the narrow hallway when Brandenbury grabbed Ilene by the arm as she tried to squirm her way past. "Where do you think you're going, witch?" His voice was cold, full of fury.

"Let go of me!"

Ilene twisted and pushed, trying to pull free, but he was much too strong for her. Brandenbury yanked her off her feet and slammed her against the wall again, snarling, "Shut your mouth, you—"

"Charlie, what's happening here? Take it easy, man. What are you doing?" It was Parker's voice now, one filled with shock and disbelief.

"You shut up, too," Brandenbury grunted as he struggled with Ilene. Then with a sudden rotating motion he threw her against the opposite wall, smashing his fist into the side of her face. Ilene's head snapped to one side, and she slumped to the hall floor.

"Charlie—Charlie—hey, come on, man. Take it easy!"

Itana was standing to one side, watching, saying nothing, as Parker made a halfhearted attempt to pin Brandenbury against the wall. Grace dropped to her knees beside Ilene. Ilene moaned, the left side of her face already puffing with what would surely be a dark bruise, perhaps even a broken cheekbone or jaw. Her lip was split open and blood trickled down the side of her mouth. Grace fought against dizziness as spiking bursts of adrenaline mixed with too much alcohol pounded through her brain.

This can't be real. The man is crazy! They're all insane!

How long had she been in the room? How long in the hallway? Time lost all sense of reality. First BJ. Now, Ilene. The sight of her lying there unconscious on the floor had numbed her mind. She couldn't think. How long? Minutes? Seconds? She flashed back to the broken window.

BJ!

Grace scrambled to her feet, glaring at Parker. "Don't let that maniac near Ilene again, do you hear?" Struggling to control the shaking in her voice, she pointed at Brandenbury. Her eyes blazed with anger as she pointed to the Lebanese diplomat. "The same to you. Keep him away from her!"

25

Grace pushed past the others, running back the way she came, her hand on the banister as she flew down the steps, across the room and through the entry door. Once outside she hesitated, getting her bearings, hearing someone running up the path from the direction of the dock. She turned away and hurried to her right.

The terrace ended at the corner of the house with a series of steps dropping down to a flagstone patio and garden. There in the shadow-light coming from a first floor window, Grace saw Bonnie Jo lying motionless on the stones, her body splayed awkwardly and surrounded by broken glass.

"No, no, no," she whispered over and over, hurrying down the steps and across the flagstone. "Oh, God, please no, no, no!"

She dropped to her knees, oblivious to shards of glass scattered about in the dark shadows. Each second passed like the chimes of a clock on the hour.

Adagio. Unhurried. Sonorous. Deliberate.

She stared down at her best friend, crumpled grotesquely on the flagstone terrace. Two deep scratches on her neck continued down a shoulder where her dress had been torn away in the struggle. Blood oozed from a glass-cut across an otherwise flawless cheek and from another deep slice a short way above her knee. *Could that have happened from falling? No. It must have been upstairs while they were struggling. He did this! That maniac—*

Reaching out her hand, she pressed trembling fingers against her throat. No response. Nothing.

BJ's deep, round eyes, always dancing with fun and laughter— everything in life a party— stared back at her now.

Caesura. Interrupted. Empty. Lost.

"Oh, BJ, BJ, BJ," Grace choked out her anguish over the still form of her friend. "This can't be. You can't be dead."

Bonnie Jo's only response was a small dark stain pooling onto the flagstone from her slack mouth, framing her face in a hideous half-halo.

Gone.

Beyond her touch.

Her mind refused to accept whatever was next. There was no next.

Not for BJ.

Not now. Not ever.

Oh my God, what have we done?

A shadowy figure flashed across her peripheral vision and loomed over her.

She looked up at a man she did not recognize. He had a gun.

Where had he come from?

The rancid taste of fish and sweets and too much alcohol exploded without warning. She leaned forward. Hands on flagstone. Gagging. Heaving. Wiping phlegm and saliva with her fingers. The stranger grasped her shoulder with one hand until the nausea passed.

"What happened?" he asked, bending down over Bonnie Jo's body, feeling for a pulse, for any sign of life.

"What happened?" Grace echoed, hearing her voice start to rise hysterically. "What happened? That ... that ... maniac up there ... tried to ... she was fighting him off ... he ... she fell from that window!"

Even as she said the words she looked up again at the second story window and then back to the patio.

No, that can't be. It couldn't have happened that way.

Bonnie Jo's body was too far out to have fallen by accident. She was at least five or six meters away from the house. Grace stared up at the window again, her mind racing back over the terrifying events of the last few minutes.

BJ's voice ... "You're hurting me!"... sounds of scuffling ... then he must have hit her ... the silence ... the sound of glass breaking. Had she been unconscious when ...

Her thoughts flashed to the upstairs room with the old-fashioned floor lamp ... the jagged glass shards in the window frame ... another wave of horror swept over her.

There's only one way she could have fallen this far from the house.

"Stay right here," he ordered, his voice hard and gruff. He turned away and disappeared around the corner of the house, calling to someone as he hurried out of sight.

How many of these people are there anyway?

She stared down at her friend.

Oh, BJ!

Then the nausea returned a second time. She spewed another repulsive mixture of food and alcohol onto the flagstones.

More voices filtered through the broken window above her. Shadows moving back and forth across the opening. A face appeared and quickly vanished. Someone cursed repeatedly. It was Parker's voice, angry, frightened.

"Charlie, what on earth were you thinking, man? We can't be found here like this. My wife will kill me! And my people. This will ruin me when word gets out that I ... that you ... "

His voice trailed off in a plaintive moan.

Then she heard Itana. "What's the plan, Charlie?"

The plan? Charlie? It was the first time Grace had heard the Lebanese diplomat call their host anything but Mr. Brandenbury. *What plan? What are they talking about?*

"This guy says the woman downstairs is dead. He's already checked her out. What were you thinking anyway? Was this something you planned without telling me?"

"She said 'no'!" Brandenbury's voice bellowed. "I brought her up here, and she said no!"

"So what? The woman said no. Did you have to get physical with her?" Parker sounded incredulous.

"They're all alike," Brandenbury snapped back. "Look. She drew blood, the little tart!"

"What are you talking about, Charlie?" said Parker. "These are university women. They're different. They aren't like the others."

"She actually had the cheek to say 'no' to me," Brandenbury repeated, paying no attention to Parker. "Me. Charles Brandenbury! Then she scratched me with those talons of hers. Look."

"But she went through the window."

"She was trash, that's all. You know what you do with trash."

"You're not serious." Grace heard Parker's voice explode with incredulity. "You threw her out the window? Oh, come on, man. Tell me you didn't do that. Tell me it was an accident!"

"What difference does it make?" roared Brandenbury. "She was garbage. Now she's dead garbage. Nobody says 'no' to Charles Brandenbury. Nobody! And that includes you, mister."

There was a long silence.

"So what are we going to do?" Parker asked at last, the question edged with fright.

"We get rid of her."

"What?"

"We get rid of her."

"But the other two will talk and then … "

"You're not listening. We get rid of her. And we get rid of the others, too. They won't be talking to anyone."

"But, Charlie, the police … "

"There are no police on this island. And don't worry about the ones on the mainland or the coroner either for that matter. They belong to me. I own them, Mr. High-and-Mighty Senator. While you've been up there in Washington schmoozing the ladies and kissing babies, I've been taking care of business. They are all bought and paid for! Not that it'll make any difference. These three just met up with a really bad accident tonight, that's all."

"But what about your people? They're going to know what's happened," Parker protested. "One of them already does. Even you can't cover this up."

"Shut up, Noah. The men working here tonight are loyal. One hundred percent. They do what I say, all right? All my people do what I say. Have you got that? All of them. Now give me a hand with this one."

From below the broken window, Grace heard it all.

This cannot be happening! She's still up there. With them!

"Ilene."

No answer.

She cried out again. "Ilene!"

Then she heard Brandenbury call out to someone else.

"The other one is downstairs. Go get her, and shut her up."

Seconds later she heard a door open and slam shut on the opposite side of the house.

The lump in her throat refused to go away. Her mind and body seemed out of touch. On her knees beside her friend, Grace stared up at the window in disbelief. *We get rid of them? A really bad accident? What are they saying?* Conscious of the rancid taste in her mouth, she swallowed and gagged again, spitting out the phlegm collecting in her throat. *No, no, no ... this can't be happening to us. They're going to ...*

The chill of death cut through the sultry summer night like an arrow tipped in ice, driving deep into her chest, taking her breath away. Then numbness. She was shutting down.

She could feel it.

She just couldn't stop it.

The sour taste returned and she retched. She needed to vomit again, but there was only the sound of her gagging.

This cannot be happening!

Swallowing once more to rid herself of the lump in her throat that would not go away. Knowing. Fearing.

He's coming back!

Do something.

I don't know ... What can I do?

Save yourself.

Her heart pounded—a wild, erratic staccato, like a deer that senses the crosshairs of the hunter's riflescope.

But I can't leave her ... Oh, God, how can this be happening?

A last despairing look at BJ's lifeless form. The thought of Ilene ... up there ... alone ... with them.

Get away from this place. Run!

Scrambling to her feet, she turned to her left, stumbling as the sole of her high-heeled shoe slipped on broken glass. As soon as her hands and knees hit the flagstones, she was up again, running toward what looked to be a dirt path that led away from the house. With a desperate glance over her shoulder, she plunged headlong into the late night darkness, each step fueled by an incendiary mixture of panic and adrenaline.

Run.

A tsunami wave filled with fear and remorse swept her along the trail. There could be no stopping now. No turning back.

Run!

The path narrowed. Thorny brush stems lashed at her face, scratched her arms and legs, tearing at her dress as she flew past. A canopy of sugar pine closed over the path, making the darkness darker still, slowing her headlong flight. Eyes wide, hands extended in a vain attempt to split the darkness, she pushed deeper into the woods, straining to find her way.

RUN!

A shout from the house. "She's gone!"

"She can't have gotten far. Go after her. Don't let her get away!"

The second voice she recognized instantly.

Brandenbury!

Unnerved, disoriented, she groped her way along the path; her only sense that of heading into the island's interior.

Where am I going?

No matter. Just keep moving.

Away from that nightmarish house!

At last she stopped, bending down to remove her shoes. She clutched them in one hand and pressed the other against her knees, sucking air, heart pounding as she strained to hear the inevitable.

Footsteps.

At the sound, she bolted again, terrified. They were coming. She knew they would be. Getting closer. The words echoed in her ears. "Don't let her get away!"

What is going to happen to me?

Frantic now, running through the darkness she didn't see the sharp bend in the trail until it was too late. Her ankle gave way as she plummeted head first off the path, sliding and rolling down a steep slope into a brushy thicket until coming to a sudden stop against the base of a tree. Stunned. Breathless. Unable to move.

Above her, amongst the trees along the trail, a light bobbed back and forth. She could see it. Someone was running. She could hear it. The light drew nearer. She could hear his heavy breathing. The footsteps slowed as they came closer to where she lay. And now she knew. Accepting the inevitable.

They're going to kill me!

145

— **Part Three** —

We are so largely the playthings of Fate in our fears.

To one, fear of the dark,

to another, of physical pain,

to a third, of public ridicule,

to a fourth, of poverty,

to a fifth, of loneliness—

for all of us our particular creature lurks in ambush.

— Hugh Walpole

I said to myself, "There is surely no fear of God in this place, and they will kill me because of my wife."

—Abraham

Genesis 20:11

26

The shrill ringing startled her. It rang a second time. She lunged for the phone, knocking it off its platform and sending it skittering wildly across the end table as she made a futile attempt to catch it before it hit the floor. Groping along the carpet in the dark, she finally retrieved it.

"Hello?"

She waited for the caller's voice, struggling as she did to free herself from the all-too-familiar nightmare terrors into which she had descended. There was no answer. She looked at the receiver to be sure she was holding it right-side up.

"Hello," she repeated. "Are you there?"

Still nothing.

Grace glanced at her watch with a sudden twinge of apprehension. She had left a message with Maggie. And Brad had promised to call.

But it was eleven-thirty.

"Hello, Grace."

She sat motionless, unable to breathe. Was she awake or was she still in the midst of her hellish dream? Suddenly, the fear she had been reliving moments before slammed into her like a hammer pounding wood. Her eyes widened in the darkness. She was awake all right.

"We've been looking for you, Grace." A man's voice, his tone sardonic, taunting. "We've looked for you a long time. You've been a very bad girl."

"Who ... are ... you?" Grace's jaws clenched as she tried to steady her voice, willing herself not to drop the telephone again. That's what she wanted to do. Drop it. Throw it away. Make the Voice disappear.

"Are you afraid, Grace?" the Voice asked. "You sound as though you might be. At least a little. But then you have good reason to be afraid, don't you? If I were you, I'd be afraid. I'd be very afraid."

"Who are you?" Grace repeated, leaning forward, clutching the telephone with both hands. "What do you want?"

"You're good, Grace," the Voice went on, ignoring her questions. "Much more devious than we thought at first. As a matter of fact, we are very interested in knowing how you did it. We want to know all about where you've been and what you've been doing these last seven years. We need to have a little talk, Grace. In fact," the Voice paused, "we insist on it."

"I have nothing to say to you," answered Grace, crestfallen, as she stared into the darkness of the living room, her sense of entrapment spiking through the roof. "Just leave me alone!"

"Don't hang up, Grace," the Voice admonished.

"There's nothing I can tell you."

"You don't understand," the Voice remonstrated. "Now that we've found you, we do need to talk. I'm sure when you've had time to think about it, you'll want to as well. The truth of it is, a lot that happens from here on out depends on your cooperation. For example, it will certainly be in the best interests of your Reverend Weston for us to talk. You know ... Bradley? Your boyfriend? Your lover? And those precious little children. They really are beautiful, Grace. What are their names again? Nancy and David, I believe."

More hammer blows, this time to the stomach!

Oh, God, please don't let this be happening.

But it was happening. And there was nothing she could do about it.

Grace's fantasy of a safe and secure desert refuge, tucked away from the rest of the world where no one would ever find her had been a house of cards after all. Shame and fear leaped over the Wall she had constructed with such vigilance, freely darting in and out, tugging, terrorizing, paralyzing her ability to think with clarity. Her long-feared and very personal *Day of Reckoning* had arrived at last.

"I do hope you've not carelessly talked about past events to anyone, Grace," the Voice went on, "especially to your little family."

Why are we sitting here talking like this? You found me so why don't you just kill me and be done with it? Isn't that what this is all about?

"It would be a shame to involve them in something that's none of their concern now, wouldn't it?"

That's it. That's the reason you want to talk. You're keeping me alive because you're afraid I've told someone about you, and you need to know who it might be!

"Grace? Are you still there, Grace?"

"Yes, I'm here. Where else would I be?" Her sudden revelation had awakened a sharpness in her voice.

"Please, Grace, please. Don't sound so bitter. Let's try to be civil about this, shall we?"

Who are you? Not Brandenbury or Parker. I'd know it if you were.

"Or would you rather I called you Taylor?" the Voice asked. "That's a nice name, Taylor."

You're not Itana either. His voice was raspy from too many cigarettes. But I've heard your voice before …

"A very nice name in fact. Which do you prefer that I call you?"

A silent pause fell between them as Grace fought back the dread she felt and tried to focus.

149

You're not Reynolds. You must be one of Brandenbury's other hirelings.

"Talk to me."

Did I see you that night? Your voice …

"Pouting or becoming angry isn't going to get us anywhere."

No southern accent. But there's definitely something familiar—would I recognize you, if I saw you again?

"What do you want?" she asked at last.

"Oh, nothing much. We just need to talk about that unfortunate little accident you were party to a few years ago."

"Little accident?" Grace shuddered, eyes shut, as she struggled to keep her voice down for fear of waking the children. Her next words fairly spat themselves out. "You call *murder* a little *accident*? Whoever you are, you and that animal you work for must have been in hell, and as far as I'm concerned the quicker you go back, the better!"

"Now, Grace, please. Let's not call each other names. Calm down and relax. I only want us to get together so we can talk things out."

"I'm not meeting with anyone. I told you, I have nothing to say."

"Oh, I think you underestimate yourself on that," the Voice responded with a sinister chuckle. "Besides, you really don't have a choice in the matter, you know. You're not calling the shots anymore. Anyway, you wouldn't want anything to happen to the Reverend now would you? And I think those really are two of the handsomest children I've ever seen. Don't you agree?"

Grace felt her throat constrict. It was difficult to breathe again. The Voice had mentioned Brad and the children twice now. He was leaving no doubt. They were in serious danger if she failed to do what they asked.

"By the way," the Voice droned on in its muffled, yet syrupy fashion, "did you like your picture? I thought it was a very good likeness."

Grace took a deep breath.

"All right, whoever you are." She forced out the words as her mind raced, desperate for some bargaining chip, however small. "Here's something you'll want to think about. You like to take pictures? Well, so do I. In fact, I have pictures. Pictures of that night."

There was a noticeable hesitation on the other end.

"You're bluffing."

"You wish," she retorted.

"No one brought cameras that night."

You were there!

"Mr … our mutual friend never allows cameras. Not at his private residence. Not unless … " the mysterious caller's words trailed off.

"Unless what?" demanded Grace.

"Unless they're his own," the Voice finished defiantly.

Grace's mind raced over what this implied.

Of course. Why haven't I thought of that before? There were hidden cameras. Brandenbury takes his own private collection of pictures. The man's a pervert on top of everything else.

"I guess he did this sort of thing often then. I'll bet he still does. Does he get his kicks from making dirty videos?"

The Voice did not answer, but Grace's mind was spinning now.

Maybe it's more than that. If he had compromising pictures, he could use them to incriminate his guests later on, to blackmail them. That's it, isn't it? This is not about me. I'm nothing to him. He gains control of a lobbyist or a senator—or anyone else he can turn into an easily manipulated pawn. Maybe even … a president of the United States!

That awful night seven years ago—and today's announcement of Noah Parker's candidacy for the presidency. The two dissimilar events came together like a coupling of train cars. The enormity of what she was thinking took her breath away!

"Believe it or not, I don't really care what he does with his pictures," she went on, mustering up as much false bravado as she could. "The fact is I've got pictures, too; pictures that will blow his camouflaged power dreams to kingdom come. We're all right there. Together. With your boss and his precious little yacht in living color!"

"Prove it." The Voice was back again.

"Sure," said Grace, her voice now brimming with contempt. "I'll just hand them over, with a list of the names and addresses of people who'll get copies of them, together with my handwritten testimony about what went on that night if ever anything happens to me."

The Voice was silent.

Grace waited.

"Well, well," he said at last, "you're quite a determined little schemer aren't you?" There was another pause with the only sound that of the Voice breathing into the telephone. Then he continued, "If you are telling the truth, and I have my doubts about that, how do you suggest we resolve our little impasse? I suppose you believe your cooperation is worth some money?"

"I just want to be left alone!" Grace's voice was rising, trembling with emotion. "And I want to be sure you'll do everything in your power to keep me and Brad and those two children healthy. I've seen what happens to people who get close to that filthy creature you work for. You may not want to believe me, but it's the chance you have to take.

"A full accounting exists, so deal with it. I have named the ones who were there, plus I have the pictures on a very incriminating digital filmcard featuring your boss, his little white yacht, my friends, and me. He told the authorities that he never saw us before. Remember? But the pictures say differently. And those monogrammed napkins— the ones imprinted with the picture of your boss' house? Did you count them after dinner to be sure they were all there?"

"Now I know you're lying, Grace," the Voice shot back, but a hint of uncertainty had crept into his tone. Grace sensed she had scored another hit with her napkin bluff.

He doesn't want to let me know it.

"You don't have anything of the kind," the Voice went on. "You couldn't have."

"Oh, but I could," she responded with a surge of confidence, "and you know it. You don't think an innocent little Southern belle, ready to graduate from the University and face the cold, cruel world, would spend an evening with three of America's 'most powerful' and not manage to take away some souvenirs to remember it all by now do you, Mr. —what did you say your name was?"

I know that voice! But where ...

"Meet me in an hour," the Voice commanded, ignoring her question. "We'll discuss this further. My employer is offering to be your benefactor. He will pay you very generously for your cooperation. He just wants to be assured that your remembrances of what went on that night are the same as his."

I'm sure he does!

"I can't do that."

"You must."

"You know I have the children here. I won't leave them alone."

"You don't seem to understand, *Grace,*" the Voice spoke her name with a tinge of derision now. And coldness. She was trembling again as fear crowded out her fleeting surge of confidence. He was in control, and she knew it. "This isn't a game. We're very serious. If you know what's good for you, you'll cooperate fully. A great deal of money will be provided you, enough so that you never have to work again. Nor will your boyfriend for that matter. But, if you try anything— anything at all, I promise you the outcome will not be pleasant."

"I'll meet you tomorrow." She gripped the phone, sensing that she'd held her own, if only for a short time, and there was nothing further to be gained. "Five o'clock."

"No. Make it later in the evening. Drive out to the wash along Fred Waring Avenue."

"Absolutely not, Mr. Whoever-You-Are. I may have been young and naive seven years ago, but I've grown up. Five o'clock in broad daylight in front of Broadmores. That's where I work, as I'm sure you already know. How will I recognize you?"

There was a brief pause while Grace held her breath, sensing the Voice was making up his mind whether or not to accept her offer or force her hand. She knew forcing her hand wouldn't take much. She was all bluff.

"Dark glasses, a green and tan sport shirt. Khaki slacks."

Grace covered the phone with her hand and let out a sigh of relief. Maybe she had just gained some control over her situation. Then it hit her. She *knew* a man who wore dark glasses, a green and tan shirt and khaki slacks!

"Fred?" Grace said incredulously.

The Voice chuckled. "Rye bread sandwich and mineral water. Missed you today."

Grace struggled to regain her composure as the reality of her situation continued to sink in. *I've been sitting with the enemy ... we've been eating lunch together!*

"And, Grace ... "

He paused.

"Don't try to be smarter than you really are. You're way out of your league. Go to work tomorrow just like always. Don't change your schedule in any way. Play it straight, and do as you're told. Don't call the authorities for help. My employer owns half the cops in this state and the FBI, too. We'll know if you try."

Is that actually possible? Surely he's bluffing. Still ...

"And the other half won't believe your bizarre story anyway."

That's probably true.

"Contact them, and you'll be very sorry, Grace. Do we have an agreement?"

"Yes," she said softly.

"Oh, there is one other thing I almost forgot. How utterly rude of me," said the Voice. "Have you heard from the Reverend this evening?"

Grace's grip tightened on the phone.

"Grace?"

"Yes—I mean, no, I haven't."

"Then perhaps this will help you sleep a little better."

She tensed as she heard a click followed by a short burst of static. Then a voice, strange and far off. Yet so very familiar and close!

"Taylor. What's going on? These guys said you and the kids are in the hospital. Are you all ..."

Click.

For a long moment Grace sat perfectly still, incapable of moving or even breathing as she tried to cope with the numbing implication of what she had just heard.

"Feel better, Grace?" asked the Voice. "I knew you'd be happy to know that Bradley is with us now. He's in good health at the moment, and he'll be quite relieved to learn that you intend to keep him that way."

The Voice chuckled.

"What ... what have you done with him?" Grace choked out each word through clenched teeth, her voice quivering.

"Ah, ah. Stay calm, Grace. I advise you to stay calm and collected. *Very* collected. We expect you to go through your day tomorrow just as you normally would. You'll be watched every minute. In fact, you're

155

being watched right now, as I'm sure you've already guessed. We're way ahead of you on this so don't try to run off. You did that once before, but it's not going to happen this time. Do exactly as you're told and Bradley will be all right. Just think of your lover boy as an insurance policy. You've not been very trustworthy in the past, and we want to know you can be counted on to do as you are told. You understand, I'm sure."

"If you hurt him, I'll…"

"Now, now," the Voice responded, mocking her feeble ultimatum. "It won't do any good to threaten or try something foolish. Remember, what I told you. Your benefactor is willing to pay handsomely for your cooperation. But if you refuse? Well, I can assure you that you stand to lose a great deal. Goodnight, Grace."

"Wait …"

Click.

Grace's eyes rimmed with tears as she sat holding the phone in her hand. Slowly she replaced it to the handset and sank back into the sofa. Then a movement in the darkness brought her to attention.

"Taylor?" a tiny voice called out, "was that Daddy on the phone?"

Grace let out a sigh, trying to calm her jittery nerves. "Yes, honey, it was your Daddy."

"Is he all right?"

Grace hesitated before deciding one more lie would be better than the truth. She couldn't be in any more trouble with God than she was now. "He's fine, sweetheart. Go back to sleep. It's late." She held her wristwatch up close to see the time. *A quarter to twelve.*

"Are you okay, Taylor?" asked the tiny voice. "You sounded like you were mad."

Grace went to Nancy and picked her up and held her tightly against her breast. *She feels so good this close. So warm and innocent. And now she's in danger, too. And David. We're all in danger. How could I have ever let this happen?*

"I'm okay. I've just had a long day, that's all. Don't worry. I love you, sweetheart."

"I love you, too," Nancy said with a sleepy yawn. Grace carried her back to her bed and pulled the sheet up under Nancy's chin, then made sure the ceiling fan was on low.

"Goodnight. Sweet dreams, darling."

She looked in on David who lay facing the wall, wearing only his pajama bottoms, having kicked off the sheet in his sleep, if it had ever been over him in the first place. The fan was on, but it did seem warm. She checked the air conditioner. It was set to go on at eighty-five degrees, which in the Coachella Valley's dry desert air was more like seventy-five where she had lived in the Bay area before moving here. She lowered it to eighty and went down the hall to the master bedroom.

The message indicator on the phone by the bed was blinking red. She didn't think it had been on before. *Maggie?* Pressing the button, she waited.

You have one message. Monday, 7:35 p.m. Then a familiar voice boomed into the darkened room.

"Hello, Grace. This is Fernando Ravez. I don't want to alarm you or anything, but Brad was called away during the dinner hour, didn't say anything about where he was going and didn't come back. The hostess said he left with two highway patrolmen. I'm at our hotel room now, but he hasn't returned and there's no word. His car is still here, too. Has he been in touch with you? I thought maybe there might be something wrong at home. If you get this message, please call me at this number."

Grace stared at the phone until finally pressing the save and the off buttons. The light went out. How had she missed this message? Had the phone rang? She couldn't remember hearing it. She put her hands to her face. *Oh God, what is happening to me? My nerves are shattered.*

She reached for the reading lamp, then hesitated. If they really were watching the house, and she suspected they were, she'd rather they didn't know what part of it she was in. So instead, she turned on the ceiling fan and stood for a long moment directly beneath it, closing her eyes. This had always been comforting to her. Like an evening breeze. A ceiling fan was one of the little things she had come to appreciate since moving to the desert.

Stepping out of her shorts, she laid down on the bed, unable to undress any further. *They* were too close for that. Watching. And they had Brad!

How had they managed to do it? Fernando said there were two highway patrolmen. "Your benefactor owns half the cops in this state."

Curling on her side in a fetal position, Grace reached out and ran her hand slowly over the emptiness—where he should be. This was his bed. It was going to have been ours soon. Together. Then she turned onto her back and stared up at the dark ceiling.

Dear God, I have done a terrible thing to this family. Why did I ever come here in the first place? I should have known better. Now what am I going to do?

A breath of air from the ceiling fan's slow rotation moved across the bed as tears ran unchecked across the bridge of her nose, along the contour of her checks and down through loose strands of hair, dampening the pillow.

Where are you, Brad?

Guilt, remorse, and shame crashed around her, over her, deep inside her. Like trees falling in a dark forest.

Oh God, I'm so sorry. So very sorry!

27

5:21 pm:

"Hi, Maggie. Don't forget that you're on to interview the rabbi in the morning. He called to confirm that you'd be there. Confidentially, I think he likes you. Bye."

Thanks a lot, Beth. I love you, too.

5:53 pm:

"Hello, Sarah? It's Jennifer. Karen and I are here at the Beach House. Aren't you driving over for dinner tonight? We'll wait a little longer. See you."

Lot's of luck, Jennifer. The name is Maggie, like the recording says, and next time I hope you call Sarah's number instead of mine.

7:43 pm:

"Hello, Maggie. It's Retha Fisher. I guess we'll have to take a rain check on Friday. I just got word that Joni has gone into labor. She's a month early, and her husband is in Germany on business. I'm catching a flight to Seattle tonight. Sorry. Catch you later."

How old is Retha's little sister anyway? Let's see. When Joni Free did

159

her concert at the McCallum—could that have been two years ago already? I think that I read she was thirty-six then. Well, I hope everything turns out okay. Why didn't you leave your contact number, Retha? I'd check on you tomorrow.

10:45 pm:

"Maggie? It's Taylor. I'm staying over with Brad's children while he's in LA. Please call me when you get home, even if it's late. It's important. Thanks."

Maggie glanced at the clock by her bed. A quarter to twelve.

She dried her face and hesitated, staring at the phone. Then she picked it up and dialed. *What could be important enough to wake up Taylor at this hour?*

A busy signal.

Well, at least she's still awake. Young people stay up until all hours, I guess. Oh well, better them than me. This day has gone on long enough. All I want to do is go to bed.

She stood at the bathroom sink removing her earrings. It had been a long day.

After a full day in her cubicle at the *Sun*, Mary Magdalene Hinegardner had spent the evening at the plush Weston Resort Hotel, on business rather than pleasure. Maggie had covered a fund-raising banquet that promised aid for refugees in Pakistan and Afghanistan fleeing terrorism, as well as other victims of religious persecution fueled by the Taliban insurgency. Feeling a bit combative today, Maggie wondered about the pressing needs that existed among low-income Hispanic families in her own area, but saw no point in raising the issue in this setting. It would be inappropriate. Pugnacious. Whatever. Maybe she would bring it up in the article itself. It was a topic never far from her mind. She had stirred the pot before and felt quite capable of doing it again.

San Francisco Bay area pastor, John Cain, had been an engaging banquet speaker. Nearly four years ago, he'd been thrust into the international spotlight when his congregation was attacked and his young daughter kidnapped during a synchronized strike by radical Islamic Jihad terrorists. His family had been at the forefront of a series of riveting events taking place concurrently in Israel, Boston and the area community of Baytown. Maggie remembered having followed the story for months. It made the Reverend Cain much more interesting to her than he might otherwise have been, and with a couple of phone calls, she'd managed a commitment for a personal interview following the banquet.

Maggie liked the challenge of her work, though interviews could sometimes be tricky. Cain, however, turned out to be very personable, and the interview had gone well. He came across as sincere and the featured project of Assist International also passed the muster of Maggie's critical eye. She had even written out a check herself.

But instead of spotlighting the speaker as simply being another Coachella Valley fundraiser among the way-too-rich-and-famous, Maggie was pondering how to do an article on ordinary volunteers, the ones who worked with such diligence behind the scenes to make events like these a success. These were the nameless, unheralded people without whom an occasion like this would never happen. Like the young woman at the registration table. Her nametag said 'Josie.' Maggie had paused long enough to show her press card.

"Glad to see you, Maggie," Josie said, smiling brightly, glancing at the press card. She handed over a ticket and a peel-off badge with Maggie's name and identity as a *Desert Sun* reporter already inscribed. "I noticed on the tags that you were coming. I always enjoy reading your column. Doing a story, I presume?"

"Always," Maggie replied, glancing a second time at the young woman whom she still did not recognize. "That's why I keep fighting this waistline. Too many of my stories have free dinners attached."

The young woman laughed, looked admiringly at Maggie's trim figure and said she wished she had Maggie's problem. Before she could respond, Josie had turned her attention to a couple who had followed Maggie into the hotel. Maggie stepped to one side, smoothing the badge onto her dress as she studied the receptionist. Here was one of those persons who felt they knew her well enough to call her by her first name, but with whom she had no reciprocal relationship, not even an acquaintance.

This happened quite often as a result of Maggie's name and picture appearing in her regular *Sun* column on the religion page, and every so often, on the editorial page while writing about Coachella Valley business and political ethics. But it always left her uncomfortable, as though in being known but not knowing, she was missing out on something important. Well, she probably was.

Most of her relationships were pretty one-sided these days. She had tried "fitting in" during the first months following Pete's death, but trying had proved to be just that—more "trying" than actual "fitting in." Being a couple with Pete had always made their social life comfortable, something she'd come to expect. She relied on it, never imagining how difficult it would be without him. But the more she tried, the more wearisome it became. After a while, she began making excuses when old friends invited her to dinner or a movie.

Maggie made a living asking people questions about themselves but seldom did anyone offer up to her any more than some innocuous comment like: "I'll bet you really miss Pete, don't you?" *Hello, what do you think?* Or, "You're working too hard these days, Maggie. We hardly see you anymore." *If you really want to know, I am working too hard. I'm working too hard in order to fill up my days because I miss him so much. Only that's not what you want to hear. You want me to say I'm adjusting well and everything is okay even when we both know I'm not. Too much honesty can be uncomfortable. And if I'm honest, tonight I'm feeling really sorry for myself, so knock it off, Maggie.*

Mona Collins from Channel 3 News had been there tonight. Beautiful Mona. Always managing to look like she'd just stepped off the cover of *Vogue*. Maggie had acknowledged her with the prerequisite smile and wave, but nothing more. What was it about that woman that made her teeth grind? Maybe it was Mona's oversized ego, always requiring reassurance that she was being appropriately seen and adored.

Well, she lives in the right neighborhood. We have more than our share of people who adore themselves around here. Maggie smiled to herself. *And if I hadn't waved, she'd be calling me tomorrow to find out why. Thankfully, I saw her and saved myself the trouble.*

Hanging her dress in the closet, she paused, looking through her wardrobe, trying to make up her mind tonight about what to wear tomorrow. But she was too tired.

She tried redialing.

Taylor's line was still busy.

Okay, Taylor, I'm tired and you're talking, so whatever it is can't be that important. It'll have to wait. I'm down for the night. I'm sure you thought I'd be home before now anyway. I'll catch you in the morning.

Maggie reached around the closet door and took her nightgown off the hook.

Tuesday—0415
north of Asheville, North Carolina

163

Harold Justiss Jones turned over in bed as the lights on the landing pad lit up, glaring off his bedroom window. Pushing himself to a sitting position, he ran a hand over his close-cropped, gray-black hair. He knew someone must have activated them from the house. There were two switches for these powerful lights, one in the main house near the servant's quarters and the other in the garage below his studio apartment. He dropped back, put his face in the pillow, and closed his eyes against the glare.

Five minutes passed before he heard the steady beat of rotor blades, a sound that had been an important part of much of his adult life. Especially his other life, the one he had lived before this one. The sound signaled the arrival of *CB One,* Charles Brandenbury's private helicopter. It was the only bird that ever landed here. Unfortunately for Harold, the pad was located just outside his living quarters and was activated on an irregular schedule any time of the day or night.

He had not been told to prepare for this arrival, so he didn't bother going downstairs. But he did get up and go to the window. He'd seen Randle Martin land the Hughes 500E chopper numerous times before. He was good. Like Harold, he worked for CB Enterprises full-time. Harold knew him just well enough to know he didn't like him. The man had a nasty ego as big as the sky and thought he was God's gift to chopper pilots everywhere. He was always bragging about adventures he had experienced during tours in Iraq and Afghanistan. Well, ol' Harold Justiss knew something about those places and some others, too, that were at least as bad, but he kept it to himself. Thankfully, Martin and the chopper almost never stayed around after making a delivery, as a rule heading back right away to the Asheville Regional Airport to await his next round of orders. That was fine with Harold.

This morning turned out to be no exception. *CB One* had barely touched down before the door opened, and two men jumped out.

They reached back to help a third person from the aircraft and then headed up the walk toward the main house. Harold couldn't make out much more than that it was some guy they were helping. He appeared to be airsick. Or more likely drunk. He thought maybe one of the helpers might be Ray Larson. Ray was another ugly cuss. Harold wondered what it was that brought them out to the Farm at this hour.

He started back to bed, stopped, looked at the tossed-about sheets, and then veered off toward the kitchenette instead. There, he yawned and stretched. He poured some water into the coffeemaker. It was early, but he might as well have a cup anyway. He'd never get back to sleep with all the noise from *CB One,* idling outside his window.

It was fifteen minutes before Martin and the Hughes 500E finally lifted off and headed south over the hills in the early morning darkness.

165

28

Maggie smoothed her silver gray hair and gave a final approving glance at her reflection in the bathroom mirror. At fifty-six years of age she was still attractive, her figure trim and firm from regular workouts at the fitness center. Usually she did not concern herself with the physical reminders of aging. Outside of a few "twinges in the hinges" that were becoming more evident of late, Maggie approved of the way her body served her and endorsed it with customary self-assurance and poise. Even lines at her mouth and eyes that no longer responded to makeup the way they used to, appeared to have been created more by laughter than by the passing of time. But this morning she didn't feel like laughing. She'd gotten in late, slept fitfully and had arisen early. This morning, she *felt* old.

She switched off the makeup lights. The morning's silence, disturbed only by sounds of her own moving about, had stirred the smoldering embers of a fire deep within—awakening memories she could feel in her heart, but never touch again.

Oh, how she missed the touches.

Those times when Pete would suddenly appear in the bathroom

166

entry, cup in hand, catching her half-dressed in front of the mirror while completing her makeup routine. His familiar wolf-whistle was always low and filled with boyish wonder, as though he had stumbled into Maggie's boudoir for the very first time. That's the way it had been on their last morning together. Sixteen months ago today.

"So, you're going to mingle with the hoity-toity today, are you?" Pete had said, gazing approvingly with a half-grin as he took another sip of coffee.

"You are correct, sir, and I hope you are properly impressed. I'll be there along with everybody that is anybody. It's *the* place to be seen today, and I intend to see them all. I even managed a ticket for Taylor, did I tell you? She's taking some extra time at lunch to join me."

The Frank Sinatra Golf Classic always drew an interesting contingent of celebrities and celebrity-watchers to the Coachella Valley, as part of an annual fund-raising event for the Barbara Sinatra Children's Center at Eisenhower Hospital in Rancho Mirage and the Desert Hospital in Palm Springs. Maggie had also landed an interview with one of the country's brightest political stars who had flown into town two days earlier to play in one of the tournament celebrity foursomes.

"Got your list of questions ready for the Senator?" asked Pete, anticipating her thoughts. He had always been good at that.

"You bet I do. Worked them up last night while you were snoring." Pete laughed.

"Do you ever get tired of it, Maggie?"

"Does anyone living near a volcano ever get tired of its erupting?"

Pete chuckled again. "I can't be that bad. You know what I mean. You really get a kick out of this stuff, don't you?"

"I do. More now than when I first started. I love chasing stories. Ink in the bloodstream and all that. You can rest assured that I will have at least as much fun today interviewing and hobnobbing with the rich and famous as you will beating your brains out on the tennis court. And I'll smell a whole lot better than you when I'm finished."

"Actually, you win the 'smell' contest already," he said, nuzzling her neck with a kiss. "I'm going to pour me a little more Java and then I'm out of here. Got time for another cup?"

"Sure," Maggie said, stepping into her dress and drawing it up over her shoulders. "Here, help me with this, will you?"

Pete set his cup by the sink and began working the small buttons through even smaller buttonholes, up the contour of her back to the base of her neck.

"Who are you playing with this morning?"

"Chuck and Al and Gary."

She smiled at Pete's likeness in the mirror as he signaled he was through. Kissing her lightly again on the throat, he reached for his cup and headed for the kitchen.

"I'll pour," he said.

"Be with you in a second."

They enjoyed the last bit of coffee—there was only enough left for a half-cup each—together with a piece of toast and fifteen more minutes of uninterrupted conversation. Small talk. Even a little handholding. Now, *that* had been unusual. They didn't often hold hands at breakfast time. But they had that morning. Odd how some things remain forever etched in memory.

Maggie closed her eyes, savoring the moment again.

He was there. She could smell the sunscreen he rubbed on his face, arms and legs. It always reminded her of Hawaii. Then he got to his feet, kissed her good-bye, picked up his racquet and water jug and was out the door. There was not the slightest inkling that this day would be different from all others.

The luncheon had provided its unusual moments—including an unusual incident with Taylor, a woman much younger than Maggie, but with whom she had become acquainted during the past few months.

She and Pastor Brad were becoming very much of 'a thing' at church. It had seemed a perfect opportunity for them to do something together. She was sure Taylor would not be able to afford the stiff luncheon price and since her own meal was gratis, she purchased the extra ticket herself.

Maggie hoped the time spent would encourage their friendship. But in the middle of the luncheon, something strange happened. Something inexplicable upset Taylor. She didn't say what it was—just turned pale, as though she had seen a ghost or something, excused herself and rushed out, leaving Maggie surprised and perplexed, wondering what to make of it. There was work to do, however, an important interview to conduct and a follow-up article to write. She would check on Taylor later.

That afternoon, midway through the first draft of the article, her mobile rang. She felt the shock in Gary's voice reach out to her through the phone. "Maggie, where are you right now?"

It was all she had needed in order to know something terrible had happened. The only words she had been able to utter in reply were, "It's Pete isn't it?"

As it turned out, Pete did not play tennis that morning. Gary had been unable to make it. Some kind of a last minute thing with one of his clients. He was in the insurance business. A friend for years, he handled the entirety of Pete and Maggie's insurance portfolio—cars, home, life—everything. So they had rescheduled their match for four o'clock.

Pete had been warming up with the others for about ten minutes. Just like always. Then he stepped to the baseline, called out, "Service— these go," tossed the ball in the air and drew his racquet back to serve. In that instant of full body extension, the way Gary described it, his knees appeared to lock. He lurched backwards with nothing to break his fall.

It hadn't mattered, really. It was over before his head hit the hard court surface.

Chuck, a radiologist by profession, had rushed to his side and administered CPR. Paramedics were on the scene within minutes. But there was nothing any of them could do.

Pete was gone.

A massive coronary at sixty-one years of age.

"Oh, Pete, I do miss you so much."

She reached over to put some bread in the toaster, thought better of it, took a bite of the soft crust instead, then stuffed what was left in the disposal, rinsed out her cup, and placed it in the sink.

Five minutes later, she locked the front door behind her and walked to her car, pausing long enough to rescue the morning paper from a bougainvillea bush where it had crash-landed on its flight into the driveway. She'd been too busy yesterday to even look at a paper. Now, unfolding it she glanced at the headline story, raised an eyebrow in surprise and murmured, "Well, well. What do you know?" Dropping the paper onto the car seat, she settled in behind the wheel.

Sixteen months ago in her interview with Noah Parker, the Senator had denied that he was giving any thoughts to running. *I guess time has a way of changing all of us,* she mused. *Time and death. Opportunity for the Senator. For me ... not so much.*

Mary Magdalene Hinegardner reached for the ignition as the unwelcome shadow of depression crowded in around her. She hated beginning mornings like this and debated whether or not she had the energy to fight it off. Or even if she wanted to. Glancing at her watch, she sighed again. A meeting with her boss at ten. Two articles due that were not finished. Another fund-raising banquet to cover this evening and an interview with the speaker following the dinner.

It was going to be another one of those days.

29

Grace sat up with a start.

How long had she been asleep? She held her watch so that she could see it without turning on the light.

A quarter to seven.

Something had awakened her. She strained to listen, but there was only the soft, swirling sound of the fan above her bed. She got up to check again on the children. Nancy had not moved since Grace had tucked her in. David was sprawled across the bed, his head against the wall. It must have been David. Relieved, she moved him back to the center of the bed. In the early morning light, she proceeded to check all the doors and windows one more time. Just to be sure. Let them sleep a little longer.

She scooped some Starbuck's French Roast she'd purchased yesterday into a filter and turned on the coffeemaker. Yesterday? Is it really only Tuesday? It felt as though a year had passed. At least. In a matter of minutes, cup in hand, Grace returned to the sofa. Only this time Brad didn't feel close to her at all. She was alone again. Alone and desperate. It was the way she had been seven years ago when her world had suddenly disintegrated. Only then she'd been able to run. This time there was nowhere to run to.

Each swallow reminded her of how it felt to run, run as hard as you could, for as long as possible, for what seemed like forever until your lungs burned, and you couldn't catch your breath, and in spite of giving every ounce of yourself, you still lost. That's how it was right here, right now. Her run was over. She had nothing left. She was beyond terrified … beyond any hope of escape.

— PART FOUR —

The tragedy of it is that nobody sees the look of
desperation on my face. Thousands and thousands
of us, and we're passing one another without a look
of recognition.

—Henry Miller

"This body of ours had no rest, but we were
harassed

at every turn—conflicts on the outside, fears within.

But God, who comforts the downcast, comforted
us by the coming of Titus."

—The Apostle Paul in 1 Corinthians 7:5-6

30

How long had it been? A minute? Five? Her eyes opened to the darkness. The light was gone. She rolled over and slowly got to her feet, feeling her head where she had banged against the tree trunk. There was no blood but even a touch was painful enough to make her wince. Somehow, during the fall, she'd managed to hang onto her shoes. She glanced about in panic.

They didn't see me. But they'll come back. They won't give up until they find me. I've got to keep moving! She knew she was trapped if she didn't do something. Shoes in hand, she climbed the slope, stepped across the path, and headed off to her left into a thick, wooded area.

Rocks and prickly plants hurt her feet but there was nothing else she could do. She had not gone far before catching sight of her pursuer, slowly making his way back along the trail, his light piercing the forest darkness, first on one side of the trail, then the other.

Don't move.

Dropping to her hands and knees, barely mindful of the rough ground and loose stones and the brush and briers tearing at her dress, scratching her arms and legs, she waited. Holding her breath, she listened as the lone pursuer with flashlight bobbing up and down in his hand, passed by again. With a sigh of relief she watched the dark figure of a man hurry on along the trail back to the house.

Quietly, Grace got to her feet and headed in the opposite direction, moving down what seemed to be a gradual slope through a trackless maze of trees and undergrowth. She caught her breath as off to her left the entire estate surrounding the house was suddenly inundated with light. Powerful floodlights dispelled the night's dark shadows, reaching all the way to the dock and feeding the panic that ate at her mind and body like a Pac-Man video. Pac-Man had been her father's favorite computer game. Grace couldn't believe she had just flashed that memory from her childhood. The mind played tricks at the strangest moments ... and then she was back.

Ilene! What should I do, Ilene?

The outline of the house through the trees revived concern for her friend whom she had left unconscious in the hallway. Ilene always knew the right thing to do. She was the steady one of the three. The one the others took for granted as their acknowledged leader. The one she and Bonnie Jo had come to rely on in matters of judgment. But tonight her sophistication and common sense had failed her. She had been fooled, too.

I need you, Ilene. What should I do? I can't leave you here by yourself. And I can't help you either!

Grace peered out from behind a tree, torn by indecision as to what to do next. She watched as two men made quick work of searching the immediate floodlit area, relieved that they seemed unsure now about which direction she had gone. One of them was carrying a gun. One like drug dealers and mobsters of all kinds in the movies seemed to have and use in abundance. The other one looked as though he was talking to someone on a cellular or radio of some type. She couldn't tell from this distance.

Then the front door opened.

She recognized the dinner jacket. It was Itana—backing through

175

the doorway—followed by Parker. They were carrying ... *oh, dear God* ... a flash of lemon-colored silk caught Grace's eye as they stepped into the light. *Ilene!* Her best friend's name sliced through her mind in a silent scream.

Brandenbury was the last to emerge. He stood by the door, peering into the darkness beyond the floodlights. He was looking her way. Could he possibly see her? No, not from where he was standing. She didn't think so.

The black dress was helping her blend into the shadows.

Though the evening was warm and muggy, she could not stop shaking. Near hysteria. It was hard not to fall apart. Even breathing was difficult. Surrounded by sugar pine and underbrush, Grace still felt naked and exposed.

Where are they taking you, Ilene? I can't let anything happen to you. I've got to get out of here and get help!

Driven by sheer terror she started moving again through the brush and the trees, the delicate outer material of her dress ripping and tearing on scraggly shoots and branches as she plunged farther into the dark woods. She thought she was moving north, but couldn't be sure. Brandenbury had joked on the way over about "Mount Daufuskie, the highest point on the island, being only thirty-five feet above sea level." Most of the offshore islands in this area were relatively flat. She assumed Brandenbury was correct and that this place was no exception. She thought she heard someone behind her again, but kept on moving. If anyone was there and she hesitated, she was dead for sure!

She skidded to a halt. The forest ended without warning. Just ahead, the landscape swayed with a gentle movement that was almost invisible in the darkness.

Water!

The Intracostal Waterway.

To her left she could see the floodlit dock, at least a hundred meters or more in the distance. There was no way to get to one of the speedboats. Even if she did, she would have no idea how to operate it. It was hopeless.

Listen!

From the distance off to the right came the eerie moan of a foghorn.

Hilton Head? No, that's too far away, isn't it? There must be a horn somewhere on this island. Or maybe it's over there on the mainland. Is that what it is? The mainland?

Her hearing, heightened by the adrenalin rush powering through her body, gathered in something else as well. The all too familiar sound of someone pushing through the woods behind her.

They must have picked up my trail!

Glancing down, she felt her dress with her free hand, the other still clutching her shoes.

Of course. I have to be leaving signs all over the place. I might as well call out and tell them where to find me.

No need. Someone did it for her. "This way," a voice shouted out. "She came this way."

Whoever it was, he was much too close. She caught sight of a light bobbing back and forth among the trees in the direction from which she had just come. In minutes they were sure to find her. Grace looked around in desperation, running her hands through her hair. She felt a shudder run through her body. There was only one way left for her to go.

As quietly as possible, she sprinted across the hard clay bank, hoping that she was not leaving telltale tracks, and slipped into the water. Its warmth came as a surprise at first, but soon cooled as she swam further into the channel, still holding onto her shoes. A few meters out, she stopped stroking and let her shoes go. If they didn't sink, the chances of their being found out here were slim. They'd drift away in the direction of the current toward the open sea.

Grace looked up, grateful that there was only a half-moon tonight, too small she hoped to reveal her whereabouts. It looked as though thin wispy strands of fog were being drawn toward the sultry mainland. Maybe a rainstorm coming?

Then she saw him!

The shadowy figure had stepped out from the trees without her hearing. He was standing at the river's edge, about ten or fifteen meters nearer the dock than where she had entered the water. Could he see her?

Silently, she sank into the depths.

31

Grace was an excellent swimmer, having competed on her high school swim team three years running. As long as possible she remained under water stroking her way farther out into the channel. When her lungs refused to wait any longer, she broke the surface with hardly a ripple. Clearing her nose and taking several deep breaths, she looked back.

There was no sign of her pursuer now. Maybe he had given up. Or maybe he was still there in the shadows somewhere. Waiting for her to show herself, to give some clue as to her whereabouts. The thought caused her to shiver.

Floating quietly on the water's dark surface, she tried to gauge how far out she had come. It was hard to tell. Fifty meters? Maybe seventy-five. It was too dark to see the opposite side. The current was not swift, but it continued to carry her away from the dock area.

How far across is it? I've got to keep going.

Just then one of the speedboats roared into action behind her. Turning, she watched as it broke free from the dock and headed down river away from her. Then a second boat started its engine. It left the dock, making a wide turn into the channel before pointing its sleek, low bow in her direction. There was no doubt in her mind now as to where her pursuer had gone.

179

A powerful beam of light from the boat swept back and forth across the water. They were looking for her. She waited, timing her move until the boat's searchlight was almost upon her. Then kicking hard she dove beneath the surface. The boat passed close enough for her to feel the motor's vibrations in the water.

Stroke ... Stroke ... Stroke ...

When she surfaced this time, the speedboat was about five hundred meters distant and turning back. Glancing in the opposite direction, she noted with relief that the first boat was almost out of sight. There was activity on the dock, however. Several people were gathered there, milling about.

The second boat had turned and was slowly making its way toward her again, its powerful, dreaded light moving back and forth, still trying to root out some sign of her in the channel's murky depths. This time she would have to be even more careful.

Inhale.

Exhale.

Again.

Force the lungs to expand.

A deep breath. Now dive!

Deeper this time.

Stroke ... Stroke ...

She heard the low rumble of the boat's motor coming nearer. In an instant it was directly over her, the powerful light penetrating to a depth that frightened her as it swept across the water.

Get away!

Stroke ... Stroke ...

The boat was more measured and deliberate this time. And in the same direction she was swimming. Had they spotted her? She altered her course and went deeper, though her need for air was becoming critical.

Stroke … Stroke …

The light was there still, only farther off to her left.

I can't do this much longer.

Stroke …

I've got to have air.

Stroke.

Now!

Grace broke the water's surface, gasping for breath. The speedboat was just five or six meters beyond her, slow-moving, in the direction of the dock. Thankfully, the noise of the engine had muffled her surfacing. She decided that the river current must still be pulling her in the opposite direction. As the light swept back across the channel to the right of the boat, she caught the outline of the opposite shore. Relief swept over her as she neared the point of exhaustion.

I'm not that far from the other side. Inhale. Exhale. Deep breaths.

She let the water cover her once more, afraid that swimming on the surface, she might be discovered.

Stroke. Stroke.

Something brushed against her shoulder.

The water was too dark to make anything out, but a chilling thought crept through her mind.

Alligators!

Grace fought back the sudden panic that struck every nerve ending and let loose every childhood fear. The Intracoastal Waterway was supposedly too salty to make such an unwanted run-in a possibility. At least that's what she'd been brought up to believe.

Having grown up around Georgia's many lakes and ponds, she knew these ugly swamp denizens preferred fresh to brackish water and lacked the salt-extracting glands of crocodiles. They were not supposed to be able to survive for any extended period in salt water.

But a year ago she'd dated a young man who'd grown up around Beaufort, and he had assured her that these coastal waterways were full of alligators. Was he right? She'd not given it much thought. Until now. It hadn't been important to her then. But now the possibility piled another layer of fear onto her already beleaguered mental state.

Grace saw the shore when she surfaced for the final time. Tall undergrowth close by and the darker outline of trees well off in the distance. Looking back across and down the channel she watched the first search boat returning to the dock. The men who had so narrowly missed discovering her whereabouts seemed to have given up as well. Their boat was also headed in that direction. The estate floodlights that had minutes before turned darkness into daylight were no more. The second boat drew up alongside the dock and cut the engine.

The silence was sudden, broken only by the distant foghorn's mournful sound and the murmur of voices that carried across the water's surface from the dock.

Grace pulled herself up onto a rock at the water's edge, gasping for air, exhausted from her perilous swim. Her new party dress, now soaked and torn, clung to her body. She shivered as an invisible night breeze gusted over the waterway. Soon her whole body was trembling. The more she tried to regain control, the more she shook.

She knew that it was not the water's temperature or the physical exertion. Those were not her problems at the moment. It was the shock and the sheer terror she had held at bay that was crowding in on her now, battering her body like an abusive lover. With a groan, she began sobbing deeply. Her body convulsed with muffled sounds as she wept, wanting to scream but afraid to cry aloud, certain that someone would hear and discover where she was hiding.

Poor BJ. And Ilene ... are you all right? I just ran away and left you there with those ... those murderers! I deserted you to save myself.

A shroud of guilt and despair as dark as the night itself wrapped around her tangled thoughts.

What else could I do? If only I could get some help ... but where? Brandenbury claims he has the police ... even the coroner ... in his pocket. I heard him tell the others. And after this I believe him. Who can I trust? After what's happened tonight, certainly not the rich and powerful. And not our nation's elected officials either. He's probably bought them all off, too. He could do it.

As jumbled, irrational mental images piled on top of one another like people trying to escape a sinking ship, swarms of tiny flying gnats discovered their first-ever human visitor. Inundated, Grace tried brushing them away to no avail. All at once they were everywhere, on her arms, in her mouth and eyes. Quickly she slid off the rock and into the water until it was over her head. Completely submerged, she waited, thinking an alligator might be better than the bug swarms. When she surfaced the gnats seemed fewer in number, but still presented a potent presence determined to make her invasion of their world both short and miserable.

Her attention turned back to the dock across the way as one of the speedboats started up again. Then so did the other. She climbed back out of the water, the gnats all but forgotten for the moment, as she watched the two boats angling out into the channel. Her fears mounted once more as she watched them turn and head in her direction.

They seemed in no hurry this time, idling side by side for a minute or more as someone stood and moved about in the boat on the left. It was hard to determine what they were up to from this distance, but she kept watching as the man who had been standing, settled back down behind the wheel.

Suddenly the boat on the left roared out into the river. She shrank back into the tall grass, certain that she had somehow been detected. As the boat continued to pick up speed, she watched to her amazement as the driver stood up and leaped into the water. The second boat slowed to a stop beside the bobbing figure as the now driverless speedboat hurtled up the channel, gradually arcing to the left. It was heading straight for her hiding place!

Grace crouched low, watching the scene unfold in disbelief, horrified that she had been found out and mystified at what was happening. Seconds before reaching her, the speedboat appeared to hit something beneath the water's surface. She threw herself down as the boat rose up out of the water and with a loud roar veered crazily past her before slamming into the embankment. The impact propelled it up into the air a second time before coming to rest, half-buried in the tall swamp grass. The engine wound into a high-pitched metallic scream, lifting the stern for a final moment before dropping down again, forcing the prop to grind itself into the dirt and silt.

Still petrified at the noise and violence she'd just witnessed, Grace covered her ears to drown out the boat's futile attempt to pull free from where it lay impaled, completely out of the water, its fiberglass bow burrowed into the mud. At last the engine sputtered and ground to a stop. Mercifully, all was silent again.

Unnerved, she watched as the second boat slowed to observe the remains of its runaway sister. The two men idled the engine and spot-lit the scene while Grace lay just beyond its glare in the tall grass, face to the ground, afraid even to breathe, fearful of being discovered at any moment. The light revealed the path the boat had gouged into the embankment, a short few feet from where Grace lay hidden. She could hear the men laughing, but their words were indistinguishable. Then the light was turned off. Slowly the boat turned about and then roared out into the channel once more, heading back to the dock.

What was that about? This is madness. I don't understand any of what's going on here! Why would they just destroy a boat like that?

Cautiously, Grace rose to her feet and made her way along the slippery embankment. She was straining to see the outline of the boat's stern when she tripped and fell. Struggling to her feet, her hand brushed against the thing she had stumbled over. It was soft. She bent forward for a closer look. The dark of night tightened around her soul as her visceral moan of surprise and horror absorbed the final unthinkable outcome of this night of evil.

No!

Hair awry, face scratched and muddy, Bonnie Jo stared up at her through sightless eyes.

And then Grace knew. Falling to her knees, her stomach churned and she threw up for a third time, or was it the fourth. She had lost count as she knelt retching and gagging uncontrollably.

No, no, no, no ...

Crying, she pounded her fist into the soft earth. Then, crouching down, she half-walked, half-crawled to the remains of the speedboat. Over and over, she whispered to herself, "Please, God ... Please, God ... "

Grasping the side of the boat, she pulled herself up and looked. Numbly, she stared at Ilene's body, draped part way over the Plexiglas windshield. Grace didn't have to go any closer to know that she was dead, too.

BJ and Ilene. Gone!

The earth spun. Slowly at first, before picking up speed. Grace felt herself being sucked under by its swirling movement. She closed her eyes as the spinning increased, choking back the bile that continued to rise from some unaccountable depth inside her. Her legs gave way, and she sank into the mud and the dirt and the darkness.

She did not feel the first drops of rain.

32

Grace opened her eyes to an inky darkness and the surreal sense that—she was moving somehow. And yet she knew she wasn't.

Cautiously she lifted her head. *Where ... am I?*

BJ? Ilene?

The sensation lingered. The nothingness. The suspension in darkness and space ... floating ... and then reality pounded its way through the dark, spilling over into a jumbled pattern of stark, traumatizing images. Images of life and death, blood and brokenness! Meanwhile a thousand crickets announced their hidden presence all around her. The dread recollection of the horrors of this night spread through her like toxic waste, killing everything that had been good.

Water lapped against her outstretched hand as raindrops ran in rivulets down her still form.

The tide ... must be rising. How long have I been here?

She lifted her arm to look at her watch. It was too dark. Her arm was wet and sticky with gray pasty clay. Even turning her head was painful. She stared upward at the sky. There were no stars. The moon had disappeared as well.

It was all so strange. So unreal.

A lightning bolt slashed downward into the swampland, followed in an instant by loud peals of thunder roiling through the blackened

186

sky. Within seconds what had been a smattering of rain became a torrential downpour. Still, she did not move.

The lightning flashes and rumbling thunder continued as the downpour swept across the island and onto the marshlands, soaking everything in its path. And as quickly as it had come, it was gone. The core of the storm had passed, turning into a steady rain. The deluge had soaked Grace through to her skin, cleansing, purging. Then the rumble began again. Only it wasn't above her this time.

It was lower down. On the water!

Pushing herself to a sitting position, she peered through the rain and the darkness. On the opposite side of the river, the yacht on which she and the others had traveled to the island only hours before was moving away from the dock. She watched as it made a slow, wide turnabout and headed back in the direction they had come.

They are going back to Savannah. Maybe they've given up looking for me.

Her feet slipped in mud and shallow water as she struggled to her feet. Out of the corner of her eye, she caught a glimpse of something. Something to her left, moving toward her.

Grace drew back from the water, bumping against the stern of the beached speedboat as she did. She froze, a new alarm clawing at her throat as she prepared to defend herself ... from what? She didn't know. Waiting ... waiting ...

Nothing!

Tension dissipated slowly, releasing the nerves and muscles of her body. She was shivering.

I must be going crazy. It was just a piece of driftwood. Hang on, Grace. Don't lose it now. Get hold of yourself.

She looked over to where Bonnie Jo had been thrown by the boat's impact. A groundswell of shame and remorse swept over her again.

187

What if it was an alligator?

Grace could not bear the next thought entering her mind. She knew that it could be an alligator. Or some other animal. If not now, then soon. She felt her way along the water's edge, until she stood beside BJ's still form, now half submerged by the rising tide. If left here, the tide would take her out to sea. Grace shuddered, closing her eyes in desperation. She had to do something. Raindrops mixed with her tears as she stooped down and slid her arms under those of her dead roommate and best friend—struggling to lift her. The riverbank was soft and slippery, difficult to stand without falling.

Knees bent beneath her weight, Grace half-carried, half-dragged Bonnie Jo to the boat, struggling to lift her up onto the splintered bow. The gruesome task finally done, she leaned against the boat, unable to bring herself to look at her two friends, instead staring at her own bare feet and mud-streaked legs while catching her breath.

What happens if those men return? Will they come back? If they do it's got to look as though this is the way they ended up. If they know someone put BJ up there they'll know I'm still alive. They won't stop looking until they find me.

A quick search of the boat gave no encouragement. She found a tackle box and some empty beer bottles and coke cans, but no flashlight. Grace wiped away the mud as best she could. She scooped up salty river water in one of the bottles and splashed it on Bonnie Jo's legs and dress, wiping at the mud and filth with her free hand, as though in some absurd and pathetic way, preparing her for burial. When she decided there was nothing more she could do for either BJ or Ilene, she retraced her steps as best she could in the dark.

It looked as though the rain and the tide had already erased most of her earlier footprints and even now was lapping over the place where Bonnie Jo's body had been thrown by the boat's impact. By this time, Grace's eyes had grown accustomed to the darkness, and she attempted to back track, doing her best to make certain that not a single footprint would remain visible. The deluge had turned into a steady warm rain, leaving Grace totally drenched, as soaked as she had been while swimming in the river.

I can't stay here. In the morning they'll come back for sure. Someone will. They've staged all this to look like an accident. They'll claim that we stole the boat or something. I heard him say he had the police ... even the coroner "in his pocket." How did we ever let ourselves get involved with this ... this madman? What sort of fiendish monster is he anyway?

Resolved in her own mind that she'd done her best to displace any evidence pointing to her having been there, Grace looked around one last time. She wished again for a flashlight, but there was none. Nor was there anything else of value to take with her.

Nothing, except her two best friends.

She ran her hands over Ilene's body first, then Bonnie Jo. They were cold and wet. And dead. She threw her arms over them and laid her face against their still bodies.

"How can this ever have happened, guys?" she cried softly. "A few hours ago we were laughing and carrying on together—full of dreams. And now this. I still can't believe I'm standing here talking to you, and you can't hear me. You're both ... gone! God, how could you let this happen? If you really are up there somewhere, why didn't you save us?"

Something broke inside her, and once more, she sobbed as rage took the place of fear. "But you're not there are you? You never were. You're not there, and my friends are not here. And I'm left all alone." Her voice sounded tiny, like a small child lost in the forest. Well, that's what she was, wasn't it? Lost. The shock of everything that had happened was settling in now, crushing and overwhelming her already spent emotions. As she turned away, her mother's face flashed through her mind.

We were supposed to drive home Thursday after Commencement. You guys, we're supposed to graduate on Wednesday. Now what's going to happen? What will I say to your parents? Will I ever get out of here and see them again?

"Come on, Grace," she whispered to herself, "you've got to move. You can't stay here."

Peering into the rain, she tried picturing in her mind the surrounding area. Her shoulders sagged as she contemplated just how little she knew about where she was. On a map, it might look simple enough. But a map she didn't have and in its stark reality, finding one's way back to civilization without a boat in this region of murky swamps with its twisting rivers and unfriendly wildlife—especially for a city girl—well, it was an impossible task!

She was in South Carolina. At least she thought she was. Out here it was hard to tell where Georgia stopped and South Carolina began. What the terrain was like farther inland she could only surmise. This was the Low Country at its worst and its wildest. The dread of being lost for days in this marsh wilderness, perhaps never finding her way out terrified her. There were wild animals; too, though she wasn't exactly sure what might be living in these coastal wetlands.

She knew there had to be other homes on Daufuskie besides Brandenbury's, and she remembered the Senator having mentioned that at least one private country club had been constructed for those mainlanders wealthy enough to afford it. Maybe there were more. But the fact was, she didn't know and she was too frightened to go back. What if she managed to swim across undetected, but the first person she asked for help turned out to be another one of Brandenbury's men? He already had a United States senator in his pocket. Who else might there be? No. He was too well connected on Daufuskie for her to take the chance on going back there. In fact, the man was too well-connected, period. The question kept repeating itself. How had they ever gotten themselves involved with these evil men?

Infuriated over having been so foolish and stupid, Grace tried pushing aside her growing sense of hopelessness, using her anger as fuel for planning what to do next. She decided her best chance would be to stay near the shoreline. There was no beach to walk on. The vegetation grew down to the water's edge and when the tide rose, as it would twice every twenty-four hours, much of what was above water at low tide would be covered over. That much she knew. She had thought earlier that the tide must have been coming in. How long ago was that? She wasn't sure.

Even if there had been a sandy beach she couldn't take the chance of being caught out in the open, or that her tracks might be discovered. She had to reach cover. She remembered a stand of trees and tall reeds that she had seen on their way up river. How far back was that? Staying here in this place, come daylight, it would be impossible for her not to be seen. But even before she started, she realized that like a tropical rain forest, the undergrowth she was standing in would make walking through this pathless maze impossible.

She had to keep the water channel in sight and on her left. That way she wouldn't get any more lost than she already was. Or would she? Water routes twisted and turned and intertwined in serpentine fashion through this land of swamps and forest. She'd seen maps of the area before. But not detailed ones. Anyway, it didn't matter. She had no map now. No compass. No way of knowing for certain where she was. Her best chance would be to reach the tree line and watch the sun's path when morning came. If she could get her bearings and keep moving south, eventually she would have to come out at the

191

Savannah River and could decide what to do from there.

Grace took one last look at the lifeless forms of her two dearest friends, hardly discernible now in the darkness and the steady rain. "I'm so sorry I have to leave you here like this," she whispered. "Good-bye, Ilene. I love you. I love you, BJ." Choking back her grief, she turned and walked away.

33

At first, moving through the brush and reeds on bare feet seemed impossible. Stickers poked her legs and mud sucked at the tender soles of her feet and ankles; stones bruised and broken seashells scratched and cut, now and then breaking through her skin. But fear drove her on. Fear of being discovered by Brandenbury. Fear of being lost forever in this horrible place. Like two warring factions, fright and desperation raged inside her as she pushed on.

As the night dragged on, the impossible slowly became the unbearable. Nothing was going to be easy about this trek. Her greatest concern at the moment was reaching cover before daylight. Her corresponding fear was leaving an obvious trail for someone to follow. It appeared as though moving through the thicker marsh undergrowth would make it the most difficult to follow, if anyone decided to try. And it would give greater protection from being seen by anyone overhead. As much as she wanted to be rescued, for now at least, every other human being on earth was a potential enemy. She didn't want to think about the non-human beings whose homeland she was invading with each step she took. But they were her enemies, too.

As she made her way through the darkness, her first concern was the Brandenbury estate. Even though she would pass it on the opposite side of the river, dread of the people there had become so all-consuming that part of her wanted to walk in the opposite direction to avoid getting any closer. Yet she hesitated to do so. She had no idea what walking north might entail. Or even if she could stay on track. Would she find anyone to help her? What was out there in that direction anyway? This way at least, she stood a better chance of sooner or later returning to familiar territory. South, she decided, was her only real choice.

The low dock lights were still on, their soft glow extending into the channel from the opposite shore. The outdoor floods remained darkened. The estate appeared quiet, peaceful, a place of tranquility. *Certainly not the site of a double murder!*

No one appeared to be moving about, but through the trees she saw that lights were still on inside the house on both the first and second levels. She wondered if Brandenbury and the others were still inside. Probably not. Her guess was that the yacht heading south had carried the three men out of the area. But she was certain that his henchmen were still over there—somewhere—and they'd be looking for her again at first light.

For the next several hours she struggled through hostile terrain made doubly difficult under a starless sky. Progress was slow. What had taken an hour to traverse by boat had become a hopeless passage. It felt as though it took forever just to put the dock lights behind her. Once past the Brandenbury estate she stayed near the dark expanse that was the New River, winding its noiseless way through the swamp. Her eyes grew accustomed to the night, picking out sights and shadows, catching a sparkle of light on the river's surface on those rare moments when the moon peeked out from behind dark clouds.

The tide continued rising as she slogged through muck and mud, sometimes up to her knees. Where the terrain was high enough to remain above the tides the ground became firm again, but undergrowth was still so thick that she often had to maneuver around rather than through it. On several occasions when the marsh became impossible to traverse, she swallowed her fear of an inadvertent waking of a sleeping alligator and went into the river, swimming across or around these difficult stretches. As frightening as stumbling onto an alligator in the night was to Grace, the terror she felt at being discovered out here in morning light by Brandenbury's men was greater by far.

Her shoes were long gone, no doubt all the way to the ocean by now. High heels would have been of no value here anyway. That she wasn't dressed for the occasion was painfully apparent. Now, looking down at what remained of her dress she longed for a pair of hiking shoes, some jeans and a long-sleeved shirt. Her present attire had been created for indoor dining and socializing, not trudging through a miserable marshland in the dark of night. Unapologetic for not serving its owner more suitably, the dress continued to self-destruct in the mud and on broken branches and spiky brush stems.

The trackless terrain she had viewed hours before from the safety of the yacht had become a hellish place, not only filled with death and horror, but with strange and frightening living things, things she had begun to remember from books she had read. Some of these "living things" were huge and dangerous. Alligators. Wild pigs. Deer. Bear. Puma. Even the thought of majestic eagles and egrets soaring overhead brought little comfort. Her uneasiness caused every untoward night sound to set off an alarm inside her that made her heart beat like a long distance runner at the end of a race. Each time she had to decide whether to run, hide or stand still.

Oyster shells along the marsh banks, unavoidable in the darkness, broke beneath her weight, some sharp enough to leave painful cuts on the bottoms of her feet. Unsure how much longer she could do this, several times she tripped and fell into the mud, sinking into the ooze and watery slime.

She lost count of how many times the rain stopped, then resumed again, before passing over altogether, turning the lowland night into a huge sauna. Swarms of gnats and mosquitoes feasted on every part of her tender skin.

Something huge in the darkness thrashed its way through the nearby reeds and brush. She froze.

Was it attacking or running away?

Shaken, Grace listened for some indication, hoping it was a deer or another animal more frightened of her than she was of it, though the way her heart pounded that hardly seemed possible.

Her thoughts kept returning to the wrecked speedboat and Ilene and Bonnie Jo. She wished over and over that she might be with them. Then all this would be over and there would be ... what? She didn't know. Did anybody? Was there really a God out there somewhere? Anywhere? Maybe, but she didn't think so. Heaven? Not tonight, anyway. Tonight there was only hell.

The sky put on a uniform of pale gray, and the first thin edge of the sun's fiery rim was on the horizon by the time she reached the tree line. An hour later and with the sun on the horizon, she heard the telltale flap-flapping sound of an approaching helicopter. Grace was near total exhaustion. She barely had time to duck beneath the cover of a tree before a red and white Dolphin II Coast Guard helicopter flew past, low over the water and near enough to the shore for Grace to see the pilot and two other men inside the open doorway.

She desperately wanted to rush out into the open and wave and catch their attention. But she didn't.

What if they belong to Brandenbury like the others? He probably sent them out here. Are they looking for me? Who am I ever going to be able to trust after this? Who around here isn't or wouldn't like to be on his payroll if given the chance? If you have enough money, you can buy anything. I guess I'm living proof of that, aren't I?

Grace swore repeatedly as she rehearsed again the brazen stupidity that had earlier seemed no more than a simple lark, an impulsive adventure.

If I do get out of here, what then? Will anyone ever believe me? Anyone with half a brain will think I'm lying—making all of this up.

The helicopter disappeared from view in the distance, and Grace resumed her trek. The coming of daylight did much to dispel the uncertainties and terrors of the previous night. The landscape was so flat she was surprised to be able to see the tips of Savannah's tallest structures outlined against the skyline. Yet the distance and the difficulty of the terrain in between brought little hope. Being able to see where she was going made walking less demanding, but her feet had become a never-ending source of tenderness and pain. She moved farther away from the shore for now, careful to stay well-hidden from passing aircraft or boats.

The whole affair seemed ludicrous. She was the victim, yet here she was running and hiding as though she were the criminal. Her anger finally boiled to the surface. She shook her fists and screamed at the empty sky, "I didn't do anything wrong!"

Her cry of defiance sounded feeble and unconvincing, even on her own ears. In her heart she wasn't all that sure. Guilt stalked her like some grotesque swamp creature. She told herself that it wasn't right for her to feel guilty. It was undeserved. She was the victim. She and BJ and Ilene. Those men out there were the guilty ones. Yet with every step, guilt came closer. It surrounded her. Suffocated her.

"This was not my fault!" she cried out, her voice sounding brittle and insubstantial in the trackless marshlands.

197

Yet she'd participated in an evening that had ended in murder.

"That still doesn't make it my fault," she whimpered.

But her denial of guilt felt hollow. Empty. Down deep, she wanted—needed to feel guilty. To be held accountable. To be punished. Her two best friends in the whole world were dead while she was still alive. It was necessary to inflict some kind of self-guilt. Some lashing punishment that would leave her soul bleeding until it consumed her.

I ran away and left Ilene ... by herself. She tried pushing the awfulness out of her mind, but it would not go away. How could it? *She was still alive when I ran down to BJ. I know she was. When did they kill her?*

Nausea roiled in her stomach.

And now I've run away from my friends again, leaving them unattended at the boat crash site.

Devastated, every step she took seemed meaningless. Where was she going? What could she do? She kept trying to grasp what had happened, how yesterday's promise had become today's hellish pit.

Yesterday had been perfect. The three of us headed out to conquer the world. How could everything have gotten so out of control so quickly? I should have done something differently—anything that would have saved Ilene and BJ. Why didn't I follow my intuition? That's what I should have done. I know it. I should have said no to this whole thing. But I didn't. And now they're dead. Ilene and BJ are dead. And it is my fault!

Grace spent the day heaping additional loads of blame and guilt onto her already overburdened psyche, all the while sensing the futility of it. But she couldn't stop. Her thoughts ran together in a kaleidoscopic loop. The same horrible pictures over and over. They were gone. Forever. For the first time—even more so than when her father had died—Grace felt the enormous burden of her own mortality. Nothing would ever bring them back. That realization altered her existence as well as theirs. Its finality was more than she could comprehend. Or accept. It was so ... so incredibly unreal. Somewhere down deep she understood there was nothing she could have done—nothing except run.

And yet ...

As the day wore on so did the reproach and self-recrimination. The sun shimmered overhead like a suffocating furnace. All around her the low country was steaming from the heat and dampness of last night's rainstorm. At last she slumped to the ground beneath a scrubby pine, her face, arms and legs raw from the incessant attack of insects and overexposure to the sun, her entire body emotionally and physically exhausted. Leaning back against the gnarly trunk, Grace nodded off in a troubled sleep.

She awoke to sounds of the helicopter again and watched as it made two additional passes back and forth, near the place where she lay hidden. She felt certain there was no way for them to see her. At the same time, she hoped Ilene and Bonnie Jo had been discovered by now, finding some measure of comfort in imagining that their bodies had been removed by the helicopter crew and that they were on their way home. That must be what had happened. She forced herself to believe it. At least their remains would be safe from becoming food for the swamp's animals and insects. That was something. More than she could say for herself, actually.

Grace moved on. Fatigue, mixed with anxiety and despair, took its toll. Most of her skin was exposed and pocked with countless mosquito, gnat, and chigger bites. She brushed away numerous ticks but was certain she had not gotten them all. There was no escaping the assault of these tiny flesh ravishers. Scratching and rubbing only increased her discomfort. And her feet were cut and bleeding.

She stopped and began tearing strips of cloth from what was left of her dress. Wrapping the strips around her feet, she bound them as best she could, all the while fearing infection, asking herself why she had not been thinking more clearly and done this sooner. And the sorrow of her predicament increased exponentially.

What is going to happen to me?

As the afternoon's relentless heat bore down, Grace's only relief was to risk exposure by dipping in the cool coastal channel water and then to scurry back to cover.

After a while, she arrived at the edge of a shallow stream. With a weary sigh she dropped to her knees, cupped her hands, and scooped the water to her swollen lips, half expecting it to be salty from the nearby sea. She was both surprised and relieved. It was tepid, not icy cold, but it was refreshing. Longing for a drink, she forced herself to sip without hurrying. Then on hands and knees she crawled forward until she lay submerged in the water, letting it trickle over her, cooling the fiery bites that dotted her body.

Even at that mosquitoes continued circling the exposed portion of her face with maddening resolve. She swatted at them half-heartedly, having long since given up on avoiding their constant attack. After several minutes she sat up in the stream, unwrapped her feet, rinsed the dirty cloths, and bent to the task of washing them, cleaning the cuts and sores as best she could. At last she stood, letting the water continue to bathe her feet while she checked the sun's position for direction. Sitting, she wound the damp cloth strips around her feet again and left the stream to resume the treacherous journey south.

How many streams and rivers and water channels had she crossed since escaping from Daufuskie? Six? Ten? Had there been more? It seemed so, but she couldn't remember. Were there still more ahead? No doubt. Some were shallow enough to wade, others deeper, forcing her to swim the short distance to the opposite side.

She'd seen two alligators, the first about one and a half meters in length, sunning itself on the muddy bank of a deep water channel. The other she hadn't noticed until there it was. So close, she almost walked right into it, its beady eyes staring at her from a small muddy hole filled with brackish water. Having heard somewhere that an alligator could outrun a horse in a ten-meter race, Grace beat a hasty retreat.

Her strength was ebbing. She could feel it. No food. Limited water sipped from muddy streams while using her hands to filter as best she could. Only God knew how unhealthy it might actually be. And he wasn't saying. He probably didn't care anyway. If he really was up there somewhere running the world, he was doing a mighty poor job of it. If he was paying attention like the preachers said, then where had he been hiding out the last twenty-four hours?

Mulling over bitter thoughts regarding the conspicuous lack of divine intervention in the world's ills in general and her own in particular, Grace guessed it was about three or four in the afternoon when she first sighted what had to be the north point of the Savannah River. She couldn't be sure, because her waterlogged watch had long since stopped telling time.

Her spirits rose at the sight of the Fort Pulaski National Monument's familiar walls on the far side of the river, well off to her left. Civilization at last. She could even see the tiny outline of the American flag flying over the fort. A huge feeling of relief swept over her. She was still a long way from safety, but at least it was something recognizable, something that she knew.

She had visited the red-walled fortress once, its battlements still pocked with the effects of cannonballs hurled by attackers from the North as they approached Savannah by sea during the Civil War. A proud but worn-out sentinel, long since rendered useless by time and man's voracious need for newer and better ways of killing each other. Yet there she stood. Stubborn. Uncompromising. Refusing to step down from her vigil at the mouth of the Savannah River. It felt as though she was somehow encouraging Grace not to give up as well!

Baked by the sun and longing once more for a drink, Grace sat down to rest and to study the lay of the riverbank. Well beyond where she was sitting, in the direction of the sun, it looked as though the river was the narrowest. How far across? It was hard to gauge. Several hundred meters to be sure. Struggling to her feet, she headed toward that point. It took what she guessed was another half hour, maybe more, to reach her destination.

Grace wondered about waiting until after dark before attempting what she knew she had to do. She had to cross over to the other side, to more familiar territory. Swimming that far in the dark in her weakened condition, however, didn't sound like a good plan at all. She had to rest. She'd need every ounce of her remaining strength to make it. But she also needed to cross over before dark. She didn't want to spend another night exposed out here. Maybe when the sun was lower. If she went then, she would be harder to spot. That was important, too.

Grace was still paranoid about being discovered by anyone, other than on her own terms. If only somehow she could get back to the university, to her apartment. That was all she could think about. These last hours of her life had caused every latent animal instinct to surface within her. She had to get back to civilization without being caught and turned over to the police. Brandenbury's words still rang in her ears—"the police belong to me!"

Burrowing deep down in the reeds to rest before crossing, Grace nodded off into a fitful suspension of reality. Exhaustion numbed her flagging spirit, and sleep came quickly.

34

There was nothing unusual about this day in Beaufort, South Carolina. Warm salt tides splashed gently against the riverbank beneath the afternoon sun. A solitary egret stalked the shallows of the high tide, while warm sea breezes stirred tree leaves along the somnolent, narrow streets of the old town. Few parking places were available. It was still early in the season, but tourists were already making their way to Beaufort's picturesque shores, with its milieu of Carolina antebellum houses and fragrant gardens laced with pink and gold and red flowers, interspersed among manicured hedges. Ornamental grasses swayed on the gentlest of breezes coming in from the sea. Just another sleepy day in Beaufort.

Lonnie Graves sat eating his lunch on the terrace of The Bank Grill & Bar. It was later than he'd planned, and he should have been on his way an hour ago, but he continued to dawdle, savoring his second bottle of Sam Adams. Not his favorite beer, but not bad. And it was ice cold. He liked that. Draining the last drop, he put the bottle down on the table, leaned back, and stared across Bay Street to the marina and the marshes beyond. It was hot today, and steamy humid after last night's thunderstorm, no getting around it. Maybe it would be cooler on the open water. He hoped so. With a sigh he got up, paid the cashier, and trudged off toward the marina.

He wasn't looking forward to this trip. It was a necessity, though, and it should save him some serious bucks. Besides, he'd have a night on the town with an old buddy before heading back. That was worth something. Maybe they'd meet some women and have some real fun. Yeah, that'd be good. He smiled as he thought some more about that. Looking up at the sun again he wiped the sweat off his forehead and adjusted his dark glasses. One last thing to do before getting underway. Stop by the store for a six-pack.

Twenty minutes later he released the lines, tossing the rubber dock fenders onto the deck. Then he jumped onboard and stepped up to the wheel. Throttling forward, he eased away from the other nearby boats and out into the river. As the Egg Harbor's barnacle-covered hull pushed through the water, seagulls squawked and squealed, diving back and forth overhead.

Lonnie pointed the bow toward the bridge between Lady's Island and the Old Fort. As he adjusted course, one of the lines he had tossed on board dropped part way back into the water. The boat's wake tugged persistently at the line until just after passing beneath the bridge, the fender attached to it dropped into the wake, bobbing unnoticed alongside.

35

Grace started at the unexpected blast of the horn.

She opened her eyes in time to see a huge container ship coming up on her left. It loomed like a floating skyscraper as she stared at its rusty green hull. A black and green tugboat nestled in against her port bow, with a sister tug trailing along a short way behind. At first she panicked. In her exposed position in the tall marsh grass, someone on the ship's deck could easily see her. Taking a deep breath, she lay back, comforting herself in the realization that it would cause a crewman little concern even if he did. Maybe he would think she was the "Waving Girl" come alive, the legendary woman who stood at the Savannah River's edge waving to each vessel coming and going, waiting vainly for her sailor lover's return from the sea.

Ebel Ali.

Though she didn't recognize the ship's flag, some indecipherable lettering after the two English words on her bow confirmed its Arabic origins. Red and green shipping containers were lashed to her deck, most of them marked UASC, whatever that meant. No matter. She was sure the ship's crew was intent only on getting safely into the harbor before dark.

She stirred as a breeze swept through the tall grass, bringing with it the smells of the river. It had gotten cooler since she first dozed

205

off. But the humidity stuck to her body like steam from a Turkish sauna. Grace stretched, every muscle aching. The soreness was raw and painful and had long since penetrated every joint and muscle in her body. Her feet were beyond pain. Swollen and bleeding, they were her greatest concern. She had to keep going, but infection seemed inevitable by any standard of luck or reason. Sitting at the river's edge, she washed them again as she had done throughout her ordeal.

Carefully she lowered herself into the cool water, clinging to a tree root, paying special attention to the direction of the current. The tide was going out. That was not good. Maybe she should wait. How strong would its pull be? Even here, close to shore, she could feel its power. It had to be stronger farther out. Grace crawled back up onto the riverbank and studied the unwelcoming expanse of dark water. If it swept her to the mouth of the river or beyond, then she was finished. She would not have the strength to resist being carried out to sea. However, the thought of dying no longer seemed as repugnant to her as it once had. Maybe, just maybe, if there really was an afterlife she might find her friends there. In fact, it might be a great relief to just lower oneself into the water and just ... drift.

For a long time she stared at the river, at the variety of flotsam floating past, headed for the open sea. At last, steeling herself with an involuntary shiver, she slipped back into the muddy water. This time she let go of the root and kicked away from the bank.

She was well away from shore when she began feeling the full force of the current. With every minute, the river became more compelling, much stronger than she had expected. Long, firm strokes kept her moving forward, but she felt herself being drawn sideways at the same time. Toward the sea. Panic stripped away the few remaining layers of self-control, like the peeling of an onion.

No!

She fought back, willed herself with a sense of the inevitable, and settled in.

No!

She did not dare let go of herself! Either she made it or she didn't. This was it. Only one thing she knew for certain. She could *not* afford to squander her meager supply of strength. It had been skimpy enough to begin with, without permitting it to fuel her dismay at the undeniable drag of the tide. Grace stuffed her growing apprehension and settled in.

Stroke ... Stroke ... Stroke...

Her mind drifted back to the high school swimming pool where every afternoon during swim season she worked out with the team. She thought about Janice and Karla. Cindy and Laura Lee. They had been great pals. Always together.

Stroke ... Stroke ... Stroke...

Stay between the lines! Her coach was shouting. *Keep your body straight. I said straight, Grace! All right, the turn is coming up. Get ready to kick out. Now! That's it.*

Stroke ... Stroke ... Stroke...

Don't drift, Grace. Don't let yourself drift. Stay out of the other lane!

Stroke ... Stroke ... Stroke...

The seconds dragged by, hours formed a single minute.

Stroke ... Stroke...

Her body settled deeper into the flow of the river. Her arms grew more and more weary.

It's going to be too far after all.

Stroke ... Stroke ...

Too much.

Stroke ... Stroke.

I can't ... do it, coach.

Stroke.

Tired ... so sorry ...

Stroke.

And then she felt it! An almost imperceptible release from the main current's thrust. It wasn't much at first, but it caused her to look up. She shook the water from her eyes, surprised at how close the opposite shore seemed to her now. She'd been afraid to look before—afraid she might not make it. But it couldn't be more than fifteen or twenty meters now. She'd come farther than she had thought.

Yes!

Stroke. Stroke.

She attacked the river with every last bit of adrenaline in her body. *I can make it ... I ... will make it ...*

Stroke! Stroke! Stroke!

After what seemed like another eternity, her spent body brushed up against a submerged clump of reeds. Weak from fatigue and spitting out river water, she grasped at the reeds, using them to draw herself in against the river's edge. With both hands she struggled to pull herself out of the water and, giving up her last bit of energy, dropped exhausted on the slippery embankment. Rolling onto her back, Grace lay on the weeds and marsh grass, gasping, sucking in mouthfuls of air as she stared up at the sky. Clenching her eyes shut, she squeezed out the last remains of the river, hardly able to believe it. She was still alive. She had made it across the Savannah!

The container ship's horn sounded once more, this time well off somewhere in the distance, beyond seeing. A sudden breeze stirred the tall grass, like a field of ripening grain, causing it to shudder and quiver around her as though startled by her presence. She imagined she might well be the first human being ever to lie down at this place. But what place was it? She didn't remember her geography well enough to know anything other than that she was on the city side of the river now. Her mind drifted with the current. *Yes!* Exhausted, she nodded off in fits and starts.

She guessed that twenty or thirty minutes must have passed by the time she pushed herself to a sticky, filthy, sitting position. The little that remained of her dress clung to the contours of her body in torn strips. Caked with mud, her skin was a massive display of bites and scratches and bloody sores. Grace rose to her feet and steadied herself against a pine tree.

Crickets. Sounds of water. The sun, a reddish-orange, settled behind an endless sea of green. The monotonous drone of another boat's engine somewhere in the distance. Looking back in the direction of the sea, she saw nothing but river. The boat she heard was somewhere out there beyond her line of sight. She turned her attention back to a more immediate problem—the never-ending onslaught of flies, gnats, and mosquitoes. Her nightmare revisited.

With a groan, she doubled over as a sharp pain knifed its way through her stomach. How long since she had eaten or had anything to drink? Anything other than dirty river water? Her lips and tongue were parched and swollen.

I've got to keep going. Move it, Grace. Don't quit now.

But quitting was a constant temptation as she resumed her barefoot trek through the murky marshlands. She was limping now, the wrappings she had made to protect her feet had been left behind on the opposite side of the river. Her left foot was becoming more painful as time wore on. Eventually, she came to a small stream that appeared shallow enough to wade. Checking first to make sure it was safe, she crossed over.

She continued pushing through more brush and reeds, fighting off the ever-swarming insects until she emerged from a dense grove

209

of trees and undergrowth. Sagging to her knees in the marsh grass that stretched out before her, she stared straight ahead in disbelief. A hundred meters or so distant there was another water channel. Looking around from this vantage point she suddenly realized that she was still not on the mainland. Her heart sank. How could this be? She had swum across the Savannah to only to find herself on another island!

The channel in front of her looked to be a span of twenty or maybe thirty meters wide, maybe more, and deep enough to require swimming if she was to cross it. And the ever-present question: *Are there alligators?*

She'd been lucky so far. She wiped at her face with the back of her hand. Besides, what other recourse did she have? Maybe the opposite shore was the mainland. If she kept going in the direction the sun had just set, she had to get there at some point. Didn't she? Grace watched as a small thread of white smoke rose against the orange sky, beckoning her toward the outline of tall downtown buildings away in the distance.

So close. Like trying to reach the moon.

She had to keep moving. With a sigh of resignation she resumed her agonizing trek, each muscle and every body part demanding an accounting, limping with every miserable step as she made her way toward the water's edge.

36

Lonnie Graves powered down the vessel's twin diesel motors, squinting into the gathering darkness. He was running about eight knots against the current, and once the sun dropped beneath the horizon on the river, darkness would come rapidly. There was still a little light left, but he wanted to be sure he didn't miss the Elba Island Cut. The entry point was well marked, however he was beginning to feel the effects of the amount of alcohol he had put away on the trip to Savannah.

He remembered having a few in town at lunchtime—had it been two beers or three? He wasn't sure now. Anyway, he'd chugged down several more since then. It had been a hot day. Most times, he could put away a six-pack and never miss a beat, but for some reason this evening he was feeling light-headed. A cup of coffee would be good, but he didn't want to go below right now to fix it. He blinked his eyes a couple of times, paying close attention to where he was on the river. He didn't want to have to double back. Turning the wheel, he made a slight course adjustment, keeping an eye on the port side for the Cut while at the same time checking the nautical chart in front of him.

"There you are," he muttered to himself. He saw the navigation lights up ahead and made out the Cut opening in the gathering darkness. "Guess I should have started earlier. But we'll make it all right now, old girl."

211

He took another long swig of Sam Adams, smacking his lips as he tossed the bottle at the garbage pail along with four others. The bottle missed the can and began rolling across the deck. He left the wheel for a brief moment and reached down to trap the bottle against the base of a storage hatch. Then he tossed it again.

Two points!

Lonnie was feeling better now. Beer made the boredom of this trip more palatable. He took the wheel in hand once again. Another hour or two and he'd be there.

Weak and once more nearing total exhaustion, Grace focused in on each stroke. Her shoulders burned and throbbed with every thrust. She was halfway across the channel when she heard something behind her. Looking up, she saw the boat bearing down on her. Too late to get out of the way!

Her first instinct was to pick up the pace and swim for it, but her energy was gone. And there was no time. Whoever was at the wheel must not have seen her. Instinct kicked in. A split second push to the right, just as her eye caught something skipping along the water, and then the boat was upon her!

Twisting away as the hull swept past, she felt something brush against her shoulder. She saw it again out of the corner of her eye, skimming along beside the boat. Coming straight at her.

A line!

On instinct she lunged for it, reaching up as it passed over her, whipping through her hand, stinging and burning as she tried to hang on. Her grip closed on the rubber fender as it slammed into the heel of her hand, halting the line's biting slide through her fingers.

The boat's wake choked her as she was yanked forward, her body twisting and bouncing until she managed to flip over onto her back and grab hold of the line with both hands. The deep rumble of the engines pounded in her ears like the heartbeat of a leviathan monster risen from the deep to devour her. Diesel fumes burned her nostrils. She coughed and spit and gasped for breath. But she clung to the line!

Pulling on the line and fender, she managed to raise the upper part of her body out of the water long enough to wrap one twist of the line around her wrist. Then she settled into the water on her back, careful to keep away from the boat hull as much as possible.

Now what? What have I done?

Afraid to let go for fear of being sucked beneath the boat, she could make out the crust of barnacles, inches from her shoulder, ready to scrape and cut her unmercifully. And, of course, there was the matter of the twin engine's propellers churning through the water no more than a meter from where her feet and legs dangled helplessly. She gritted her teeth together.

Stay with it, Grace. This boat is heading for Savannah. If you can just hang on a little while longer, it'll take you home!

Only Lonnie Graves wasn't headed for home. At least not yet. Unaware of his latest "catch," he guided the boat on a diagonal course across the South Channel, the body of water that separated Bird Island, from which Grace had just departed, and McQueens Island to the south. Moving the throttle ahead a bit, Lonnie increased the speed as he lined up on the Cut that ran through McQueens Island.

Once through the Cut he throttled back again, working his way west toward the Wilmington River. Once on the Wilmington, he turned south and focused on the final leg of his journey, heading toward Thunderbolt and the Palmer-Johnson Boat Works. His buddy, Wally, worked there and had arranged for him to use one of their rails for the bottom job. Tomorrow they would pull the Egg Harbor out of the water and work on it together. With any luck they would finish by nightfall. Lonnie liked Wally. He was a fun kind of guy. After they were done, a night out on the town would provide a partial payback for the favor.

Reaching for the lone bottle that remained close at hand, he tried to remember the last time he and Wally had been together.

Grace's arms felt like they were going to tear away from their sockets; blood circulation seemed almost non-existent having been pulled up and backward over her head for so long a time. Time passed with agonizing slowness, an eternity in this watery hell.

How much longer can it be?

There was no way for Grace to know where she was. Nor did she care any longer. All she could think about was hanging onto the fender line. An occasional star peeked through the ever-darkening curtain of night. The water around her grew dark as well. And there was the ever-present boat on her left, like a Loch Ness monster, dragging its helpless victim to a watery lair.

The feeling was gone from her arms and hands now. Her jaws had been locked together for so long that her teeth ached. Her upper torso felt as though each muscle had been separated out and stretched on a rack. Grace wished again and again that she had never seen the boat or its line dragging through the water. Just when she couldn't continue any longer like this, she felt herself sinking deeper into the water. The boat was slowing. And then after what seemed like another forever, it stopped altogether.

Lonnie watched to determine whether or not the bridge operator had noticed him. After a bit he saw the man wave from the door of his work shack. Wooden traffic arms dropped at either end of the bridge, and a few minutes after that, the bridge itself began to open. While he waited, Lonnie finished off his last beer.

Grace released her grip on the line and treaded water, drifting away from her impromptu "water taxi." Where the line had been wrapped around her wrist, the skin was raw to the touch. It stung as she lowered her hand into the water. Her back and shoulders ached with each move she made.

Where am I anyway?

It was dark except for a few house lights along the shore. This was not downtown Savannah for sure. *But where?* Looking up, she saw the bridge and understood why the boatman had stopped. It clanked and groaned as it opened to let her unknown benefactor through. From her position, however, everything looked strange. Surreal. She was still lost. One thing she did know. She couldn't do again what she'd just done.

She pushed farther away from the boat, feeling the soreness all through her body—in particular, the shoulder and arm that now and again had bumped against the boat during her watery journey, in spite of all she could do to keep from it.

She made her way through the darkness to the river's edge. Completely spent from her ordeal, she required near superhuman determination just to pull herself up out of the water and flop onto the bank. Though she had no way of knowing for sure, this final stint in the waterways must have lasted for almost an hour.

Careful to stay low and out of sight, she crawled away from the bank to where three palmetto palms offered her shelter. Dropping down onto the dirt and pebbles beneath one of the palms, all her physical and emotional reserves consumed, she curled into a soaked and shivering ball and immediately fell asleep.

37

Grace awakened with the muscles in her back cramping in painful spasms. Scrambling to her feet, she stretched out, bracing against the tree. It was still dark. How long had she been sleeping? The little that remained of her tattered clothing was damp and cold and crusted with dirt. She continued pressing against the tree for several more minutes, stretching as best she could to ease the discomfort.

Gradually, the pain subsided and she turned to look back at the river. The boat was gone. The bridge was back in place. All was quiet along whatever body of water this was. That was good. But she was very much out in the open here. Come morning, in her present condition, she was sure to be reported by one of the homeowners whose houses she could see across the road. There was nothing else she could do here. So she started walking.

Off to one side, she saw a sign. *Causton Bluff.* It wasn't a name she recognized and surmised it to be some kind of suburban housing development. Across the river, she could see the lights of an industrial area. And beyond the lights, still well off in the distance, was the solacing glow of the city against the black sky. She kept moving along the river's edge.

On she went, until sometime in the early pre-dawn, she paused along yet another creek and gazed hungrily at the sight of buildings on the opposite shore and the dark outline of boats clustered together.

A marina.

Coming closer, while staying in the shadows away from lighted areas, she made out a single-story building that she surmised was a clubhouse or gathering place of some sort. It was surrounded by a small parking lot rimmed by low cut shrubbery. Boats rested on trailers in the parking lot. A large, yellow, two-story metal building loomed behind them. Catwalks provided access onto several floating docks. At least fifteen or twenty pleasure craft were moored alongside.

Grace noticed one in particular, a large boat, farthest out into the estuary. At first she recoiled, reminded of the *Brandenbury* that had carried her into this nightmare she'd been living for the past two nights. But a closer look assured her that it wasn't the *Brandenbury*. This was a different craft altogether. And it was large enough to have a good-sized cabin below. While she couldn't be sure, it appeared there was no one on board. At this hour in fact, there didn't seem to be any security or anyone around the marina, period.

Still, not wanting to take a chance on being discovered by a night watchman hidden somewhere in the shadows, she slipped into the water and made her way around to the floating dock. Listening for a time to be certain no one was about, she grasped the side of the dock and pulled herself up until she lay flat on the wooden planks.

Dripping wet, she got to her feet and shifted to where she could see across the cruiser deck.

Empty.

Grace climbed over the low railing and onto the wooden deck.

Now I'm trespassing for sure. After all I've been through, who cares? I'm already so far outside my comfort zone I may never get back.

Moving quickly to the cabin hatch cover, she tested it, careful not to make any noise. *Was there someone sleeping inside?* No. It was locked from the outside with a padlock and clasp. Looking around, she spotted what looked like a toolbox. It wasn't locked. Inside she found a large screwdriver. She wedged the screwdriver under the clasp and lifted. It took less than a minute to rip the lock and clasp away. It fell onto the deck with a thud. Grace glanced around again. Still no sign of anyone. She had come too far to turn back now. She had to take the chance.

As quietly as possible, Grace slid the door upward and peered down into the semi-darkened interior. With a relieved sigh, she felt her way down the steps and into an empty cabin. Her hand brushed against a light switch. She flipped it and was surprised to see the room light up. She turned it off. There was enough natural light filtering in to enable her investigation.

If there's electrical power, then maybe there's water, too.

She reached into the tiny shower and turned the valve. A stream of lukewarm water spewed out of the handheld nozzle.

Yes!

Stripping down, she stepped in. There was soap in the container.

And shampoo!

For ten minutes she washed and luxuriated in the water spilling over her depleted body. Even though her skin burned and itched with every touch, the clean water was a welcome relief. It spoke of civilization. It was incredible.

Turning off the shower, she stepped out and looked for a towel. A small hand towel was all that she found. With a gentle patting motion she moved the soft material across her tender skin. So many cuts and bruises and bites. The slightest bit of rubbing felt as though she was on fire.

Dropping the towel on the floor, she stepped across to a set of storage drawers located under twin bunk beds. Her mind felt clearer than it had for hours, prompting her to pause for a moment and survey her situation. Picking up the towel she retraced her steps to the entryway and the shower, wiping the places she remembered her hands having touched. *Don't take chances. Keep them guessing. No fingerprints to tell anyone I was here and that I'm alive.*

Using the towel as a glove, she opened one of the drawers. Spying some women's underclothes, she started to reach for them.

Wait.

She pulled out the other drawer. In it were men's things—shorts, shirts, socks and underwear.

Give them one more thing to think about, Grace. They'll know somebody's been here. Take some guy stuff. It'll make them wonder. They'll think a man did this.

She looked at her own underclothes. Filthy, sweaty, buggy.

Hold it. What's that?

Grace reached down and picked up the tightly rolled hundred dollar bills.

Oh my goodness. I'd actually forgotten about you.

Feeling around her discarded clothes, she found an identical roll still lodged among her tattered under things.

Maybe there is a God after all! Am I glad I decided to bring you with me! You could come in very handy before I'm done.

Carefully she laid the twin rolls of $100 bills on the counter. Then she remembered something else and felt around the waistband of her tattered dress. There it was. She withdrew the small tube of lipstick. And something else.

BJ's filmcard!

It had to be water-damaged. Grace swore softly.

It's probably worthless. Still ...

Laying these two items on top of her other possessions, she

219

returned to the drawer and pulled out a lightweight, multicolored rayon shirt. A pair of men's walking shorts—too big—but with the belt she found rolled up in the corner of the drawer, they would do for now. Some socks and a pair of tennis shoes from inside the tiny closet. Again, several sizes too big, but better than remaining barefoot. Besides, her feet were so swollen with infected cuts and bites. Bigger would be better. At least for now.

The battery-powered clock near the galley sink said five-fifteen.

I'd better get out of here.

Using the towel once more, she checked the refrigerator. It was empty except for a large bottle of mineral water, which she removed. In a cupboard she found a box of crackers and a jar of peanut butter. She spread peanut butter onto some crackers and began eating and drinking alternately, all at once realizing just how hungry she had become. Suddenly, she tensed.

What was that?

Grace stopped chewing, her mouth still full of crackers and peanut butter.

Footsteps. Outside on the catwalk.

Someone is coming.

Sweeping up her clothes, she wiped the water bottle, the peanut butter jar, and the knife and started for the cabin hatch.

The money!

Darting back to the counter, she scooped up the money rolls along with her lipstick and the filmcard, stuffing them into a pocket in her newly purloined shorts.

"Honey?"

A woman's voice!

She sounded close by. Grace stood motionless at the steps, listening.

"Yo!"

A man's voice, farther away, probably still on the shore.

"Have you got everything?"

"Almost. All except for the box of books and the laundry," the male voice answered.

Grace licked her swollen lips. She was seconds away from being discovered by the owners of the boat. A trespasser. A thief. And who knows what else?

She heard the woman walking on the forward deck now. Apparently, she'd not yet noticed the open cabin entrance.

I'm dead!

"I'll come back for the other stuff," the woman called out.

Grace heard her jump down onto the floating dock, her footsteps echoing dully on the wooden planks.

"I forgot the truck keys, too, babe. Lock up and bring them with you when you come." Now Grace could hear the man walking along the dock.

"Will do." It was the woman's voice now that was the more distant of the two.

It's now or never!

Grace crouched down as she tiptoed up the steps, pausing to peek out of the open hatch. Carrying two cardboard boxes balanced on top of each other, the man was two thirds of the way along the catwalk and coming straight toward her, head down, concentrating on his footing.

If he looks up ...

She was quick. Up and out of the hatch, careful to keep the cabin between her and the man. Sliding over the starboard rail, opposite dockside, she made a tiny splash as she dropped into the water. Still clutching her own clothes with one hand, she kicked and stroked under the stern toward a second boat tied further back. She surfaced behind the smaller vessel just in time to hear a shout.

"Sandy. Someone's broken in here!"

"What?"

"Someone's been in our boat ... and not very long ago. They used the shower. And there's a wet towel!"

The woman was running back along the floating dock just as Grace ducked around the last boat in line, staying in the shadows as she swam toward the shore. She heard their voices, excited over their discovery of a break-in, calling back and forth as she climbed out of the water near a fuel pump under a Texaco sign at the end of the dock. Her feet made squishing sounds in the oversized shoes that she hoped no one could hear. Fortunately, no one else seemed to be about this early.

Crouching, she ran along the perimeter of the parking lot past a sign that read, *Savannah Bend Marina*. Crossing the road and into a grove of trees, she ducked down out of sight. Grace moved along a wide semi-circle that took her away from the excited voices of the boat owners. After about fifteen minutes, trudging through the trees and undergrowth she came upon what appeared to be a highway and a large bridge crossing the river.

This has to be a main road into town.

Looking back, she could still see the marina. There was a light on now in the cruiser's cabin. Mindful once again of potential danger, she climbed down the embankment until well under the bridge superstructure. Among empty beer cans and plastic bottles and cigarette butts she spotted a small, depression-like cavity behind one of the concrete piers. Checking first to make sure there was no one or nothing else living in it, she knelt down and pushed her old clothes as far up inside the cavity as she could. Standing once more, she listened for any sounds that would indicate she was being followed. There were none.

The adrenaline she had been living on was spent. She needed to rest, to think about what her next move should be. Looking around, Grace decided that the best place to hide for a while was right here. It appeared safe enough. A lot safer than anyplace else she had been during the last two nights. Ripping apart an old discarded box she formed up a kind of makeshift cardboard mattress between her and the sloping earth.

It was a strange feeling.

So this is what it's like to be one of America's homeless. A vagrant. On the run.

Lowering herself onto the cardboard she concentrated on relaxing the joints and muscles of her body. Listening to the rumble of traffic passing back and forth over her head, Grace closed her eyes and waited for the dawn.

38

Every haunting scene had retold the murder of her two best friends, played out with Blue-Ray vividness that provoked a cold sweat. She tried to pray, but there was little direction and no solace whatsoever in her prayers. Her spirit was too low to reach all the way up to wherever God was at the moment. He seemed withdrawn, distant, unapproachable. In the last few hours, her life had once again become the giant mistake she'd tried so hard to put behind her. She had never been able to forgive herself for leaving BJ and Ilene behind. And if she could not forgive herself, could she ever really expect God to do so? She had thought so, but now everything had come crashing down on her. The panic she had felt as she ran for her life that night was back.

The more she worried, the more depressed she became. Finally, she roused herself as best she could and came to the only decision she could think of. Breathing one more prayer to a God who seemed absent for the courage she did not have, she took a quick, cold shower in preparation for the day ahead. As much as anyone could whose husband-to-be was now a prisoner of killers. Killers who were stalking her, watching her every move.

At seven fifteen, she awakened David and Nancy, prepared a simple breakfast of cereal and toast, and waited while they finished getting ready to be dropped off at the daycare center.

Grace was teetering on an emotional wire, and she knew it. Brad could be anywhere by now. Desperation gnawed away at her, eating up huge quantities of energy. But it was not just Brad. She and the children were also in danger. These people weren't kidding. She was certain that whoever "they" were would be monitoring her every move to see if she did anything out of the ordinary. She was a minnow swimming in an ocean full of hungry sharks—and she didn't want to keep thinking about it. Going down that road left her paralyzed, unable to deal with what was happening. Instead, she forced herself to concentrate. She needed a plan.

At seven fifty-five she packed the children into the car and backed out of the driveway, on the lookout in both directions for some signs of the enemy. There were none. She half-expected the car with the photographer to be back in the same place as yesterday. It was not. David and Nancy were their usual selves, chattering, arguing, teasing, seemingly unaware that anything out of the ordinary was taking place around them. That was good. *Keep things as normal as you can for as long as you can.*

At the school daycare center, she followed the children in and gave each of them an extra long hug. She watched them run off to the play area, her emotions raw at the thought that this could well be the last time she would ever see them. Then she spoke to the director. "I'm not certain, Mrs. Fernandez, but I may have to work late today. If that's the case, I'll ask Maggie Hinegardner to stop by and pick the children up. Do you know her?"

"The name sounds familiar, but … no, I don't think so."

"She's the ethics and religion reporter/columnist for the *Sun*. Very attractive. Gray hair. In her fifties. Attends our church."

225

"Oh, yes, now I know who you mean. I knew that name was familiar. She did an article about a month ago on the overall effects of childcare on preschoolers. I read it to my staff. It was very good. I'll watch for her."

"Thanks. If I do have to work late, she may come in the afternoon right after school and take them home with her. I don't know what her schedule will be."

"That's fine. No problem. Thanks for letting me know. You do remember that classes are being let out early today and tomorrow. End of the year schedule."

"That's right. I'd forgotten, but thanks for reminding me. I remember Brad reading the notice the kids brought home, now that you mention it. One o'clock?"

"Yes. The children will come here or to the playground after one."

"All right then. Have a good day."

Grace started out the door, paused, and turned back to face Mrs. Fernandez. "It will only be Maggie or me. No one else."

Mrs. Fernandez smiled. "Don't worry. You know how careful we are about only authorized people picking up the children."

"I know," Grace smiled nervously. "Thanks."

"You're welcome," Mrs. Fernandez answered, noting as she did Grace's uneasy manner. "Is everything all right, Taylor?"

"Everything's fine, thanks. I'll see you later," Grace answered.

Mrs. Fernandez watched curiously as Taylor walked across to her car and got in. She shook her head and turned her attention back to a small boy and a girl in the far corner of the room. They were squabbling over whose turn it was to ride the wooden horse.

"If all our difficulties could only be as tiny as yours," she said, separating the two and then kneeling down to give them a much needed lesson in the art of negotiation.

39

Grace checked the mirror repeatedly for signs of anyone who might be following her, but she saw nothing out of the ordinary. If they really were out there, and she had no doubt that they were, then they were good. Very good. That thought frightened her still more.

It was for that very reason she had waited until arriving at Broadmores to use the telephone. Her phone at home could be tapped. Brandenbury had no limits. He could do anything. Well, almost anything. She didn't think he was good enough to know which phone line she might be using at Broadmores—nor whom she might call from there. But his weaknesses were few. One slip-up on her part could prove fatal—and unfortunately, now not just for her. How could she stop this monster and get Brad back safely? Was there a way?

For hours, her mind had been racing down every pathway, every alley, every mental side street or boulevard that looked as though it might be going somewhere. Her strategy, if she could call it that, was inadequate at best and a fragile one at that. She had made her decision. There was no plan B.

Get in touch with Maggie. Have her take the kids to her house. Or to the Clouses. They have two of their own about David and Nancy's ages. Either way should work. These people can't possibly know about Maggie. They'll be safe with her.

Then she would deal with the Devil.

Her eyes were rimmed with a redness that refused to go away no matter how many eye drops she applied. An observant coworker might have assumed she had had a hard night, or at the very least, a tiff resulting in a good cry. They wouldn't be missing the truth by much. Grace glanced at the clock. Ten to ten.

A quick look around reaffirmed that Broadmores' furniture department was ready for another business day. Jim and Kaylin were already on the floor standing over by Carpets, talking and laughing about something. She gave the two of them a quick look as she picked up the phone and began touch-dialing. She did not bother to check the large *Desert Pages* directory on top of her desk. This number she knew by heart.

"Hello? Maggie here."

Grace placed her elbow on the desk and rested her forehead against her hand, overcome by the mixed sense of relief and weariness that often comes to the long-distance runner.

"Hello, Maggie—it's ... Taylor."

"Oh, hi, Taylor. I was just getting ready to call you. I got your message last night. It was after eleven-thirty, though, by the time I got in from covering a big fundraiser for refugees."

"That's okay. I understand."

"I tried calling twice anyway, but your line was busy, so I went to bed. What's up?"

"Sorry to bother you, Maggie, but I need to see you."

"Sure, okay, let me think. I'm just heading out the door right now to turn in my story. I wanted to take the rest of the day off, but you know what they say. No rest for the wicked—especially wicked religion reporters. Lowest form of life on the news food chain, you know." There was a short pause. Grace knew Maggie expected a light-hearted response, but she stayed silent. "Okay then, I have to swing over to the Temple for an interview with Rabbi Shapiro. I'm meeting him at eleven. I'm supposed to be back here for an editorial luncheon at twelve-thirty. Does after two work for you?"

"I need to see you," Grace repeated, unable to hold back the anxiousness in her tone, "right away."

She was certain that Maggie would sense her stress and so made no effort to hide it. Maggie's brief silence on the other end of the line was the signal that, indeed, she had come to attention and was waiting for more.

"Is something wrong?" Maggie's tone changed to one of concern.

Grace leaned forward, resting both elbows on the desk as she ignored Maggie's question. "Just listen. Please meet me at work as soon as possible. Okay?"

"Okay," Maggie answered, her voice steady and calm. "Okay, sure. I'll come as soon as my interview with Shapiro is over. I'll tell the boss I have to skip the luncheon. I can get there a little after twelve. Is that soon enough?"

"Yes. I'll be on the floor. And, Maggie, when you come in, just act as though you're a customer, okay? Don't let on that we're friends."

There was another pause, then, "Taylor, what's going on? Are you all right?"

"No, actually, I'm not." Grace's voice quivered as she fought with her nerves, trying to stay in control. "But I can't talk now. Not on the phone. I'll see you at noon."

"Taylor, I ... "

Grace put the receiver down, cutting Maggie off. She glanced at her watch again. One minute past ten. The store's entrances were open. She waited to see if anyone looked suspicious, if anybody she did not know came off the escalator onto her floor. Five minutes went by—then ten—while she dusted and straightened up the showroom from the night before.

She paused to say something to Kaylin just as Mrs. Willis reappeared at the top of the escalator and waved, pointing toward the Henredon sofa she had exclaimed over the day before. Grace knew the signs. This one had "sold" written all over it. Any other day, she would have been pleased. But today wasn't like any other day.

40

Maggie tapped her iPhone date book symbol with her finger and closed her computer. Taylor had hung up on her. Just like that. And while Taylor had been known to show an occasional quirk now and then during their emerging relationship, this was not like her. Something was definitely wrong.

Though more than twenty years her senior, Maggie had become good friends with Taylor. That friendship was growing, as was Taylor's relationship to the man who was Maggie's minister. She thought it was only a matter of time before the two of them made it official. Early on, Maggie had picked up on Taylor's need for an older friend, a kind of mentor mother. Maggie had been happy to be that person since she and Pete had no children.

She wondered if something had blown up between her and Brad. Maybe the thought of being thrown into the role of pastor's wife and mother of two small children not her own had finally caught up with her. While Taylor seemed almost artful in keeping her true feelings hidden, Maggie had recognized the signs of insecurity from the beginning. Call it a sixth sense or women's intuition. Maybe it was the reporter in her. Perhaps it was because she carried some of that same uneasy restlessness in her own spirit. She often told herself that it takes one to know one.

They had talked about this some as their friendship deepened. When Maggie teased her with the idea of becoming the Desert Community Church's "first lady and an instant mom," Taylor had just laughed and said she was sure that was the farthest thing from Brad's mind. But it was a demure laugh, and Maggie knew she had hit a nerve. Brad's first wife, Helen, had been much loved and was in some ways quite different from Taylor. She'd grown up as a pastor's daughter and had become much more experienced in the ways of the pastorate and the pastor's home, no question about that. She had become, in death, a hard-to-live-up-to-legend in the minds of many at the church. Including Taylor.

The emotion in her voice had been obvious, and Maggie had accepted this at face value, although she had the distinct impression there was something more that Taylor was leaving unsaid. Whatever it was, if there really was something, had remained a closely guarded secret up to now. Maggie surmised that maybe everyone had a secret of some kind, something that they were unwilling or unable to share.

Knowing that both Taylor's parents and Brad's mother had passed away and that Brad's father had retired and was living in Florida, Maggie decided it would be her mission to help fill that "older woman" space in Taylor's life.

It had been a pleasure from the very start and, she felt, rewarding to them both. Taylor had proven to be a delightful, albeit at times melancholy individual, bright and caring, a hard worker. What is there not to like? Maggie asked Taylor that question often when trying to shore up her dwindling self-confidence.

There were weeks when Maggie felt as though Taylor was making real progress. Yet on occasion there was a desperate plea in her eyes. But for what? Understanding? Reassurance? Maggie was never sure. She was certain of one thing, though. Their friendship had been a definite God-send to Maggie helping to ameliorate part of the supreme void in her life resulting from Pete's death.

In fact, that's how it started—it was Taylor who had sought her out at the time, offering help and compassion during those first few weeks after the funeral. It hadn't taken long for them to hit it off, despite the difference in their ages. In fact, they decided the difference was one of the reasons they enjoyed each other so much. Over time, and in a healthy way during the ensuing months, their roles had reversed.

Maggie, always the strong, driving force in her marriage to Pete, reverted once more to being the feisty, energetic, albeit a touch earthy and gray-haired reporter on ethics and religious life for the Coachella Valley communities. An anomaly in the newspaper business, Maggie's work had gained the respect of both her publisher and her readers throughout the region.

She and Pete were unable to have children, a fact that had been a major disappointment to them both. But they compensated. He went on to establish a respected and successful accounting firm of his own and she, looking for something to do to fill her own well, wrote a couple of novels that were still unpublished and yellowing in a file cabinet in her office at home. In the process, however, she discovered she had a talent for interviewing people and, after several tries, managed to get some "freebies" published in *The Desert Woman*.

Her breakthrough as a serious reporter came with a series of investigative articles on the fiscal problems plaguing one of the local school districts. Maggie's research and the articles that followed had resulted in the exposure, indictment, and subsequent conviction of the district's business administrator. It turned out that over a period of three years, he had clandestinely transferred over one hundred thousand dollars of school funds into his own checking account in order to pay off gambling debts incurred at local casinos.

Shortly after this exposé, the *Desert Sun* offered her a full-time job as a reporter. Her "beat" was to be the diverse and often complex issues of ethics and religion in the Valley communities. It wasn't exactly what she'd hoped for, but it was a foot in the door, a place to begin. Forty-four years old at the time and her creative writing career going nowhere, she leaped at the chance. Twelve years later, she was still doing ethics and religion—her name and the subject matter having become synonymous to the *Sun's* subscribers.

Then one day, as they were leaving Le Peep's Restaurant on El Paseo Drive, Maggie, on impulse, had thrown her arms around Taylor and declared her to be "officially adopted." Taylor became the "daughter" Maggie never had and Maggie took over as "deputy mom." A classic win-win for them both.

And just now her "daughter's" voice had sounded strained. And something else crossed Maggie's mind. Had she ... could she have been ... frightened?

Maggie gathered up her purse and briefcase and started for the building exit. *There really is something wrong, isn't there, Taylor?*

41

At five minutes before the hour, Grace breathed a sigh of relief as Maggie appeared on the second floor, stepped off the escalator, and strolled through the bedroom displays, giving every appearance of an interested shopper.

"Can I help you?" Grace asked. Maggie stood back to admire a particular lamp, mounted on the wall beside a bed display.

A short distance away and well within earshot, Jim Flessing glanced over the shoulder of a young Hispanic woman in her thirties who for the past twenty minutes had been looking at living room furniture. Grace caught his eye and lifted her hand in acknowledgement.

"I like this lamp," Maggie declared in a tone so deliberate that Grace wondered for an instant if she actually intended to buy it. She recovered quickly, however, noting the questioning look of concern in Maggie's eyes.

"Yes, it is beautiful, isn't it? Is it the sort of thing you've been looking for?"

"Well, I do like it ... but I'm not exactly sure. What else can you show me? I've been here before, and I don't think any of the others

235

you have on the floor are suitable. Any catalogs, perhaps?"

"As a matter of fact, we do. May I ask your name?"

"It's Hinegarder," Maggie responded, playing along. "Maggie Hinegarder. And yours?"

"My name is Taylor, thank you for asking," Grace answered, pointing to her name-tag. "Come over here, Ms. Hinegarder. I'll show you what we have. The catalogs are at my desk."

"What's this all about?" Maggie whispered, walking a step behind and to one side of Grace as they made their way across the showroom. "I feel a little silly, you know? What are we doing anyway?"

Grace didn't answer, her attention captured by a male customer engaged in conversation with another sales representative. She sat down at her desk with Maggie across from her. Her hands were trembling. She fumbled inside a drawer for a moment and then placed a catalog between them on the desktop. Maggie waited.

"I want you to listen carefully to what I'm about to tell you," Grace began, her voice quivering. "Don't ask questions right now. Just listen."

Maggie nodded, absently turning the pages of the catalog as though she were searching its contents. Grace glanced beyond Maggie toward the male customer. He had moved closer and was sitting in a brown wingback chair, conversing with Kaylin Martin regarding available fabrics and colors, patting the armrests with his hands.

"I don't know that man talking to Kaylin," she whispered, "but I think he may be one of them."

"One of *them*?" Maggie repeated. "One of *whom*? What are you talking about?"

The man in question had moved away from Kaylin now and was walking up behind Maggie.

"Yes, may I help you?" Grace said and jumped to her feet, startling

Maggie who turned to look over her shoulder.

His face and arms were thin and sallow, definitely not one of the suntanned locals. Straight black hair, a pencil-thin mustache, white slacks, and a flowered sport shirt that would have been more at home in Hawaii than in Palm Desert.

"Yes. I couldn't help but notice you ... Ms. ... "

"Carroll. My name is Taylor Carroll."

"Ah, yes. Ms. Carroll. That's the name your associate mentioned. You look so familiar to me. I thought we might have met before."

Grace felt her face growing warm.

"No, please, that's not a pick up line or anything," the man said, smiling, but his eyes were cold and penetrating. "Actually, Carroll is not the young lady's name that I met in—in Seattle, I believe it was. Yes, it must have been Seattle. Unless that is your married name?"

"I'm sure we've never met. I've never been to Seattle. Now if you'll excuse me, I have a client."

The man glanced at Maggie for a long moment, then looked again at Grace, a thin, vapory smile on his face. "Of course, please excuse me for interrupting. My mistake. Thank you, and have a nice day." He took a step back, turned, and walked away.

Taylor slumped back onto her chair, her eyes following the man as he made his way toward the escalator, pausing once at a sofa to feel the cushions and toss pillows the same way any interested customer might do. He glanced in her direction once more before turning away. Their eyes met for a moment, then he disappeared down the escalator.

"He *is* one of them, I knew it—I knew it," she repeated. She looked at Maggie despairingly, rolling her pen back and forth on her fingers.

"Who is '*them*,' Taylor? What are we talking about here? And what could you possibly have that *they* want?"

Grace didn't answer. Instead, she waved Kaylin over. "I need to get out of here for a while."

"Sure. Are you okay?"

Grace gathered up her purse. Her hands were shaking.

"I'll be all right. I just need some air. Kaylin, this is Maggie. A friend of mine. We're going to get something to eat. I ... I didn't take time for breakfast this morning, and I think I need something to settle my stomach. It's a little upset."

"Sure, no problem. Take all the time you need. Don't feel you have to rush right back. It's been pretty slow around here anyway, at least until half an hour ago. Jim and I can cover. I brought my lunch with me. Nice meeting you, Maggie. Enjoy."

"The pleasure's mine," Maggie answered, following after Taylor, who was already moving toward the escalator.

Maggie started to say something as the escalator approached the main floor, but Grace held up her hand, waving off all conversation for the moment. She scanned the scene below, tense as a deer in the woods on the first day of hunting season.

Grace hesitated as they stepped onto the main floor, her hand brushing Maggie's arm. "I'll go first. You wait a minute or two. Then meet me at Cedar Creek Inn."

Maggie started to protest, but instead said, "Okay. See you there."

Grace walked to the front entrance, and once through the glass doors, continued down the street.

The Cedar Creek Inn was located in the next block. Taylor sat at a small table, well back along the wall, facing the doorway.

Moments later, Maggie, following a hostess, joined her.

"Manuel will be your waiter, ladies," said the hostess. "He'll be along shortly. Have a nice lunch. My name is Sylvia, if you need anything."

"Thank you, Sylvia," Maggie said.

Across the table, her obviously troubled young friend made no effort to break the silence between them, her eyes darting toward the entrance, then back to Maggie. And Maggie suddenly realized why she had chosen to be seated here. They were well away from the door, but she could keep her eye on it.

Okay. What is going on?

"Ladies?" A young man with an order pad in his hand appeared at their table. "What will it be today? A glass of wine or beer to begin with? We also have iced coffee, tea, lemonade, Cokes?"

"Thanks. I'm ready to order. I'll have a half-Caesar," said Maggie without bothering to look at the menu, "and an Arizona tea, lemon-flavored. Some water, too, please."

"Half-Caesar, a lemon Arizona, and some water. And you, ma'am?" He looked at the woman across the table, nervously fingering the menu.

Closing it abruptly, she passed it to the waiter. Maggie noted that her hands were still unsteady, her face pale and drawn. "I'll have the same."

"Thank you. And my name is Manuel."

"Thank you, Manuel." Maggie offered a courteous smile as he walked away, before turning back to her young companion.

"Okay, Taylor, out with it. What in the name of peace are we doing here? What is going on? You're behaving like ... well, just tell me what this is all about."

Taylor's hands were clenched in front of her on the table, knuckles white. Her eyes darted about the room before finally settling in on Maggie.

"Please, just listen to me," she began. "I know I may look and sound paranoid, but I'm not, Maggie. I'm not. At least not the way you might think. I am in trouble." She paused and took a deep breath. "And so is Brad," she continued. "They've got him. He's been kidnapped!"

"Kidnapped?" Maggie blurted. "Come on, Taylor, be serious."

"Shhh, please," Taylor cautioned, threading her fingers together and squeezing them into a tight ball. "Maggie, I ... there's some things I have to tell you. Things about me that you need to know. Things that even Brad doesn't know."

Maggie waited, her eyes fastened on Taylor's face, watching her lips tremble once again. She was making a valiant effort to curb whatever anxiety and fright that she obviously was feeling. The pain that filled her eyes took Maggie by surprise, forcing her to instinctively steel herself for whatever was to come.

"I'm not who you think I am, Maggie." The words came out as a whisper. Taylor blinked, a single tear spilling through her mascara onto her cheek. As soon as she said it, she glanced up at a couple passing their table, walking behind the hostess.

"Whatever do you mean?" asked Maggie, her voice low and intense. She leaned forward, returning the troubled gaze that clouded Taylor's countenance with one of her own. "What are you talking about?"

"That's it. I'm telling you that I'm not who you think I am, but I *am* the reason Brad has been kidnapped."

"How do you know he's been kidnapped?"

"They called me last night. I heard a recording of his voice. He sounded so ... so ... " her voice faded with a ragged sigh. Then she let it out. "And my name is not Taylor."

Maggie stared at her.

"It's Grace Nicole Grafton. And I'm not from North Carolina like I've told you before. I'm from Atlanta, Georgia. Seven years ago, I was about to graduate from Georgia Southern when my roommates and I went to Savannah for a day on the town. We met a man there who paid us each a thousand dollars and bought us all new clothes so that we could be dinner companions for his boss and two other men."

Maggie sat open-mouthed, astounded at what she was hearing. This was not the Taylor Carroll she knew. Had she gone over the edge somehow?

Taylor was trembling again, her eyes tracing over the restaurant's growing clientele. "The man in the store. He is one of them, I know it—I know it," she repeated, desperation engraved on her tense features.

"Who are '*them*,' Taylor ... or Grace ... is that really your name? Grace?"

Grace nodded.

"And not Taylor."

Grace shook her head and looked away.

Maggie leaned back in her chair, absorbing what she had just been told. It wasn't often she was caught this off guard, but this was truly off the charts. Then she leaned forward. "What do you have that *they* want?"

"That night—seven years ago—those people murdered both of my friends."

"Oh, my Lord. You're not serious!" Maggie sat back in her chair again, stunned by what she was hearing. Tears ran freely down Grace's cheeks. For a moment Maggie was numb. Then she reached across to touch Grace's clenched fists. "Oh, my dear sweet girl. You are serious, aren't you? Are you telling me the truth?"

"Yes, I'm telling you the truth. They were going to kill me, too, that night, but I managed to escape. But as far as they're concerned, I'm still a problem because I know who they are. I kept running because

I knew no one would ever believe me, Maggie. Not the police. Not the FBI. No one!"

Maggie's mouth dropped again. She shivered. The air conditioning was too cold. She glanced around the room herself, suddenly alarmed, looking for the stranger who'd been standing behind her in Broadmores. Thankfully, he was nowhere to be seen. Her astonishment gradually reverted to a professional skepticism. This could not be possible!

"No, Taylor … Grace … whoever you can't be telling me the truth. You're pulling my leg and you're about to come up with some crazy punch line. Right?"

Grace shook her head. And from her expression, Maggie knew that this was no joke. In her mind, at least, this was real. She was serious. Dead serious.

"Your name is not Taylor? It's 'Grace'? And you say you were involved in a double murder?" Maggie repeated, incredulous. "Why wouldn't the authorities believe you if this actually happened? Surely there was an investigation. People just don't go around killing other people in cold blood and have everybody promise to forget about it."

"He does."

"Who does? Who are you talking about? Is it that weird guy in the store?"

Grace hesitated, then her eyes bored into Maggie's with such intensity there could be no doubting what she said next, as unbelievable as it sounded.

"One of them is a man named Itana. Talal Itana. He is supposedly a diplomat from Lebanon to the U.N." Grace hesitated then looked directly at Maggie. "The others are Senator Noah Parker and Charles Brandenbury"

"Oh, my goodness," Maggie sat back in her chair, feeling as though she'd just been struck in the face. "This is too bizarre. You can't mean this. Are you sure, Taylor ... Grace? I'm sorry. I don't know what to call you. Are you absolutely sure?"

"As sure as though my life depended on it—and it has for the past seven years. Now I've dragged Brad into this mess along with me. And I'm frightened for the kids, Maggie. These men will stop at nothing. They are powerful and ruthless and deadly. They're capable of doing anything. Especially Brandenbury."

"Incredible," Maggie breathed, sitting straight up and staring wide-eyed at Grace. "Parker's running for president—and the polls and pundits think Brandenbury could very well be his VP choice. If what you're saying is true ... "

"It's true, Maggie, as God is my witness. It's *all* true. But it is so incredible that even you, my very best friend, are having a hard time believing it. Think what chance I would have with total strangers."

"Okay ... what shall I call you then? Taylor ... or Grace?"

Grace looked down, pursing her lips tightly. "My name is Grace."

Maggie sighed. "It's going to take me a little while to wrap my brain around all this ... Grace. But, you've got to understand. This *is* hard to believe because—well, it's just so totally unbelievable! You're my friend. You are in love with my pastor. And now you're telling me that my pastor has been kidnapped and that America is about to put a pair of murderers in the White House?"

"That's exactly what I'm telling you. And now they've found me. I don't know how, but they have. So, I have to get the children to a safe place and then try to get Brad back."

Maggie drummed her fingers quietly on the edge of the table. "Can you prove any of this? Is there any hard evidence?"

Just then, Manuel reappeared and placed their teas and salads onto the table.

"Anything else I can get for you ladies?"

243

"No, thank you," Maggie said, feigning a smile while her heart pounded with a combination of outrage that such a thing could ever happen and disbelief that it actually had.

"Signal if you need anything. Enjoy your meal," Manuel said as he turned away.

Grace picked up her fork, pushing it aimlessly through the salad before laying it to one side without taking a bite. Leaning forward, elbows on the table and hands locked together, she began telling her story.

Unhurried. Step by step.

And Maggie listened.

At first with a professional skepticism that was gradually being subsumed by the enormity of what she was hearing. Soon she sat open-mouthed as with growing horror she absorbed the implications of this young woman's story.

Grace's words flowed across the table with depth and swiftness; words that had been locked inside her "adopted" daughter for seven long years. Words about her two best friends. A hotel in Savannah. A man named Reynolds. A yacht. Daufuskee Island. Her swim across the channel. A driverless speedboat hurtling in her direction. BJ. Ilene. Their lifeless bodies hurled up on the beach. Her consuming guilt over having abandoned her friends, still intense and unappeased … as though it had happened yesterday. And in a way, it had.

— PART FIVE —

He who fights with monsters might take care lest
he thereby become a monster. And if you gaze for
long into an abyss, the abyss gazes also into you.

—Friedrich Nietzsche

During my second year of nursing school our professor gave us a
quiz. I breezed through the questions until I came to the last one:
"What is the first name of the woman who cleans the school?"
Surely this was a joke. I had seen the cleaning woman several times,
but how would I know her name? I handed in my paper, leaving
the last question blank. Before the class ended, one student asked if
the last question would count toward our grade. "Absolutely," the
professor said. "In your careers, you will meet many people. All are
significant. They deserve your attention and care, even if all you do
is smile and say hello." I've never forgotten that lesson. I also learned
her name was Dorothy.

—Joann C. Jones

A kindhearted woman gains honor, but ruthless
men gain only wealth.

—Proverbs 11:16

245

42

The sun's promise of another brutal day was a foregone conclusion by ten-thirty. Grace wiped the back of her hand through the sweat on her face and gazed longingly at the Highway 80 bridge crossing over Turners Creek, linking Talahi Island with Whitemarsh Island.

She surveyed the scene from the shelter of a yellow pine grove. Across the highway and to her left, a black man stood smoking a cigarette while cars and trucks lumbered over the bridge in both directions. What concerned her most, however, was the patrol car parked off to one side of the Talahi approach to the bridge. Was it just coincidence? Or were they looking for her? She couldn't take the chance of finding out so she waited. Finally to her relief, the car moved onto the roadway and headed across the bridge, disappearing from sight.

Then came the really unnerving part. Walking across the bridge span to the other side. If she was challenged by anyone while on the bridge there was no place to run. Grace forced back her anxiousness and started out, trying to look as natural as possible in her unnatural clothes and this unnatural setting.

Once across the bridge, she breathed easier as Saffold Drive eventually became Victory Drive. When she saw the Highway 80/26 sign, she began to get her bearings. It was still a long way to the parking lot in the center of the city where they had left Ilene's car.

What if they've already found it? And what would she do if it were still there? She didn't have the keys.

Maybe she'd better try for a bus depot instead. But a bus to where? The closer she came to things familiar, the more confused she felt herself becoming. Civilization was a welcome dream after the nightmare she'd been through. But its reality was worrisome, too, bringing with it a fresh set of dangers that crowded into her beleaguered mental state as she crossed the Bonaventure Road intersection. Her "borrowed" clothes had long since dried in the hot sun, though beneath the shirt and shorts, perspiration ran freely along every crevice of her body. Bone-tired and finding it more difficult to keep placing one foot ahead of the other, she decided it was now or never.

As she walked along she put out a thumb, something she'd never done in her life before, hoping to catch a ride that wasn't a policeman. A few cars slowed as drivers gave her the once over before accelerating and continuing on. Then an old pickup rattled across the bridge, passing by Bonaventure, slowing as it drew nearer to Grace and coming to a stop a short distance beyond her. As fast as she could make herself move, she stumbled up to the passenger side and looked in through the open window.

"What on earth you bin doin', girl? You looks like the las' rose o' summuh an' we ain't even got to summuh yet!" The heavyset black woman behind the wheel, dressed in an old checkered shirt and overalls that were faded from too many washings, laughed at her own joke.

Taylor leaned her head against the car door.

"Come on, you po' thing. Git on in heah outa the heat. You don' look like you gonna to make it much further anyway 'less'n you sits an' rides a spell."

Grace pulled open the door, waiting just long enough for the woman to push a pair of fisherman's waders off the seat and onto a floor already cluttered with "stuff"—fishing tackle, some netting, and a bucket full of fresh shrimp. It was anybody's guess as to when the last time was that the passenger side of the old pickup had been cleared out.

"Come on, get in," the woman urged. "Don' worry. You cain't hurt nothin'. Ah keep on tellin' Sammy—tha's mah boy— clean up this mess, but he don' an' ah don' either. Fo'tunately, as you can see, it ain't no bother to the shrimp. They was jus' hangin' 'roun' waitin' fo' me this mornin' down by Turners Creek Bridge. Yessuh, they liked ma net real good this mornin'."

She laughed again as Taylor climbed in. The gears ground as the woman steered the pickup out onto the road. Taylor leaned back against the worn seat and closed her eyes, too exhausted to talk.

"You looks mighty thirsty, girl. They's some water right down theah by yo feet. In that canteen."

Grace picked it up, unscrewed the metal cap, and drank deeply, oblivious to the water leaking through her cracked lips and trickling down onto her shirt. The driver, meanwhile, eyed her with suspicion.

"Hon, you looks like you jus' spent the night in hell! Where you been to git so all scratched an' bit up so bad?"

Grace took a last long swallow from the canteen. The water was warm but no matter. It was clean.

"In the marsh."

"In the marsh? Well, ah kinda figured somethin' like that," the woman responded with a shake of her head. "But what on earth was a pretty white thing like you doin' by yosef out in the swamp. Thas' what ah'm askin'?"

248

"I got ... separated from my friends," Grace answered. "And then I became lost."

"How long you been out theah?" asked the woman, braking for a signal light. As they waited for the light to turn green she reached out a hand. "By the way, mah name's Ellie. Ellie Fitzgerald. A good ol' Irish name, hon, 'cause they was a good ol' Irishman somewhere back in mah husband's family woodpile that took it on hissef to add a new limb to the family tree, if you knows what ah mean." She chuckled again.

"Two nights," Grace mumbled, staring out the window as they passed a row of Palmetto palms. "I've been out there two nights."

Ellie Fitzgerald remained silent. When Grace glanced her way again, she saw the woman studying her out of the corner of her eyes as they rattled along the thoroughfare. A little way farther they turned onto Harry Truman Parkway.

"You got a name, hon?"

"Sorry. My name is ... Nicole." Grace caught herself, but not without a slight hesitation.

Why didn't I think about that ahead of time?

"So where's home ... *Nicole,*" the woman emphasized the name. "From the looks o' you, I better take you theah right now. You ain't in fit shape to do no mo walkin, tha's fo sho."

Grace hesitated again, unsure about how to respond. Her entire focus until now had been on survival, on getting back to Savannah. So much so that she'd not planned anything beyond that. Now she was here and at a loss as to what to do. Or say. She cursed under her breath and glanced over at the driver.

I'm too obvious.

Ellie Fitzgerald confirmed the same in the next breath.

"Honey, it ain' none o' mah business, ah know. But you looks to

249

me to be in some kind o' trouble. So, whatever yo name is ... wha'd you say it was again ... *Nicole?* If that *be* yo name, it's fine by me. But if you is really in trouble, hon, you better say so 'cause we ain' that far from mah house now. The Man upstairs sho let you come to the right mama, I kin tell you that. I *knows* trouble. Mah middle name is 'trouble.'" Ellie chuckled, her eyes dancing with the kind of knowing wisdom that comes from tough streets and hard times.

"I ... I guess ... could I come to your house for a little while?"

Ellie gave her a hard, appraising look as the pickup slowed for another intersection. Then she nodded and without a word turned left off the Parkway onto Henry Street. Then right onto Harmon. Grace leaned back again, closing her eyes. As exhaustion took over, her hands began to shake. She tried to control them but soon her whole body was trembling.

"Are you on somethin', girl?" Ellie asked with a sudden sternness in her voice. "If you is, you betta speak up right now 'cause I ain' foolin' 'roun' with no crack-head. I got betta things to do!"

"I ... I'm not on anything ... honest," Grace stammered. "I ... I just can't quit ... shaking. Sorry."

Ellie stopped the pickup under a giant live oak in an old neighborhood that had clearly seen better days. Two-story row houses were stacked against each other on both sides of the street and painted with bright blues, pinks, yellows, and greens, an effort on the part of the residents to improve the aging appearance of their homes. Ellie got out and came around to the other side.

Grace sat with her arms clenched against her body, trying to regain control as tears started rolling down her cheeks. She was falling apart. Even her teeth were clacking together.

"Come on, girl," said Ellie, opening the door and reaching in for her. Her big hands pulled Grace from the truck and into her arms.

Grace's body continued its convulsive movements as she yielded to the woman's firm grasp, her only clear thought one of surprise at *what was her name? Ellie? Yes, that was it*—at Ellie's strength and that a woman with black skin was holding onto her. That had never happened before. Not that she could remember anyway. Just then a young man, shirtless and muscular and wearing a pair of faded denim shorts, sauntered out onto the front porch.

"Sammy, come heah an' help me," Ellie called out. The young man bounded down the steps. Grace watched as he jogged toward them. The shaking had begun to diminish, but her legs were like jelly. No matter how she tried, they refused to hold her up.

"Help me get this po thing inside."

"Here, give her to me."

He has a nice voice. Strong. Like his body.

Grace closed her eyes as Ellie released her to the young man. She felt herself being lifted effortlessly and carried toward the house. As they started up the steps, she opened her mouth to protest, to argue that she was sure she could walk, when a wave of sickness erupted in her stomach. She turned her head and retched. The phlegm and a subsequent fit of coughing left a disgusting residue in her mouth. It had been all her body could summon from the depths, all there was left. She fell back, helpless in the young man's arms. They were up the steps and inside the house before she could say anything more.

She steeled herself against the sick sensation of being lowered onto something.

I must really be losing it.

The young man released her and stepped back. As this latest nauseous surge subsided, she opened her eyes again and looked up.

251

43

Pillows of various shapes and colors lay scattered across the old couch. Some had been pushed off onto the floor to make room for her. A large white doily was draped over the back. To her surprise, although she couldn't say exactly why she was surprised, it looked fresh and clean. Maybe it had been the chaos in the old pickup. Maybe it was ... something else. The truth was she'd never been in a black person's house before. Maybe she had just assumed that ...

From her prone position, Grace turned her head and looked around the room. The furnishings were spare and modest in appearance and the rugs on the hardwood floor looked worn. But everything was clean. In fact, she surmised with total accuracy that she was undoubtedly the dirtiest object in the room.

At that moment, Ellie trudged through the doorway, puffing, carrying the pail of shrimp in one hand and her waders in the other. All the while the young man standing opposite her had not uttered a word. Grace guessed him to be seventeen or eighteen, his dark face expressionless as he watched her.

"All right, hon," said Ellie as she returned from the kitchen. "Let's git you in the bathroom an' run some water in the tub. First thing you need is a bath to soak that theah grunge off. From the looks o' them bites an' all, we'll make it jes' a few degrees above cool so's it'll not git yo skin so all fired excited an' upset. Sammy, git Nicole heah a drink o' water, please. I think she's a mite dehydrated."

"Where'd you find her, Mom?" the lad asked as he returned with a glass of water and some ice. Grace offered a weak smile as she guided his hand and the glass to her lips.

"Out on 80, headin' back into town from Turners Creek," Ellie answered from the bathroom where Grace could hear water splashing into the tub. "Help her outa them shoes, Sammy, an' bring her in heah."

Grace watched the young man unlace her stolen shoes and ease them from her feet. Then he peeled back the socks, his eyes widening as he saw the condition her feet were in. He started to reach for her but she waved him off. "I think ... I can make it," she said, struggling to sit up. "Please ... let me try." She dropped her feet over the side of the couch and, seeing the crust of dirt and caked mud that she left behind, tried to scoop it up. "I'm sorry ... "

"Don't worry," the young man said, taking her hand. "I'll get it later."

Grace tried to steady herself as she got up. All at once the room rotated in a half circle. She felt his arm slide around her as she started to fall. He grasped her firmly at the waist and drew her against him.

"Sorry. Thanks," she mumbled as he guided her swollen, shuffling bare feet across the room. Leaning against the bathroom door, she worked at catching her breath, coming to terms with the weakness she felt throughout her body. It was as though once she had started to let go, all her muscles and joints and nerves had begun falling apart, leaving her quivering and totally spent.

Ellie gripped the side of the tub and pushing herself up from her knees, she stepped back. "Think you can git on now by yoself?"

Grace nodded.

"Then turn the water off when it's full, hon. I put in a gen'rous po'tion o' soda, too, fo them bites. Soak as long as you want. I'll be checkin' back in a few minutes to make sho you is okay. Le's go, Sammy."

The door closed behind Grace.

Bracing herself against the sink, she listened to the sound of the water flowing into the tub.

A toilet stool!

She sat down on it, mouthing a silent thank you to whoever invented the thing. Looking around the room, she noticed a small screened window above the tub. It was open. When the tub was well above half-full she reached over and shut off the faucet. With the water turned off, the only sound was the whirring of a floor fan moving warm air toward the tub. At least the air is moving, she thought. Slowly she unbuttoned the stolen shirt.

Moments later she lowered herself into the tub. Leaning back, she luxuriated in the extravagance of water clear enough to see herself in, water that left no worries about what else might be in it with her.

This must be what heaven would be like, she thought, closing her eyes, *if there was one.*

"How you doin,' hon?"

Grace awoke with a start. Ellie was standing in the doorway. "You best not sleep too much longer in theah or you'll be lookin' like one o' them shrimp I brung home."

Grace shook her head, staring down at her submerged body. The water was cloudy now, not clear like it had been when she'd first stepped in.

Ellie bent down to scoop up the dirty clothes Grace had dropped on the floor.

"I know yo're tired, chil', but wash up now. See the shampoo? It's right theah. Yeah, that's the one. Use as much as you want cleanin' out that hair an' I'll dry it when you is done. Heah's a robe to put on. Come on out when yo're ready. Then maybe we can talk some. An' don' worry 'bout them bites. I'll work on 'em after we dry yo hair. Marcy, girl, I ain't never seen nothin' like that in all my years. You ain't got two square inches that ain't been all chewed up!"

The door closed again. Grace finished bathing and washing her hair, her sunburned scalp almost too tender to touch. Dabbing at her red, raw skin with a towel, she slipped into a thin cotton robe.

"In theah, chil," Ellie pointed toward another room as soon as Grace opened the bathroom door.

This bedroom had to be Ellie's, Grace decided as soon as she walked in. A queen-size bed covered with only a sheet and some pillows at the headboard. On the nightstand was a picture of a man standing alongside a younger version of the boy she had met earlier. It was propped up between a reading light and a Bible. A closet without doors, located to the left of the bed, was jammed with an assortment of inexpensive-looking clothes and shoes. An ancient four-drawer dresser with some missing knobs and an attached mirror that was cracked in the lower left corner stood against the wall next to the closet. Opposite, a screened window was open, though it brought no relief from the mugginess outside.

Ellie closed the door behind her. "All right, Nicole, lay yo'sef down. First thing, we'll start out with is them feet. Let me have a looksee."

"What?" Grace stared at the large black woman standing between her and the door. A renewed stab of fear and uncertainty pressed against her temple.

"Yo feet, chil,'" Ellie repeated. "Lay down on the bed. We gots to deal with them cuts and bites befo you git any mo infection than you already has. Come on. Lay down. I won't hurt you none. Well, as little as possible anyway."

For the next twenty minutes, without another word, Ellie concentrated on disinfecting the wounds and bites on Grace's feet, attaching band-aids to the deepest lesions. Slowly she worked her way up Grace's right leg, then the left. Propped against pillows, Grace watched the dark fingers move back and forth across her sunburned skin, so pale by comparison, sorting out which bites were gnats and mosquitoes and which were ticks or chiggers.

"Hon, I'm puttin' nail polish on these heah chigger bites 'cause they's most likely a little blood suckin' rascal inside got his livin' room all set up an' gettin' ready to make you even mo' mis'rable than you already is. 'Sides, I seen five ticks makin' their livin' offen you so far an' they ain't no fun either. They prob'ly worse in fact. I know you don't think that's possible, but trust me, sweety, it truly is. An' I ain't *nevah* seen nobody with mo' chigger bites on 'em than you got."

"I believe you," Grace answered. "I picked up some chigger bites when I was a little girl playing in the woods behind our house. They became infected and swelled up like golf balls on my ankles."

"An' when you that allergic they'll do it agin if we don' git along heah an' serve 'em up some eviction notices." She continued working. "All right now, you kin git them private places on yo own, but you better turn over an' let me git at yo backside."

An hour and fifteen minutes later, Grace was robed again and sitting in the kitchen, devouring a ham and cheese sandwich and a glass of iced tea. She noticed breakfast dishes stacked off to one side of the sink, but the pail of shrimp had disappeared. Ellie Fitzgerald sat across from her, fanning her brow with a folded section of the *Savannah News Press.*

"Thank you, Mrs. Fitzgerald. This sandwich is just what I needed. And I can't seem to get enough to drink."

"You were near drained dry, girl ... an' the name is Ellie. Ain't nobody in this heah neighborhood calls me 'Mrs. Fitzgerald' 'cept fo ol' Arnold, when he stops to pick up the garbage. Works fo the city an' lives a block down the street from heah. He bin callin' me 'Mrs. Fitzgerald' since ever I kin remember."

"Sammy is your son then?" asked Grace, wiping breadcrumbs from her mouth with a paper napkin.

"He is fo' sho," she said proudly. "A good boy, too. Jus' survivin' in this heah part o' town is a near miracle these days what with drugs an' gangs an' all. He's goin' to graduate in a few days. Top ten percent o' his class, too. How 'bout that? Goin' on to Savannah State in the fall. His daddy would sho be proud o' him. Sammy's goin' to be somebody, I jus' know it. God got his han' on that boy!"

At the mention of "graduation" a shadow fell across Grace's mood. She caught the look in Ellie's eyes and knew she had sensed something, but Ellie said nothing. Instead, she offered her mysterious hitchhiker some more iced tea and another sandwich. Grace declined the sandwich, but accepted the tea and then leaned back in the chair to stare at an invisible spot in the middle of the table.

"You think we's ready to talk yet?" Ellie asked softly, leaning forward in her chair. "You in some kind o' trouble, ain't you ... *Nicole?*"

Grace sighed, lifting her eyes until she took in Ellie's penetrating gaze. "Grace. Nicole is my middle name. My name ... is Grace Nicole Grafton. I'm a graduate student at Georgia Southern."

Ellie stopped fanning herself, her gaze fixed and unwavering. She was not smiling as she unfolded the newspaper and pushed it across the table. "Would this be the same Grace Grafton you's talkin' 'bout?"

Grace stared in disbelief at the morning paper. There, in the top left hand column of page 2, she saw her recently-posed-for-graduation photo smiling back at her.

44

STUDENTS KILLED IN BOATING ACCIDENT.

The *Savannah News Press* headline declared its macabre message in matter-of-fact journalistic fashion under the black-and-white news photo of a Coast Guard helicopter. Grace was certain it was the same one she'd observed the first morning following her escape from Daufuskee Island. It was shown here with a rescue team removing the body bags containing Ilene and Bonnie Jo's remains.

> *Early Sunday morning, passing boaters notified the Coast Guard of an accident along the IntraCoastal Waterway near Ramhorn Creek and the New River, opposite Daufuskie Island.*
>
> *A Dolphin II search helicopter crew was dispatched from Hunter Army Air Base in response. The air rescue team discovered a speedboat, registered to billionaire Charles Brandenbury, located along the South Carolina shoreline a short distance from the Brandenbury estate's private docking area on Daufuskie Island.*
>
> *According to the Coast Guard, the speedboat reportedly crashed into the shoreline while running at an excessive rate of speed. The bodies of two female passengers were found in the boat, both apparently killed instantly from the impact.*

Police have identified the occupants as Ms. Ilene Hunter and Ms. Bonnie Jo Senter, graduate school students who were scheduled to receive their degrees with high honors this Wednesday from Georgia Southern University in Statesboro.

School officials indicate that the two women were living off campus with another graduating honors student, Ms. Grace Grafton. Only two bodies have been recovered. Police and school authorities have been unable to locate Ms. Grafton who has been officially reported as missing. It is unclear whether she was with the others at the time of the accident, but the Coast Guard has confirmed that a search of the waterway is continuing. Police are asking anyone who may have information concerning Ms. Grafton's whereabouts to contact them.

Charles Brandenbury was reached for comment on Sunday in Savannah as he was leaving the Hyatt Hotel. Mr. Brandenbury had checked into the Hyatt's VIP suite overnight before continuing on to his island retreat. He spent the day cruising with friends on his yacht, including Senator Noah Parker of South Carolina. He had been unaware that one of his speedboats had been reported missing. Upon hearing the details of the accident he was deeply moved by the deaths of the students and expressed concern and condolences to their families.

Mr. Brandenbury, through the Brandenbury Foundation has been a generous contributor to GSU's Scholarship Fund. School authorities confirmed that recently the GSU Business School received $500,000 from the Brandenbury Foundation to fund a joint faculty exchange research and

259

teaching project with educational institutions in developing Third World countries.

Autopsies of the two students will be performed. Meanwhile, rescuers report the presence of half-empty liquor bottles in the boat. Small amounts of cocaine and marijuana were also recovered from the scene.

It remains unclear as to how the students might have arrived on Daufuskie Island, a destination readily accessible only by water. Authorities surmise they may have come to the island on a tour boat out of Hilton Head or were left on the island by a third party. A subsequent weekend joyride apparently ended tragically when the driver lost control. The bodies of the two women were flown to Memorial Medical Center in Savannah.

Grace stared in shocked disbelief at pictures of Ilene and Bonnie Jo. And next to Bonnie Jo, her own face smiled back at her. She looked up at Ellie whose countenance was that of someone clearly anticipating an answer to this mysterious conundrum that had capped off her early morning shrimping expedition. Grace dropped the paper onto the table. Tears filled her eyes. "I guess you're probably wondering what happened."

"Actually theah is a couple o' questions that have crossed mah mind," Ellie responded dryly. "Were you theah with those girls?"

Grace nodded. "But my friends were already dead before that boat ever crashed."

Her impromptu hostess stared hard into the eyes of her ragamuffin guest. Grace could feel her mind searching and probing and knew she was trying to decide whether or not she was telling the truth. She took another sip of tea.

"All right, Ellie, what I'm going to tell you will be hard to believe.

I can hardly believe it myself. But I swear in God's name—assuming there is one out there somewhere—what I'm about to say is the truth."

"Theah is a God, honey chil'," Ellie said softly. From the look in Ellie's eyes, Grace was certain the jury was still out when it came to believing her. "An' he'll let me know if you is pullin' on my leg. Anythin' but the Bible-truth now an' you is out that front door an' into the hands o' the police faster than a greased pig!"

Grace forced a grim smile at her hostess' colorful warning. "Ellie, I only wish I could have met you under more pleasant circumstances. When you say God will let you know, I think you mean it. I promise. Only the truth."

She spent the next thirty minutes recounting the events that in the past forty-eight hours had violently taken the lives of her two dearest friends and altered her own life forever. She wept while describing Bonnie Jo, lying twisted and lifeless on the flagstone patio; and again over the shock of discovering the bodies of her two friends in the wrecked boat.

Without elaborating on her escape across the channel and her journey through the marsh, she paused to recount the details surrounding breaking into the boat at the Savannah Bend Marina.

"I've never done a dishonest thing in my life," she declared, "and now I'm guilty of breaking and entering and stealing. I'm a witness to a double murder, and I'm afraid to go to the police. Brandenbury told the others there that he had the police 'in his pocket.' Those were his exact words. 'In his pocket.' Not only the police, but the FBI and even the coroner, too. Ellie, I'm so frightened I don't know what to do. Those men are evil. And they're powerful. Especially Brandenbury. There's nothing he can't do. Even murder. How in God's name did we get mixed up in this? Ilene and BJ. He killed them! And he'll stop at nothing now until he finds me."

"First of all, yo problems ain't got nothin' to do with 'God's name,' hon, unless yo callin' *on* his name instead o' cursin' *in* his name. It's time you learned that fo a fact. 'Sides, maybe this big shot billionaire daddy thinks the 'gators got you," mused Ellie as she reached for the newspaper. "You gone through more than most could imagine, hon, 'specially 'fo a city girl. I ain't never heard o' nobody trudgin' through them marshlands barefoot like you done."

"May I have the article?" asked Grace.

Ellie drew her hand back.

"Sho, hon," she said, "though I don' know what in the world fo."

"Maybe no reason, I don't know. It's the only reality I've got that's associated with the last two days. These were my best friends, and now they're gone. Murdered ... " Her voice trailed off.

"Darlin', I think you betta get yo'sef out o' town fo awhile," said Ellie, reaching for the telephone on the wall behind her.

"What are you doing?" Grace's eyes widened with alarm.

"It's okay," she said reassuringly as she dialed. "I'm callin' Sammy. He's over at his girl frien's house an'—hello. Sandra? How you doin' chil'? Good ... well, tha's mighty fine, hon ... say, would you get Sammy an' come over heah right away? Thanks, luv'. 'Bye now."

She put the phone back.

"You really got yo'sef into a potful o' trouble on this one, ain't you?"

"Then you believe me?" Grace hesitated, dreading the answer to the question.

Ellie eyed her steadily and then nodded. "I believe you, hon. Ain' nobody goin' to go through what I see you lookin' like jus' to make me believe some fool lie. Now, you got any place you can go? Yo folks, maybe?"

"My mother lives in Atlanta, but I can't go there. I'm afraid to even call her. People like Brandenbury can tap phones, can't they? Wouldn't that be the first place he'd look for me, or have I watched too many movies? No, I think that's the first place they'd expect me to go back to if I was alive. And the police will go there to ask questions. It's better if Mom doesn't know where I'm at for now, don't you think? I know thinking I may be dead will devastate her, but I can't call her. Not yet. It's crazy, isn't it? I feel like *I'm* the murderer. Why am I the one that's so scared and not them?"

Ellie ignored the question. "We got to git you some clothes."

"I've got money," Grace said, "only someone might recognize me from my picture if I go out shopping."

"No problem," answered Ellie, "I think Sandra may be 'bout yo size."

At that moment Sammy opened the front door and waited as a lovely teenage girl with braided hair, huge dark eyes and skin the color of mahogany, slipped past him into the living room. Ellie picked up a pencil and a piece of paper. "What're yo sizes, hon? We'll send Sandra and Sammy downtown to buy you some things."

Grace smiled gratefully at Ellie and the two young people who proceeded to pour themselves glasses of iced tea. They had to be curious, never taking their eyes off her, but all the while not saying a word. Grace knew Sammy must have briefed the girl about the strange white woman her mother had picked up along the road. She gave Ellie her measurements.

"Then maybe I can catch a plane or a bus out of town tonight."

"Don' be foolish, chil'. By now Mr. Money Bags has got every taxi an' bus an' airplane in town covered with men lookin' fo you. By the way, how you feel 'bout bein' a brunette or a redhead? Take yo pick. The younguns here kin git that stuff, too. Meanwhile you take yosef off to bed fo some shut-eye while I fix up some o' them shrimps fo

263

supper. After you gits some rest maybe you kin start thinkin' a bit clearer. You goin' to have to, darlin', if you wantin' to git out o' this one alive. Trust me—I know 'bout these things. You don' make it through life in this part o' town without knowin.' Ain't that right, kids?"

Sammy and Sandra nodded, grinning like participants in an inside joke that really wasn't funny at all.

"Maybe Sammy an' Sandra kin drive you down to Jacksonville after supper. It's only a couple o' hours from heah. You kin catch a bus down theah to Miami or Birmin'ham or wherever. I doubt anybody be lookin' very serious fo you in that direction. Least not yet. Okay, Sandra, heah's what we need."

She handed the girl the penciled list and Grace pulled out two one hundred dollar bills.

"Hold on," said Ellie, pushing her bulk away from the table as she grabbed the bills from Grace and headed off toward her bedroom. Moments later she returned with a handful of twenties. "If these two black kids show up flashin' hundred dollar bills in the department store, security's goin' to be all over 'em, askin' questions, maybe even accusin' 'em o' bein' drug pushers or some other fool thing. Twenties is betta. Now don' waste time, you two. Buy in a couple o' different stores. You close enough in size, Sandra. Make 'em think you buyin' fo yoself."

Sandra nodded. "Okay, we won't be long." Flashing Grace a smile, she and Sammy headed for the door.

As soon as they were gone, Ellie turned to Grace and said, "All right, Grace Nicole Grafton, off to bed now. You kin use mine. You gonna need some sleep. I'll wake you up when supper's ready.

45

Grace was sleeping, so she did not hear Sandra enter the bedroom. It was not until Ellie knocked on the door to call her for dinner that she saw the clothes stacked neatly on the foot of the bed.

Bras and panties. Two shirts. A pair of jeans and one pair of soft denim shorts. Socks. Canvas walking shoes a size larger than her normal size to accommodate her swollen feet. The basic toiletries. Hair coloring—she examined the package—a dark brown. Receipts and money left over. And a not-so-new canvas athletic bag that she thought must belong to Sammy or Sandra. Quickly she slipped on her new clothes, and wearing the shorts and one of the loose-fitting shirts, Grace joined the others at the table.

She was surprised when Ellie asked Sammy to say grace. Even more surprised to hear the young man pray. It was a simple prayer, yet confident and sincere, without hesitation. He must have done this before. Something stirred inside her when he asked God for her safe journey. *I didn't think teenagers prayed any more. Not like that. At least not out loud in front of other people.*

She couldn't remember the last time anyone had prayed for her. At least that she knew about. Not since her father died. Grace had stopped attending the little church near their home long before that, except for special occasions like Christmas and Easter when her parents went along with her. But her father's funeral was the last religious service either she or her mother had ever attended so far as she knew, except for some of her friends' weddings.

She had brought up the idea of going to church on the first Easter after his death. Her mother just stared at Grace for what had seemed the longest time, her eyes filled with so much sadness that she had never forgotten that moment. Then without a word she had turned away into her bedroom and closed the door. That was it. They never talked about church or God or religion ever again.

Grace was suddenly very hungry. Ellie's fried shrimp, green leaf salad, and vegetables were consumed with little conversation as the four of them emptied the plates and bowls that Ellie had prepared. Steaming black coffee followed a dish of ice cream topped with chocolate syrup.

"You best be rinsin' that hair befo you leave, hon. Use the bathroom. Sandra, give her a hand. Sammy, go get the pickup filled up an' ready to go. I'll clean up these heah dishes."

Grace sat on a small stool as Sandra, mindful of her tender scalp, was careful as she worked the color into the roots of Grace's hair and then combed it throughout. After a wash, Sandra proceeded to cut and style it into a short pixie cut. Her hands moved with a confidence that surprised Grace for someone so young. She asked no questions. Grace wasn't sure if she had been told not to or what, but she was grateful for the silence and time to think about what was next. The entire transformation took less than an hour.

At last, Sandra handed her the mirror and stepped back. Grace was startled at the dramatic change in her appearance. Her skin, where it was not burned, looked almost alabaster against the contrasting dark brown hair. The pixie cut made her neck look longer, drawing attention to her strained appearance and the taut lines around her eyes and mouth. But the transformation had been well done.

"Thank you, Sandra," said Grace, "you did a great job. Where did you learn all this?"

"Can't afford a beauty shop in my family," she replied, "so you learn to do for yourself."

When Grace and Sandra walked into the kitchen, Ellie looked up from the sink. The dishes were drying to one side, and she was busy cleaning the remainder of her morning catch. Shaking the water off her hands, she came over to give Grace a closer inspection. Circling slowly she smiled, giving a nod of approval. "Good work, Sandra. Our girl looks like a brand new person."

Sammy and Sandra excused themselves and went outside. Grace glanced at the wall clock. Ten after eight.

"It's time, chil'," said Ellie. "You got to be gittin'. She went to the sink and rinsed, wiping her hands dry on an apron that tried its best to cover her ample waist. "You'll be in Jacksonville by 'leven. If you misses the bus, them two'll drop you off at a motel near the bus station an' come straight back home."

"Are you sure?" Grace glanced at the door leading out to the porch.

"Don' you worry none 'bout them two. I trust 'em one hundred percent. They got Jesus in their hearts an' good sense in their heads. They'll git you theah an' git themselves home—no problem. I'd take you mysef, but I don' see so good at night no mo."

"What about Sandra's parents?"

"I talked to her mother while you was sleepin'. Jus' tol' her I had somethin' our kids needed doin' together. Tha's all. Everythin' is all right. You only got one thing to worry 'bout, honey chil', an' that one thing is yosef. Soon as you gits theah hightail it to wherever you thinks you gonna be safe. You know yet where you might be headin'?"

"As far away as I can for now anyway. I think maybe California."

267

Ellie studied her for a moment, thinking. Then she took a pencil and began writing on a scrap of yellow paper. When she finished she handed it to Grace. "This heah is my brother's address in Oakland. An' his phone number. He runs a gas station downtown. His name is Wendal Brown an' he gots a wife named Tara. She's one o' them Polynesian ladies from out in Hiyawaee someplace. They got two boys. I ain't seen 'em—oh, in maybe five yeahs now, but they's good people. I'll call out theah tonight an' let 'em know you is comin'."

"Ellie, I've dragged you into this far too much already. I can't possibly ... "

Ellie shrugged her off with a wave of her meaty hand. "Trust me, girl, you goin' to need some mo hep when you gits out theah."

"But ... "

"No 'buts' about it. You in a heap o' trouble an' it ain't goin' away when you reaches the Savannah city limits. You got some powerful people upset now an' as scared as you is 'bout *stayin'* alive—they's jus' as scared that yo might still *be* alive, so you gots to keep movin' on. An' you call Wendal when you git theah, you hearin' me now?"

Grace heaved a sigh of grateful resignation. At first she'd thought of LA. That had to be a big enough place to get lost in. But this gave her a new direction—and a ray of hope. Someone to meet her at the end of her run. She nodded her agreement as she took both of Ellie's hands in hers.

"I will. How can I ever thank you, Ellie?"

"By not gittin' caught, fo one thing," her rescuer chuckled, "'til somebody figures out who the real murderers are. An' by stayin' out o' trouble from now on, fo another. I think you right on waitin' some befo callin' yo momma. I know she gonna be worried sick, but don' take no chances on givin' yosef away. If the police come callin' then she don' know from nuthin'. When you sho you outa heah an' away

268

from wherever they be lookin', then call her. But be careful. An' don' try reachin' me neither. I don' want Sammy mixed up in this any more than he is."

"Will you at least let me pay you something for all you've done?" asked Grace, hesitating, not wanting to offend.

"'Course not," Ellie answered with a wave of her hand. "You know Jesus—he tol' this story 'bout a fella that got beat up by robbers real bad an' was left to die in a dark alley on the edge o' town. The 'big boys' with their fancy cars an' 'doctor-this-'n-that' in front o' their names saw him theah, but they was too busy to stop an' help. Fo'tunately fo him though, some fella by the name o' Good Sam happened by an' he took that beat-up fella in an' cared fo him an' everthin'. Even paid his hotel bill, mind you. I'm not sho 'bout how it all turned out, but I do know that theah Good Sam made Jesus a pretty happy fella that day. You heah what I'm sayin', chil'?"

Grace nodded. "I think so. 'Good Sam' picked me up this morning and cared for me all day. Now, 'Good Sammy' is about to take me across the state line to Florida. I'll bet you've made your Jesus a pretty happy fella all over again, Ellie."

Ellie laughed and kissed Grace on both cheeks.

"Now gather up yo things an' git on out o' heah. Wait. I got one mo thing I want you to have."

Ellie went to an old chest that stood on one side of the living room. The top right drawer. When she came back, she handed Grace a small book. "Put this in yo bag, hon. You ain't got no readin' material fo later an' you got a long ride ahead to California so maybe this'll help pass the time. By the way, don' mention to them two where you goin'. The less they know the better it is fo 'em, if you gits my drift."

Impulsively, Grace threw her arms as far around Ellie as she could get them. Tears of gratitude welled up in her eyes and spilled down her cheeks. "I'll never forget you, Ellie. I promise you that. Thank you so much for everything!"

Ellie's chin quivered with emotion. She brushed one hand over Grace's hair and the back of her other hand across her own eye. "I'm prayin' fo you, chil'. Ever' day from now on I'll be puttin' yo name up there to The Man. You jus' count on that. Ever' day he'll be lookin' after you where evah you go."

"Thank you, Ellie." Grace didn't know what else to say to this strange, wonderful black woman who had, on the spur of the moment, pulled up alongside whatever was left of her life that morning and stopped to take her in. Grace hugged her again, her final words spoken softly, forming a question for which there was no answer. "Whatever would I have done today without you?"

Minutes later, Sammy, Sandra, and Grace were crowded into the pickup truck. It rattled and bounced its way along Harmon Street before turning right on Victory Drive and heading toward Interstate 95. Three and a half hours later, Grace was registered in a nondescript motel, within walking distance of the bus depot in Jacksonville, Florida.

They had driven to the depot first so that Grace could check the schedule. Because they arrived later than expected, Grace insisted that Sammy call Ellie to let her know they would be late in returning. While he and Sandra huddled together at a telephone booth, Grace went to the ticket window.

She asked for the closest cross-country connection to the Bay Area from Jacksonville. She had already missed today's last departure, however, and the Greyhound bus did not leave again until nine thirty-five the following morning.

The agent explained that there would be transfers in Tallahassee, Dallas, and Los Angeles, where a connecting bus would take her the rest of the way to San Francisco. The tickets would set her back $233, and she would not arrive until early Friday morning, but, after briefly mulling over her options, she decided to do it. A night in a motel would help to refresh her body that was, at this late hour, once again feeling the tell-tale signs of exposure, shock, and fatigue. She paid the fare and walked to the exit where Sammy and Sandra were waiting.

Three blocks from the bus station, they pulled into an inexpensive looking motel. The elderly Hispanic woman on duty, speaking with a heavy accent, looked Grace over with a practiced eye as she filled out the registration. The room would be $65 and she could stay until three the next afternoon if she wanted to.

After hugging the two youngsters and telling them how much she appreciated their help, they said good-bye. She watched the old pickup make its way out of the parking lot and onto the street. When the taillights had finally disappeared into the night, she turned and made her way along the outdoor walkway to her room.

As soon as she closed and locked the door, Grace took off all of her clothes and began filling the tub. Her bites and sores were on fire again, but once she recovered from the shock of sinking into the tub full of tepid water, the relief she felt was exquisite. Leaning back until the water was up to her neck, she closed her eyes.

She wasn't sure how long she'd been dozing when a sudden, loud sound caused her to jump! Her heart pounded as she twisted around, grabbing at the edge of the tub with both hands.

What was that? Where am I?

Then slowly she sank back into the water.

The blaring noise was coming from the radio by the bed. The room's last occupant must have set the alarm to go off in order to catch a bus or a plane or whatever, and then failed to reset it before leaving.

Grace rose slowly from the water, dabbed dry with a towel and padded into the sleeping room on bare feet. The bed squeaked as she leaned across to turn off the radio. Pulling back the thin cover, she checked out the sheets. They appeared to be clean.

Sitting on the edge of the bed, she spread out the ointments and the Band-Aids that Ellie had generously supplied for her cuts and bites. She shook her head in amazement. Ellie had even remembered to include nail polish for any enterprising tick or chigger that might have eluded their earlier search. Unscrewing the cap of the first jar, she began smoothing the healing cream onto her skin.

Her mind drifted back to the bus terminal while her fingers continued working their way up from her feet and ankles. She decided that the long journey didn't sound as bad now as it had at first. Passenger check-in procedures at airports made her too vulnerable, though flying would have been her first choice. Besides, she was sure that the walk-up fare for a flight to San Francisco would be prohibitive. This was better. More anonymity. Less expense.

Just then something caught her eye. While unpacking her newly acquired canvas bag, the one that Sandra had given her, she'd placed Ellie's gift book on the nightstand. She had smiled upon realizing she'd been handed a small Bible. How many years since she'd held one of these in her hands? She recalled having been given a cheap copy of a children's New Testament as a prize for attending all five days at a weeklong summer Vacation Bible School in the little church where her father's funeral had been held. Now she noticed something else.

What is this?

Something was sticking out from the pages, mid-point in the book. She opened it up. There were the two $100 bills that she'd given to Ellie in exchange for $20s. Grace blinked as a tear broke across the rim of her eye and spilled onto her cheek.

Oh, Ellie. I don't believe it. In the last forty-eight hours I've met the worst of all people. And the best! What caused you to want to help me like this? I guess you want to be sure that I look up your 'Good Sam' story for myself.

Turning it over, she traced the softness of the worn imitation leather cover with her fingers, remembering as she did Ellie's firm, but tender touch. *Well, one thing's for sure, Ellie, you've already introduced me to the guy in real life.*

Then something broke inside. Flashbacks filled her thoughts like pictures on a movie screen. She watched and listened to Bonnie Jo, head thrown back in infectious laughter—and felt Ilene's hand squeezing hers, putting her mind at ease.

Everything's going to be okay, Grace.

Lowering herself to the pillow, Grace wept for her friends.

46

The noon crowd had thinned out, leaving the two women with empty tables on either side of them. Their salads lay wilted and half-eaten. Maggie ordered a second Arizona tea, mesmerized by the story that spilled out from Taylor like dirty water through a broken dike. Except for a clarifying question now and then, she just listened, amazed, stunned at the recounting of Taylor's narrow escape from that island off the East Coast—what was its name again? Daufauskie? And her incredible trek back to civilization!

At first she had listened with a reporter's instinctive skepticism, in spite of her friendship and love for the young woman who sat across from her, discernibly crushed and seared by the retelling of her own story. Gradually however, Maggie's skepticism melted away as she became immersed in Taylor's ... no, not Taylor's ... *Grace's* saga of survival. She shook her head as if that would replace the name of this person she was no longer sure she really knew. The same lovely face, now overwrought with stress, her eyes red-rimmed with telltale signs of sleeplessness. *Unbelievable! And yet ...*

Grace had twisted the napkin into tight folds as she spoke. Now she clenched it with both hands and looked up. "That's my story, Maggie. That is my awful, horrible, hellish story."

For a long moment, the two sat in silence, staring at each other.

Grace spoke first. "Do you believe me?"

"Taylor ... sorry, *Grace*. It may take me a while to get used to the name. That is the most bizarre story I've ever listened to. And Parker is mixed up in this? The guy who could be our next president? Do you realize what you are saying? I know this guy. I interviewed him once. Wait. It was at the Sinatra event that we went to together. And you suddenly jumped up and ran off. You saw him there, didn't you? The day Pete died."

For just a moment Grace glanced away, her eyes taking in the few remaining patrons in the restaurant. Then she looked back at Maggie and nodded.

It was the look in her eyes, the torture, the utter desolation and sorrow that dispelled any remaining vestige of doubt for Maggie. Some things you just know.

Catching Grace's anxious glance at her watch, she asked, "Do you have a plan? Why are you telling me this now? Am I in it?"

Grace frowned, nodding her head again. "I need help, Maggie. The understatement, I know. You are the only person I could go to. I need you to go to day care and pick up David and Nancy. I want them safely out of the way. Will you take them home with you? Or to the Clouses? Please? These people are watching every move I make. I need to be sure the children are safe."

"What about our friend?"

"You mean the man that was in the store? If he's still hanging around, I'll keep him busy long enough for you to slip away. My lunch break was over long ago. I have to get back. You were just a customer, remember. They don't know you. Get your car—here is the address— go there right now, and pick them up. I've told Mrs. Fernandez—she's the director—that you might do this if I had to work late. Get them to a safe place and then call me at work. I'm supposed to meet the man

275

who called me last night at five o'clock in front of the store."

"You're meeting with these people?" Maggie gasped. "Face to face? Oh, Grace … don't do that. Call the police. Get some help for goodness sake. Don't do this on your own. It's too dangerous!"

"I have to. Look. Who besides you is going to believe such a cockamamie story as the one I've just told you? These are some of the most powerful men in the world. In six months they'll own this country. Especially Brandenbury. He's worse than Parker. He probably owns the police in this town right now. If he doesn't, it won't take him long to buy whomever he has to in order to get to me. I can't go to them. Nothing can stop him. I'm telling you, Maggie, Brandenbury is the personification of evil. He killed BJ and Ilene, and I think he enjoyed doing it!"

Maggie shuddered reflexively before posing the question that had been troubling her for the past hour. "Okay, I have to ask you this. Now that they've found you, why haven't these people already killed you?"

"I wondered about that myself at first, but this morning I realized why. It's because they don't know yet whom I may have told my story to. And now they think I might have pictures of that afternoon with all of us together. They're concerned about it. For their own protection, they need to know these things."

"Do you have pictures?"

Grace hesitated.

"I've got a digital film card," she said at last. "It was badly soaked in the water. I kept it, but I've never tried to use it. I was afraid to. It may sound crazy, but I could never bring myself to see if the pictures were still there. Too many bad memories. But I told the guy last night that I have pictures and that I've left my written testimony in places that will automatically be made public if I am killed. In other words, that's my insurance policy. At least for the moment."

"Have you done this?"

"I wish," said Grace. "Actually, I have written the details in a diary. It's in a safe deposit box in the Bay Area where I used to live. But I've been afraid to tell anyone. Only two other people know about the diary or the film card or the safety deposit box."

She reached into her purse and withdrew a small key.

"Now I want you to have the only other key in case … in case something happens. Would you? I didn't lie to the man. I just shaped the truth to fit my need at the moment. Like I've been doing for the last seven years."

Maggie took the key and cradled it in her hand, at the same time glancing at her watch. It was one-thirty. She studied the crestfallen look on the face of the young woman across the table, a woman she had thought she knew, but now wasn't at all sure.

"Everything's going to be okay," Maggie said in as reassuring a tone as she could muster, dropping the key in her purse. Scooting her chair back, she reached for the check. "And I'd better get going if I'm going to pick up the kids."

She stood for a moment, shaking her head as she looked at Grace. "This is the most extraordinary story I have ever heard—and I've heard some beauts, kid. Remember, I'm a religion and business ethics reporter. If this is all true, and I'm accepting that everything you've told me is, then, girl, you are in such deep trouble!"

She started to reach out and squeeze Grace's shoulder, then stopped short, attempting a reassuring smile. "I almost forgot. I'm the 'customer,' not your friend. So, I'll take a rain check on that lamp in your department, sweetie, which as you know here in the desert means 'there's not a snowball's chance I'm going to buy it.'"

Grace offered a weak smile at Maggie's attempted humor.

"I'll go get the kids right now," said Maggie, "and I'll let you know when we get home so you can rest easy as far as they're concerned. You take care of yourself and call me just as soon as you've met with your night crawler ... or caller ... whatever sort of vermin he is. Just be careful, okay? I still wish you'd call the police. I really don't think you should be doing this."

"What choice do I have? They've got me in a vice. If I notify the authorities, they'll kill Brad."

"Maybe you're wrong about that."

"I'm *not* wrong. I've been wrong about a lot of things, but not about this. You'll call me the minute you get home?"

"Count on it. Take a deep breath. You've got enough on your plate. Trust me."

"I do, Maggie, I do. You're the only person in the world that I can trust now. That's why I came to you."

Maggie let out a sigh and nodded, placing a $20 and a $10 bill on top of the check, then turned and walked briskly out of the restaurant.

47

When the sallow-looking shopper in the flowered shirt saw Maggie leave, he touch-dialed 1-704 on the cellular phone, adding the private direct-line number he'd been given on his arrival in the area. Moments later, a male voice boomed in his ear.

"Yes ... that's right, sir. Her friend just came out of the restaurant. They've been in there over an hour ... What? No, we already ran a check on her. She's a reporter for the *Desert Sun* ... yes sir ... yes sir ... religion and ethics ... my guess at what she's up to? Well, Sammy says the preacher's girl friend talked real tough last night. I think there's a good chance she's got something written down somewhere ... no sir ... no sir, I don't know whether or not she's told the reporter anything. Jon couldn't get a table close enough to overhear their conversation. This isn't getting any easier, though.

"Reynolds confirms that there was a camera there that day all right ... you recall seeing it, too? Yes ... he says he got it away from her and dumped it ... that's right. Says he took the filmcard out and destroyed it along with the camera. He thinks she's bluffing, but we can't take that chance ... yes sir, I know ...

"The kids? Like the report says, Weston has got two—a boy and a girl. They're his actually. The wife died some time back. The oldest is ten or eleven. What? Are you sure? Yes sir, of course. Certainly we can.

You think it's really necessary? I see ... certainly, of course you're right. If we make the whole litter disappear, then the mama kitty won't be able to stay away ... We'll get on it ... My guess is she's gonna try to make them vanish herself. Maybe that's what the meeting with the reporter was about. Not about spilling her tale, but covering it."

The man chuckled at his little joke.

"Okay, we're ready. I'll have them picked up right away. What about the reporter? What shall we do with her? All right. Yes sir, as soon as we can make it happen. The plane is waiting back here at Bermuda Dunes. They just got in an hour ago. We're keeping the flyboys hopping. Yes. Consider it done."

The woman had already disappeared from view around the corner by the time he disconnected. Quickly, he tapped a different set of numbers.

Across the street from Broadmores, an Asian man in white shorts and a brown shirt swallowed the last bit of iced tea from a plastic cup, pulled the small cellular phone from his pocket, and brought it to his ear on the second ring.

"Yeah?"

He listened for a full minute, his gaze trained on the parking area in front of Broadmores.

"Okay, I see her now. She is getting into her car ... a blue Acura, California license number ... 2 FDB ... she's heading out in your direction. Do you see her? Good. Is Aziz there with you? Tell him to follow her ... You'll wait for the target? All right, I'll get the other car and pick you up when you're ready."

48

Grace came out of the Cedar Creek Inn and started back along El Paseo Drive. A few doors down the street, she saw him out of the corner of her eye. It was the same man, the one who had approached her in the furniture department, standing on the opposite sidewalk, smoking a cigarette.

I was right. He is one of them. He's watching me and wants to be sure I know it!

Her fear became mixed with anger. She cleared her throat and looked the other way. Worries about Brad glutted her thoughts. She was enraged at being stalked like this; infuriated at having allowed herself to be found out.

How did they do it anyway? How did they find me? This sort of thing happens in squalid little African countries. Or the Middle East. Maybe in Iran or some other hate-peddling society. But not here. Not here in the USA. And not by somebody who wants to be president and is prepared to kill me in order to get there!

She recalled a time she'd been filled with optimism, about to graduate and face the world with all the tools she had been told were needed to conquer it. How long ago had that been? At least a lifetime. Maybe more. Grace had struggled so long to contain her memories that she could hardly remember the days before her life had been reduced to simple survival and little else.

"Before Brandenbury" seemed like a distant fairytale. Just staying alive had occupied her attention ever since she had met him. And there were days when it had not seemed worth it. This was one. Several times she'd been tempted to end the lonely misery her life had morphed into. Yet she had never been able to forget a total stranger's tender care. Ellie Fitzgerald had changed her life. Along with the many long nights spent alone with Ellie's worn, imitation-leather Bible, until she had finally uttered the first honest prayer that she could ever remember. A prayer of such deep regret and sadness, asking for forgiveness. Then five years later when she had met Brad, at last her world seemed to have righted itself for good.

Hesitating, Grace stepped into a small, very exclusive dress shop and stood quietly in the store's air-conditioned interior, trying to sort out her options. Were there any? *Common killers have hunted me these last seven years on their way to the White House. I let myself be dumped into the middle of a high-stakes political crap game and didn't even know how to roll the dice!*

"Hi, there."

Grace started at the sound of the clerk's voice.

"Sorry. I didn't mean to disturb you. Go right ahead and look, it's okay," the woman said. "If I can help you with anything, just let me know. We've got some really great clothes on sale today."

"Thanks." Grace flashed a polite smile and made a pretense of looking through the clothes hanging on the rack nearest the window, while keeping an eye on the man in the flowered shirt. As she watched him, an overwhelming world-weariness passed through her mind like a riderless dark horse.

America is about to choose. And if the pollsters are right, the good citizens are about to put two murderers in the White House. That's the deal, isn't it? It's not about being red or blue or even purple. Color doesn't really matter. Not in skin or in politics. It's about character and wisdom and the ability to choose well. I messed up my life seven years ago. In those days, the world was a little playing around, a little lying, a little cheating didn't matter all that much if no one got hurt, whether in one's own life or in the oval office. But we were wrong. The collective conscience was successfully seared, and I bought the lie, just like a lot of my friends. We were being primed for the big time. Who would have thought something like this could be happening here. Some place else, maybe. But not here. Not in America. And especially not with me. A nobody. A not so innocent innocent. But it is happening, isn't it—and it does matter. Now I'm next on the list of persona non grata, and so is the country, and no one out there has a clue.

She glanced down at her watch to check the time. When she looked up again, the man was gone. Vanished. He was out there, though. Like a renegade cancer cell, she knew he was still there. Somewhere. Hiding. Able to kill when he is ready. Grace stepped back into the afternoon heat and headed toward Broadmores. She felt the man's eyes following her, even though she couldn't see him.

Brad, where are you? Are you all right? Are you still alive? I'm so sorry, sweetheart. This is my fault! How many times have I said that? But it's true, isn't it? No, I should never have come here. I never should have let myself think I would marry you, Brad. I knew better. I just wanted so much to be with you. This is all my fault!

It was going on three when she reappeared on Broadmores' second floor, but it was impossible to concentrate on what she was supposed to be doing. She kept glancing at the phone on her desktop. *Maggie should have called by now.* Jim was still on his break. Kaylin Martin was busy with an elderly couple when Grace spotted a middle-aged woman with far too much of herself packed into a pair of fitted jeans, looking through the display area for pictures and frames. With a sigh, she dropped her purse back in the drawer and headed in her direction.

49

Maggie drove away from the day care center with David and Nancy and their backpacks in the back seat. In her mirror, she could see Nancy fumbling with her safety belt.

"Are you okay back there, sweetie?" she called. "Can you find the buckle?"

"I've got the buckle, but I can't make it work," Nancy replied.

"Here," said David, grasping the shortest section of the belt in one hand while reaching across with the other, "give it to me."

"No, David, I can do it," Nancy declared, pushing him away.

"But you're not doing it," David said emphatically as he snapped the buckle in place. Nancy gave her brother the coldest pouting look she could for having just experienced "one-upmanship" from an older sibling.

Maggie turned off Palm Desert Boulevard onto a two-lane side street—a shortcut leading to Bob Hope Drive. With her attention divided between the roadway and the two children in the rearview mirror, she didn't notice the car until it had already pulled alongside, keeping pace. Out of the corner of her eye, she glimpsed a man in the passenger seat looking in her direction. The car sped up and began passing. Maggie glanced back to check the children again just as the car cut sharply in front of them, forcing her to swerve to avoid being hit.

"Look out!" she cried out instinctively at the driver who could not possibly hear her and the children in the back seat, who could and did. Gripping the steering wheel with both hands, the car careened up onto the sidewalk and crunched solidly into an electric pole. The impact released the car's safety air bags, slamming her back in the seat, stunned. It happened so fast—how long she couldn't tell—in actuality, only a matter of seconds.

There were men's voices coming from both sides of the car now. They were shouting something to each other.

Thank God, they stopped to help.

Maggie stirred slowly, releasing her grip on the steering wheel, trying to regain her full senses. Then the driver's side window exploded, spraying tiny glass shards into Maggie's face and lap.

Before she was able to move, a hand reached inside and released the lock.

"Come on," *A man's voice, sounding gruff.*

"No—wait." *David's voice. Good. He's okay.*

A scream—"No!" *Nancy's voice. It's okay, sweetheart—they're just trying to help.* Maggie started to turn around, wincing at a sharp stinging above her eye as she did. The initial shock was subsiding now, and her first instinct was to reassure the children.

"No! Cut it out! Maggie!" *David. Sounds frightened. Well, of course he's frightened. What child wouldn't be?*

Her hands throbbed from gripping the steering wheel at impact. Everything seemed to be happening in slow motion.

Were minutes passing? Or only split seconds?

Maggie reached over and opened her door just as a man brushed past her.

A man's voice again. "Car coming. Let's go."

"What about the woman?"

"Forget her. It's too late. Come on."

Wait!

They were running back to the car.

They have David and Nancy!

The children were screaming and kicking against the men as they were pushed into the Mercedes.

What are you doing?

"Wait! Stop!" Maggie's voice returned as she screamed, half-falling out of her car and stumbling toward the Mercedes. The driver jammed his foot on the accelerator. Tiny bits of gravel shot back at her, forcing her to turn away, shielding her face. A small stone ricocheted off her arm as the car sped down the street. She stood dumbfounded for a moment, blood seeping down from a cut on her leg, watching helplessly as the car turned left and disappeared from view.

No, no. The license number. Get the number.

But the car was moving too fast. She thought it was a California plate, but couldn't be certain, even about that. It had all happened so quickly. Moving unsteadily, she hurried back to her car where she stood for a moment gathering herself together. Then she slammed the palm of her hand against the door.

"No!" she shouted helplessly into the air at no one and everyone. Just then another car came to a stop behind her. The young Hispanic driver jumped out and ran up to her. Maggie squinted at her through dazed eyes, her hand against the swelling lump already forming on her forehead.

"Are you all right?" she asked. "Here, let me help you. You're hurt."

Maggie sat down on the ground, staring at the empty street as the woman ran back to her car, reached into her purse, withdrew a cell phone, and dialed 911.

50

Grace was quietly falling to pieces. *Maggie should have called before this. Where is she?* She picked up the phone and dialed the daycare center.

"Hello, Mrs. Fernandez, did Maggie come by yet?...She did? ... She signed the children out at two fifty-five? ... Okay, thanks ... no, there's no problem. I'm sure they just stopped for ice cream or something. Thanks. Bye."

Grace put the phone down and stared disconsolately across the showroom. It should have taken no more than fifteen minutes for them to reach her house. Unless they *had* stopped for ice cream. Jim was straightening up the floor tile display and Kaylin was still busy with her customer. For Grace, a silent alarm had gone off inside and was rapidly turning her stomach into a tight knot. Just then the telephone rang. She grabbed it up.

"Hello?"

The voice on the other end sounded muffled. Was she crying. Or in pain?

"Grace, I'm sorry."

287

It was Maggie.

"Maggie, what's happened? Are the kids okay?"

There was a brief pause before the answer came.

"Some men forced my car off the road. They've taken David and Nancy."

For an instant Grace sat stunned, speechless. "Taken?" she said at last. "Maggie, what do you mean 'taken?'"

There was no response, only silence.

"You mean they've been kidnapped, too?" Grace whispered.

"I'm sorry," repeated Maggie, her voice thin and anguished, not at all sounding like her normal self-assured self. "It happened so fast. There was nothing I could do."

Grace sagged into her chair in disbelief. "How ... what happened?"

"Two men—there might have been a third person driving. In fact, I'm almost sure of it. They forced me off the road and we crashed into a pole. The air bags went off. For a few seconds I was stunned. But I did see *two* men. At first, I thought they had stopped to help us. Then they opened the doors, dragged David and Nancy out, and put them into the car that ran us off the road. It was silver. A Mercedes, I think, but I'm not sure. It all happened so fast that I didn't even get the license number."

"They've got David and Nancy." Disbelief and the hopelessness of her situation fully set in. She slumped forward with her elbows on the desktop and buried her face in her hands. "Then it's over."

"Listen," it was Maggie's voice again. "You've got to call the police. This thing has gone way too far. It's out of control."

"No!" Tears sprang from her eyes as she gritted her teeth and spit out the words, covering her mouth with her hand. "Don't you see? These people impersonate police officers. That's how they got Brad. They may even *be* police officers. I can't go to the police!"

"But Grace ... "

"No! Even if we found some police or FBI who were the good guys—and even if they believed my story, which is unlikely—they'd do an Amber Alert and go after them. David and Nancy would be dead and gone before they even got close. Brad, too. Don't you see that? It's too late!"

They were both silent for a long moment.

"Where are you, Maggie?"

"They brought me to Eisenhower Emergency."

"Are you hurt?"

"Just a bad bump on my forehead. A small cut on my leg. Not a big deal. I'm going to be sore, that's all."

"Who?"

"Who what?"

"Who took you to the hospital?"

"The police. A young woman stopped to help. She called in the accident. The paramedics were there in ten minutes. I had to fill out a report. One of the officers was kind enough to bring me here."

"Did you tell them about the kids?"

"No. I wanted to. I really think I should have but after what you told me, I wasn't sure what to do. Grace ... "

"Stop! Don't say a word, Maggie. Not to anyone. Nothing more than you absolutely have to. I'll be there as quickly as I can. Fifteen minutes. Are you free to leave?"

"Yes."

"I'll be right over."

She hung up the phone and motioned to Jim. "A friend of mine was just admitted to Eisenhower. She's been in a car accident. I've got to go get her and take her home. She doesn't have any family in the area. Would you take care of things for the rest of the afternoon?"

289

"Sure'" said Jim, "no problem. It's pretty slow anyway. Are you okay, Taylor? Was your friend hurt badly?"

"She'll be all right. Hit her head I guess. She's been shaken up pretty good, that's all. You'll handle the lock-up tonight?"

"Don't worry. I'll take care of it. I know you said earlier that Brad is away. Does someone have his children?"

Grace didn't answer as she scooped up her purse and hurried toward the employee's exit, pretending she must not have heard. Oh well, it was a dumb question. Of course someone had the children.

51

The four-door sedan, windows darkened, accelerated smoothly onto Interstate 10 at the Monterey onramp, heading east, moving through heavier-than-usual afternoon traffic with ease, passing three large tractor-trailer units and a motor home as the driver maneuvered from right to left across the multi-lane roadway. Once in the left lane, he set the cruise control at 70 mph, the legal limit for this stretch of highway. He kept an eye on the rearview mirror, but there was nothing out of the ordinary.

In the rear seat, David and Nancy were squeezed between the two men who had pulled them from Maggie's car and forced them into this one. It was a nice car, David thought, his eyes running over the gray leather interior, as well as what he was able to see of the dashboard through the opening between the front seats. It even smelled new. He'd ridden in a car like this once. It belonged to some people at church. Will and Sarah Rogers, a nice older man and his wife. They were from somewhere up north—Wisconsin or some place like that. They came to Palm Springs every winter. He remembered riding in it once. It had a new smell, too, like this one.

The driver was wearing his safety belt. There was no one in the front seat opposite him. Nancy sat huddled in David's arms, crying softly. At first they had fought back, kicking and yelling, trying to twist away from the grip of their abductors.

Abductors.

It was a word David was all too familiar with. One he had learned at school. He and Nancy had been cautioned, both at home and school, never to accept rides from strangers. Well, they hadn't exactly accepted this ride, had they? He felt a sudden protectiveness toward his little sister and a fierce sense of pride at the way in which she had fought back.

She had surprised the man dragging her into the car by kicking him in the groin. He had grunted in pain and almost lost hold of her in the process. But the men were both strong and rough. Too much for the children. It was over almost before it started. They were shoved onto the backseat of the car that had swerved in front of Maggie. The men wedged them in from either side, slamming the doors shut. David heard the tires spinning in gravel. He felt fright and helplessness swirling in the pit of his stomach. Twisting around, he looked out the rear window as the car leaped forward, glimpsing Maggie running after them, waving her arms.

"Where are you taking us?" David demanded.

The three men remained silent.

"Tell us where you're taking us!" he demanded again, this time shouting out at the top of his voice.

"Shut up, kid," growled the man next to him.

"You can't do this to us, you know," David went on bravely as he tried twisting away from the man's grip. "This is against the law. You're going to be in big trouble."

"I said, 'shut up.'" The man emphasized his point by jabbing David's stomach with an elbow.

"Ouch!" he yelled, catching his breath. "That hurt."

No response.

David could see that they were headed east on the freeway. He reached around and drew Nancy closer as she buried her face in his chest, still sobbing softly.

"My dad will get you for this." David tried to make his voice sound as confident and as threatening as he could muster.

No response.

"Why are you doing this?" David asked, deciding to try a different approach. "Our family's not rich. My dad's a preacher."

The man next to Nancy shifted in his seat and slapped David across the face with the back of his hand. It was a stinging blow that snapped his head to one side. David yelled in pain.

"You were told to shut up, kid. Now, shut up! Another word out of either one of you, and I'll really smack you."

David rubbed the side of his face with his hand. Nancy was crying harder now, looking up in dismay at him. He pulled her closer, determined to protect his sister in whatever way he could. It's what his dad would want him to do. And Taylor, too. Anyway, where was he? And Taylor. Did Mrs. Hinegardner and Taylor know what was happening to them? He remembered hearing Mrs. Hinegardner call out just as they were being thrown into the car. He closed his eyes and began a silent prayer the way he'd been taught at home and in Sunday school.

Jesus, please, please help us ...

The driver handed a cellular phone to the man sitting next to David.

David watched as he punched in some numbers. A local call? He was good at numbers and was able to remember most of these. Then the man held it to his ear and began to talk.

He studied the man's features, trying not to look directly at him. Hairy hands and arms stuck out in David's mind. They looked unusual, because of the man's pale skin. He had a mustache and lots of dark hair, combed straight back. He was wearing white pants and a dumb-looking shirt with flowers on it. And glasses. Dark ones. David hadn't noticed that before. He looked around at the others. They were all wearing dark glasses.

He turned his attention back to the man with the cell phone. There was something else. Two weeks earlier, David's dentist had recommended braces. Ever since then, he'd been noticing people's teeth. As the man talked, he noticed his teeth, especially the bottom ones. They were uneven. And they were yellow—the kind of yellow people get from smoking cigarettes. That's what he smelled.

No one was smoking at the moment, but this one was definitely a smoker. He could smell it on the man's clothes. The one beside Nancy was Asian. Chinese, maybe. Or Japanese. He wasn't sure. He wore white shorts and a brown shirt. David's confidence grew with the awareness that he could recognize these men later, when the police caught up with them. In fact, he was sure that he could identify all three.

What?

David's mind refocused on the man with the cellular.

What was it he had just said?

The man handed the phone back to the driver, glaring at David as he leaned forward. In a flash, David's growing confidence imploded. Something the man said just registered.

We'll be there in ten minutes—maybe a little more. Have the plane ready to fly.

He shrank back into the seat as far as he could, clinging to Nancy now for moral support as much as out of his desire to protect. He felt a new fear stirring in the pit of his stomach.

What's going to happen to us? Who are these people? Where are they taking us?

52

Grace parked well away from the Eisenhower Emergency entrance. The small lot near the entrance was always full. Parking was always a guaranteed problem any time around this hospital and its several adjacent medical buildings. Near the Wright Building, a valet was busy helping an elderly man from his car, a service provided free of charge for patients who couldn't walk long distances.

She jogged through the sweltering heat—a hundred and twelve today, along with a higher than normal desert humidity. Thunderheads loomed off to the southwest, promising at least the possibility of showers, though none had been predicted, as far as she knew. She hurried through doors marked Emergency and up to the receptionist's counter.

"A patient. Last name Hinegardner? Mary Magdalene. She was admitted a short while ago. Car accident."

The receptionist glanced down at her computer. "Right. Ms. Hinegardner is back there," she said, motioning with her hand at the same time toward a nearby hallway. "Are you family?"

"The closest to it that she has here in the Valley."

"Your name?"

"Taylor Carroll."

"Okay. You can be 'family.' Go on back. She's in the third stall. Just

295

peek through the curtain. And I wouldn't worry. It didn't look like anything too serious. She walked in with a police officer. Just some bruises and a bump on the head."

"Thanks."

Grace hurried past the receptionist and into a large, open room partitioned off by several privacy curtains hanging from stainless steel ceiling tracks. Behind each curtain was a bed ready to receive its next patient. The first one was empty, the second held a young Hispanic boy surrounded by his parents and siblings. Sure enough, Maggie was half-lying, half-sitting on the third bed. As Grace pushed past the curtain, Maggie greeted her with a look of mixed relief and trepidation.

"How are you?" she asked, putting her hand on Maggie's arm. "Are you okay?"

"Yes, I'm okay. I'll be fine," Maggie reassured her. "It's the kids we have to be concerned about. A rock cut, no big deal. When they drove off their rear tires kicked up the roadside gravel. A bruise on my knee and my hands are starting to ache like crazy. They're going to be sore for a day or two, that's all. I was gripping the steering wheel so hard when we hit the pole. I don't think either of them was hurt. I'm not sure how, but I must have banged my head against the car door when I was getting out."

"Let me see."

Maggie pulled back her hair to reveal a dark discoloration above her left eye. "It's swelling a bit, and I've got a major headache, but nothing else. It's not a concussion. They want me to stay overnight, but I said no."

"Do you think that's wise?" asked Grace. "I mean, what if you leave and then something happens?"

"Listen, dear," Maggie winced as she threw her feet over the edge of the bed and pushed herself to a sitting position. "You are in major trouble—with a capital 'T.' There is no way I'm staying in this place tonight to nurse a little bang on my head and a few extra bruises, so forget it. Understand? It's David and Nancy we have to think about. And Brad."

Grace nodded, overcome by foreboding and dismay at the thought of the children and Brad. "What am I going to do?" she asked of no one in particular, staring past Maggie at the medical apparatus hanging from above the bed on the wall.

"Well, first of all, *we* are going to get ourselves out of here and go to my house," declared Maggie. "Where's your car?"

"Along the outer edge of the lot."

"Go get it and come around to the entrance. I'll check myself out at the desk and meet you."

"Do you want me to wait for you?"

"No. Get going. We've got lots to do, and I want to get some things at my place. So do you."

"What are you thinking?"

"That you and I aren't staying in our homes tonight. We're checking into a hotel. Somewhere safe. What are you? A size smaller than me?"

Grace nodded absently, unable to get her mind off David and Nancy. They had to be frightened to death.

"Okay, we'll find a change of clothes for you at my house. I don't want you going back to Brad's or to your apartment. Just hurry and meet me out front."

Grace turned and pushed back through the curtain. Moments later, she was outside, swallowed up once more in the hot breath of early summer heat that held the entire Coachella Valley in its grip.

53

Following a brief stop at Maggie's to pick up come clothes and toiletries, the two women drove to the nearby city of La Quinta. As they made their way along Eisenhower Drive, they were careful to watch for anyone who might be following. Before checking into the La Quinta Resort Hotel under the names Beverly Carson and Karen Swifthurst, Maggie and Grace withdrew enough cash from an ATM to pay for one night and have some cash in hand. She declined the clerk's request to imprint her credit card for additional charges.

"We'll pay cash if we eat here. And if anyone should call or stop by asking to see us, please don't let whoever is at the desk give them our room number. Call us in advance. We have a bit of a husband problem to work on tonight, if you know what I mean."

The clerk glanced up at Maggie, saw the bandage and her discolored temple, and looked down again quickly, acting as though this was a normal request, something she heard everyday.

Who knows, thought Grace, standing a step behind Maggie and to one side. *Maybe it is.*

She looked around the spacious lobby interior, her gaze gathering in the dark wood beams, the stone fireplace and big screen TV, as well as the overabundance of lounging chairs, art, and colorful throw rugs. *Any other time and this would be a paradise,* Grace thought as they left the registration area and followed after the bellman's golf cart in their car. She had been to this tennis resort once for dinner with Brad and recalled that Dwight and Mamie Eisenhower had made this their desert home following his tenure as President of the United States.

The bellman led them around to the back of the resort complex, past clusters of white stucco one and two story, tile-roofed units—each situated near beautiful, placid swimming pools scattered throughout the grounds. Lemon, orange, lime and grapefruit trees with white-painted trunks hugged the lanes and sidewalks, spreading their branches over bougainvillea vines bursting with purple and red floral bracts, framing each building with the beauty of desert flora.

"This way," the bellman said as he stepped away from the cart and opened the courtyard gate. "Your unit is over here, to the right. Number 119."

Within minutes they were inside a room with twin beds, bath and shower, closet and TV. All the basics. Pleasant, but unlike the grounds themselves, nothing out of the ordinary. That was okay, however. Golf and tennis amenities—even the restaurants were not important today. It was simply a place to hide, regroup, and decide what to do next. That was all.

"Is there anything else you will need?" the young Latino bellman asked pleasantly.

"No thanks," Maggie answered. She handed him a generous tip and stood in the doorway until he disappeared through the wrought iron garden gate Closing the door, she set the lock before turning to look at Grace.

"How are you feeling?"

"Like I was the one who ran my car into a pole, instead of you," she groaned, dropping onto one of the beds. "By the way, where is your car? In all the rush, I forgot to ask."

"I don't know. The policeman said he'd have someone tow it in, wherever 'in' is. I'll call later and find out."

Maggie stretched out on the other bed, resting her head against one of several large pillows. Grace got up and crossed the room, sitting down on an upright wooden chair.

"I just can't believe this is really happening," she said at last. "It's all so unreal, so horrible. Last Sunday at church, everything was normal, Maggie. I sat with the kids. Brad preached about forgiveness. He made it seem so real."

"Yes. His message was good as usual," Maggie agreed. "I liked the way he developed the story."

"You mean about Jesus washing feet or about the woman caught in the act of adultery? The one those self-righteous Pharisees dragged out to challenge Jesus?"

"Yes to both."

"Well, right now I'm not too sure about the foot washing business, but—meet the woman, Maggie. You're looking at her. She is me!"

"Come on ... lighten up. Whatever you did back then was a long time ago. You've gotten older and wiser. A lot wiser. And speaking of forgiveness, you know how completely God forgives when we ask. Whatever you were guilty of in the past, you know he's forgiven you. You know that, don't you?"

Grace hesitated, and then said, "Yes to the God part, at least intellectually I understand that. But, Brad? Well, that's another matter."

"He doesn't know about these people? Not anything at all?"

Grace grew pensive. "No. Not a word. I wanted to tell him at first—when I started to realize where our relationship was going. I know I should have. In fact I tried more than once. I was scared, though. I kept thinking that if he knew who I really was, he wouldn't want me. Then I made excuses. What could he or anyone else do? What was done was done. History. I had really begun thinking these madmen were so out of my life that they were just a horrible memory. After all, it's been seven years. And then Sunday, when Brad proposed again, I wanted so much to say, 'yes,' and I almost did. I let down all the bars, Maggie. I love him so much! But instead, I told him I had some personal things to work out, that it wasn't about my love for him or the children. It was about me. And I promised to give him my answer tonight when he came home from LA. When I went home Sunday night, I knew. I had to tell him. It was a mistake. It was too big a chance. *I'm* too big a chance for anyone. I knew I had to tell him why and then leave town."

Grace shook her head. She lifted her hands and then dropped them in a gesture that signaled the helplessness she felt as tears carved muddy rivulets through the mascara on her cheeks. Maggie watched but made no effort to intervene.

"I was so sure they would never find me. And now this. What am I going to do, Maggie? I am so messed up. What ever am I going to do?"

"You're going to get hold of yourself for one thing," Maggie said finally, her tone firm and unyielding. "You're going to quit beating yourself up. And then we're going to figure out what to do next. Aren't you supposed to meet with one of those people at five?"

Grace wiped at her face as she glanced at her watch. Twenty minutes to five.

"Yes. Oh, yes. I forgot about the time! If I hurry, I can still get there." She stood and reached for the keys she'd tossed on the nightstand.

"No!" Maggie declared as she pushed herself to a sitting position. "You're not going anywhere."

"But ... "

"I said, no. Just stop. You're not going to meet with anybody. Get that through your head. You're running on impulse right now. They've got you on a string. If you show up, they'll know that they've won. What can you do anyway? Offer to give yourself up in return for Brad and the kids? If they don't kill you on the spot, you'll be dead as soon as they've extracted from you the names of all the people you've told your story to. And they will get *everything* from you."

"But you're the only one ... " Grace stopped suddenly. "No, that's not true. There's Ellie Fitzgerald in Savannah. And her brother and his wife ... "

"If these people are the killers you say they are, then this Ellie woman is a goner. If they get control of you, she's a walking dead person. So is her brother. Me, too, for that matter. They'll get our names out of you one way or another. And they're never going to let Brad and David and Nancy come back to tell how they were kidnapped by a United States senator who also just happens to be running for president along with his billionaire business friend!"

"You make it sound even worse. And you keep saying, '*If* these people are killers ... ' do you still not believe me, Maggie? Guess I wouldn't blame you if you didn't."

Maggie sat quietly for a long moment, staring at Grace. Then she shifted off the bed to a standing position. Turning her back on Grace, she walked toward the shuttered window and peeked outside.

"I am going to be stiff and sore tomorrow, I can tell you that for sure. I know I'm not shaking hands with anyone real soon either. They're starting to swell a bit." Maggie paused, flexing her fingers as she turned to face Grace. "All right. Enough of this 'poor me' stuff. I want you to hear this and hear it good. Are you listening?"

Grace nodded.

"Really listening?"

"Yes, I'm really listening."

"Okay. Your story is so absolutely crazy that, if I didn't know you, I'd say you were a case for the nut house. But I do know you, *Taylor*—although not as well as I thought. And I'm getting to know this 'Grace' person you've introduced me to. And as nearly as I can tell, this is one very strong person. Yes, I do believe you. As incredible as all this sounds, I believe you. Every word."

Grace leaned back against her chair as, little by little, the tension released its grip on her body. She sighed, dabbing with a tissue at the messy dampness on her cheeks. "Thank you, Maggie," she whispered. "Thank you. I don't feel strong. Actually, I feel anything but strong. But thank you for that undeserved vote of confidence. I feel ashamed, that's what I feel. Ashamed and defeated. Lost and scared out of my wits. Like a total coward. That you believe me is huge."

"Don't just thank me," Maggie admonished. "Just go put some cold water on your face and then let's try to plan our next move. You've been on the run for seven years. Your only defense during all this time has been anonymity. Now that's gone. Get that through your head. You no longer have anonymity. And you have no defense. You've been exposed. Every desperate defense you've clung to in your past is gone. So are Brad and David and Nancy. There's only one thing you have left."

"What are you talking about?"

"Seven years ago you went on the defensive to stay alive. You ran from, hid from, lied about, did every possible thing you could think of, and created a whole new persona. That's over. You can't do that anymore."

"I understand. So what are you saying?"

"I'm saying we've got to go on the offensive. It's time you turn the tables on these monsters. They think they know who you are. They think they've got you. But they don't know you. You've changed, girl. You've changed since they saw you last. You've grown. You know more. You're smarter. You've become a follower of Jesus—albeit somewhat flawed, but who isn't—you have a guy in your life who loves you and wants to marry you. And you have two kids who are counting on you. Somehow, we've got to snag the upper hand and put these miserable excuses for manhood on the defensive."

"But ... "

"Will you just stop it with the 'buts'?" Maggie's tone was surprisingly sharp. "Go wash your face. Get it together. Forget how rotten you feel right now. We don't have time for you to feel sorry for yourself. We have to trust God. One hundred percent. Brad and the kids are depending on us to be strong. We are their only hope! So go on. And when you've washed up, I think I've got an idea that might get us started. But we have to hurry."

Grace doused cold water on her face without bothering to replace her makeup. Maggie grimaced at the pain in her shoulders as she hugged Grace, patting her reassuringly. Then they hurried out the door to the car.

It was nearly half past five according to the Red Robin Restaurant clock on the wall, when Grace placed the receiver back on the pay phone and sat down in the booth across from Maggie. Their first counter-attack had just been launched. Now all they could do was wait to see if it was successful.

"Okay, young lady," said Maggie, "you've done all you can do for the moment. We just sit here now and wait. While we do that, I know there's more to your story, and I want to hear it all. But first, let's order something."

Grace started to protest, but Maggie held up her hands.

"I know you're not hungry. I'm not either. But we need to keep our energy level up, so let's order a sandwich and split it. Then I want the rest of your story. But before you start, I want to ask you an important question."

Grace waited, as their waitress appeared with a young blonde woman in the same style company shorts and shirt uniform beside her.

"Hi. I'm Rachel, and this is Cindy. She's training this evening. Are you ladies ready to order now? Or do you need more time?"

"Thanks," said Maggie. "We'd like to split a crispy chicken sandwich and a green salad. Vinegar and oil on the side please. Just water to drink."

"Great. Anything else, just let us know." The two moved on and began taking orders at a booth across the way and over two.

Maggie's attention was full on Grace once again. For a moment neither person spoke. Then Maggie asked, "Do I keep on calling you Grace? Are you really ready to become Grace again? Or are you still living in Taylor's skin?"

Grace clasped and unclasped her hands. It was a simple enough question, but with profound implications. Grace stared at the tabletop, cupped her hands to her mouth in prayer-like fashion, then let them drop. Drained but resolute, she looked up at Maggie. "Grace. Call me Grace. I thought she was dead. Maybe she will be before this is over. But, if you don't mind, my name is not Taylor. Not anymore. It's Grace. Grace Nicole Grafton."

Maggie smiled as she reached across and grasped Grace's hand. "Good. It's nice to meet you, Grace Nicole Grafton, come back from the dead. Now it's time to start redeeming Grace. Hey, I like that. Redeeming Grace. You were born again and baptized as Taylor Nicole Carroll, right?"

Grace nodded.

"Okay. So right now let's say you are born again *again*. The Lord is with us and this is his business. Redeeming grace." Maggie dipped her fingers in the water glass and drew a watery cross on Grace's forehead. "I am no ordained minister and this glass is not exactly a baptismal ... for that matter the Red Robin is not exactly consecrated ground, but I now baptize you Grace Nicole Grafton, in the name of the Father and the Son and the Holy Spirit!"

Grace smiled and wiped her eyes. Maggie chuckled, drying her fingers with a napkin. "I can't believe I just did that."

Both women burst out laughing. But the impromptu moment quickly passed.

"You know, the Bible teaches that God's redeeming power is both instantaneous and ongoing. Back whenever you gave yourself up to Jesus, that was the 'instant button.' A kind of Redemption 101. That started up an eternal relationship with God. Since then the continuous action part of redemption has been at work in you. Twenty-four seven. He's at work in your life right now. So stop with the 'I'm such a worm' stuff and suck it up!"

Grace's smile was weak and strained.

"While we're waiting, I want you to tell me everything," Maggie continued. "Pick up with what happened after you left this Ellie person's house. And don't leave anything out. If I'm going to help you, knowing what took place back then may make a difference now. Whether or not it does, I still want to know."

Grace sighed, shaking her head in an effort to clear out the jumble of disconnected thoughts and bring some sense of order back into her life. She was emotionally exhausted. The events of seven years had come crashing down on her during the last twenty-four hours, like an avalanche in winter. She shivered as she closed her eyes—and was there again ...

54

With the downshifting of gears and the hissing of air brakes, the Greyhound bus rolled to a stop well inside the terminal. Twenty-one passengers exited from a bus designed to carry twice that many. Most stood by patiently, waiting for someone to begin unloading their luggage, watching as the young black couple that had boarded in Los Angeles was being attacked by a gray-headed man and woman, with three small children in tow.

The children took turns jumping up and down with arms outstretched as they ran in circles around the others. The gray-heads did not even try to conceal the "thank heaven mom and dad are finally here" look on their faces.

Two girls, in their late teens, laughed and squealed with excitement as boyfriends in Army uniforms stepped up to hug and kiss and otherwise brighten up what had turned into a very cool and damp early Friday morning in downtown San Francisco.

One of the last to exit the bus was a young woman dressed in a short-sleeved shirt, jeans, canvas walking shoes, and sunglasses despite the light rain. She held a blue canvas bag in her right hand.

"You're going to freeze to death," observed the the gray-haired woman who had been sitting two rows in front of her for the last several hours. The passenger smiled, running a hand through her short brown hair. With the other, she held up a canvas bag in silent testimony to the fact that there was a jacket inside, which in actuality was not true at all.

By the time she reached the sidewalk, Grace was shivering as the damp wind cut through the thin material of her shirt. The old woman had been right. She wasn't used to this. Pausing, she checked her surroundings, listened to the noise of cars and trucks and still more buses coming and going, watched as people with heads down, seemed to push their umbrellas ahead of them in the wind, brushing past without a word.

A brisk walk of several blocks put some distance between her and the bus station. Soaking up her first sights and sounds of the City by the Bay, she stopped once again to look around. This time not at the sights, but as she had so often the last few days, for anyone that looked suspicious—someone who might be paying her unwarranted attention. It was a familiar habit now, one that was quickly becoming routine.

No one appeared to be following or acted even the least bit interested in her. She hadn't really expected anything. Still, there was relief when she came to the corner and headed toward the entrance of a small hotel.

She was conscious of the doorman giving her the veteran people-watcher's once-over as she waited for a man and woman to exit behind a bellman with their luggage. Checking her out. She kept her eyes averted, forcing herself to believe that, to him, she was just another tourist and not the runaway witness to a double murder on the opposite side of America.

Once through the door, Grace brushed off raindrops pearling on her blouse as she strolled across the lobby toward the sign denoting public restrooms. Before entering, she stopped at a public phone.

Glancing back to the entrance she caught sight of the doorman and sighed with relief. He had turned away from her and was busy scrutinizing someone else coming through his hotel doorway.

Reaching into her pocket, she withdrew a scrap of yellow paper, wrinkled and smudged from too much sitting, but still legible. She dialed the number that had been hastily scribbled a few days earlier. A moment later, she dropped the amount of requested change into the phone slot. Her conversation was short, her voice too low to be overheard by passersby. Returning the receiver to its place, she turned away and pushed open the restroom door.

Nearly an hour had gone by when she looked up from one of the lobby's three small sofas, where she sat skimming the morning edition of *The Chronicle*. A middle-aged black man, with a slim athletic build, walked through the main lobby entrance and paused to look around. Brown sweater and slacks, a silver streak through short, dark hair—just like he'd said over the phone.

She laid the paper aside and got to her feet. The man spotted her and headed in her direction. Grace gathered up her courage, hoping she wasn't making another mistake, that he really was who she thought he was. Her confidence in her ability to judge strangers—especially men strangers—was at an all-time low these days.

The man put out his hand. "I'm Wendal. Do we have a mutual friend?"

"We do," answered Grace, grasping his big hand as firmly as she could, while doing her best to make sure her voice did not shake. Clearing her throat, she continued. "She's your sister. Her name is Ellie Fitzgerald. She lives in Savannah."

He nodded. "Ellie was sort of mysterious when she called the other day. Said you're in a bit of trouble and need some help. Didn't

310

tell me your name, but said if there was any doubt, I was to ask you about a story she told you just before you left."

Grace smiled and felt herself beginning to relax for the first time in days. "That has to be the one about 'Good Sam.'"

The man smiled then and nodded in apparent satisfaction. "Is that bag there the sum total of your earthly goods?"

She nodded.

"Give it here, and let's go. My car is parked down the street a ways."

55

The second-hand Datsun purred smoothly as they made their way out of San Francisco and onto the Bay Bridge, heading toward Treasure Island. "We've had this car for three years now, and it don't burn a lick of oil." Wendal's accent was not as "deep South earthy" as his sister's, but she recognized certain earthy similarities in the speaking style that were not unlike that of the woman who had befriended her just days before. They rode in silence for a time after Grace acknowledged that this was her first visit to the Bay Area and, yes, she hoped to find work here soon.

"Ellie said you might be needin' some papers."

"Papers?" Grace repeated with a puzzled look.

"Yeah. Birth certificate. Driver's license. Social Security number. Papers."

Grace's mind whirled. She had worried about this during her journey to the West Coast. She'd never been this far away from Georgia. How did one go about creating a new identity that passed for the real thing? Even if only for a little while. Until she could sort things out and decide what to do about Brandenbury and Parker and Itana. Could she get a job without revealing who she really was? Maybe no one would look for her out here. It was a chance she figured she'd have to take sooner or later in order to survive.

Uncertainty twisted her stomach in knots every time she wondered, always skeptical about the outcome of all this. No matter how hard she tried, Grace could not shake the vision of Ilene and Bonnie Jo's dead bodies. That horror followed her into fitful dream sleep. Twice on the bus she had awakened with such a start that she'd jabbed her seat mate with her elbow. With a determined effort, she tried putting them out of her mind for now. But the uncertainty of her circumstances remained strong, driving her ever deeper into a sense of hopelessness. Now, Ellie's brother had brought up the subject that she'd been trying to avoid. It triggered all the negative, frightening feelings of the past few days. Of course, he was right. And what other choice did she have but to trust him?

"Yes, as a matter of fact, I do have need of 'papers,' as you call them. Do you know how I might go about getting them? I ... I've never done anything like this before," she concluded lamely.

Wendal was silent until they were off the bridge and speeding southeast along Interstate 580. "Yeah, I think I kin help you on this. It's been a while, mind you."

"What do you mean?"

"Ellie probably didn't tell you 'bout me for fear o' scarin' you off." He glanced her way. "I'm an ex-con. Spent three years in Quentin. Unlike most o' my friends inside, I was guilty as sin."

Grace stared at the man, wondering what she'd gotten herself into now. Uncertain as to how to respond, she remained silent.

"Oh, I didn't own up at first, mind you," Wendal went on, "but one day the chaplain—he got to me with all that 'Jesus-stuff,' you know? I guess bein' aroun' Ellie, you got a little taste o' that, too, huh? Well, long story short, I gave my life to Jesus while I was in the Joint an' now my wife an' kids—we's all Christians. Go to church ever' Sunday an' read the Bible ever' day. I'm livin' a whole different life now than the one I had before. Got a good job an' everything. Manage a real good service station over here on this side of the Bay. In Oakland. A few months ago, we even bought a house in the 'burbs. So, I got to tell you I was kinda surprised when Ellie calls an' says you was comin' an' that she wants me to break the law again so's I kin help you out."

Grace started to respond, then stopped.

"You wouldn't happen to have five big ones on you, would you?" he asked, looking serious now.

"Five big ones?" Grace repeated.

"Yeah. Five hundred."

She hesitated. Was she really safe? Of course not. If she were safe, she wouldn't be riding through Oakland on Interstate 580 with a total stranger. An ex-con, yet. Was she about to become another one of those California crime victims she used to read about in the newspapers back in Statesboro? The worst thing to happen to anyone in Statesboro was a failed exam. At least that's what Ilene used to say. All that had changed now. This was uncharted territory. Flying blind. Swallowing her anxiety, she nodded. "Yes, I have it."

"Good," he said without smiling. "You know, you are gettin' a bargain 'cause my boy usually charges three, four times that much. But he owes me an' he'll do it for five. He's the best. Give it to me when we git to the house. I gotta tell you, I ain't real crazy 'bout this, 'cause if I were to git caught doin' it, the chances o' me gettin' throwed back in the slammer are a whole lot higher than winnin' the lottery."

"Why *are* you helping me?" Grace asked curiously, uneasy as to what the answer might be. "You don't even know me."

Wendal shrugged. "Next to Tara an' my boys, Ellie's the only family I got. She's stayed by me through thick and thicker all my life.

314

Lucky for you, I owe her big time. I know what a stickler she is 'bout stayin' on the right side o' the law, so when she tells me we got to break the law to protect you from whatever or whoever's out there ... well, now, that's somethin' I ain't never heard from my sis before. The real question is, why you is so important that she believes that strong about taken' care of you."

He guided the Datsun off the freeway and followed the loop around to a street leading into a suburban residential community. The city limits sign said *Baytown*.

"I thought Ellie said you lived in Oakland."

"Like I said, we moved six months ago. She ain't been out here for a few years, so she thinks everything east o' San Francisco is Oakland. We wanted to git our boys outa where we was livin' an' into a better neighborhood. This is closer to where Tara works, too. An' to our church."

Out of the corner of her eye, Grace studied her black savior, conscious of the exaggerated tension in her body, hands clasped tightly in her lap. She remained silent as Wendal turned down a street separating rows of older, single-story homes with lawns in front and cars that looked newer than the houses parked in driveways. They rolled to a stop in front of a modest-looking ranch style with a partial brick front and a white double-garage door.

"Well, here we are," announced Wendal as he turned off the engine and opened the door. "For the next few days, 'til you git on your feet, this is home sweet home. Come on in."

Grace could feel the rapid beat of her heart as she stepped out of the car, her mind racing as it had so often in the last few days. Even the pavement felt different. What was she doing here? What if this was all a ruse? An evil trick. *What if they're all conspirators in league with Brandenbury, and he's paying these people to get rid of me?* Her recently

315

acquired paranoia was in high gear again, and her mouth felt as dry as a desert. She shouldered her bag and fell in behind Wendal. Then the front door opened and a chunky Polynesian woman stepped out on the tiny cement porch, dish towel in hand and a smile on her face.

"Hello," she said, extending her free hand, eyes sparkling with a warmth and friendliness that surprised Grace and went a long way toward dispelling her natural instinct to turn and run. "I'm Tara. Welcome to our home."

Grace took her hand. It was warm. That was the first thought that flashed across her mind. Warm … and safe.

Inside, Grace found herself in a small living room furnished with throw rugs scattered over a carpet that had seen better days. The furnishings consisted of a well-worn sofa and chair, a TV, two old-fashioned floor lamps and a large, wooden coffee table. Through the door on the right, she glimpsed the kitchen with a table and chairs off to one side. To her left, a narrow hall led to the bedrooms and bath.

Tara showed Grace to a tiny room that she said belonged to their youngest boy. Posters of race cars and a machine autographed picture of San Francisco Giants pitcher, Tim Lincecum. The room had been vacated in anticipation of her coming. She felt awkward at the inconvenience her presence in this small house was already causing, but said nothing. A few minutes later, they sat around the kitchen table drinking iced tea while the two women made small talk.

Wendal was silent. Listening. His eyes never left their guest's face. Tara did most of the talking, telling Grace about their family, the community, her job at the Chevron Corporation in San Ramon. At times, their conversation seemed forced, as it does when strangers are thrown together. Grace tried to focus on what was being said, grateful that her hostess did not ask many questions outside of those related to Ellie and Sammy. The chitchat talk finally drifted into an awkward lull. Wendal's fingers quietly drummed the tabletop as he leaned back in the chair.

"I'll need the money," he said at last, matter-of-factly.

Grace cast a nervous glance at Tara, then back to Wendal. Her mouth opened, then closed without a word. Reaching into her pocket, she withdrew the bills she'd already counted out in the bedroom. Five wrinkled one hundred dollar bills. She handed them to Wendal.

"Does this leave you anything?" he asked.

She nodded, grimacing. "A little. But I need to find a job as quickly as I can and get out from under foot. I really appreciate your kindness and willingness to help, but ... " her voice trailed off.

Tara reached over and placed her hand on top of Grace's. "Listen, hon, we know about trouble in this house. And we know what it feels like when you've hit bottom and then someone comes along and helps you get up again. We also know it's a lot more blessed and a whole lot easier to give than it is to receive. We've been on the receiving end a lot in our lifetime. Now God seems to be saying that it's payback time. And you're the one he's sent our way to collect.

"Wendal and I aren't sure if we should be doing what Ellie has asked us to do. In fact, truth be told, we know it's not right. It's against the law. And we are taking a big chance here. You need to know that. I'm having a hard time knowing whether for sure this *is* God or not. If it is, he's got a pretty strange way of doing things, I'll say that. But when Ellie called, she insisted that somehow God had brought you along and made you her responsibility. You just have to know Ellie to appreciate that. She is some woman!"

"Yes she is," agreed Grace.

"She said you're like the person Jesus talked about when he said, 'I was hungry and you gave me something to eat, I was thirsty and you gave me something to drink, I was a stranger and you took me in.' So they asked him when they had done that, because none of them could remember, and he said, 'When you did it for the least of these, you did it for me.'"

They were silent for a moment, looking at each other.

"She's right. I guess I qualify for being one of the 'least of these,'" Grace said at last.

"Ellie said you were in some bad trouble, and for whatever reason you can't go to the police for help. Wendal and I don't want to know what's happened unless you decide you need to talk about it. In fact, Ellie said she knows the 'why' in all this and the less we know the better anyway. One thing's for sure, though. Wendal knows how to get what you need, so don't you worry."

"What do you want us to call you?" It was Wendal who spoke up. "I guess you notice that we don' know what your name is. Ellie wouldn't say. She been real mysterious about this whole thing. So don' tell us. Not your real name. We don' want to know. You need to git used to a new one anyway. Have you picked one out yet?"

Grace delayed giving an answer, as she sat back in her chair.

A new name? A different identity? I still can't believe all this is happening!

Her troubled look betrayed the fears and anxieties warring inside her.

"Yes, I have," she sighed, putting a hand to her lips as if to keep back the words that had to be spoken. "My name is Taylor Nicole Carroll. Two 'r's,' two 'l's.'"

"Where was you born, Taylor Nicole Carroll with two r's and two l's? Make it somewhere in the South 'cause we can hear 'South' in your accent. But pick another city an' state than the one you was actually born in. Make sure you're familiar with it, though, in case someone from wherever it is asks you somethin' about it sometime."

Grace paused. "I was born in ... Durham, North Carolina."

"What year? Don' make it the actual year. You look like you could be twenty-eight. Maybe twenty-nine. Thirty might be pushin' it some."

"1985. June 7, 1985."

"All right, Ms. Taylor Nicole Carroll, born June 7, 1985, in Durham, North Carolina—from now on that's who you is. You got to start thinkin' that an' believin' it 'cause you ain't the person you was before comin' here. Got that?"

"Yes," Grace said softly, her words a reluctant whisper. "I understand."

56

The next few days passed slowly for Grace. She took short walks through the neighborhood, nodding now and then to a teenager mowing a lawn or other walkers in sweats or joggers in shorts she met along the way. She stared at the television in the evenings without really watching. Read employment opportunity ads in the newspaper. It didn't matter what she did, though. Ilene and Bonnie Jo were everywhere present in her mind.

When she closed her eyes and tried to relax or sleep, her mind became filled with every monstrous detail of their lifeless bodies draped across that boat. She replayed the ugly sounds of the upstairs struggle—and there was always the breaking of glass. Over and over.

On the second evening after her arrival in the Brown household, Tara accidentally dropped a water glass in the kitchen sink. The sound of it breaking had been traumatizing enough to send Grace to her room in tears.

At first she tossed and turned in her borrowed bed, waking with fits of crying through the long nights. The loneliness was draining. Coupled with what she thought might be clinically identified as post-traumatic stress disorder, it ate away at any sense of well-being. It was as though she had just returned from combat and battle fatigue had set in. In a way, that was exactly what had happened. There were, in these first days of hiding and not running, times when suicide felt like the lesser of evils. Hopelessness pinned dreary pictures, framed with feelings of strong guilt and worry, on the walls of her mind. She had no appetite. She was losing weight. Then at last, the reservoir of tears dried up. Disappeared, though where to, she could not say.

On her fifth day in Baytown, she stood in front of a pay phone near an Albertson's Super Market and dialed her mother's phone number in Atlanta. It was time. She needed to talk to her, no matter what Ellie had said. To reassure her. She'd make it a short call. Just long enough to tell her to walk down to the Days Inn at the corner and wait for a call there. Then they could talk and she would explain everything that had happened. She felt terrible that she'd waited so long. Anyway, her mother was no doubt sick with grief by now.

No answer.

She hung up and tried again.

Still the same. No answer.

Where do you suppose she is?

She decided to try again the following morning.

The next day, after several more futile attempts, Grace dialed information and got the number of the Days Inn, where her mother worked as a cleaning lady. After being connected to housekeeping, she pretended to be a cousin visiting from out of town and asked if she could speak to Ellen Grafton.

"I'm so sorry to be the one to tell you," said the supervisor. "But Ellen ... passed away."

The news of her mother's death hit her like a hammer.

Her knees gave way.

Grace sagged against the booth in shock, unable to speak for a moment, struggling desperately to stay coherent. "How?"

321

"Somebody, we don't know who ... murdered her in her apartment."

"No," she wailed pitifully. *No!* The silent scream shattered her soul. "Not Mo"—Grace caught herself—"not Ellen." There were no tears. Only numbness. Suspended in unreality. This couldn't be. *No!* There must be some mistake. And yet, she knew it was. The only real thing in her world anymore seemed to be pain and death. "When did it happen?" she asked finally, her voice cracking, sounding hollow and distant as she spoke into the phone.

"The police are still investigating," the supervisor went on, "but they believe Ellen was killed sometime after she went home from work—on the seventh or maybe early the next morning."

June 7th. The day after her mother's birthday. *While I was still lost in the swamp—they went after my mother, and they killed her!*

"She'd been dead about twenty-four hours when they found her," the woman's voice droned on. "It's all so sad. It's been in the Atlanta papers and on the local news shows, but there's so much violence going on in the world. Maybe you haven't seen it where you're from. Where did you say that was again?"

She's suspicious.

Grace ignored her question. "Where was she found?"

"In her apartment kitchen. They also found some drugs and more than three thousand dollars in cash in her bedroom. It was done execution-style, the papers said, whatever that means. Shot in the back of the head. They're calling it a 'professional hit.' None of her neighbors saw or heard anything out of the ordinary, but because of the drugs and the money, they've ruled out the idea that she might have surprised a burglar.

"None of us can believe it, of course. Ellen mixed up in drugs? It's foolishness as far as I'm concerned, but they think she might have been dealing in drugs—or maybe holding them for her daughter. I guess they found enough to be worth about $4000 on the street."

There was a brief silence as the supervisor waited for some sort of response, then she went on. "Did you know her daughter? Her name is Grace. I met her once when she was on Christmas break from college. Ellen was always talking about her. She was so proud of that girl, you wouldn't believe. She had planned to go to her graduation down at Georgia Southern the week she was killed. This whole thing is just too terrible. She could probably have used the money they found, but if you knew her like we have all these years, why, you just know she couldn't be any drug dealer. And she certainly wasn't a user either."

Grace leaned her head against the telephone, saying nothing, trying desperately to make her mind work coherently. *Mother is dead? Oh, God, I am responsible for my mother's murder!*

"If that isn't enough grief by itself," the supervisor went on, "now her daughter has disappeared and the authorities think she may be dead, too. Her roommates at the university were both killed in a boating accident. They think Ellen's daughter might have been with them, but there's been no trace of her yet. The Coast Guard believes she could have fallen out of the boat and was done in by alligators or something. Maybe washed out to sea by the tides. I guess they found drugs and alcohol in the boat, too."

Dear God—what is happening? Everyone close to me is dying! But not Mom. She didn't do anything!

Grief swept over her like a wind howling in winter, whipping and tearing everything away that was dear to her.

Why did they think they had to kill my mother? What could she ever have said or done to hurt them? I knew the police might ask her questions, but she couldn't tell them anything—because she didn't know anything! I just never thought that ... Her mother's supervisor—*former* supervisor—

323

was still talking when Grace managed to place the receiver back on the hook and take a few unsteady steps to a wooden bench situated in front of the store, near the entrance. She sat down.

I shouldn't have waited. I should have gone to her, at least called her—warned her. I should have done something! It's my fault! But, I had no idea. I was so busy thinking about myself. I killed her! Oh, God—what have I done? I've killed my own mother!

Grace lost track of time as she sat motionless on the bench. People coming in and out glanced in her direction, but nobody stopped to ask if she was all right. Why should they? How could they possibly know what was happening to her—how her life was being ripped to shreds? Worse yet, if someone did stop to ask, she couldn't say anything.

She stared at the cars in the parking lot, at housewives and mothers with small children coming and going, without really seeing any of them at all. Even her anonymity was bittersweet. She felt sadness in the fact that no one was here to comfort her and help her make sense out of the devastating grief washing over her. And yet this unfamiliar namelessness was undoubtedly the only thing keeping her alive.

If they murdered Mom, then they won't stop looking until they find me.

How much time had passed as she sat there? Did it matter? Did anything really matter? A mother and teenage daughter passed by, each with a sackful of groceries. They were arguing. Defeated and drained, Grace got to her feet. Once one of Georgia Southern's most vibrant, beautiful, and energetic female graduate students, she shuffled off to her temporary hiding place.

57

Wendal was late coming home from work that evening. Grace and the boys had gone ahead with supper at Tara's insistence. Grace had said nothing about her tragic news and picked at her food, unable to answer the look of questioning concern in Tara's eyes. She had remained by herself in her room all afternoon, coming to supper only at Tara's repeated urging.

Eddie and Zak had just been excused from the table to finish their homework when they heard their dad's car turn into the driveway. Moments later, he came through the front door, stopping to kiss Tara, roughing the boys' hair as they clung to his legs and clamored for attention, apologizing for being late. After the boys had resumed doing homework on the floor in the living room, Wendal came over to the table, looked across at Grace and winked. He handed her a plain brown envelope.

"I brought you home somethin', Taylor. I know you think you spent a lot o' money on this, but this much work with this kind o' quality normally goes for much more than what you paid. You got a deal, girl. Actually, my friend owed me special an' this was my time to collect."

Grace peeled back the tape, opened the envelope, and spread the documents in front of her. They were all there. The things she'd been waiting for. A California driver's license, replete with a color photo vaguely resembling her likeness. In red letters above it the reminder of its expiration date. A birth certificate. A Social Security card. She stared at them. Though she was no expert in these matters, it was hard to believe how genuine they looked.

She looked up at Tara, then at Wendal.

"They're the best," Wendal assured her. "You're official now."

Official!

Her gaze returned to the documents. She brushed her fingers over them, not wanting to touch them, to pick them up, to own up to what they said about her.

I'm Taylor Nicole Carroll now.

Suddenly she felt something cold against her arm. It was Tara, reaching across with a pair of scissors.

"Cut up your old driver's license if you still have it. And anything else there is that might identify you with your past."

Grace—*Taylor* looked crestfallen. She pushed the scissors away. "I don't need them. I don't have it anymore. I ... I left it ... everything behind—"

She hesitated.

Her voice was low and quiet now. She glanced into the next room, making sure the boys were beyond hearing her next words.

"Everything ... " she said again, and then finished softly. "The night my friends were murdered."

For a long moment the others at the table didn't so much as breathe. Wendal and Tara stared at her, shocked. It was obvious her subdued revelation had rocked their wildest unvoiced imaginations.

With hands that wouldn't stop shaking, Taylor Nicole Carroll ... with two 'r's and two 'l's ... gathered up her new identity documents. Pushing away from the table, she went into the living room, walked past the boys without giving them her usual smile, and closed the door to her borrowed bedroom behind her.

Wendal and Tara were still at the table five minutes later, talking to each other, their voices low and filled with concern, when Taylor came back into the kitchen carrying her small canvas bag.

"What are you doing, Taylor?" asked Tara, jumping up and moving around the table toward her. Wendal was on his feet as well. The boys watched with puzzled expressions from their places on the floor.

"I need to go."

"What are you talking about? Go where?"

Zak started to get up, while Eddie shifted onto his knees, their wary expressions indicating they sensed something was wrong.

"I'm not sure. Anywhere. I've caused all of you more than enough trouble. Now you know my situation. You know I can't take the chance of putting you or ... them—" she looked down at the two boys—"in any further jeopardy."

Wendal stepped forward until his face was only inches away from hers. "Tell me, Taylor—an' understand I'll know if you're lyin', 'cause I done lived with the best liars in the world—did you do it? Did you ... hurt your friends like you say they was hurt?"

Wendal's eyes were hard and penetrating. Taylor wanted to look away, but she couldn't. He held her there—waiting for her answer.

"No," she said, shaking her head. "I didn't do it. I barely managed to escape myself. But I know the men who did it. They are looking for me, and they are very powerful. Some of the most powerful men in America. And now, today ... " Grace hesitated and looked at Tara, then down at the floor.

"What about today?" Wendal pressed her.

"I ... I learned today that ... my mother ... the same thing ...

327

happened to her." Taylor's voice broke, and eyes that had been dry until now suddenly spilled over with tears. Her shoulders shook as at last she began to cry.

Wendal glanced at Tara whose face was lined with concern and compassion. Taylor, though aware of how forlorn and devastated she must look to them, could do nothing to control it. The boys were standing next to their dad, watching and listening, asking in whispers as to what was going on and why Taylor was so upset. Tara's soothing tones hushed them, and she pulled them closer to her.

"You're tellin' the truth," Wendal said simply, reaching his hand out to take her arm, "so you ain't goin' nowhere. Not tonight anyway. 'Cept to bed. We'll talk some more tomorrow. Meanwhile, you need to unwind and get some rest. Tara here will get you something to help you sleep. Some herbal tea, maybe. You ain't goin' nowhere else tonight. You hear me?"

Grace nodded, wiping at her tears with the back of her hand. Tara handed her a tissue.

"Maybe now you got your papers an' everythin', you kin start lookin' for work in a day or two."

Tara moved over next to Taylor and took the bag from her trembling hand. She slipped her arm around Taylor's waist, guiding her past the boys and back into Zak's bedroom. "You get undressed and go to bed. I'll bring you something that'll help you sleep. Okay? I'm so sorry. I think later on you're going to need somebody to talk to. So we're here for you. Don't ever forget that. You and I and Wendal, we're friends now. And friends stick together, hon—no matter what!"

58

"Friends stick together, hon—no matter what!"

That amazing statement of acceptance and undeserved trust carried Taylor Nicole Carroll, nee Grace Nicole Grafton, through the following days of grief and sadness. Anything that identified her past life was gone. She was becoming used to answering to "Taylor." This was her life now. If she was to survive, she had to deal with it. Accept it. Live it.

Taylor remained at the Browns' home for three more weeks while looking for a job. In the end, she found work as a summer replacement with a furniture company in San Leandro, taking the place of one of their sales people who was on maternity leave. Her salesmanship proved to be of such high quality that when the person she replaced returned, a new permanent position was created for her.

After saying good-bye to the Browns, Taylor boarded for several months with an elderly San Leandro widow. Eventually, she was able to rent a small apartment of her own in Baytown, about a mile from the Brown's home. Baytown was newer and felt safer to her than living closer to the more urban Oakland area.

One day while at work she accepted Tara's telephone invitation to visit their church. The following Sunday, she went, joining them afterward for lunch. She looked forward to seeing the Browns and their boys. Going to church with them would be a small price to pay. It had been a long time since she'd been inside even an empty church, and the whole idea made her nervous. Nearly six months had passed without a hint that her true identity was suspect. Though she had a good job, she remained reclusive, uncomfortable when faced with the prospect of mingling with large crowds, fearful that somehow, through some fluke, someone might recognize her.

Her life had taken on its aura of isolation after her move to San Leandro. The loneliness grew deeper as time passed, becoming more pronounced after she moved into her own apartment. Taylor's only friends, besides the Browns, were the people with whom she worked. Even then, she didn't socialize except at company functions where her presence was required. The darkness that existed inside movie theaters suited her just fine as a place to get away from the walls of her tiny apartment, and she spent more time going to movies than she'd ever done before.

Breaking up the boredom, Taylor spent evenings surfing the Internet at the Baytown Regional Library. She searched Georgia and South Carolina online newspapers for any backdated articles pertaining to her or the murders of her mother and friends. There proved to be little information beyond what she already knew.

One story in the *Atlanta Journal-Constitution* did mention that the FBI had sent her description and photograph to law enforcement agencies throughout the country as a routine exercise, readily admitting that there was little likelihood of Grace Grafton ever being found alive. It seemed that authorities in general assumed she had been with her friends at the time of the accident, fell overboard, drowned, and was swept out to sea.

From pictures published in newspapers and shown on television, the store clerk had identified Bonnie Jo and Ilene as having purchased the items they were wearing at the time of their deaths. They told the clerk that they were buying new outfits for a party at Georgia Southern following their graduation. The missing roommate was also identified as having been with the others in their shopping spree.

Since the presence of alcohol and drugs was confirmed at the scene of the accident, authorities postulated that Grace Grafton could have fallen or been thrown out of the boat and into the water, the strong currents and tides in that locale causing her remains to drift into the open sea.

That theory was plausible enough and okay with Taylor if, in fact, that really was the concurrence of law enforcement officials. She wondered how much of that hypothesis had been bought and paid for by Charles Brandenbury in an attempt to discourage further investigation while he launched his own search for her.

Was it paranoia that caused her to think this way? She wasn't sure, but she didn't think so. Not after what she'd heard him say that night. Not after what she had been through since that night. Not after what they had done to her mother. Her anguish over her mother's murder was at times overwhelming. Deep down, she wanted to go to the authorities and tell them everything that had happened. Wasn't that what you were supposed to do? But Brandenbury was too all-powerful for that, to say nothing of a United States senator named Noah Parker. No way was she going to take that chance.

She didn't know how to assess the Lebanese diplomat, Itana, but she knew he was every bit as evil as the others. These men seemed to be almost godlike in terms of power and influence. If they found her they would sweep her under the rug like a piece of lint. There was no way that anyone would believe her accusations against men of such high reputation. She would not be safe even if she appealed for protective custody. These people were too well-connected. They

331

would find her. She was certain of it. And once they did, she knew she would have no chance. Her life would be worthless. And very short.

Her apprehension and mistrust of the establishment was nearly total now. She was sure that Brandenbury's billions could reach right across America and buy whatever he needed in order to find her. Did he really think she was dead? Taylor desperately wanted it to be so, but doubted that this was the case. And that doubt fueled her perpetual uneasiness.

It was in this frame of mind that Taylor Nicole Carroll showered and dressed for church on an overcast Sunday morning, taking Ellie's Bible from off the shelf above the small, but brand-new color television she had purchased three weeks before with the help of her employee discount. She did not want to chance a credit check, so she had waited until she'd been able to pay cash.

Taylor felt extremely vulnerable concerning background inquiry of any kind. When she had to handle the matter of former employee reference checks, she made up a story about having spent two years in Europe, traveling with friends, working here and there only when they needed money. She'd started as a fill-in, with minimal background check. By the time she became a permanent hire, nobody challenged her, and so the fictitious European adventure became part of her personal story.

This morning, Wendal and Tara were waiting for her on the large patio in front of Calvary Community Church. They waved to catch her attention. Strains of music drifted through the open doors, mingling with the soft fragrance of flowers that girdled an attractive water display. Blossoms were flourishing in pots placed in befitting style under trees, all of which summoned unexpected feelings of childhood happiness and innocence; an innocence lost since bending to her mother's anger at God, following her out the church door, never to return until today.

Now that innocence had been replaced with—what? A feeling of guilt? A betrayal of loyalty to the inheritance of her mother's displeasure at the Divine? Or did it go deeper than that? Was it her own guilt that was rushing to the fore, tempting her to turn away while there was still time? To head for Starbuck's instead? But it was too late. There was Tara, already coming toward her, all smiles and hands extended in welcome. Nothing left to do but hunker down and get through the next hour. At least, she hoped it was only an hour.

Tara hugged her, kissing her lightly on the cheek.

"The boys are in Children's Theatre," Tara announced as they walked toward the doors, "so it's just Wendal, you, and me for now. Normally, we all go to discussion groups afterwards, but we thought that, since this is your first visit, we'd skip that today and have an early lunch at home. Is that okay with you?"

Taylor nodded, sensing that if she spoke her voice might betray the emotion she was feeling. Wendal shook her hand, and they walked inside. The auditorium appeared full at first glance, but they managed to find three seats together in next to the last row. The congregation had already begun singing, and to Taylor's surprise, the words to the songs were projected on two large screens that were lowered and raised electronically.

Though most of the songs were unfamiliar, she did recognize one hymn, *Fairest Lord Jesus, ruler of all nature* ... They sang these words without instrumental accompaniment. Listening, Taylor experienced being engulfed in the amazing four-part harmony. As she drank in the harmonic beauty of the combined voices of choir and congregation, Taylor fought a losing battle with tears spilling down her cheeks. In her peripheral vision, Tara glanced at her but said nothing.

The minister, a man named John Cain, gave a stirring message.

Taylor was surprised that he didn't yell the way she remembered the preacher doing when she was a youngster attending church and Sunday school in Atlanta. This man spoke in conversational tones, leaving her with the impression of one intelligent person having a conversation with another. A conversation about God. The way he related his thoughts about God to everyday life drew Taylor in, breaking down some of the barriers she had built up before coming. But not all.

He spoke from the Gospel of John about "being the friend of God." To her surprise, it all made such good sense. During the closing prayer, when Pastor Cain asked people to consider making a commitment of faith in their hearts to God, Taylor found herself wishing she could, while at the same time steeling herself to get out the door as quickly as possible after the last "Amen."

Later on, after lunch at the Browns' home and some table games that included both Zak and Eddie, Taylor thanked Tara and Wendal for the invitation and prepared to leave.

"Don't feel pressed to do so, Taylor," Tara said warmly, "but if you'd like to join us again at church, you'd be very welcome. It was nice having you there with us. We got used to having you in our little family, and now we miss you."

"Thanks. Actually, I enjoyed it. More than I thought I would. It's been a long time for me between churches. I liked your pastor, though. He seems pretty normal, if you know what I mean. If you want to know the truth, for a while there, it felt like he was having a one-on-one conversation with me and nobody else."

"That's the way we feel just about every Sunday," Wendal injected. "I guess if you kin turn jailbait like me into a believer, you got somethin' goin' for you. When you think you're ready, Taylor, give it another shot. That is, if you ain't afraid to look God in the eye an' talk over your troubles with him.'"

"Wendal!" Tara's tone was reprimanding. "Don't pay him any attention, Taylor. He's a tad too direct, but he means well."

"I know he does," Taylor replied with a smile. "And so do you. How can I ever repay the both of you for the kind of friendship you've shown me from that very first day?"

Then she did something she'd never done before—to a black man. It ran counter to all she'd been brought up to believe by parents she now understood could only be classified as racist. Beliefs she had glossed over, even as a well-educated "liberated" woman, had in recent months been shaken to the core. She took Wendal's strong arms in her hands and leaned forward until her lips touched his cheek, first one and then the other. "You're a special man, Wendal Brown," she declared with a smile. Stepping back, she turned and gave Tara a warm hug and kisses as well.

"Bye, guys," she waved to the youngsters who were in the other room watching television. Both boys jumped up and ran to give Taylor hugs. To Tara and Wendal she added, "I'll call you."

Taylor spent the rest of the evening in her apartment, reading Ellie's Bible. About nine o'clock that night, she came across a story in Luke's Gospel, chapter nine. She read it once, then again, her eyes growing moist, smiling to herself all the while. It was the story of the Good Samaritan.

Good Sam.

It wasn't exactly the same version she remembered hearing from Ellie, but the essence was there. In truth, as she reread the story the third time, she graded Ellie's version as being more memorable.

Months later, Tara informed Taylor that she'd won a dollar from Wendal after Taylor's first visit to their church. Wendal had bet that Taylor wouldn't follow up with the promised phone call and another visit to their church. He lost. Taylor had called Tara the following Thursday and asked if she might sit with them again on Sunday.

Before long, she had become a regular attender, all the while careful never to give outward expression to what she was feeling inside. Inwardly, however, it was a different story. Being among people of faith was strangely comforting. For the most part, she preferred solitude and anonymity. She wasn't antisocial by nature, but strangers continued to jar her. She still kept a constant eye out to see if anyone looked at her with more than casual curiosity. But it was different somehow, being there in church. She had begun singing with the congregation instead of being content to just listen. And she looked forward to the congregation at prayer, though she couldn't explain to herself exactly why. Standing in reverent silence as someone led the prayer time from the pulpit was ... comforting.

She had been reading Ellie's Bible every day since that first Sunday, especially the New Testament. And one night alone in her tiny apartment, she sat for a long time staring at the wall ... and found herself praying ... asking God for forgiveness.

Once she began, it was like a dike that was breached by floodwaters as she sought forgiveness for so many things on so many levels. She began with that terrible night at Charles Brandenbury's island estate, seared forever in her memory. Beyond having made an impulsive and foolhardy choice, she knew she had not been responsible for what had happened. Who could have possibly known? But it had happened and she continued carrying a huge weight of guilt. Guilt for the stupidity of their choices that day. Her choices! Guilt for leaving her friends behind. For being the only survivor. Guilt over her mother's death. Guilt for so many things that would never go away, not in a lifetime of asking God for forgiveness. Perhaps he could forgive, she thought sadly, but she knew that she would never be able to forgive herself.

Still she prayed. At first it felt strange. She wasn't even sure she was going about it the right way. Mostly, she prayed 'thought' prayers in her mind. After several days, she caught herself shaping silent words on her lips. And then one evening she knelt by her bed and said her first audible prayer. Though she spoke softly, the words reverberated around the room. No one had ever spoken out loud here in her bedroom. Not even Taylor. Why she had not at least talked out loud to herself she couldn't say. But the sound of her voice surprised her. And after the initial shock, she felt warmed somehow, not simply by the sound of her own voice, but something else. Could it be that God was actually listening? That he really heard her praying? Was it his presence that she felt just now?

Taylor gradually became more at ease talking to God about her situation. Prayer was an opportunity to voice her anger, her deep anguish and loneliness, something she never permitted herself to do with anyone else. Only Wendal and Tara knew about her past. When Grace finally was baptized, along with a small group of other adults and two young teenagers, she joined Calvary Community Church as Taylor Nicole Carroll. And slowly, she began to expand her new world. The church's adult singles group provided her with several new friends, though she always managed to stay aloof in relationships and never dated anyone seriously.

In the spring, nearly two years after her arrival in California, Taylor accepted a sales position at the new Broadmores of San Jose, an upscale department store chain that rivaled Nordstrom in customer enthusiasm. Work continued to consume most of her time and energy, and in her first year at Broadmores, she became the top producer in her department.

Three years later, that factor had been a primary motivation behind management's offer to relocate Taylor to Southern California.

A new Broadmores was opening in Palm Desert, near Palm Springs, the following January. They wanted to establish their new sales force in the best of traditions by placing their top California producer on the team. The new salary and commission scale was good and living in the desert sounded both different and exciting. Taylor was ready for a change.

It had been five years since a frightened young traveler had stepped off a bus in San Francisco. Five years since assuming a new identity that broke forever with her former life. Five years since losing it all—her mother, her best friends, her plans for the future—everything because of one terrible mistake. It was time to start a new life in a new place. Another giant step away from the reminders of the past that had brought her to the Bay Area in the first place.

After all, there was nothing she could do to stand up against the likes of Brandenbury and Parker. Nothing at all. They were too influential. Too powerful.

She had come to terms with the idea that God had forgiven her for her part in that awful night. At least, she felt that way most of the time. But she could never forgive herself. The best she could do was push it to the back of her mind, behind a carefully constructed imaginary wall. Gone but not forgotten. When she thought about it for any length of time, her secret was like a heavy weight. It struck painfully at the core of her new life.

The few who thought they knew her, chided her good-naturedly about her long work hours and short social life. She knew that she appeared to others as though she was driven to succeed. But there was so much more to it than that. There remained a dark secret that stained her past and controlled her future, one that those who thought they knew her now could never comprehend. It was not a matter of being *driven* to succeed. It was a matter of *outrunning* the past.

A thousand times she'd thought about going to the police with her story. And a thousand times she stopped short.

Maybe confessing everything to God was enough.

Yes, going to the desert would be a good thing. New places. New faces. A new future. It was something she needed. Maybe there she could slow down. Stop running. Make a life. Maybe the hot desert sun would burn out whatever residue of the past continued to cling to her.

Maybe there she could forget.

59

Fours rings ... and then her voice, steady and clear.

"Hello. This is Grace Grafton. If you're the person who called earlier about a meeting, and you still wish to speak with me, call this number before six-thirty. If I've not heard from you by then, I will be giving an interview to an editor and reporter from the *Desert Sun* and will be unavailable until much later. The number is ... "

The recorded message concluded with the familiar beep indicating it was now time to leave a message. The man, wearing dark glasses and a green and tan sport shirt and khaki shorts, was standing a short distance from Broadmores' main entrance, He pressed the "off" button on his cellular, a puzzled look on his face. Checking his watch, he looked at the hastily scribbled number before stuffing it in his pocket, then dialed a different area code and number.

"I've been stood up," he said moments later. "Yeah. She left a number. Said I could reach her there before six-thirty. After that she claims she's going to the newspaper ... that's right ... yes sir. No, I don't at all. She does work for the Sun ... yes sir ... sure ... okay, got it."

The man slipped the phone into his pocket, at the same time wiping a thin layer of perspiration from his forehead. He swore at the heat and wondered why anybody in his right mind would choose to live in this desert, especially during the summer. Then he walked next door to a coffee shop, went inside, and ordered a triple-shot iced coffee. He needed a jolt and some time to sort out his thoughts.

✶ ✶ ✶ ✶

Grace checked her watch again for what seemed like the hundredth time. Five minutes to go. They had tried the salad and chicken sandwich, but Grace could hardly touch the food. She was looking anxiously at Maggie when her cell phone began ringing. Her hand hovered as she waited for two more rings before picking it up.

"Hello?"

"Is this Taylor Carroll?"

The Voice!

"No," she answered, releasing a quiet sigh of relief. "This is Grace. Grace Grafton."

There was a brief hesitation on the other end of the line. Then the Voice said, "Okay, *Grace,* tell me something that lets me know for sure."

"You called last night and played a tape of Brad Weston's voice. Your name is Fred. At least it was when we were eating lunch on the bench together. And today you and your rat pack kidnapped Brad's children."

Another pause.

Grace held her breath.

"Listen, lady, you stood me up. Do you have any idea what you're doing? I really hate being stood up. Now you've not done anything silly like asking the police in on our little conversation, have you?"

"First of all, my name is not 'lady.' It's Grace. Call me that again, and I'll hang up."

Maggie smiled and gave her a thumb's up.

"But to answer your question," Grace continued, "of course not.

341

Besides, what good would it do?"

"If I even see a meter maid headed in my direction writing parking tickets, those kids and that preacher you love so much are dead. You got that?"

Grace shuddered at the cold, matter-of-factness with which the Voice spoke. "Yes," she replied, clutching the phone with both hands. She was shaking. Maggie was beside her, and she held it far enough away from her ear so that she could hear as well.

"Why didn't you show for our meeting?" the Voice asked.

"I told you. You've taken the children. Before I talk to you I want to know they're okay."

"They're okay."

"How do I know that?"

"You just have to trust me."

"Oh, sure. No problem there at all."

"Don't be cynical."

Grace didn't answer.

"And don't play games with me. I am very close to losing my temper here. Trust me, you don't want that to happen. The brats are fine—for now anyway. They're just being kept as collateral until you give us what we want."

"Why? What good are those children to you?"

"One can never have too much insurance, if you know what I mean. Just give us what is ours, and we'll give you what is yours."

"And what do I have that you think is yours?"

"The pictures and the names of anybody you may have talked to about this unfortunate little incident. That's all. Then you and everybody can go on living long and normal lives."

"And if I don't?"

"You don't really want to go there now, do you?"

Grace remained silent. She didn't want to go there.

"So, let's start over."

"Okay, you can begin by telling me what you've done with my children." Grace was still shaking, but her voice was strong. Maggie nodded again, patting her shoulder.

"*Your* children? Don't you mean your boyfriend's children?"

The thought suddenly struck Grace that this was the first time she had ever said to anyone that David and Nancy were her own. Had it taken something like this for her to realize what they truly meant to her? That they were part of her now? Or was this simply the first time she had confessed aloud what she had kept secret for so long; how much she wanted them to be her children and not just Brad's? She didn't respond to the caller's implied taunt. Instead, she breathed a little prayer and steeled herself.

"Okay," the Voice went on, appearing to be satisfied that he had scored a disarming punch, "here's what we want."

"No!" Grace's voice was low and firm, surprising even her as she felt a sudden unexpected strength coming from somewhere. She looked at Maggie. Her eyes were closed, her lips moving. And it dawned on Grace where this feeling of strength was coming from.

"I have enough evidence to link your boss to the murders of my two friends, Mr. Whatever-Your-Name is. I know you're working for Charles Brandenbury. At the very least, I can cast a very large shadow of suspicion over any political ambitions he may be planning to foist on the country. And if you're one of Noah Parker's lackeys, when I go public he can kiss his presidential candidacy good-bye. Even if you find me and kill me after the fact, it won't stop the incriminating information that I possess from becoming public. And your presidential aspirant will never *see* the inside of the president's quarters, much less live there."

She could hear the man's raspy breathing on the other end of the line.

"If you really had anything," the Voice said finally, replacing his earlier surliness with a more mollifying tone, "you'd have turned it over to the police years ago."

"I was too frightened to go to the police years ago," she answered honestly. "But that was before you kidnapped Brad and the children. You thought you were so clever—but the truth is you are really, really stupid. You stepped over the line. When you took these innocents, you successfully removed the only restraint that has kept me from exposing your boss—or bosses—and their devious political plans. When that happens, the stink will bury them. I'll do it, too. Don't make the mistake of thinking that I won't!"

Grace felt Maggie squeeze her arm. She looked at her. Maggie was smiling still. A fresh wave of courage lifted her spirit, like a surfer catching an unexpected wave. Where had that come from? Was it false bravado? Or something else? She glanced at Maggie again. Her eyes were closed once more, lips moving in silent prayer. Grace turned her gaze back to the wall, staring at an imaginary point, willing herself to concentrate. She was sure now of the Source of her boldness.

"So here's what I want," she continued. "Are you listening?"

There was no answer.

"I want to meet with Terry Reynolds. My guess is that with all that has gone on the last couple of days he's not far away. I'll bet he's in town. Anyway, you get him. He got me into this mess, and he's the only one I'll meet with now."

The Voice swore angrily. "You're an insane little broad, you know that? You're playing with fire!"

"Now that's not at all nice," Grace said, her voice now taking on the reproving tone. "Name calling isn't going to get you anywhere.

Listen to me. The only way you've got a snowball's chance to get what your boss wants is to get Terry Reynolds here to talk with me. Face to face. Alone. And fast!"

Maggie's eyes were open now, and she was nodding her approval again. She ran her finger across her throat as a signal that it was time to cut off the conversation.

"Will you be at this number?"

"No. Give me a number where I can reach you in an hour."

She could hear the muttering of curses and name-calling. At last he spoke up. Grace scribbled the numbers on a napkin. Before she could say anything further, she heard the click that indicated the Voice had already hung up.

Grace laid the phone on the tabletop. She was trembling as she turned to look at Maggie. Maggie leaned in and gave her a gentle hug. "You were good, Grace. Really good. In fact, you were sensational. You sounded confident. Forceful even. Fortunately, he couldn't see your hands and knees shaking."

They both laughed, releasing the tension of the moment. To Grace it seemed like an eternity had come and gone since yesterday morning.

"We don't want to hope for too much too soon," Maggie went on, "but you have the upper hand, at least for the moment."

Emotionally drained, Grace sat quietly staring past Maggie's shoulder at the busy atmosphere of the restaurant. Waiters, busboys, customers. Organized chaos. Her eyes shifted back to Maggie. "Do you think they might have traced this call? Could he tell where we are the way they say they can on television? Am I being paranoid or what?"

Maggie sat for a moment, saying nothing. Then she tossed her napkin down alongside her water glass. "Take the battery out of your phone. Now."

Just then their waitress appeared. The trainee in the same style company shorts and shirt uniform stood beside her.

"Would you like some desert? Our Mountain High Mud Pie is delicious."

"Thanks," said Maggie, withdrawing a $20 and $10 dollar bills from her purse and placing it on the table, "but we're going to have to pass. My friend just received an emergency call and has to go."

"I'm sorry," Rachel responded, stepping back as Grace opened the cover of her cell phone and removed the battery. "I hope everything is okay."

"So do we, Rachel," Maggie declared as they headed for the exit. "So do we."

60

The phone kept ringing. *Five, six—come on—seven.*

"Hello."

Thank God, it's him.

"It's been over an hour."

"Meet Reynolds at the College of the Desert campus main entrance on Monterey Avenue at eight o'clock."

"No. I'll meet him at the church. Here's the address."

"Never mind," the Voice grunted. "We know where it's at."

"There's a bell beside the door marked *Offices*. I have a key to the church and Brad's office. Tell Reynolds to ring three times. I'll unlock."

"You're way out of your league, Grace. You know that, don't you?" the Voice declared with undisguised disdain.

Ignoring the affront she replied, "I don't want to see you or anyone else. Tell Reynolds to come alone."

There was a hesitation. Then without another word, the Voice hung up.

Grace put down the phone in their room and turned to Maggie

who was perched on the edge of the bed.

"You're doing great," said Maggie. "You sounded like you were in charge. You've turned a corner, Grace."

"I'm not sure about that. I'm still so scared I shake like a leaf, Maggie. I hope he can't hear in my voice how frightened I am that all of this is going to …"

"Don't go there, Grace. You can't permit yourself to think like that. Listen to me. You didn't sound frightened. And that's the important thing right now. Even the way you looked while you were talking was different than a couple of hours ago. Stay in control. Brad and the kids are depending on you. For that matter, so is the whole country, if they only knew it."

"Don't say that."

"Are you ready?"

"I've got to go to the bathroom."

"Hurry. We need to get going."

When she emerged, Maggie was waiting in the chair nearest the door. As she started to get up, Grace motioned to her to stop.

"I've been thinking, Maggie. I can't involve you in this anymore than I already have. I know what we've talked about, but I think I should do this alone. You've already been through too much today, and it's all because of me. So, I want you to stay here until I get back."

"Just when I thought you were beginning to think straight, don't go south on me now, young lady," Maggie retorted as she got to her feet. "If I had a daughter, do you think I would just wave good-bye, send her out among killers and wait for her to come home by eleven? Of course, I don't have one. And you don't have a mother, so we're stuck with each other, sweetie. Get the picture? Besides, there's something I forgot to tell you."

"What's that?"

Maggie reached into her purse and withdrew a small .38 caliber handgun.

"Where did you get that?" Grace asked incredulously. "Don't you know it's against the law to carry a concealed weapon? Besides, you're too ... " Her voice trailed off.

"Too old?" Maggie smiled. "Pete was determined that I knew how to protect myself. He didn't like me to be traveling around the Valley at all hours of the day and night, interviewing people neither of us knew. So he made sure I took lessons. I'll have you know, I'm not a half bad shot. And, in case you are wondering, I have a permit to carry."

"I don't believe this. You should be home taking care of ... " Grace stopped short again, realizing what she was on the verge of saying was inappropriate to their situation.

"Taking care of my grandchildren?" Maggie finished again. "The only 'grandchildren' I ever hope to have were kidnapped this afternoon. On my watch, no less. So this isn't just about you anymore. It's about us. We've got to get Brad and those two precious children back, so let's go."

Maggie opened the door. Grace shook her head in wonderment and followed after her, closing the door behind them, making sure for some unknown reason as she did, that it was securely locked.

61

Late afternoon
Near Asheville, North Carolina

Sixteen miles north of the city limits, on Interstate 70, a dark-colored limousine passed the *Jupiter/Barbersville Next Exit* sign. The driver let up on the accelerator and coasted down the off ramp to the stop at the bottom of the slope. Turning right, the car passed another sign, this one warning, *North 197 pavement ends 10 miles ahead.*

The driver and his lone passenger continued eastward along the valley floor, though more slowly than before. He knew that traveling too fast on this stretch that wound back and forth with its sweeping curves and valley vistas, upset the stomach of the man sitting behind him, and he surely didn't want that to happen. The risk increased whenever he was driving his passenger at night. And though the late afternoon sun belied that possibility, it was one cussing out he didn't intend to get, no matter what.

On both sides of the road, the parade of foothills seemed to kneel in deference to the mountains shaping the distant terminus where earth met sky. A shallow river danced and sparkled its way over pebbles and stones, creating an occasional miniature waterfall, though not so dramatic as the ones in his favorite part of North Carolina's Blue Ridge Mountains, beyond the small community of Brevard, an hour or so to the west.

Still, it was a scene of stunning beauty, especially at this time of day. One that gave the limousine's driver a peaceful feeling each time he drove through this valley. He thought that it must be true for his solitary passenger as well, but he wasn't sure. He doubted that the rich white entrepreneur seated behind him had ever, in his miserable life, confided anything so personal as "a feeling" to a black man. Certainly never to Harold Justiss Jones.

After following the river for several miles, Harold braked to a near stop in order to negotiate the turn taking them over a narrow bridge. Once across the river, they passed by the gatehouse with a mere wave of the hand, and then beneath a gold-lettered arch declaring this to be the main entrance to the Brandenbury Horse Farm. Once it became known that *the* Charles Brandenbury had purchased and was developing this site for his personal use, an influx of tourists and local gawkers from Asheville and the surrounding area had forced the erection of the small gatehouse and the staffing of it twenty-four hours a day by uniformed security personnel.

The heart of the 50-acre spread extended downward from a high knoll overlooking the valley and the mountain foothills beyond the river. White split-rail fences, stables, grazing areas, corrals, and riding paths zigzagged over the landscape, much the same as any horse farm possessed by a wealthy owner.

There was one difference at the Brandenbury Farm, however, in the shape of two and a half meter-high, parallel fences encircling the property, the outer fence topped with prison-roll wire. The approximately two-meter distance separating the fences provided Brandenbury's kennels of trained Dobermans with their nightly

351

work zone, terminating on either side of the gatehouse, making the gatehouse the only auto access to the property.

The narrow drive leading to the main house wound upward through a curving hollow sandwiched between two rolling hills. Other than his own self there were few things in life that Charles Brandenbury loved. This place was one of them. Brandenbury himself had mused that sentiment enough times for Harold to realize his own polite silence encouraged Brandenbury to think out loud.

"It's always nice to come back," the lone rear seat occupant murmured to himself and the surrounding environment as he gazed out the side window at lush beds of grape hyacinths, pansies and crocus. "By this time next year, this will be the nation's new 'Camp David.'"

Evidence of spring's late arrival was still visible on the estate, though groundskeepers had obviously worked hard to repair last year's unusual winter flailing. Heavy rain, snow, and ice had caused serious damage to several trees, especially those planted more recently as a "reforesting America" statement of Brandenbury's "personal concern" over the world's environment. Not that he actually cared all that much, but it resonated nicely with the green voters he unaffectionately dubbed the "Ben and Jerry crowd," whose social and environmental concerns ran all the way from Burlington, Vermont, to the Amazon rainforest. More folk to impress and manipulate. Little things like this went a long way. "Some of those trees won't make it," Brandenbury noted to no one in particular. "I'll remind the gardener to have them replaced."

In the shadowy side of a particularly gaunt-looking pine, an India Blue peacock was engaged in a showy mating dance, loudly proclaiming his proud virtues to a hen that appeared bent on ignoring him completely.

Two white mourning doves nodded their agreement from a side-by-side perch on the last fence post, just before the road opened out onto a wider driveway. The limousine's tires always sounded different here, rolling off the asphalt and onto an expanse of red brick encircling a large water fountain in back of the main house. The uneven vibration of tires on the brick surface gave off a certain "special" sound, impressive to the ears of anyone upon first arriving.

The area for additional guest parking sloped down and away from the far side of the drive and was almost completely hidden from view behind tall trees and daffodil foliage. So was the detached garage and equipment shed. This square, replete with painted markers and landing lights, doubled as a landing pad for *Air-CB,* Brandenbury's private helicopter, used whenever he wanted to reduce travel time between the Farm and Asheville's Regional Airport, a good hour away by car, on the south side of the city. *Air-CB* also served to transport important guests from Washington or New York or any other power-laden metropolis of the world, people who often flew in to visit the man who was rapidly becoming a Las Vegas odds-on favorite to be named the party's vice-presidential nominee on a Noah Parker ticket.

The automobile came to a stop in front of a brick path leading up to the main entrance of this out-of-the-ordinary hilltop farmhouse. Setting the brake while letting the engine idle, Harold got out, and with a slight limp, made his way around to open the right-rear passenger door. "Welcome home, Mr. Brandenbury," he said, smiling and doffing his chauffeur cap. "I hope you found the ride to be pleasant and relaxing this evening."

Brandenbury brushed past, giving no indication that he had heard him. Harold's head dropped slightly at the snub, stacking the silent insult in the back of his mind along with the large pile of other put-downs he'd packed away during his lifetime. He said nothing further,

353

though his lips tightened at the lack of at least an attempt at polite response.

Harold Justiss Jones didn't like it, but he'd gotten used to it. He called it "white Southern attitude." He allowed that it was better now than when he was growing up as a kid in the country outside of Augusta, and later on in Charleston. But there was still a long way to go. It was one of the reasons he had enjoyed the military so much.

Twelve years of "being all he could be" had put Harold on the ground in the Iraq War and also as part of the American contingent assigned to keep peace in that hellhole they called Afghanistan. Army life had treated him to a greater sense of fairness and less overt racism than he'd experienced anywhere else. It hadn't been perfect, but then what was? He'd still be a soldier if it hadn't been for the land mine that had taken out his jeep and driver and left him with a broken-up leg.

Now this was his life—most likely all it would ever be. An honorable discharge. A small disability check every month. Enough to get drunk on but no one to do it with. And a job as chauffeur for a rich white dude who bought power with money and exhibited no real feelings for other people at all. At least none he'd been able to see since coming to work here. Unless, that is, they had something he wanted. Then he wined and dined them until he got whatever it was. And as soon as he got it, it was over.

There was a certain brutishness about his boss at times. He'd seen it on some battle-hardened comrades-in-arms. Hardened by so much death and destruction that the thread of human decency was lost and killing became an end-in-itself. He knew Brandenbury had never served, but still it was a trait not to be overlooked.

That's the one thing Harold had discovered about being a chauffeur. Chauffeurs see a lot and hear a lot more than the people they work for ever give them credit. All the seeing and hearing Harold had done had caused him to realize that his boss was, to put it politely, a slimeball. It didn't take an Army shrink to bring him to that conclusion. And there would be no changing that. No point in expecting him to change. But he rationalized the pay was decent even if the man wasn't. And you didn't have to like a guy in order to drive him around.

The hood over the engine felt warm to the touch as he shuffled around to the driver's side, pausing for a last glance at his employer who was opening the door to the house. Sliding in behind the wheel, Harold reached down and released the brake. With one hand, he guided the limousine around the fountain and into the garage.

62

The heavy oak door opened onto a marble entry. Even though it was his home—well, at least one of them— just like a first-time visitor, Brandenbury's gaze was drawn toward the living room glass wall, strikingly visible from where he stood. It wrapped around to the right, beyond his immediate line of vision and into the adjacent family center. An unobstructed view jutted out from the hill, its sweeping elegance affording the privileged that came here with a breathtaking northwest to southeast vista of white fences, thoroughbred Arabian show horses, the river, and the forested mountains in the distance.

The house was a sprawling two-story affair created out of wood, stone, and concrete, comprised of six bedrooms, five baths, formal living and dining rooms, a family center, and a small ballroom for "power parties," as he liked to call them. A suite of private offices and the master bedroom were located on the upstairs level.

The servant's quarters were also on the second floor, above the kitchen, at the southwest end of the house. Here, the cook and the maid shared a small apartment with kitchenette, living area, and separate baths and bedrooms. Other than the chauffeur, who lived in a studio apartment above the garage, the groundskeepers and all other workers lived away from the farm. Some came to work for Brandenbury from struggling little "farmettes" that one could see now and again along the banks and hillsides extending down to the river. Others came from small towns off 197 or the Interstate, and one, a horse trainer, from as far away as Asheville.

He poured himself a drink at the wet bar and then strode across the room to look out the glass wall. He smiled as he caught sight of Prince Valiant, grazing in the lower pasture. One of the things he liked to do, after an "obstacle" had been removed, was ride. Sometimes two or three hours, always by himself. It cleared his mind. Helped to prepare him for whatever—or *whoever* was next.

With his first *whoever,* he'd actually been surprisingly nervous.

He and Barbara had spent a quiet evening at home on the maid and the cook's night out. How he had hated that woman. The more accolades he received for being a business genius, the more withdrawn and indifferent to it all Barbara had become. There were no children, nor would there ever be. After several unsuccessful years of attempting to propagate the Brandenbury line, they had gone to their doctor for help. Subsequent tests revealed that it was Brandenbury who had the problem. He was diagnosed as being sterile. He would never be able to produce an heir.

The whole idea that there was something he could not do galled and angered him. Since he needed someone to blame, Barbara became the target. She tried reasoning with him. It wasn't the end of the world. Thousands of men and women were incapable of having children. The difference in their case was that they could easily afford to adopt a child—a dozen children for that matter. They were blessed.

But Brandenbury would have none of it. Barbara just didn't understand. An adopted child would not be *his* child. His seed. Therefore it would not be perfect. If she had not been so argumentative, so unyielding, she would have understood that. But no. She persisted. Adopted children could be even more special than one of their own, she argued. Couldn't he see that?

Nor did she approve his secret mission in life. Power was like a magnet to him. He would sell his soul for it and, in actual fact, had done just that. Soon after 9/11, a golfing partner who worked for a technology firm in Charlotte had approached him. Would he be interested in meeting with a small group of business owners who were looking for someone to lead their organization through these difficult times? Of course. He had nothing better to do.

During the months that followed, he reconciled himself to Barbara's total ignorance. Her stupidity. This woman to whom he was married was not at all worthy of the greatness of Charles Brandenbury. She was clearly incapable of comprehending his destiny. It was her fault. It had to be. He needed what she could never give to him. There would never be a perfect little heir to the empire his genius was creating!

At first, he vented his disappointment by being verbally abusive. Yet there was nothing bad enough he could say to her or about her that would assuage the emptiness left by his "secret flaw." After awhile, he chose to ignore Barbara, engaging in numerous one-night stands and short-term sexual encounters with other women. When Barbara decided to confront him with his unfaithfulness, he acknowledged it without holding back, showing no shame or remorse whatsoever. Even taunting her with intimate details of some of his scandalous liaisons. Especially the ones he thought would hurt her the most.

Trapped and mortified, Barbara pleaded with Charles for a divorce, but to no avail. That would be another acknowledgment of failure—and failure was out of the question. No. A divorce was certain to tarnish his public image. Even if he could pile most of the blame for their marital demise onto Barbara, he envisioned that he would still be made to look bad. And looking bad was intolerable for the great Charles Brandenbury.

The result had been Barbara's continued emotional withdrawal. The more she withdrew the more she drank, relying on alcohol to deaden the hopelessness and helplessness that she felt in her now pointless life. Brandenbury routinely pounced on the weaknesses of others, and Barbara would be no exception.

He made it a practice to seize on Barbara's fragility as his chance to rid himself of the hollow drag she had become in his personal and professional life. He made certain there were always generous supplies of wine and liquor available at all of their residences—the Farm, the mansion in Asheville's exclusive Biltmore Forest, and the island estate.

When Barbara made one final attempt to turn her life around and stop the abuse of alcohol, Brandenbury was right there, calling in a personal substance abuse counselor to work with her in the privacy of their home, so as to "spare her any public humiliation." It was clever all right. A carefully contrived facade.

The climax to their relationship came following a merciless week of spiteful derision during which Brandenbury had taunted and humiliated his wife with criticisms and caviling that drove her ever nearer the edge. Maybe he couldn't create another human being, but he was cunningly capable when it came to destroying one.

That night, in a depressed mental state and with Charles' incessant encouragement, Barbara poured herself a drink. Then another. And another. Brandenbury sat watching, egging her on as he swirled the wine in his glass, always generous in replenishing hers while adding little or none to his own. He needed his mind to be clear.

The rest turned out to be surprisingly easy.

Once Barbara had slipped into a dreamless stupor, Brandenbury lifted her from her chair and carried her out of the master bedroom to the top of the staircase. His first thought had been to push her off the balcony. At the last minute, he changed his mind. Pressing moist lips against her forehead, he smiled down at her as her eyes fluttered open. She stared at him, curious at first, puzzled at his sudden tenderness. Then she returned smile for smile and lifted her face toward him in grateful response to his affectionate gesture, not realizing she had just received the kiss of Judas.

He held her eyes in his for a long moment. Then, without a word, he pitched her.

Watching her helpless body tumble down the flight of steps, he continued smiling in the knowledge that he'd made the right choice. An accidental fall down the stairs would be believable.

Descending, each step slow and deliberate, he gazed at her twisted form that lay sprawled at the bottom of the staircase. He paused briefly, the toe of his slipper a scant inch from her face. He resisted the impulse to kick and smash her beautiful face to a pulp, but that would have left injuries too suspicious. Kneeling, he felt for a pulse. At first it seemed there might be a faint one. He wasn't sure, so he waited a few minutes and tried again. All the while, every part of his body tingled with excitement, as if he were connected to an electric current. The feeling was indescribable! He'd never experienced anything like it before. Taking a deep breath, he pressed his fingers along the base of her throat again.

This time, nothing.

No sign of life.

Satisfied at last, he stood to his feet and stepped over Barbara's still form, reaching for the telephone that rested on a small table against the wall. Picking it up, he turned and looked at Barbara again. The tingling in his body had begun to subside. In its place a kind of hollow emptiness. No regret, no sorrow, no guilt. Nothing. No feeling at all. Just empty. He stared at her for a long time.

He had just taken the first step in what he knew would, of necessity, be a long journey. He had removed an impediment of doubt and failure, with the same dispassionate manner of a physician removing a tumor or a dentist, an abscessed tooth. It was something that had to be done, and he had done it. Several more minutes passed before he dialed 911.

Eighteen additional minutes went by before the paramedics arrived to be greeted by Barbara's suitably distraught husband. A half hour after that, the cook and the maid returned home from their night at the movies to discover that a terrible accident had befallen the mistress of the house.

A tragedy attributable to her own private hell.

That's what people had said once word was leaked from a reluctant husband that Mrs. Brandenbury had long been suffering from alcoholism and addiction to prescription drugs and had been undergoing recovery treatment.

Charles maintained a fitting charade of sorrow and despondency over her loss. There were numerous social and professional callers to express fitting attitudes of solace, though none could truly call themselves "friends" of the grieving husband. Such close, deep relationships were not permitted. They were too dangerous. Close relationships required intimacy. Confidentiality. Trust. They made people too vulnerable, and vulnerability was something Charles Brandenbury could not afford.

Not now.

Not ever.

He swallowed the last of his drink, relishing the burning sensation in his throat and the glowing feeling in his chest. He started to replenish his glass, thought better of it, and set it on the end table near the room's large, leather sofa. Then he returned his gaze to the window.

361

Since the occasion of his wife's unfortunate demise, there had been other obstacles in his pathway to power. Senator Burton's airplane crash had been the result of a "mechanical failure," thanks to the excellent skills of Randle Martin, Brandenbury's personal helicopter pilot and aviation mechanic. Then there had been that cleaning woman in Atlanta. A fruitless, inconsequential "offing," as it turned out, but no matter. Brandenbury thought Hitler was right. There are some people who shouldn't be permitted to go on living. Worthless, non-contributors to society. Anyway, he'd rewarded his man, Sammy, with a week in the Caribbean islands for that one. An added bonus for doing a good, clean job.

It was the way he maintained the members of his inner court. Terry Reynolds, Ho San, Sammy Vespatti, Randle Martin and Dempsey Vallbrick. And to a lesser degree, Cavanaugh and Larson. While he had no family, per se, these men were his family. Each received executive-level salaries and benefits, plus periodic "surprise" bonuses. Like Sammy's week in the islands at a top of the line resort with all the women and any other extras that money could buy. It was the stuff that resulted in unquestioning loyalty and obedience.

For reasons never disclosed to the Atlanta citizenry, local police had re-designated the cleaning woman's murder to low priority. Conveniently drug-related. A spokesman pointed out that more pressing cases had stretched the city's beleaguered crime prevention capabilities to the maximum. That homicide department reckoning had cost Brandenbury a few dollars as well, but like anything else of real value, it had been worth it. It had been necessary because of the woman's daughter. Grace. She had been a beauty. Not the Hollywood-style looks of the Senter woman, the one they called BJ, but a beauty nonetheless. And unlike the others, she had gotten away.

For a time, Brandenbury had hoped that Grace Grafton had

drowned or, better still, become a victim of alligators in the hostile swamp. Still, the lack of a body caused him concern. No detail was too small. If she really was still out there, neither he nor the Ultimate Dream was safe until she had been found and disposed of permanently.

Bonnie Jo Senter's death had been the one most like that of his first wife. She'd been much younger, of course, and incredibly beautiful. A beauty he wished he'd had more time to enjoy. But that same "electricity" had been there while they fought. He'd glimpsed the panic in her eyes as he grasped her, hauling her from the floor. He had loved that! Her lips had formed a silent whisper—"please, no." But there was no way he was going to stop. This part was the best! His thoughts had flashed to Barbara as he flung the woman through the windowpane and watched her disappear into the night.

Ilene Randle? He'd discovered something about himself through all the mayhem. Her death had not been the same thrill. She'd been unconscious when he delivered a fatal twist of the neck. There was no questioning that he preferred looking into the eyes of his victims. Observing the instant the iris widened with the sudden realization that they were about to die. That was the moment he enjoyed most of all.

The thrill of an event like the one this past weekend in Louisiana was not so much. If he could have been there to observe first hand the pandemonium and violence, then maybe. He wasn't sure since he had never witnessed something like that on such a grand scale. This much he knew. There was nothing like looking into their eyes. That was the best.

Brandenbury sank into his favorite leather club chair, placed his feet on the matching ottoman and settled back to wait the arrival of his expected guest. He knew it would be a few hours yet, but he needed to ponder things, to work out in his mind the subsequent sequence of events. Then he would get a few hours sleep.

Grace Grafton's escape from his island estate, and the interval of years during which she had failed to come forward with accusations, caused him to think she had most likely been discreet in telling her story. It was even possible that out of fear she had spoken to no one about it. But he had to be sure. There could be no more slip-ups. Things were happening much too rapidly now. The prize was too important. The Ultimate Dream was near at hand.

At first, he'd planned to do away with the Reverend Weston as soon as he was satisfied that all useful information had been wrested from him. In the past few hours, however, he'd changed his mind. And he had added two more small ingredients to the recipe, thus insuring an outcome that would be to his liking.

The good Reverend would remain alive until the woman who'd caused him no small amount of personal anxiety and frustration over the last seven years was standing in front of him, within his grasp. *Nobody gets the best of Charles Brandenbury.* He would find out what he needed to know. That would be easy ... and pleasurable. Then he would simply make them ... disappear. All of them. Without a trace. When he and the Grafton woman met again, this time would be the culmination of a much-deserved payday for all the expense and inconvenience she had caused by running away.

He glanced at his watch, then picked up a copy of the *Charlotte Observer's* business section and proceeded to run his finger down the NYSE columns, pausing every so often to determine which of his primary holdings had gone up or down in value during the last twenty-four hours.

63

Grace's heart pounded at the sound of the doorbell announcing the awaited arrival of her nemesis. The church alarm system had already been coded out. All that was left to do was release the exit bar and open the door. That and face the man who seven years ago had led her and her friends into an unforgettable night of madness. Once again, mental pictures of Ilene and BJ flashed through her mind, fueling her faltering courage. Her anxiety over Brad and the children pushed her the rest of the way.

From her position near Brad's administrative assistant's desk, she could see across the dimly lit entry to the set of double doors leading outside. Through the clear glass, she made out the shadowy figure standing outside. She tried to see past him, her eyes searching the darkness for some sign of an accomplice, but there was nothing. Satisfied at last that he appeared to be alone, Grace emerged from the darkened room on feet that were unsteady, concentrating on each step as she crossed the entry and pushed down on the exit bar. The door opened. Terry Reynolds walked in. The door closed and locked automatically behind him.

Grace backed away, staring at Reynolds as she felt for the wall with her hand. His body language seemed loose and relaxed, like a college student waiting for his date to show. Just the opposite for Grace, as a further spike in apprehension tightened every muscle. She caught her breath as, for the first time since that day, she stood face to face with the abettor in the murder of her two friends, aware of his nearness, the smell of tobacco on his clothes, the chill of old fears creeping along her spine, while in turn his cold eyes glanced up and down the hall, then lingered with open admiration on her face and body. She became conscious of her hands, clenched into fists.

Reynolds, dressed in a sports shirt, slacks, and sandals, did not give the appearance of carrying a weapon, but she thought he probably was.

"You're still as beautiful as ever, Taylor—or I guess it's back to Grace again, right?" He grinned and took two steps toward her, stopped, and held out his hand as if he expected her to take it. Grace didn't move. Slowly he let his hand drop. "Like your hair this way. Very becoming actually."

Still, Grace didn't attempt to respond.

"It's been a long time."

"Not long enough," she said at last, her voice thin and taut, eyes brimming with hostility.

"Hey, you need to know how sorry I am that things have worked out like this for you. I mean it could have been anybody. Really. It just happened that you three were there that day and ... well, it wasn't ... " he extended his hands and shrugged.

"Anything personal?"

"Right. It wasn't anything personal. The boss was just workin' his agenda, that's all."

All at once her fears gave way to a rage boiling up from somewhere deep within her, fueling the pain and bitterness and anger that she'd struggled to keep closeted for seven long years. "And exactly what was his agenda that night, Mr. Terry Reynolds, or whatever *your* name really is? Boy's night out on an island with three easy women? Was that it? Only instead of going to all the bother of taking them home after the party, let's just kill them and dump them like so much worthless garbage, right?"

"Now, please, Grace. I think you're ... "

"Shut up! Just shut up and listen." Her voice shook with anger. "The 'garbage' your boss and the others threw away that night was what was left of my two best friends. They had a future. We all did. We'd worked hard to prepare for it. We wanted to make a difference in the world. We wanted to get married, have kids, and be grandmothers someday. That's what my best friends wanted. That's what we all wanted. We just wanted our lives—and you took that from us!"

Reynolds face grew hard, his gaze never leaving Grace. He took another step toward her.

"Don't!" she commanded sharply, holding up her hands. "Don't come any closer. Remember, anything happens to me, and your boss' dreams of sleeping in Mr. Lincoln's bedroom disappear with the help of a filmcard and a front-page story. If that should happen, my guess is he'll hold you responsible for that, don't you think?"

Reynolds hesitated, seemingly considering his options. Then he stepped back. Grace released a quiet sigh of relief.

"It is the White House, isn't it? That's what this has been about from the beginning."

"Well, darlin', when opportunity comes fallin' out o' the sky into your lap, you got to do what you got to do. You might say it's kinda like a divine anointing."

"I assume you're speaking of my former dinner partner. How is dear old, smooth-talking Noah, by the way? Still sleeping with pretty girls whenever he's out of town carrying out the nation's business?"

"Noah's become one of America's most loved senators, if you know what I mean," Reynolds responded with a wicked grin at the double entendre.

"And now he wants to be America's 'most loved' president."

"Well, some men just have greater needs than others, that's all. It isn't anythin' new, darlin'. Surely you're not goin' to fault ol' Noah for a little carnal concupiscence?"

"And this 'opportunity' that fell from the sky—could that also have been a senator named Elwood Burton?"

Reynolds face registered surprise at that.

"It was, wasn't it? Isn't it just so interesting to see how good old Noah Parker was standing there in the wings at just the right time. In fact, it borders on being downright amazing, don't you think? A not so 'divine anointing' when you begin to add it all up. I'm guessing you made sure God had all the help he needed to bring that poor man's plane down, right? Aren't you just God's little helper!"

Reynolds shrugged and kept on smiling.

"How did you find me?" asked Grace.

Reynolds looked away for a moment, a smile returning to his face. "Have you ever heard of the fortuitous concourse of circumstances? A sort of random turn of events? That's what it took, darlin.' I was the one who spotted you, actually. A couple of weeks ago in the *Sunday Los Angeles Times*. There you were in all your glory. Your hair was different, like it is now, but it was that same beautiful face. I would have missed it if I had not been out here over the weekend, doing something for my boss. I was having breakfast at my hotel when I read the story. What are the chances?"

Grace's heart sank. What were the chances? She had tried to avoid the picture, but Brad had insisted. The *Times* reporter was working on a human interest story about the uniqueness of their singing group, comprised for the most part of non-professionals doing popular radio commercials for release in the LA basin and around the country. The picture featured the singers and their spouses or significant others. The story and the photo had run in the Entertainment Section two Sundays prior.

She shook her head in disbelief. *What lousy luck!*

"So now it's come to this, Terry," she said at last. "I want Brad and the kids back—safe and unharmed."

"That's not a problem," Reynolds smiled.

"So why go to all this trouble? Here I am. What more do you want? What's your price?"

"The filmcard you say you have, we want. Any pictures or negatives you may have layin' around your apartment, we want those, too. We want the names of anyone to whom you have told your version of what went on that night on the island. And your word that you'll keep as quiet as a little church mouse from here on out, just like you've done for the last seven years. You plannin' on bein' a pastor's wife an' all, that last part shouldn't be so hard. Keepin' confidences is part of the deal for bein' married to a preacher, isn't it?"

"So the only thing I have to do is give up the photographs and any friends in whom I may have confided, and then trust you people to keep your part of the bargain?"

Reynolds shrugged.

"If I agree to all this, how do I know you'll give them back?"

"You said it yourself. Trust?" Reynolds grinned again as if the word constituted a joke worth laughing at. Then he gave her a steely look. "Get real, Grace. You've got no choice. You're out of options. If you don't do it, you'll never see your preacher and those beautiful kids again, I promise you that. If you come through for me, though—and give my boss everything he wants, well then, I guarantee that you'll be seein' 'em in a matter of hours."

"You killed my mother!"

Reynolds blinked at this sudden turn in conversation. "It seemed like the right thing to do at the time. I'm sorry."

Grace trembled once more with anger. "You are a snake, Terry Reynolds, an unfeeling despicable snake. A beast. Pathetic and spineless!"

"Sticks and stones," Reynolds chuckled in blithe disregard to her pain and hostility.

Grace glared at Reynolds, shaking as she worked to control the impulse to tear apart this worm of a human being, an impulse she knew would result in her own swift demise. She was no match. She knew it. This, together with her understanding that she represented Brad and the children's only hope caused her to relax her clenched fists..

"Okay, then," she sighed in an expression of final resignation. "There is someone I've told. She was driving Brad's children this afternoon when your goons forced her off the road. I'm sure by now you know Maggie Hinegardner. She's a member of our church and a reporter for the *Desert Sun*. I've told her everything."

"Okay. Who else?"

"I've given you the name of one person. If you and the man you work for hadn't taken Brad and the children, even she wouldn't know. But now she does, thanks to you."

"If you'd tell her, why wouldn't you tell others?"

"You're right, of course. I may be just as devious as you and your friends. I could be lying through my teeth. Maybe I've already told my story to twenty other people. How will you know for sure? Trust? When you build your world on lies, it's hard to discern if someone is telling you the truth, isn't it? Like, for example, how do I know you'll keep your end of this 'Judas' bargain?"

"You're certain?"

"About what?"

"You wouldn't lie to little ol' Terry now, would you? About not having spilled your guts to anybody else other than your reporter friend? Can we trust her to be discreet?"

"Trust?" Grace snapped. "It's a stalemate, Terry. I guess we have to trust each other in order to get what we both want."

Reynolds laughed. "You've got chutzpah, I will say that."

"Why, I didn't think a southern gentleman like yourself even knew what that word meant," Grace replied, mimicking Reynolds' southern accent icily.

Reynolds glowered at her. "So where's this filmcard and the pictures? If you've written stuff down, where is it?"

Grace stepped back.

Reynolds came closer.

"Stop," Grace ordered. "Wait while I go into Brad's study."

Before Reynolds had a chance to say anything, Grace whirled and walked back through the study door. She did not turn on the light.

As she disappeared into the shadows, Reynolds moved quickly. He bent down and drew a small handgun from a holster strapped to his ankle. Stepping to one side for a clearer view, he raised the weapon, pointing it toward the open doorway.

What happened next was a blur. Like a movie fast-forwarded.

Maggie stepped out of the janitor's closet directly behind Reynolds. He started to turn, but it was too late. His gun hand wavered for a

371

split second. Time enough. Like a home run hitter, Maggie swung the cast iron skillet she had retrieved minutes earlier from the kitchen.

A single gunshot reverberated through the small church office entry. The bullet slammed into the wall, inches from the study door. Reynolds twisted sideways, slumping onto the tiled floor, his gun skidding back toward the entry doors.

Grace came out of the study, her face drained of color, and stood opposite Maggie, staring down at Reynolds motionless form between them. "You must have hit him awfully hard," she said finally.

"As hard as I could. He was going to shoot you as soon as you came back through that door." Still breathing heavily, Maggie made a conscious effort to loosen fingers that, in her excitement, had become welded to the handle. The skillet clattered onto the tile floor.

"I know." Grace's tone sounded wistful. "But ... "

"Will you stop it? Don't even think that. Get hold of yourself. You have to be strong."

Grace pursed her lips and gingerly reached down to feel for a pulse, afraid that Reynolds might suddenly jump up and grab her. Blood oozed out from under his hair.

"When the gun went off, I thought it was you."

"I know."

"I mean I thought he had shot you. Then when I saw him laying there on the floor I thought maybe you had killed him. Did you fire your gun?"

"No, it was this lowlife. I chickened out. After all that training and target practice, I still wasn't sure I could do it to another human being so I borrowed the skillet from the kitchen. That I knew I could do."

"He's still alive," Grace's voice was tentative now, still shaky from her encounter with Reynolds and the shock of gunfire, "but you really hit him hard. He's useless to us."

"What are you saying?"

"I think he's hurt pretty badly. From the looks of that wound, he may not wake up for a long time."

"We'll pour water on him. He'll come around."

"Maggie. I know these men. They are ruthless. Even if we do revive him, do you really think he's going to tell us anything? And what if he's not alone? What if someone is outside waiting for him? Maybe they heard the gunshot. And we still don't know where Brad and the kids are. If anything happens to them, I don't want to go on living."

"Come on," urged Maggie. "Get over yourself. Don't talk like that. If ever there was a time to keep it together, it is now. But you are right about one thing. We don't know how many more there are out there like him. Even if they didn't hear the shot, they may come looking, so let's go around back and get out of here."

"What are we going to do with him? Just leave him here?"

"We'll tie him up."

"With what?"

"I saw some tape in the janitor's closet." Maggie disappeared and was back in a moment with a thick role of gray duct tape. "Okay. Use this to tie him up while I make a phone call. Wrap it around his legs and pull his arms behind him. Make sure he can't get away unless someone helps him."

"What are you doing?"

"I'm calling 911."

"Maggie?"

"We can't just leave him ... Hello, I need to report a ... a citizen is holding a man who is not supposed to be here. He may have a criminal record. Here's the address ... No, my name is not important but we need you to have the police come and check it out. Thank you.'"

Maggie put the receiver back.

"You know they recorded your voice," said Grace.

"I know. But we can't just leave him here, now can we? What if he was still here when Karen comes to work in the morning? Or, worse, what if he managed to get free and hide until the office opened and then ... "

"Okay, okay. You're right. As much as the rat deserves to bleed to death, you are right."

"They'll probably take their time responding to a break in. Then when they find Mr. Reynolds it will take a few more minutes before the paramedics show up. We need those minutes. So let's get out of here before the police show up."

Grace finished wrapping the tape around Reynolds' ankles and they ran down the hall into the darkened sanctuary, across the carpeted area between the platform and the front row of seats. Here they came to a fire exit. They eased open the door and stared out into the darkness. It looked clear. At least no one was in sight.

They ran along the side of the building and through a narrow opening between a shrubbery blind and the sidewalk to where Grace had parked her car. She pushed the door lock button on her key chain. Taillights flashed as the doors unlocked. Sliding inside, she turned the ignition key and within seconds they were rolling along the street, searching the shadows for any sign of Reynolds' counterpart. She didn't turn on the lights until they had turned the corner and headed north, well away from the church.

64

The small private jet touched down at the Asheville Regional Airport at one forty-five in the morning. Both children, heavily sedated during the flight from California, had to be carried off the plane in the arms of their abductors. There was, however, nothing about their transfer to evoke undue notice.

CB-One lifted off as soon as everyone was on board, her nose dipping slightly as Randle Martin brought the helicopter about and flew north over the city, along the Interstate 26 corridor.

65

2210 local time
Palm Springs

Officers Hermano Pérez and Janet Leffler were the first to arrive at Desert Community Church in response to a 10-14 "citizen holding suspect" call from dispatch. A quick check around the building's exterior revealed an empty parking lot except for one car located near the main entry area to the church. The car was also empty.

Exiting their patrol car, they approached the building's only source of interior light, visible through the glass doors leading into the office area. Through the glass they could see a man lying face down on the floor, arms thrust and bound behind his back. Legs, too, although that had proven unnecessary. He wasn't moving. A dark path of blood trickled down from behind his ear.

"Someone didn't want this guy to get away," Leffler observed dryly.

Pérez tried the door, finding it unlocked. He stepped inside. Service revolvers in hand, they investigated the hall and any doors that were unlocked, determining that no one else appeared to be about. The man showed a pulse. He was unconscious, but alive. Leffler radioed a

901 request for an ambulance and paramedic team.

"Looks like he took one on the back of his skull."

"So it was Miss Scarlet in the hallway with a frying pan?" Pérez shook his head, looking at the iron skillet on the floor. "But who might Miss Scarlet be?"

Leffler chuckled. "Whoever she is, she swings a mean skillet."

"Dispatch did say it was a woman who called, right?"

"Yeah, but maybe she had a friend."

"Who do you suppose belongs to that?" Leffler pointed to the small handgun on the floor. He stepped over, knelt down and sniffed it without touching it. "Recently fired. Did our Miss Scarlet with the hefty swing become frightened and leave her gun behind?"

"Check out the man's leg." Pérez pointed toward the partially exposed ankle. "He was carrying. My guess? Gun's been fired? My money is on him being the shooter."

"A poor one, though. No bodies. No blood trail. Only a whack on the back of his noggin. If he was the shooter, he's going to have one serious headache when he wakes up and tells us what happened."

A short while later, the ambulance and medical team arrived, followed by two more patrol cars, pulling into the lot alongside Pérez' and Leffler's black and white. In a matter of minutes they had photographed the scene and transferred the injured man to the ambulance. With siren wailing and lights flashing, the victim or suspect or whoever he was, was headed for the trauma center.

Pérez and Leffler secured the area and waited for the investigative team to arrive and take over.

66

They were silent as they made their way along Washington Street. Both hands gripping the wheel, Grace stared wordlessly at the road most of the way. As they neared the hotel, she could no longer contain herself.

"Maggie, what if ... what if something ... happens ... before the medics get there? He wasn't moving, was he?"

"He's not going to die."

"How do you know?"

"Come on. Get a grip. I'm scared, too, but we've got to keep it together."

Grace's hands were shaking.

"If something *does* happen—if Reynolds dies—will Brandenbury take it out on Brad and the children?"

"You're in shock," declared Maggie, as they turned right off Eisenhower and guided the Mazda along the palm-lined road to the hotel.

"Stop and let me drive," Maggie offered.

"No, we're almost there. I'll be all right."

"Remember, this Reynolds character is an evil man. He was going to kill you. He fired his gun at us. I acted to protect us both. It was self-defense. He's lucky to be alive. Remember that, Grace. I'm thinking that when he wakes up, though, he may wish he'd been shot."

"Do you suppose he brought some others with him?"

"I wouldn't be surprised at anything right now. Let's hope if he did come alone, he'll still be there when the police arrive, but we won't know for sure. Not for a while anyway. You were right back there, though. We've lost any chance of discovering where Brad and the kids are being held."

"What are we going to do?"

"First things first. Let's get back to the room and settle ourselves down. Then we'll decide what to do next."

Fifteen minutes later, Maggie was leaning back against the bed pillows, sipping an Earl Gray tea that Grace had made by heating water in the room's coffeemaker. Maggie felt shaky herself, but the hot liquid was producing the much needed calming effect. The two women sat quietly, mesmerized by thoughts of the day's events that had brought them to this place.

Grace closed her eyes. *Jesus, wherever Brad and David and Nancy are, please, please watch over them and protect them. I'm begging you…*

"I have an idea," Maggie interrupted, her voice much stronger. Grace watched as she picked up her purse from the nightstand. Removing a small book, she thumbed through it until coming to whomever or whatever it was she was thinking about. She looked up at Grace.

"I first met Paul Jacobsen two years ago at the annual Southern Republican Leadership Conference. He's an investigative reporter with the *Washington Post*. The *Sun* sent me to the Convention to dig up some stuff for a feature on the impact that evangelical Christian delegates and the Tea Party movement were having on the presidential nomination process. I was there the whole week.

"At a luncheon where former President Bush was speaking, I happened to be at the same table with Paul. We hit it off right away. He's a pretty serious sort, but the guy's a good audience and laughs when he thinks something's funny enough. I guess he thought my quirky personality was a bit unusual for someone working my side of the street. I proved to be funny enough to lighten up an otherwise boring couple of hours. We had a really good time."

"Did you go out together?"

"You mean did we date? Sweetheart, those days are gone forever. Besides, the guy's twenty years younger than I am—and very married, with two cute kids. No, it wasn't anything like that. We just had a great time talking and laughing over lunch, that's all. He said that he wanted to see my story feature after the convention, so I sent it to him. We had dinner again last year. He was vacationing out here with Melody and the kids. Paul had a book hit the stores just this last month and sent me an autographed copy. I've not had a chance to read it yet, though."

"So what's he got to do with all this?"

Maggie looked up and smiled as she reached into her purse for her phone. "The title of his book is *America's Desire for White House Integrity.*"

"Are you kidding?"

"Nope."

"Do you think he'll call back tomorrow when he gets the message?"

Maggie grinned once more as she focused on punching in the numbers. "Actually ... if he's home, he'll be answering personally, right about ... Hi ... Paul? It's Maggie Hinegardner ... yeah, the one and only Mary Magdalene. What? ... well, thanks a lot, sport ... did I wake you up? I hope so."

Grace looked at her watch. Ten twenty-two Pacific Time. That meant it was nearly one-thirty in the morning on the East Coast. A look of admiration crossed her face as she watched her friend lean back against the pillows and laugh into the telephone.

Moments later, laughter had been replaced by a frown as Maggie recounted an overview of Grace's story and of the events of the past two days. "Yes, that's right, Paul ... her fiancé and his two children have been kidnapped ... No, I told you, we *can't* go to the police. By the time they sort out the details, Brandenbury will be all over us. It'll be like suing God. He'll have so many lawyers and paid-off public officials they'll put Grace away in a mental institution, if she lasts that long. And no one will ever see her future husband and the kids again. Do you hear what I'm saying? Yes ... yes ... No, I haven't had anything stronger than Earl Gray.

"One of Brandenbury's bad guys tried to kill her tonight after she told him what he wanted to hear. What? Well, I ... I hit him, Paul. No, with a skillet ... well, it was cast iron ... "

Maggie's face broke into a half-grin.

"No, I didn't kill him, but he wasn't moving either when we left. We tied him up, called 911, and then got out. No! I'm not pulling your leg. They've probably found him by now in the entry to our church office. What ... Yes, I know. It sounds crazy, but it's not. We're in a life and death situation here, Paul, and unless we turn this around right away, it'll be too late—if you know what I mean ... yes ... yes. So put your investigative reporter's hat on. Why I called was to find out if you know anything about Charles Brandenbury ... wait, wait ... hold on a sec."

Maggie looked up. "Hand me a sheet of that paper over there, will you? I left my notebook in the car."

Grace scooped up a sheet of hotel stationery from the desk and handed it to Maggie who already had retrieved a pen from her purse.

"Okay, I'm ready. Fire away."

For several minutes, Maggie scribbled abbreviated notes on the stationery, making a temporary desk out of a hotel services directory propped precariously on her knees. Her efforts were punctuated by an occasional grunt or a request "say again" and, finally, an enthusiastic "great! You're terrific Paul. What? Meet us there? Just a second." She put her hand over the mouthpiece.

"Paul wants to know if we'd be open to him meeting us."

"Meeting us? Where?"

"We're going to the East Coast as soon as we can catch a plane. I'll tell you what's up in a second. Yes or no?"

Grace's mind was whirling. "I ... I don't know. I guess so ... but ... "

Maggie was back on the phone. "Yes. Meet us there. We haven't got anything better here. I think you may be right. It's worth a try, at least. We'll get there as fast as we can. I'll call you back when we know what we're flying. Thanks, Paul ... yes ... yes ... okay ... thanks. See you in a few hours. Bye."

Grace looked at Maggie expectantly as she laid the phone on the nightstand. Maggie was smiling, but her eyes were serious. Grace could almost see wheels turning inside her brain.

"Okay. Here's the scoop. I didn't think Paul could write a book about White House integrity without having done at least some research into Noah Parker and Charles Brandenbury. He tells me that he has verifiable evidence that Parker has been womanizing for several years, albeit discretely. He guesses Mrs. Parker is suspicious, but hasn't pressed the matter. Paul thinks that maybe she doesn't really want to know for fear of what it will do to their marriage and their lifestyle—

to say nothing, of course, about the good senator's candidacy for the nation's highest office.

"Brandenbury has been extremely careful of his own image. He's one private citizen who knows how to control what the public knows about him. Paul says that your story adds credibility to his own suspicions, however, related to what he's turned up about the death of Brandenbury's first wife. It seems that Paul interviewed the guy who was working with her at the time in a private rehab program. He says that she spilled some pretty intimate and devastating details about their marriage. It wasn't the 'love and devotion' relationship that Brandenbury claimed after her death, which incidentally was declared 'accidental' at the time."

Grace nodded. She had read up on Barbara Brandenbury on the Internet while living in the Bay Area. Based on her own experience, she had wondered if it had really been an accident.

"Paul also thinks what's happened to you might even lend further credence to a tie-in with Senator Burton's death. Especially now that it has opened up the way for a Noah Parker candidacy. Nothing he can verify at this point; just a journalist's sixth sense. He knows for a fact that these two are thick and is betting that if Parker gets enough of Burton's delegates into his camp in the next couple of weeks, he's going to announce Brandenbury as his vice-presidential nominee."

"I'm certain that's what they have in mind," exclaimed Grace. "And afterward when the timing is right Brandenbury will somehow get rid of Noah Parker and then ... guess what?"

"*President* Brandenbury!" Maggie finished.

"So why are we going to the East Coast?"

"Well, Paul just got back from a political dinner in Washington that was thrown for the national press corps and paid for by our very own Mr. Brandenbury. The featured star of the show was none other than our 'much loved' Noah Parker, who, as the main speaker, outlined his personal agenda for liberating America from all its ills."

"What good will it do for us to go to Washington?"

"Not Washington. Atlanta. Paul will meet us there. From there we drive to Asheville, North Carolina."

"But why there?"

"Because that's where Brandenbury was going to go after the dinner. He has a mansion in a very exclusive section of Asheville, as well as a horse farm out of town a ways. On the north side somewhere. Paul says the man likes the farm the best. It's more isolated."

"I still don't understand."

"If Brandenbury has taken Brad and the kids, then he knows where they are. Don't you think he would want them close by? Maybe they're with him right now!"

"I don't know … " Grace hesitated. "How can we be sure? This is such a long shot. What if they're somewhere in San Diego or Los Angeles instead … or even right here in Palm Springs? For all we know, they could even be right here in this hotel. That's the trouble. We're only guessing. We just don't know!"

"We've God to be with us, Grace. To give us guidance. I think he just did." Maggie sat bolt upright, throwing her legs over the edge of the bed. "Why didn't I think of that before?"

"What?"

"When you said 'they could even be right here in this hotel,' I remembered."

"Remembered what?"

"John Cain."

Grace stared at Maggie. "My former pastor? From Baytown?"

"Yes."

"What does he have to do with anything?"

"He's here."

"You mean here? As in Palm Desert?"

"I mean here. As in this very hotel!"

Grace stared open-mouthed at Maggie.

"You remember I told you I was out late last night covering a fundraiser for refugees? Well, John Cain was the speaker. He gave me an interview afterward. He and his wife are here vacationing for a few days. He mentioned that they were staying at the La Quinta Resort."

"Okay, so he's here. How does that help our situation?"

"You surely remember four years ago when terrorists held his congregation hostage at the same time he was taken hostage with a group from his church on a tour of Israel. And Boston was threatened at the same time in a coordinated attack on Americans?"

"Sure. I was in the area at the time. It was in the world media for days. Front-page stuff. And when it was over, his little girl had been kidnapped. Yes, I've heard the story. I've even met his little girl. It's incredible. *They* are an incredible family."

"I'm calling them right now."

"Are you serious? It's the middle of the night. I've met them, but I don't know them. I doubt they will even remember I was in the church. What good will it do?"

"We need all the help we can get, girlfriend. Spiritual or practical. The Cains may be able to give us both."

Maggie dialed the front desk. "Yes, this is … Beverly Carson. I need to speak with the Reverend John Cain. He and Esther are guests here. Yes, that's right. No, I realize the time but this is a matter of extreme personal urgency. Wait. He may not know the name Beverly Carson. Mention that Maggie Hinegardner is with me and needs to speak to him right away. Yes. Thank you."

Maggie placed the receiver back on the telephone.

Grace shook her head. "I can't believe you just did that."

"Well, we'll see. They say pastors are on call 24/7, so now we'll find out."

"But he's on vacation."

"So let him deal with it. We need help. At least he can pray for us. Maybe out of his experience with his daughter's kidnapping he can give us some words of wisdom. I tell you for sure, I could use a few right now. You're right about one thing you said a minute ago. We don't know. Not for sure. But there's the old saying, 'if the mountain won't come to Mohammed, then Mohammed will go to the mountain.' Remember that? Well, that's what we're about to do. We don't know where our 'mountain' is, so we can't go to it. But, maybe we can get to the mole who made the 'mountain' in the first place."

Grace remained silent, her mind racing in circles around this new unexpected option.

"Well?" said Maggie impatiently.

"Okay," Grace declared at last. "It's all we've got."

Just then, the telephone rang.

67

Maggie picked up the phone. "Hello?"

"Hello, this is John Cain." The sonorous voice was full-flavored, rich and strong. And familiar.

"Pastor Cain, this is Maggie Hinegardner. We met last evening after the refugee fundraiser?"

"Yes," he paused then continued, "and did I forget something you needed to make a great story? It's a bit late. To what do I owe this honor?"

"No, actually, you didn't forget anything. And I apologize for calling you at this hour and on your vacation, too, but something has happened since we met. Something ... very important that I'd like to talk to you about."

"Could it wait until morning? We've already turned in for the night."

"No, I'm sorry. This is a matter of grave urgency to some of my dearest friends ... something of national importance. World importance actually. I don't say this just to get you to talk with us, but we do need to speak with you now."

"We?"

"I have with me a woman named Grace Grafton. She used to attend your church in Baytown before moving to the desert."

"Grace Grafton ... I don't recall the name."

"Perhaps it's because when she attended your church she did so as Taylor Carroll."

"Mmm. Taylor Carroll." Another pause. Then, as though checking through a mental member list, "Quiet, very attractive, a bit reclusive, yes, I remember now. She was baptized three or four years ago, maybe longer? Tara Brown was her friend. Tara and her husband are two of our youth sponsors. I believe she joined the singles program at Calvary. Then I'm afraid I lost track, but I think she may have left the area."

"Amazing recall, Pastor, I must say. She moved to the desert two years ago to take a lead sales position at Broadmores. Reverend Cain, I know it is late, but could you meet with us now? We have to leave in a short while."

Maggie heard the murmur of voices. Cain talking to his wife. Then he was back. "Okay, Maggie, I'll meet you and Taylor or Grace or whomever in the hotel lobby in ten minutes. Just give me a chance to dress and walk over. National importance? You've piqued my curiosity, Maggie. But I hope you didn't just suddenly remember our family's involvement with terrorists a few years ago and think perhaps you could get another story for your paper?"

"The truth is, your past experiences are part of the reason we need to talk. Your daughter was kidnapped. You are acutely aware of all the world events that surrounded the story of her survival. We have a similar situation going on right now, even as we speak."

For a moment there was silence, then, "I'll see you in ten minutes." The line went dead.

Grace and Maggie were sitting in front of the lobby fireplace when John Cain came striding through the door, dressed in a blue polo shirt, kaki Bermuda shorts, and Birkenstocks. Pausing, he spotted them and headed in their direction.

"Hello again, Maggie," he said, smiling as he shook her hand. "How is my new best reporter friend?"

"Fine, Pastor," Maggie replied.

"Please, if you're Maggie, then I'm John. And this would be?"

Maggie let her free hand touch Cain's arm lightly as she turned to face Grace. "This is Grace Grafton, whom I believe you knew as Taylor Carroll while she was attending your church."

Cain released Maggie's hand and held out his arms to Grace.

"How good to see you again," he said with a polite embrace. "I absolutely do remember you, of course, now that I see you again. Though I have to admit I was confused a little at first."

As he stepped back, Grace remembered that this man had always been a hugger when it came to people in the congregation, though never in a way that caused whatever man or woman he hugged to be embarrassed. He simply made you want to hug him back. It was just his way. She recalled how much that warm spirit and acceptance had meant to her during the time she had spent in Baytown.

He continued, "I'm used to women changing their last names, Grace, but you may be my first to change them both. I am guessing there is a story behind this? So sit down, please. Tell me what is prompting this sudden urge for a pastoral call after all this time has passed. So far I've heard 'kidnapping' and an intimation regarding 'something of national importance.' I'm listening, so tell me what's going on."

Maggie nodded to Grace. "Go ahead, Grace. Bring Pastor ... sorry, bring John up to date."

Thirty minutes later, the three of them sat quietly, letting the silence frame Grace's abbreviated recounting of the last seven years of her life. She studied the man's face as he sat across from her, never taking his eyes off her. Looking for what. Acceptance? Disbelief? Hope? At last John Cain leaned back into the leather chair and rubbed his face. "That is a truly incredible story, Grace."

Grace looked away.

"That is in fact a gross understatement," he continued. "Do you realize what you are saying? What the implications of all this could be, if true?"

Grace looked back, her gaze steady, jaw set, not taking her eyes off Cain. "I do," she said softly.

Cain shot a look of incredulity at Maggie. "And you believe her story? All of it?"

Maggie nodded. "There is not even an inkling of doubt. At first, I admit to having listened with the ears of a reporter who's heard every cockamamie story there is to tell. I was stunned when Grace told me that the Taylor I thought I knew was this other person, too. It's like she's formed up her own self-styled witness protection program. But I believe she's telling the truth. And Brad's children have been kidnapped. No doubt about that. I was there when it happened. They were taken right out of my car and whisked away. Brad is missing, too. That has been verified. Grace heard his voice once since it happened. Probably a recording, but we don't know for certain. We have to assume he's been taken hostage as well. A fly on the hook to reel Grace in. People have been killed. Grace's two friends. Her mother. And the man who would be our next president is up to his eyeballs in this murderous mayhem!"

Cain sat forward again and looked intently at Grace. "You

mentioned there was a third man present with you on the island."

Grace nodded. "I never got to know him all that well. Talal Itana. They said he was a UN diplomat from Lebanon. Ilene was his dinner companion." As Grace said "dinner companion," she felt a sudden heat infuse her cheeks, knowing what this man, a pastor for goodness' sake, must be reading between the lines.

"Describe him."

"The thing I most remember about the man was that he was quiet. Ilene had to really work to get him to talk. For a diplomat, he wasn't much of a conversationalist. Appearance-wise? Dark hair, dark skin, a Middle-Eastern look, handsome, well-built, I'd guess him to be in his early 40s maybe? Gave the appearance of having worked out a good deal. Quiet, polite. A full beard, well- trimmed. A scar on his cheek."

Cain suddenly got to his feet and walked away. Grace looked at Maggie. Maggie shrugged. A few steps, then Cain turned back and looked down at them both, the expression on his face becoming hard and unwavering.

"Where was the scar, Grace?"

Grace looked at Cain, her curiosity piqued at the emotion in his voice. "It was on his right cheek. Ran up through his beard almost to his ear. Gave him a rather rakish appearance, actually. I wondered about how he got it, but don't know. We weren't together long enough to ask those kinds of questions."

Cain searched Grace's eyes for a long moment. "Are you absolutely sure of your description?"

Grace nodded again. "I'll never forget the faces of those three men. They live in my worst nightmares. They murdered my friends. They would have killed me if I had not escaped. It's as accurate as I can tell you. I could recognize him anywhere. Why?"

"Because I don't believe the man you described is really this Talal

Itana. For certain he is not a UN diplomat."

Grace stared up at Cain.

"You just described a man named Marwan Dosha."

Grace and Maggie waited. All at once, the name clicked for Maggie, and she jumped to her feet. "Wait. That's one of the world's most sought-after terrorists!"

"He's the man who kidnapped our daughter."

Grace shook her head in bewilderment. "What … what are you saying?" she stammered. "That the man we were with on Daufuskie Island, the one who was Parker's and Brandenbury's friend is a terrorist? An enemy of our country? No way. That can't be. If the others knew this, why would they … " Her voice trailed off. "Brandenbury, maybe I could believe Brandenbury. He is evil personified. But Parker? The man who would be president?"

"Would you recognize him again? If you saw his picture?"

"Itana? Or whoever he is? Sure. Yes. Absolutely."

"We have no photographs. But we do have a sketch that Jessica helped generate with an FBI artist."

Grace started to stand, then sat back in her chair, thinking. "I may have one," she said at last.

Now it was Cain's turn to express surprise. "What do you mean? A picture?"

Grace described the photo shooting sequence that had taken place on the dock that day in Savannah and how the two men she was then introduced to by Brandenbury, namely Noah Parker and Talal Itana, had been in the background of a picture of BJ and Ilene standing front of the yacht they were about to board.

"Where is this photograph?"

"On a digital filmcard that somehow survived the swamp and the water and everything else. It is in a safe deposit box."

"Here in Palm Springs?"

"In Baytown."

"There is a picture of the world's number one terrorist in a safe deposit box in Baytown? That is incredulous! You have a key?"

"I gave it to Maggie this afternoon. But ... someone else also has a key. I left it with them in case something ever happens to me and I die or disappear without a trace."

John Cain nodded knowingly with a slight smile. "Wendal and Tara Brown. They have the key."

Grace forced a smile. "Yes. Not so hard to figure that one out since I permitted very few others to befriend me while I lived up there. And no one so close as the Browns. They have the other key."

"All right then, we have to let the FBI know what we know right away," said Cain.

"No!" Grace's voice was sharp as she leapt from her chair to face Cain.

Cain registered surprise. "But we have to, Grace. They need to know."

"No!" she declared, panic shaping the sound of her voice. "No FBI. No police. No CIA. No Homeland Security! No, no, no."

Cain looked at Maggie. Then back at Grace, who by this time was shaking, tears streaming down her cheeks. "I cannot go to the authorities. No, Pastor Cain. I won't do it!"

"Why would you say that?" Cain asked, his voice soothing and comforting, with the instinct of someone used to calming distraught souls.

"Because the man owns them," she answered simply. Then through tears she continued. "That night on Daufuskie Island, I overheard Brandenbury tell the others not to worry about the police or the FBI; that he owned them. And the way the investigation into BJ and

Ilene's deaths went, I'm convinced he does. The same holds true with my mother. That was all put down and shut up so quickly that there was never any real investigation into the matter. The man who spoke to me over the phone last night said the same. He promised I would never see Brad again if I went to the authorities and that they would know it because they have connections everywhere. It was the police who took Brad. Or at least they were acting like policemen. Don't you see, Pastor Cain, if we go to the police or the FBI, I will never see Brad or his children alive. They will simply disappear!"

Grace slumped down in the chair and covered her face with both hands. Maggie placed a hand on her shoulder.

"I'm the one they want," Grace said, her confession as stark and bare as a windswept plain.

Cain peered down at her.

Maggie's eyes were closed, her mouth moving in silent prayer, then they opened again as she gently rubbed Grace's neck.

"I'm the reason they took Brad and the children. They don't care about them. It's me. My diary. The filmcard. The names of anyone I may have told my story to. You are both in danger now. So are the Browns if they ever find out I told them and that they have the deposit box key. They're ruthless. They'll kill us all. There is only one hope."

"And that would be?" asked Cain.

"I have to do what I should have done years ago. Face Brandenbury. Expose Parker and this … this terrorist character, if in fact that's who he is. Brad and David and Nancy are dead unless I can protect them somehow." Grace looked up at Cain and Maggie. "I'm going to do it."

"And your plan would be what?" asked Cain again.

Grace slumped back in her chair and stared across the room. Then her gaze returned to Cain, unyielding. "You must promise me that you won't go to the authorities. Everything I've told you is in confidence.

Aren't pastors supposed to keep the secrets of the people who come to them for counsel?"

"Well, yes, but ... "

"Then that's it. I forbid you to share what I've told you with anyone else. And, Maggie, the same goes for you. It's what you news people call 'off the record,' right? So everything I've told you is off the record."

A look of amusement crossed Cain's face. Maggie laughed outright. "Grace, honey, first of all, you needed to make the 'off the record' deal before you spilled your guts to me. So now is a little late for that. Secondly, there's no way you can tackle these people by yourself. What do you think, that you're the Lone Ranger or something? Even he had Tonto!"

"She's right, you know," said Cain as he continued to contemplate Grace. "Okay, let's suppose we don't go to the authorities. Let me make a suggestion."

Grace looked at Cain, pleading for some glimmer of hope, already knowing her bravado speech was pointless and absurd. She had no plan.

"Permit me to make a phone call to a friend of mine. He is not connected in any way with the authorities. He is also one of the best security specialists in the business. I would trust him with my life. In fact, I already have. He and I went to Iran to get Jessica out. We did it without getting government permission because we knew that if we tried, they would never permit us to do what had to be done. We were then much like you are now in this situation. He is the one person who just might be able to help us. While he and I were together last, we broke more laws than you could count which is something I'm not particularly proud of."

"But you and your friend got her out?"

"In a manner of speaking. My friend and I did all we could do. But, actually it was a friend we all know who finally brought her home safely."

Grace looked puzzled for a moment, then nodded as a broad smile crossed her face for the first time since they had begun their conversation, now almost an hour ago. She brushed at the residue of tears. "Really?"

"Really. Our best Friend did it. We attempted something so big that unless God intervened, it would surely fail. We did fail. He didn't."

"What do you say, Grace, honey?" asked Maggie, bending down to look directly into her eyes.

"I say maybe I need to finally discover what redeeming grace really means. Okay, Pastor Cain, what's your idea? I know I need help. Lots of it. So what's next?"

"First, I'll break the news to Esther, and we'll start packing. I'll try to reach my friend in Seattle. I'm not sure if he'll be there or somewhere else in the world. He gets around. Then, I encourage you both to get out of here as fast as you can. You said you were going to Atlanta to meet up with your journalist friend? Go. God-willing, things haven't yet hit the fan, so you'll have time to catch a plane without being on someone's watch list. When you get to Atlanta the first thing to do is get lost. Every minute counts. Don't waste a one. I'll catch up to you. Let's be sure we have cell phone numbers. And any conversations must be short. Remove the batteries from your phones until you want to get in touch. Phones can be traced.

"We know," agreed Maggie.

"All right. But before we do anything further, let's pray, okay? We really need some divine direction here."

"From the sound of things, maybe it's already starting," said Grace. "But could we ask for some handwriting on the wall or something?

I'm frightened to death for Brad and the children. And my blood runs cold when I think of Brandenbury. He's been bigger than life to me for so long that the very thought of facing him again ... I know I have to, and I don't know if I can. Does that make any sense? We need to be certain for their sakes. And we're really just best guessing as to where we think they are. I'm scared, that's all. Terrified actually."

"And well you should be after all he's put you through," agreed Cain. "Here. Take my hands. Let's pray together."

For a few moments, the two women joined hands with John Cain and bowed their heads, quietly voicing prayers to Jesus, asking him to provide them with strength and courage and guidance. Then they asked for divine protection for Brad and David and Nancy. Their hands pressed together in an affirmation of unity as they concluded.

"Now, we need to find an airline," Maggie said. "Maybe Delta would be good. They fly into the South a lot. I think Atlanta or Raleigh-Durham is their headquarters. If they don't have something flying right away, I'll find out who else goes there. We want the fastest connection possible."

"And I'd suggest you drive a ways first," said Cain. "You have a car?"

"Yes."

"Don't try to fly out of Palm Springs. Too obvious. Go to Ontario or LAX. Or even Phoenix. That's a four hour drive from here but that might be a good thing."

Twenty minutes later, Maggie hung up the phone for the last time. Their best connection had turned out to be with Delta Airlines out of Phoenix. "Okay, we've got reservations to Atlanta. It leaves at six-thirty. That means we've got to move fast. We're fifteen minutes from the freeway at this time of night. From there it's about three and a half hours to the Phoenix."

397

"Well, we haven't unpacked anything so let's go. I've got to get gas!"

They hurried back to their room, gathered up their belongings and ran for the car.

Exactly twelve minutes later they were accelerating out of the Washington Street loop in Palm Desert and speeding east along I-10.

"What happens in Atlanta?"

"We'll connect with Paul. Get out of Atlanta as soon as possible and head for Asheville, North Carolina."

Grace expelled a deep breath. "Well, I'll say this, Maggie, when you start rolling, things do pick up speed."

"Pray for a good tailwind and no slow-ups along the way. I'm not sure about which concourse is which after we get there, but we're going to need a fast track through the airport."

"The police are going to be swarming all over our church office," Grace spoke in low tones as they swept past a tractor-trailer, and she set the cruise control at eighty. "In fact, they may already have been there and gone. And before we get to Atlanta, Jim and Kaylin will have been wondering why I didn't show up for work."

"First things first. You'd better keep an eye out for the CHP, girl. We can't afford the time if we're pulled over, much less the cost of a ticket. And we sure don't want to have to answer any questions that would tie us to what we did with Reynolds. Not yet anyway."

"We should have just left him there," declared Grace, her voice tinged with bitterness and defeat.

"Grace."

"I know, I know. I'll just keep driving and try not to get us stopped for speeding."

Grace's eyes automatically sought out headlights visible in the rear view mirror. Maggie was right, of course, but now that a decision had been made, there was no way she was going to miss their connection. Not if Brad and the children were at the other end of their journey. *Oh, Lord, please let it be so.* Traffic was light as they cruised out into the open desert. She surveyed the taillights ahead. Nothing that looked like a highway patrolman. At least not yet.

If God was watching, and she hoped that he was, Grace knew they were already in serious trouble. She and Maggie had broken more than enough laws of both God and man during the last three or four hours. She speculated on how the Almighty might be viewing their situation right now. She shut her eyes for a second, as if to close out the reality of her nightmare, before opening them again. If they lived through this, maybe she'd be able to figure it all out later. *Who am I kidding? The odds of living through all this are slim. But I don't care anymore!*

The road stretched on into the darkness as Grace kept her foot against the accelerator, and the speedometer inched past eighty-five.

68

"Hi, Maggie, good to see you again."

"And you as well, Paul," Maggie responded with a hug and a kiss on his cheek.

"Did you two come on angel's wings or what? Look at me. I hung up the phone, bought a ticket off the Internet, kissed Melody and the kids good-bye—and got here barely an hour ahead of you. Just enough time to take care of a car rental. And you had farther to travel than I did."

Paul Jacobsen was about Maggie's height, thin and round-shouldered, a receding hairline, and eyes behind wire-rimmed glasses that Grace could already feel probing her psyche. He didn't examine her as some men did, lecherously reviewing the contours of her body. Instead she was conscious of him searching her eyes, as though seeking to uncover whatever secrets might be hidden there. She knew he was sizing her up, trying to decide whether or not the story he'd been introduced to a few hours ago could really be believed.

"We didn't have angel's wings, but I am traveling with my pastor's fiancé. Maybe that's a good angel substitute. Grace, meet Paul Jacobsen, as good an investigative reporter as you'll ever get to know." Paul extended his hand as Maggie continued. "Until recently, as I told you over the phone, Grace has been known to us as Taylor

Carroll. However, seven years ago she was Grace Nicole Grafton, a young student about to graduate from Georgia Southern University with her Master's degree in Business Management. That's when all hell broke loose, Paul. She was forced to run for her life and has lived under an assumed name ever since."

"Pleased to meet you. Are you answering to Grace now? Or Taylor?"

"Grace. I'm actually having to get used to it again," Grace responded, embarrassed, accepting his hand. "It's been a while."

It was a small hand, almost feminine in smoothness. No calluses. But, there was firmness in his handshake. All the while, his unswerving gaze studied her eyes—she thought perhaps seeking the slightest indication that she might not live up to the verbal credentials Maggie had given her over the phone. It was beginning to make her uncomfortable. "I've been Taylor for so long that I'm not sure anymore who Grace is—or was. But I am trying to be Grace again, so Grace is fine."

"Grace it is then. You ladies have any luggage?" Paul asked, looking away at last as he pointed them toward the exit.

"What you see is what we've got," Maggie said.

"Good. Then, let's get out of here." Paul spoke rapidly as they hurried along the carpeted walkway leading toward the ATL SkyTrain. A few minutes later and they were at the rental car center.

"Wait here. The police may be looking for you by now, but not for me. Just stay back until I have the keys. Then follow me to the car."

Paul went to the Alamo desk and handed the woman behind the desk the rental contract that had already been completed inside the terminal. She glanced at the license number scrawled on the folder and handed Paul a set of keys.

Maggie and Grace followed Paul at a distance until they saw him

401

pause behind a blue Chevy Aveo and look their way. They hurried the rest of the way and jumped in. As Paul backed out of the parking stall, their conversation picked up again as if there had been no break.

"I know it's small but so is my travel allowance," Paul said as the others settled in. "The guy offered me a red one, but I figured that would be on every cop's radar just for being red." Once past the lot gate they moved easily into the traffic flow leaving the airport. "Anyway, before I left, I took the liberty of checking back through some newspaper archives to corroborate your story, Grace. The telephone, the computer, and the Internet are the most wonderful inventions known to a journalist. Don't take it personally. Same goes for you, Maggie. I'm paid to be suspicious of everything and everyone, and I always check my sources. I also called a reporter friend of mine in LA and asked if there was anything unusual coming out of the Coachella Valley this morning."

"And?" Maggie asked.

"I took his return call about thirty minutes ago. He told me the police found an unidentified man in a Palm Springs church last night. Person or persons unknown had kayoed the guy. Somebody made a 911 call—a woman's voice—and then split. They found a gun. Fired once. No one else around." Paul looked intently at Maggie. "The guy they found apparently has one humongous headache from a blow to the back of his skull. As of early this morning, he is still in the hospital and has not regained consciousness. What did you say you hit him with?"

Maggie shuddered involuntarily. "A skillet. Cast iron. I hope I didn't ... "

"I'm sorry. You probably feel bad, but don't worry too much. According to my friend, the guy appears to have gotten off one shot. They think he is probably a pro—had an ankle holster and everything.

His source says the gun was still there, and they dug a slug out of a wall. They'll do a check on it, but they believe it came from the weapon they found. And there were no other bodies.

"Whoever nailed the guy tied him up and then left. Police think it was probably their mysterious caller. The mysterious caller with a hot hand and a cold skillet. They have her voice on the 911, though. They also found a lone car in the church parking lot. A rental. It probably belongs to your friend. The church secretary found the cops there when she arrived for work."

"Poor Karen," exclaimed Grace.

"It gets even more mysterious," Paul continued. "Turns out the pastor of this church is called away from a dinner engagement on Monday at a Mexican restaurant in Burbank. Two state troopers were there asking for him. Then *he* disappears—along with the troopers—leaving behind a couple of dead bodies in the parking lot. An off-duty cop and his girlfriend. Shot to death."

"Did you know about those people in the parking lot?" Maggie asked, looking at Grace. Grace shook her head, her eyes filling with tears.

"Nobody knows anything regarding this missing pastor's whereabouts," Paul continued. "It's like the Second Coming took place, and he was the only one who got called up. They have his name. Brad Weston. Got it from his dinner companions who turned in the missing person report in the first place. Didn't show up back at his hotel room. He simply vanished. The cops impounded his car. It's still in Burbank.

"At first, the cops are so busy with the double homicide that they don't think much about the missing Rev. But when the guy never shows up the next day—not at his home or at the church where he's the priest ... "

"Minister," Grace interrupted. "Actually, he's the pastor. There are no priests in our church."

"All right then. Sorry. The priest thing. It's my Catholic upbringing showing through. Anyway, they start asking themselves, what's going on? So, they check with the CHP, and there's nothing. No record of any of troopers going to that restaurant on a call of any kind. It's a big mystery. There are witnesses who swear they saw the officers. The hostess is positive that this Weston fellow left with them. They walked out the door together. So what happened in the parking lot? Did the preacher kill these people? Were they fake cops? Did anyone see what happened? Did the real killers take the preacher hostage? And why would they do that? Or did he somehow turn the tables on two legitimate law enforcement peeps. It's a mystery. It's like there has been a total disappearing act. Nobody has a clue."

"We do," said Grace, gazing out the window at landscape so beautiful it hurt her to look at it, its lovely, rolling hills and trees splintered by myriad freeways, flooding her mind with familiar scenes. This was the place of her childhood, her growing-up years. She felt like a released soul coming home after having been imprisoned on the far away planet Pandora. Yet there was an unsettling strangeness about it all at the same time.

"Okay, so do I. At least I think I do," agreed Paul.

"Did you tell your friend you were meeting us?" asked Maggie.

"He wanted to know what I knew about all this. Why was I so interested? I told him I'd get back to him later. He knows I'm onto something, but I'm sure he hasn't a clue yet as to what. Or even how I might have a story cooking this far away from where the pot's heated up. But there's more, so let me finish."

"Before you do, where are we going?" asked Grace, unable to resist being amused at Paul's picturesque metaphors. She could readily see why Maggie liked him.

"There's a Best Western in Asheville. I've booked a couple of rooms there. You can freshen up and we can decide what 'Plan A' is going to be. I've got to tell you, if everything you say checks out, Maggie, we are sitting next to the biggest story of the decade. I mean Clinton had his Jennifer Flowers and Paula Jones debacles, and there's Edwards and Woods, but *this* ... "

Grace looked away, ashamed at being matched in this reporter's thinking to the tawdriness of the alleged affairs attached to these international figures. Maggie, perhaps sensing Grace's discomfort, gave her a reassuring look.

In the same instant, Paul must have realized the insensitivity of his comment. "Sorry," he said, glancing back at Grace in the mirror. "I didn't mean it to sound like ..."

"It's okay," she replied. "It's the kind of connection I imagine a lot of people will probably be making if this all comes out."

"Not 'if,' but 'when,' trust me on that. If everything you are saying is true, when this hits the fan, it will be mega big time. Anyway, as I was saying," Paul continued as the car accelerated onto an on-ramp and headed north on the Interstate toward Asheville. "The Reverend Brad Weston has vanished, leaving two bodies behind in beautiful downtown Burbank. Then this morning another guy shows up in the Reverend's church out in the Springs, bound and beaten."

"I only hit him once," Maggie said defensively.

"Whatever. Anyway, the cops try to reach the Reverend's home without any luck. They even go to the house, but nobody's there. It's empty. No minister. No kids. No nothing. When the church secretary shows, she tries calling her boss. No answer. So she wants to talk to the woman he's been dating and see if she knows anything about what is going on. There's no answer there either. Then she calls the department store where this woman works. She's not checked in which is unusual because she's never late, they say. In fact, this is her week to open up the department she works in, so she usually shows up a half-hour early to do whatever she has to do.

"Finally, the secretary calls the daycare center where the Carroll's two kids stay while the parents are working. They were picked up the day before by one Mary Magdelene Hinegardner, well-known ethics and religion guru for the *Desert Sun*. She takes the kids and heads out.

"Then someone calls Ms. Hinegardner's home. No answer there either. They call the newspaper where Ms. Hinegardner works. She's not at work. No one has seen her. The police uncover an accident report involving Ms. Hinegardner the day before. They check the hospital, but she's been released. She's nowhere to be found. And no kids either. Any connection to all of these mysterious goings-on? They have no idea. But people are disappearing or being murdered at a fairly fast clip here—even for California.

"So, the police have now got two dead bodies in Burbank and one unidentified guy in the hospital in Palm Springs. Then there's the Rev, his girlfriend or fiancé or whatever, his two kids—*and* Ms. Mary Magdalene Hinegardner. They've all disappeared. Vanished into thin air, without a trace. I mean, things are *happening* in sleepy little Palm Springs! Tell me you didn't use your real names on your airline ticket purchase."

"No choice. We had to use our credit cards. Didn't have enough to pay cash. Besides, airline security is super strict these days. You know that."

"I figured as much. That's why I wanted to get away from the airport as fast as possible. The police will be 'scouring the neighborhood,' as they say on TV. They'll be looking for the Rev, his girlfriend, and his family—and you, too, Maggie."

"Mr. Jacobsen, please," Grace's voice was tinged with irritation. "Could you stop referring to the man I love as 'the Rev?' His name is Brad."

"Sorry. And my name is Paul. Okay?"

"Of course. I'm sorry, too. It's been a long couple of nights."

"So, what we've got to do from here on is be very careful. By now, the police and the FBI and anyone else in the law enforcement industry know you bought tickets to Atlanta. I'm surprised they weren't standing in the exit to greet you. You may have just missed them. So let's not get picked up before we've had a chance to do our thing."

"And just what is 'our thing?'" asked Grace.

"That's what we've got to figure out. The drive time is about three and a half hours, so I'd suggest you both catch a little shuteye. In Asheville, we'll give you a chance to freshen up. I've made a couple of phone calls. Been checking around a bit. When we get there, we'll check again. Need to determine how things may have changed in the world in the last hour or so."

Three hours and fifteen minutes later, Paul Jacobsen swung the car off the freeway and into the motel parking lot. Maggie and Grace went straight to their room and spent the better part of the next hour showering and drying their hair. They had slept very little on both the flight from Phoenix to Atlanta and on the drive up. The red in their eyes, particularly Grace's, was pronounced. She could feel weariness and tension weighing on her like a heavy blanket. She looked at the bed, longing to climb in, knowing all the while that sleep was not an option.

Maggie was running the hair dryer when a sharp knock on the outer door caused Grace to jump. She hesitated, unsure as to whether

407

or not to open it until she heard Paul's voice and quickly let him in.

"Good news and bad news," Paul declared as he plopped down on the nearest chair. "The good news is my cell phone is still working. It hasn't run out of battery yet. Only I forgot to put in the charger when I threw my things together. Anyway, from the looks of you two, at least the shower is operational."

The hair dryer noise had stopped and Maggie stood in the bathroom doorway listening.

"Anyway, the bad news is that the police got hold of your picture, Grace. They've run it through and matched it along with some fingerprints you left behind at the … at your fiancé's house with a certain Grace Nicole Grafton who has been missing and was believed dead for the past seven years. Seems she vanished the night her roommates were killed in a boat stolen from none other than our very own Mr. Charles Brandenbury.

"About the time she disappeared, her mother was found murdered in Atlanta. You didn't tell me about that, Maggie," he said, glancing over at her. Then he turned back to Grace. "Sorry. It was labeled a drug killing. The police initially had suspected that she or the daughter were somehow mixed up in small-time drug dealing. Seems drugs and some money were found in your mother's apartment and drugs and alcohol were also in the boat from which your friends' bodies were recovered. Anyway, now we've got this whole string of dead bodies stretching over a seven-year period *and* the sudden resurrection of one Grace Nicole Grafton. By the way, there's a BOLO out on you … "

"A BOLO?"

"A 'Be On The Lookout.' The authorities have a few questions they'd like to ask. Like why have you been living under an alias for the last seven years? And what's your connection to all these dead and missing people? Things like that. They think you might know something about all these murders. Isn't that an amazing bit of detective work? There's some conjecture that maybe you're some kind of mad killer and that more bodies may be scattered over the countryside, just waiting to be found."

"Me?" Grace felt her heart sink.

"The police, and by now the FBI, probably know that you two left Phoenix together on a plane bound for Atlanta. It won't take them long to follow you here. What the authorities don't know is whether or not our Ms. Maggie here left California of her own free will or maybe the enigmatic Taylor Nicole Carroll, nee Grace Nicole Grafton, has kidnapped her, too. Or, because they're reportedly such good friends, maybe they're in cahoots together. Maggie and Grace like *Thelma and Louise.*"

"That's absurd." Maggie declared from the doorway. "What possible motive could we have?"

"I don't know—but do you think anyone really cares? The law enforcement folks are not going to take to this lightly. They smell something big going on here. They just don't know what. And one of the several bodies connected in one way or another to Grace here—that cop in LA? That's one of their own. Maybe they're witnessing the resurrection of a female serial killer. Or maybe there was an extraordinary offering on Sunday, and you took it and ran."

"Be serious, Paul."

"Stranger things have happened," he assured them.

"So what are we going to do?" asked Maggie.

"I'd suggest you finish getting dressed," Paul said dryly, "unless you plan on drawing attention to us right off the bat when we leave here."

Maggie's face colored with embarrassment. She'd been so engrossed in this latest turn of events that she had forgotten what stage of readiness she was in. Without a word, she grabbed her blouse from the closet hanger and disappeared into the bathroom.

"It's dangerous for us to stay here," Paul declared. "As soon as you're both ready, we've got to head on up the road. It will be a while before the police manage to connect you to me. I'm a wild card. They won't be looking for my car rental. They can't possibly know we're together. Not yet anyway. I registered us under different names, one room as 'Mr. and Mrs.,' and the other as a single woman. I also left a bogus car license number and paid cash. But, who knows. They might get lucky. Maybe someone spots you and recognizes your picture. Or maybe security cameras at the airport pick you out. They might even see us together. We need to move on."

Maggie reappeared, running a comb along the sides of her graying hair. "Where are we going?"

"If you're ready, out that door and into the car. Can you remember what you've touched since we got here? Try to wipe away any prints. If you miss one—well, that's tough. If the cops do show up here, and I expect they will sooner or later, let's at least make them work for it. We need time."

Hurriedly both women moved around the room wiping the closet, the desk, the bathroom, the door and door handle, anything they remembered having touched.

"Do you think they'll put together the fact that we're looking for Brandenbury?" asked Grace.

Paul shrugged. "Hard to say. The only thing that connects you is the boat that you and your friends allegedly stole way back when. I guess Brandenbury was in Savannah at the time, but maybe it'll take them a while to make the connection. That was a long time ago. They probably think you came back to meet someone you knew in Atlanta. It was your home. They'll be digging, though, that's for sure. And as prominent a figure as he is—well, who knows. They'll likely put it together eventually. Okay. Are you ready?"

They nodded and started toward the door.

"You've double-checked to be sure you've left nothing behind."

"Yep."

"Then let's get out of here and out of this town as fast as our little rental car can take us."

69

The small cafe was situated on a side road overlooking Interstate 70 near an off-ramp fifteen miles north of Asheville. Paul had spotted it from the freeway, taken the off-ramp, then doubled back across the overpass and pulled off the frontage road onto a graveled parking surface near the entrance.

Minutes after placing their orders and taking turns in the restroom, the trio gathered around a rectangular Formica-top table and stared out a window blotched with rain spots. On the freeway below, the northbound traffic flowed with hypnotic monotony along the asphalt ribbon. Cars and trucks disappearing into a sea of green rolling hills capped with a glass-like rooftop of brilliant blue sky. A halcyon setting, serene, at peace with itself and the rest of the world. On any other day, a vacationer's paradise. But not this day.

Today was a day for desperadoes. That was what Grace felt like. A day for being unsure of which side of the law you were really on. Or whether the law really mattered after all. It was compromised. She couldn't trust it. By now she was a wanted person. Assault. Kidnapping. Murder. A social pariah. A spiritual leper. Throw whatever else on the pile you could think of. Liar. Coward. Deceiver ...

The clanging of a pan dropping into the stainless steel sink behind the counter caused Grace to flinch, drawing her back to the scene inside the café. The heavy-set woman who had taken their orders was busy at the grill. A pair of grizzled old men perched on two of the six well-worn red leather stools that were bolted to the floor. They leaned into the counter, chewing away on their meal, ignoring the napkin holder in front of them, preferring to wipe now and then at their chins with shirtsleeves while washing their food down with bottles of Bud.

"Need another beer, Hank?" the woman called over her shoulder.

"Nope. Doin' fine, Hattie, thank yew," the one on the left answered, massaging a mouthful of hamburger at the same time.

"How 'bout you, Carl?" she asked, reaching to the overhead shelf for the salt container.

"No, ma'am. This here'll do it for me."

Grace, Maggie, and Paul breathed in the sounds and smells of chicken frying, hamburgers sizzling and French fries sputtering in a basket of cooking oil, turning the thin, but incontestable odor of grease into a savory mixture of smells that came to rest on the inner lining of each patron's nose.

"Brandenbury's farm is supposed to be up that valley, three, maybe four miles," said Paul, breaking the silence at last and pointing out the window in the direction of a road leading eastward through the surrounding hills, away from the Interstate. Grace could make out a small ramshackle farmhouse and a couple of outbuildings from where she sat. He continued, "I'm not sure just how far, but we're pretty close. I googled a picture on my computer, so we'll know it when we see it. There's a gate. After the others get here, I vote we drive up the valley until we find it. That will give us the lay of the land to see what to do about gaining access without setting off any alarms."

413

"Alarms?" She hadn't thought about alarms.

"Yeah, security will be pretty heavy on the property. Brandenbury isn't the kind of guy who welcomes strangers in for a free home tour."

The cook shambled around the corner of the lunch bar and headed in their direction with an awkward, rolling gait, her hands and arms laden with a full cargo of food. She obviously intended on making only one trip. A green salad for Grace. A small breadbasket with little paper-covered butter patties perched on top. Soup and a half tuna sandwich for Maggie. A cheeseburger and fries for Paul. She refilled their glasses with more iced sweet tea.

"Anythin' else, hon?" she asked, looking at Paul.

"Not at the moment, Hattie," Paul answered. Grace was impressed that he remembered the woman's name. "Maybe you can bring us the check. We have to get on down the road shortly."

"No problem," the woman wheezed, her breath coming in short little gasps. Reaching into her apron, she whipped out a pad and pencil, squinted, and wrote furiously, looking for all intents and purposes like Lebron James on his way to a slam dunk. With a flourish bordering on elegance, she tore the bill from the pad and presented it to Paul. "There you are, darlin'. Y'all enjoy your meal now, y'hear?"

"I'm sure we will," said Paul as he poured ketchup onto his plate and proceeded to pick out an attack point for the oversized cheeseburger. The woman smiled, heaved her bulk to the right, and turned back toward the grill. Paul lifted the bun and paused as juice dripped down his fingers onto the plate. "What's ahead may be dangerous, but probably not any more than this sandwich, do you think?"

The others chuckled, the moment's tension easing somewhat, along with the realization that it had been a while since their last meal. "It's not the Cliff House," Maggie remarked as she lifted a spoonful of greasy, vegetable beef soup to her lips, "but it will do for now."

Grace shuddered as Paul bit into his hamburger, then tried turning her attention to the salad. Her thoughts were not on food. She kept seeing their faces.

Brad's concerned look on Monday, when he caught her staring at the calendar.

He knew something was wrong—and I put him off.

David's curiosity over the anonymous letter with her picture enclosed.

I'm sure he sensed something, too. He's so quiet and thoughtful—he just put it away in his mind somewhere.

And Nancy. Dear, sweet, lovable Nancy.

Even she was upset when I awakened her talking to The Voice. *Are you okay? You sounded angry. I love you, Taylor ...*

"Come on, Grace." The sound of Paul's voice snapped her preoccupation. "Eat. We've all got to maintain our energy." He pushed the basket of bread toward her. "Here. Get some of this bread down. It may be a while 'til we get to our next meal."

"What do you think the chances are that Brandenbury will be here?" asked Maggie.

"That's the word I got at the dinner last night."

"Do you think Brad and the children are here, too? I mean, they could be anywhere, couldn't they?"

Paul looked across at Grace for a moment before taking another bite. Then his gaze returned to the window.

"You're right. They could be anywhere. But, I think," he said, pausing to swallow, "it's highly possible that they're here."

Grace's heart skipped a beat.

"I've been giving this a good deal of thought since you called last night. Unless I miss my guess, if he really does have them, he'll want to keep them close. Within easy reach. It could be the reason he was coming back here rather than staying over in Washington. On the other hand, maybe he just likes to sleep in his own bed. Who knows?"

"Maybe we do need to call the FBI or something," said Grace, lost in thought, fiddling with her fork in the salad.

The others looked up at her.

"You're not serious, are you?" asked Maggie, leaning forward as she stared at Grace.

"Well, I just don't see how we can pull this off. Do you? The closer we get, the more impossible this looks. I mean, really. Brandenbury is no fool. If he's got them here, they'll be guarded for sure. How will we ever get close enough to get them away from him?" Grace's eyes grew moist with apprehension. "If anything happens to them ... " Her voice trailed off.

Paul reached over and placed his hand over hers.

"Don't lose your nerve, Grace. Trust me, you're going to need it. All of it. From everything you've told me, there's no way we can bring in the FBI. Or anybody else for that matter. Not yet. And your friends are coming, right? Reinforcements. When they get here, we can decide best options. Besides, you're the prime suspect, not Brandenbury or Parker or that other guy you mentioned.

"Itana?"

"Yeah, that one. What we have to do is try to find your fiance and kids and recover them safely. That's our goal. Don't lose sight of that one thing. We're here to get them back. Okay?"

Grace blinked and tried to smile. She nodded. "Thanks. I understand. You're right, of course. It's just that I'm so ... so frightened. Not for me. Not anymore. I don't really care what happens to me. I'm fearful for Brad and the kids ... and for both of you. And now Pastor Cain and his friend. This isn't any of your battles. You shouldn't even be here taking such risks with your lives. So many people have already died. Innocent people. Some I don't even know. How can I ever live with myself if something happens to either of you?"

"We're here by choice, Grace," Maggie said, glancing at Paul, the seriousness evident in her tone. "Our choice. It's as simple as that. And we're going to be here with you until this is finished, and we can all go home."

"This slime-bucket and his Senate lackey are up to their ears in a presidential campaign, Grace," Paul reminded her. "What's happened to you will undoubtedly be repeated on an ever-grander scale if he succeeds in gaining power. And then there's this Itana guy. If he really is *the* Marwan Dosha, then these guys are all linked to terrorism big time. And so are you. You just didn't know it until now. I know it's difficult for you to think about this in global terms, with so much and so many you care for at risk right now. It sounds hokey to say it, but America has a lot riding on this, too. Shades of Osama bin Laden!"

Muffled sounds of ringing sounded off in Maggie's purse on the floor by her chair. Then it stopped. She reached for the phone just as it began ringing again. Glancing at the screen, she put it to her ear and listened for what seemed like a long time to Grace, but was in reality a few seconds, before pushing the 'end call' button and looking at the others. "They're about ten minutes from here. They'll meet us just off the freeway on the valley road."

Grace fell silent, staring at her salad. Then, taking a deep breath, she exhaled, nodding with a wan smile. "Okay, then. Let's go do it."

"First, eat some more of your salad," Paul admonished. "While I go pay our bill."

Grace reached for her purse, but Paul waved her off. "Eat. This one's on me. You can buy the victory steaks."

70

Herschel Winslow Towner III lowered the field glasses he'd packed in his suitcase before leaving home that morning. The five of them were crouched down on the ground, behind a small knoll, invisible to anyone across the valley who might by chance look in their direction.

"May I?" Grace put out her hand for the glasses.

They had been at this location for half an hour, having driven off the main asphalt road onto a dirt lane that looked as though it served a farmhouse well beyond them, up the side of the hill behind this one. No one had come up or down the lane since they had arrived. Both rental cars were parked off to one side in a swale beneath two large trees, hidden from the valley below and difficult even to spot from the side road.

Already each of them had taken several turns gazing through the high-powered lenses at magnified images of the Brandenbury Arabian Horse Farm across the valley road. The only apparent sign of human life so far had been the security guard, who every now and then wandered outside the confines of the small gatehouse to smoke a cigarette. Since their vigil had begun, no one had entered or left the premises. The sun was lower on the horizon, and in less than two hours, would drop behind the hills altogether. All at once, there was movement along the riverside of the property.

"Hold it," Grace exclaimed, pressing the glasses closer to her face, "I see something. Dogs! I see dogs along the fence line." She handed the binoculars back to Towner who quickly brought them to his eyes.

"You're right. Two of them. Look like Dobes. Big rascals, too, and I'll bet they're mean and noisy." He searched along the easterly fence line. "Yeah ... okay. Two more on the east side. They must have been in a kennel. They let them run at night between those two fence lines. I'll bet there are some more on the other sides of the property as well. Just what we need."

Paul looked at the women. "Well, I told you Brandenbury would be tight on security, didn't I? But, dogs? I never figured dogs."

"Here, let me have the glasses again," said Maggie. She looked through the lenses before handing them back to Towner. "Someone's leaving."

A limousine slowly made its way from the top of the hill toward the gate. Towner watched as it rolled along at a leisurely pace until reaching the gate. The guard was standing outside the gatehouse in full view as the limo approached. It slowed, but did not come to a complete stop as the guard waved a greeting. He bent down to say something to the driver as the car passed under the entry sign, but they were much too far away to make out their conversation.

"What do you think?" Maggie asked as Towner lowered the glasses.

The car turned left onto the roadway and began moving in the direction of the Interstate.

"Couldn't see inside. I say let's follow," declared Towner, scrambling to his feet. "Brandenbury may be going somewhere. John,

Grace, come with me. Paul, you and Maggie stay here and keep an eye out for more movement. Your cell phone still working?"

"Yes," Paul said, disappointment in his voice over being left behind.

"If he is on the move, maybe we can find out where and why," said John as they ran toward the hidden cars. "Who knows? Maybe we'll get lucky and kidnap him."

They ran back to the dirt lane. Crossing over, Grace stumbled, nearly falling, as they hurried to where the car was hidden among the trees.

"Quick. We'll take this one." Towner urged them on as he slid behind the wheel of the tan-colored Infiniti M35 that he and John had rented at Ashville's Regional Airport. "Come on!"

"We have no weapons," Grace reminded the others. "Maggie had one but she left it in my car at the airport."

"You what?" Towner looked at Grace. "She had a gun and you left it in your car? Did you have it at the church?"

Grace nodded.

"If you had it with you, why didn't you just shoot the guy?"

"I guess Maggie thought she was better with a skillet," Grace said lamely. "We had no choice about leaving it behind. We certainly couldn't take it on the plane."

"Couldn't you have at least thrown it away somewhere? I suppose it's got Maggie's fingerprints all over it, too."

Grace didn't answer.

"Okay, lighten up a little, everyone, and let's focus," urged John. "We're doing our best. All of us."

The car's wheels churned up dirt and gravel as Towner guided it up the slope and onto the dirt lane. They raced down to the main road as fast as they could without attracting undue attention. Towner made a right turn onto the highway and sped off after the limo, already lost from sight for three or four minutes.

They drove in silence, each person harboring their own thoughts, knowing there was no master plan—they were out on the edge in this, following their instincts, grasping at straws and little else.

"There!" John pointed ahead just as the limo disappeared over a hill. "We're gaining on them."

"What if they're going to Asheville ... or someplace beyond?" asked Grace. "Are we just going to follow them until they stop somewhere?"

Towner did not respond. Nor did John. *What in the name of peace are we doing here anyway?*

"Look," John exclaimed. "See that? They're turning in. We're in luck. They must be getting gas."

Towner slowed the car and turned off the highway, pulling in behind the limousine. The station, complete with two bright Irish green pumps did not appear to have credit card capability. A sign said simply, *Pay Inside*.

Towner turned off the engine and got out. He studied the gas pumps, pretending to determine what was required and which one he wanted to use. In so doing, he was sizing up the situation in the car in front of him. The windows were tinted, and he could not see inside. The front door on the driver's side had been left ajar, however, suggesting that the limo might be empty.

Towner looked behind him to find that Grace had stepped out of the car and, without waiting for the others, started walking toward the grocery store. He raised his hand to wave her back, but it was too late. A man pushed open the screen door, fumbling with his wallet as he walked out of the store. He had to be the driver.

"Excuse me."

The man looked up with a startled expression. "Excuse me,

421

ma'am," he said, stepping aside politely. "I was tryin' to get this credit card back where it belongs. I 'pologize. I surely didn' see you."

"No apology necessary. I just need some help. My friends and I have been wandering around these back roads for the last couple of hours. We got off the Interstate to check out the scenery, and now we're lost."

Towner smiled to himself at her initiative. And courage. She was diverting the guy's attention so that he could check out the car. He moved away from the pump and edged up alongside the limo, all the while keeping the driver in his line of vision—just in case. He heard the man explaining to Grace where the main highway was and that, in fact, she was not far from it.

"Could you show me exactly where we are on a map? Do they have one inside?"

"As a matter of fact, they do, ma'am. It's on the wall right inside the door. Come on, an' I'll show you." The man turned and opened the screen door for Grace. They disappeared inside.

Towner took a deep breath, wondered what he would say if someone really was sitting inside the car, then ducked his head through the door. A quick look revealed that it was empty. He'd guessed as much with the casual attitude of the driver who'd been easily distracted by Grace and who seemed in no hurry to drive away.

The limousine's interior was a rich combination of cloth, leather and even some wood. Maybe it wasn't real wood. Towner wasn't sure. It didn't matter though. This was the plushest car he had seen in awhile, even working with the megabucks folk at Microsoft back in Seattle. He pushed the unlock button and heard the rest of the door locks release. Then he leaned across and opened the glove compartment. No gloves—but there was something even more useful. A shiny, blue-black Colt .45 ACP. Towner withdrew it from the compartment. A

422

quick check revealed that it was fully loaded. Interesting.

He lowered the compartment lid and was backing out of the car when he noticed that, instead of locking shut, it had flipped open again. As he reached over to close it, his elbow brushed against the horn. It only honked for an instant, but it seemed like an eternity! Hurriedly he pushed himself out the door, dropped down between the car and the gas pumps, opened the rear door and scrambled inside on the floor behind the driver's seat. His heart pounded as he lifted his head to look out the tinted window. *Not the brightest move I've ever made.*

The driver had emerged from the store and was halfway to the car, walking rapidly. Just then, another horn honked—once, twice, three times, and Towner saw the driver hesitate The car horns actually emitted two very different sounds. Enough so they could not be mistaken under normal circumstances. But the driver had been inside, too busy, at least Towner hoped, in pointing out the route to a lovely young woman. Now, hearing and seeing a man honking the horn in the car parked directly behind, the driver stopped short, confused.

Grace diverted his attention further still as she stepped past the screen door. "Thank you, Mr. Jones," she called out after him.

He turned and smiled. "My pleasure, ma'am." Then he continued around the front of the limo and stood by the driver's door. He got in, leaning back in the seat as he fastened the safety belt. The instant he started the engine, he glanced at the open glove compartment. Leaning over and looking in, he swore under his breath. "Where's the gun?"

A split second later, Towner answered that question. He pressed the gun's barrel firmly against the base of the driver's neck. "I think this is what you were looking for, Mr. Jones." Towner spoke quietly from close behind the man's right ear. "You would do well to drive out of here as though nothing is out of the ordinary. Don't signal. Don't blow the horn. Anything unusual, and I will blow your head off with your own gun. And the car you see behind us? Those are my friends. You've already met one of them."

The limousine rolled away from the gas pumps slowly, on its path to the roadway.

"So where we headed?" asked Jones, evoking an amazingly calm attitude for someone with a gun at the back of his head.

Towner's mind was racing. "To the right. Toward the freeway. Only go on under the freeway to the opposite side. Keep going until we can find a nice quiet place to talk."

"What you got on your mind, mister? I sure hope it ain't nothin' as serious as you look. If you want the car, you kin have it, you know. Be my guest."

"Look, Mr. Jones ... that is your name, right?"

"Harold Justiss Jones ... thas' right."

"Okay if I call you Harold?"

"You got the gun. You kin call me whatever you like."

"All right, Harold. I don't want to hurt you. I ... we just want some information ... and I imagine you can provide us with just about everything we need to know. So keep on driving, and I'll tell you when to stop."

"That nice lady back there ... you say she's your friend?"

"She is today. I've only known her a few hours myself. But she's in trouble, Harold. Big trouble."

"Looks to me like we's all got some trouble here. An' you think I kin help y'all with yours? I ain't got but a few dollars, mister—you're welcome to 'em, though, no sweat—my credit card, too."

"We don't want your money, Harold. Just your help."

"You sure got a funny way of askin'."

424

"There's the freeway up ahead. Go on under."

"You got it."

"And, please, Harold—keep both hands where I can see them. Don't try to be a hero. If you do what I ask, you won't be hurt. I promise."

"I always try to believe the promises of the man with the gun," Jones replied.

Just then a car phone attached to the dashboard began to ring.

Jones glanced up at Towner's image in the mirror.

"Is that your boss?"

"Maybe."

"Don't answer it."

It continued ringing four more times.

On the opposite side of the freeway, they came up on the little community of Jupiter, a clutter of houses, mobile homes and miscellaneous cars, trucks and boats, all scattered throughout tree-covered hills with no apparent rhyme or reason. About a mile and a half up the road, Towner saw a large yellow building on the right with an unpaved open area surrounding it.

"Pull over there, Harold, and keep the driver's side away from the road."

The vehicle rolled to a stop.

"Get out. Stand over by the railing. But move slowly, and keep your hands where I can see them."

"You got it," the driver responded in an obliging tone. Towner was not impressed. He was certain that Jones' every instinct was on alert and that he would try to overpower him the moment he saw the slightest opening. Towner didn't intend to give him one.

A minute later, the two men were joined by Grace and John Cain.

The sign over the entrance to the yellow building announced that it belonged to the Jupiter Volunteer Fire Department. There were four large doors behind which Towner assumed the community's firefighting trucks were housed. In back of the building, he could see a diesel fuel tank and a garbage bin. An American flag on a pole in front of the pedestrian entrance fluttered gently in the warm breeze. It didn't appear that anyone else was about.

To the left of where the cars were parked, the property fell off sharply into a steep ravine. The hills and the trees on either side looked pleasant enough, and on any other day this might have been an enjoyable respite. Today's tension, however, made relishing such a moment impossible.

"Turn around."

Jones turned to face the ravine. Towner passed the handgun to Cain.

"I've given the gun to my friend here. He's an expert shot. I know from first-hand experience with him in Iran. And the lady and her friend are whiz kids with cast iron skillets, too, as one of your shoddy little friends found out yesterday in Palm Springs. I just thought you'd want to know that."

Towner proceeded to run his hands over the driver's clothing and down each leg. Satisfied there were no concealed weapons, he backed away.

"John, go over to the limo and sit there on the edge of the driver's seat. Keep the gun on our friend here, but stay out of sight in case other cars come by."

Cain moved over to the open door, never letting the gun waver from its human target.

"Sit down, Harold," Towner ordered. "Right there. On the ground."

Jones eased himself down until he was sitting on the ground

426

with his hands wrapped around his knees. This simple maneuver had rendered him incapable of any sudden attempt at escaping.

Just then a car came by. It did not slow down, however, and quickly disappeared around the corner. Towner motioned to Grace. "You two have already met, but I'll introduce you again. Harold Justiss Jones, this is Grace Grafton—the Reverend Brad Weston's fiancé."

71

They watched for a flicker of recognition. There was none. Jones waited, his eyes moving from Cain and the weapon he held, to Grace, then back to Towner. Towner motioned to Grace and stepped back to watch.

"Does the name Brad Weston mean anything at all to you?" Grace asked.

Jones' eye contact was steady, and for a long moment, he made no effort to respond. Finally he said, "Lady, if you're really engaged to be married to a 'reverend,' it makes me wonder 'bout the kind o' company you're keepin'."

Grace stepped closer, careful not to get between the man sitting on the ground and John Cain's line of fire.

"Have you seen Brad Weston at the farm?"

"What farm? You mean Mr. Brandenbury's place?"

She waited.

"Lady, I ain't seen no Brad Weston. Wouldn't know him if I did. He's not anywhere that I know about. An' so long as we're all just askin', let me ask you one. Who's the guy your friend there mentioned that got in the way o' your skillet? I don' know nobody in Palm Springs. Ain't never been there."

"His name is Terry Reynolds."

Grace saw the driver's eyes flicker for a split second.

He knows him.

"So what did he do to deserve gettin' whacked? I'd like to know so's I don' do the same thing here."

"If by 'whacked' you mean killed, he's not dead. He's probably still in a hospital with a huge headache. But I honestly don't care. Seven years ago, he arranged an evening with your boss and his cohorts during which they murdered my best friends."

Jones eyes widened in surprise, then narrowed again. "Get out. You talkin' 'bout *the* Charles Brandenbury, president of CB Enterprises? Come on lady, that's crazy talk!"

"It's the gospel truth."

"How do you know?"

"I was there!" Grace's voice trembled with emotion at this man sitting on the ground who worked for the murderer of her friends. She took a step forward. Jones just stared at her. "You was there."

"My name is Grace Nicole Grafton, and yes, I was there."

Jones looked steadily at her. No flicker of recognition concerning the name. His brow furrowed in puzzlement. "Hold on, now. You say you are Grace Grafton, and you got a man you gonna marry named Brad Weston, and he's a 'reverend.' Like a minister? A pastor of a church?"

"Yes. In Palm Springs. Seven years ago three of us were invited onto Brandenbury's yacht in Savannah and taken to Daufuskie Island. That night, Charles Brandenbury murdered my two friends in cold blood. He threw BJ out a second story window. While I went out to find her, he killed Ilene."

"An' you're tellin' me there was two other guys there when all this happened?"

"Yes. Senator Noah Parker and a man named Talal Itana, supposedly a Lebanese diplomat. They stood by and watched and then helped get rid of the bodies—to make it look like an accident. But it was not an accident, Mr. Jones. It was cold-blooded murder. And the man you work for is their killer!"

Jones fell silent for the moment, biting on his lower lip. Grace could tell that this bit of news had shaken him. Then he asked, "If what you're sayin' is true, lady, then what's the Reverend doin' here with the man?"

"His name is Brad Weston," she replied heatedly. "Your boss had him taken in Burbank, California, on Monday. And two more innocent people were murdered in the process."

"Holy mother of God," Jones exclaimed. "You're either the craziest people I ever seen ... or ... "

"Or what?"

Jones remained silent, staring off in the distance, his lips tight and the bones on either side of his jaw flexing in and out.

"Or what?" Grace repeated.

"The company chopper flew in late Monday night," he said at last, looking straight at Grace. "The landing pad is right outside my room, so I woke up. Don't usually come in that late, though you can never tell. Mr. Brandenbury, he uses it to go an' come from the airport in Asheville. Brings guests in that way, too. Lots o' things you can do when you got the bucks."

"What time Monday?"

"Well, it was actually early mornin' Tuesday, 'cause it was 'bout— oh, I'd say 'bout four. Maybe closer to four-thirty or thereabouts. I got up an' looked out the window. I live above the garage. They're was three of 'em."

"Could you see who it was?"

"No. The chopper was between me and them. But two of 'em was helpin' the third guy to walk. I jus' supposed he'd had too many, you know? That happens sometimes."

"So what else? Did anything else happen? Did you see anything?" Grace demanded.

"After a while, two of 'em came back. I recognized the pilot. They got in the chopper an' left."

"Two. Only two of them left?"

"Thas' what I said. I may be black, lady, but I can count to two."

"Hey, ease up," interrupted Towner. "Don't play no race card. This isn't about being black or white or green."

"Well, then, you ease up." Jones waved his hand in frustration. "You the ones who come in here like the Green Berets an' make me a prisoner of your own little war. You the ones holdin' the gun. Who're you to say 'ease up?'"

"Okay—both of you. Knock it off." Grace spoke sharply, glancing over at John Cain who sat on the outer edge of the car seat, the gun still leveled at the driver. Then she turned back to Jones.

"Is the man who stayed behind still there? Is Brandenbury there, too?"

Jones wavered, and Grace could tell he was trying to make up his mind over whether to answer that one—or at least, whether to answer truthfully.

"He's there," he said at last, "an' your senator friend was there."

"Parker? Noah Parker was at the Farm? Today?"

Jones nodded. "He showed up early this mornin'. The chopper brought him in 'bout seven o'clock. He left again aroun' eight-thirty."

Grace stepped closer. "Is anyone else there? Are there ... any children there?"

"So why you askin' now 'bout kids?"

"Because yesterday your boss kidnapped Brad's son and daughter."

431

For a long moment, everyone was silent, each person remote, shrouded by their own dark thoughts. Jones' loud expletive brought them back to the moment.

"When do you say them kids was kidnapped?"

"Yesterday. Early afternoon. They ran Maggie off the road and took the children."

"Who's Maggie?"

"She and Paul are back watching the gate to the farm. That's how we saw you when you left a while ago."

Where are they?

Jones began massaging the tip of his chin. "Ain't seen no kids. But I don't see everything goin' down. I got other things to do, you know. The chopper did come in at two or three this mornin'. But I didn't get up to look. It left and didn't come back 'til the Senator showed up. How many o' you are there anyway?"

"Did you see anything? Anything at all out of the ordinary?" Grace persisted, ignoring his question. "Was there anyone else with him? Could the children have been there?"

"No, it was the Senator. And the pilot, Randle Martin. There wasn't nobody else."

Grace's countenance fell. She looked helplessly at Towner, then at John.

"Hey."

Grace's gaze returned to Jones.

"Is it okay if I stand? I'm startin' to cramp up in this position."

"Get up," she said, watching as he pushed himself to his feet. "Mr. Jones ... "

"The name's Harold, since we're so chummy here an' all ... " He paused at the sound of a truck climbing the hill from the direction of the main highway. It came into view just as the driver geared down to

432

match his load with the slope. As the trucker came alongside the limo and the car rental, he smiled and waved.

Grace tensed.

He's going to do something.

She watched as Jones nodded and waved a greeting back to the trucker. The truck continued to grind its way past. Grace exhaled slowly, at the same time realizing that her hands were clenched into tight fists.

"You could've tried to signal that driver," she said.

"Could've," Jones answered. "Maybe should've. 'Course I might o' got my head blown off if your friend over there is as good with that gun as y'all let on. Then again, maybe you got that in store for me anyway. But there's somethin' 'bout you, lady—Ms. Grafton or Grace or whatever your name is. I spent enough time in the Army to know a con job when I see one. I learned to spot a liar a regiment away. I get the feelin' you're tellin' me the true story here. What you're sayin' blows me away, though, but I think I'm actually beginnin' to believe you. Well, I don' know 'bout them murders an' I ain't seen no kids aroun', but tha's somethin' kin be checked out easy enough. 'Sides, why else would you be here doin' all this? Y'all are crazy. 'Less maybe yo're thinkin' 'bout knockin' off the next vice-president."

Grace looked at him steadily.

"You ... you think that's going to happen? That he's really going to be nominated?" she asked.

"Maybe. Probably. Kinda looks that way now, don't it? I think he's gonna git nominated an' mos' likely they'll win. I ain't votin' for him, but I think he'll git it all right."

Grace and the others stared at the man.

"What are you saying?" she asked.

"I'm sayin' that Mr. Brandenbury is one cold fish. I don' work for him 'cause I like him. I drive the man aroun' 'cause this is the best money I kin make. Hey, for me, it ain't gonna to get no better than this. Not since I took a hit in Afghanistan. Drivin' the man around is what it is. But sometimes he ain't human, you know? He's like a machine. Methodic-like. Calculatin'. An' cold as winter. You know why else I think you might be tellin' the truth?"

"Why?"

"'Cause I was in Iraq. Got sent there the first time. Volunteered the next two times. Then one more in Afghanistan. Stupid, huh?"

"Not stupid. It sounds patriotic to me."

"Yeah, well, that's where I caught this here shrapnel in my leg. Only got one really good thing out o' all them years. I learned to be a judge o' character. You had to do it fast there sometimes, 'cause your life might depend on whether or not you can trust a guy to stay in there with you an' not run when things get hot."

"So I repeat, what are you saying, Harold?"

"Well, I ain't sayin' he done all the things you're sayin' he done. I jus' think he maybe coulda. Tha's all."

"Then why do you work for such a vile man if that's what you think?"

"Well, for one thing, ain't nobody ever said before all the cockamamie things you been tellin' me. Up to now I jus' figured he's another super rich whitey user an' abuser o' people regardless o' their color—though I think he 'specially don' like us black folk none. 'Sides, I'm askin' myself, why would you make up a story as wild and hairy as this one? An' another thing."

"What?"

"I don' really think you could lie as good as this."

"What makes you think that?"

Jones looked away from Grace and began walking slowly,

deliberately, toward John. John, who had said nothing at all up to this point, stood with feet parted, one just ahead of the other as he leveled the gun, using both hands. The gun did not move. His eyes flicked over to where Grace and Towner stood. Towner started to move toward Jones when Grace put a hand on his arm.

Jones stopped in front of John at arms length. John kept the gun steady, his finger on the trigger.

"'Cause I'm a pretty good judge o' character, thas' why."

"He's right, John," said Grace. "We're not going to shoot him. He's not one of the bad guys."

There was a collective release of tension.

Jones looked over at Grace. "You really gonna marry a preacher?'"

She shrugged. "I was. Before this all happened."

Jones nodded, a flicker of sympathy crossing his face. "My momma used to say that God works in mysterious ways. I'll say to you an' these here bodyguards o' yours that this is 'bout as mysterious as it gets. I tol' you already I don' like the man, but, if he's really done all you say he done, I sure ain't goin' on workin' for him."

Jones' fundamental repugnance for the man, until now well-hidden behind an impervious exterior, was clearly visible in his tone and facial expression.

"Give him back his gun," Grace ordered, coming to a decision.

Towner gave her a cautionary look, but said nothing. He looked at John with a shrug and a trace of a smile.

John removed his finger from the trigger, reset the safety, and let the barrel roll forward. Jones accepted the weapon, examined it for a brief moment, looked up at John, and smiled without a word. Then he moved past him and reached across the front seat to the glove compartment. Opening it he placed the gun inside and then closed it again.

435

"Good," sighed Grace as more hesitation and distrust drained away. She glanced at Towner and John. Towner also appeared relieved. John gave her a reassuring nod. She turned her attention back to the driver.

"Mr. Jones … Harold … you think that so far this is as mysterious as it gets? Before we go further, let me introduce you formally to my 'bodyguards' as you call them. Mr. Herschel Winslow Towner III, President of OCEANS Security out in Washington State and a decorated Navy SEAL. And this is Pastor John Cain from Baytown, California."

Towner extended his hand. Jones stared at Grace as he absorbed this bit of information before shaking hands. Just then the car phone began ringing again.

"I should probably find out who it is," said Jones.

"We'd like to know, too, but not just yet," Towner replied. "Come over here."

John brushed against Harold's arm as the four of them walked over to the ravine. He held out his hand then added, his countenance grim, "I would have, you know. We're fond of this girl. The missing family, too. We don't intend to let anything happen to her. Or them."

Harold's gaze was steady as he shook John's hand. "I know. I tol' you, I'm a pretty good judge o' character."

72

Light from an almost full moon defined the darkening ridges and hills that dropped all the way down to the river, itself a filigree of gold and silver and copper, shimmering with reflected brightness. Stars were starting to pop out like lanterns in a forest, showing the way, beckoning to the limousine as it moved across the narrow bridge and stopped at the gatehouse.

"Where've you been, man?" asked the guard as he stuck his head part-way through the open car window and glanced around. "They've called down here twice from the house looking for you. Mr. Brandenbury himself the last time. A couple of hours ago."

"Ran into somethin' unexpected with the car an' had to take care of it."

"Was she pretty?"

"No, not like that," Harold chuckled. "But by the time it was ready, I thought I'd get a bite to eat. Didn't have nothin' on the schedule. He say what he wanted?"

"Didn't say. You know how he is. There's been lots of activity up at the house, though. CB-One came in a while ago. What you got in

437

the back?" he asked, looking over Harold's shoulder into the rear seat area. Three boxes rested on the seat, and three more, slightly smaller, were situated behind the front seat on top of a stack of blankets.

"Some supplies I had to pick up for the man himself. You need to check?"

The guard leaned on the window's edge, his eyes on the boxes. "Naw, it's okay. You better hurry on up to the house.'"

"Is it still there?"

"CB-One? No, left not long after it landed. Maybe ten minutes was all. But you shoulda called in, man. He was one upset dude the last time. I could hear it in his tone. Your buns are going to be on the griddle, that's all I'm sayin'. You better think up some really good excuses between here and the house 'cause I don't think he's in a very good mood."

"Is he ever?"

The gate guard laughed.

"Thanks for the warnin', Jerry. See you later."

The car moved past the security gate and the guard and the dogs and on up the hill in full view of security cameras located strategically along the road as well as elsewhere around the Farm's perimeter. This place was impregnable. That's the way the boss wanted it, and that's the way it was. Until now.

Harold pressed the garage opener and let the car roll to a stop, while waiting for the door to lift. Once inside, he pressed a different button to the left of the steering column, listened for the muffled click of the trunk release, turned off the motor, got out and shut the car door. Hesitating, he thought about the gun still in the glove compartment. As he turned to reach back in and get it, a voice called out.

"Jones! The boss was looking for you hours ago. Where've you been?" The man whose voice it was emerged from the shadows and stood in the garage door entrance. "Out impressing some chick with the limo?"

"Not hard to do with this car and my good looks. Sorry, Sim, the car had a problem, and I got stranded. Took a while. What's up?"

"Come on up to the house."

"Okay. Be there in a minute."

"Now!"

Reluctantly, Harold moved away from the car and followed after him.

"The door," said the man.

"What?"

"The garage door. You forgot to close it."

"I'll get it when I come back," Harold replied, as they walked across the parking area to the sidewalk and headed for the house. Their footsteps faded into the distance and voices became indistinguishable. The door lift's timer light went off, leaving the garage interior in darkness. It was quiet again; the only sounds those of crickets outside playing their night songs.

The first movement came from beneath the blankets as a hand reached for the rear door handle. The door opened. First Towner, then Cain slid out from beneath the blankets and empty boxes they had found behind the fire station. Paul pushed the lid all the way open, rolling out from the Limousine trunk onto the cement floor of the garage. He held out a hand for Grace and Maggie as they sorted out their tangle of arms and legs and scrambled out of the cramped space to stand in the doorway.

"You were right, Grace," whispered Maggie.

"About what?"

"You said I was too old for this sort of thing."

"I did not."

"Well, if you didn't, you should have. There is no doubt that the last thirty or so hours have been the most jaw-dropping ones in my entire life. I know I've aged ten years, and on top of that, I'm going to have bruises all the way to Christmas."

"You think you've got problems," whispered Paul. "Wait until I try to explain to Melody how I spent the evening curled up in the trunk of a car with two beautiful women."

"It does sound a little kinky, doesn't it?" Maggie remarked with a giggle.

"Keep it down," ordered Towner, bending down and pulling a Glock G30S handgun from an ankle holster on his left leg.

"I didn't think you had a weapon," exclaimed a surprised Maggie.

"There's a lot you don't know," answered Towner simply. "Focus on the house. It's our next challenge."

"How will we get in?" asked Maggie.

"Those guys just went through the front door," said Towner. "I doubt there's an alarm on with people already inside. Besides, this place is loaded with security around the perimeter. They won't be expecting us. But we don't want to become the star attractions on Candid Camera, either, so be careful."

"Maggie, you and Paul stay here. I think the .45 is still in the glove compartment. Check around to see if you can find any additional firepower. But don't go outside unless I call for you. Your cell phone on?"

Maggie nodded.

"Grace, you follow between John and me. Stay in the shadows, close to trees and bushes. And don't make any noise."

They moved out of the garage and started toward the house.

"Wait." Towner stopped abruptly, causing Grace to catch herself as she stumbled into him. "Grace, you should stay back."

"No deal," Grace protested, "we go together."

"If we get caught, you are our best hope to get us out or get away. There's too many for this kind of op. One of you has to stay here."

Grace and John looked at each other.

"I need to go with you," Grace exclaimed. "You don't know Brad, and he doesn't know you."

"Grace is right," John reluctantly agreed. "Okay, I'll hang out here at the corner where I can watch the front entrance. Harold left the keys in the car, so we'll be ready for a quick exit if we need to."

"Just don't set off any alarms," cautioned Towner. He looked unsmilingly at John. Disapproval was clearly written on his face. He didn't agree, but he said nothing. Then he turned back to Grace. "You asked for it. Come on."

Grace followed as Towner struck out, crouching down, darting in and out among long shadows of dark on darker, created by the shrubbery and trees along the parking area border. Night had settled in around them. They moved quickly, and as they did, the thought that crossed Grace's mind was that this man she had met only hours ago had done this sort of thing before. Probably in places even more dangerous than this. He was swift, silent, glancing back only once to see that she was right behind him.

They edged their way past a fountain. It stood silent, its waters placid and undisturbed. Moments later, they found themselves in front of a large oak door.

"What are we going to do now?" asked Grace.

Towner shrugged and then grasped hold of the large brass door latch. He pressed the thumb-piece and pushed. Nothing. He tried again, this time more firmly. Then he looked up and shook his head.

Motioning with his hand he pointed to the far corner of the house and waved her forward.

Staying low against the house, they ducked beneath unlit windows, careful to avoid a hard-to-see sprinkler head or a security alarm trip wire. When they reached the end of the house, they stepped past the corner, peering cautiously down the full-length of its side. The moonlight was brighter here and, near the far end of the house, they saw an outside staircase leading up to a landing. Atop the landing a light could be seen through a narrow opaque window next to the door.

"What do you think?" asked Grace.

"Who knows? Could be anybody. But if Jones' description of this place is correct, my guess is we're looking at the entrance to the servants' quarters. And it would appear that somebody's home. But we're too exposed out here. Too much light and no cover. If anybody's around they'll see us and set off an alarm. I don't see it, but there's a good chance of a camera on the staircase."

Grace's eyes closed and her lips moved silently.

"What are you doing?"

"I'm praying that nobody will be around to see us."

"I had to ask," he said, shaking his head. "Okay, let's try it out and see if God is in business tonight. Keep moving. I need you to stay right behind me." They rounded the corner, running in a half-crouch to the stairs. Then up the steps as quietly as possible until they reached the landing.

Towner took a deep breath and exhaled slowly. "Okay, here goes."

"Wait," exclaimed Grace with a loud whisper as she grasped at his arm, but it was too late. He knocked on the door, four sharp raps, and then stood close against it.

Grace heard footsteps and a muffled voice saying, "I'll get it." A moment later the door opened. Towner pushed his way through as a middle-aged, plump woman staggered backward in surprise. By the time she recovered, the muzzle of Towner's handgun was pressed under her nose.

"Not a word, lady," he hissed through gritted teeth, his countenance fierce and hard. "Not a sound or you're dead!"

Grace closed the door and stepped past Towner. The woman's face drained of color. She looked as though she might faint on the spot. And then she did, crumpling to the floor with a moan as her knees gave way.

"Who is it, Sarah?"

A woman with Asian features emerged from the hallway and stared incredulously at her fallen companion and at the man in the open doorway with a gun in his hand. She turned to run. Grace flew across the room, and like a San Diego Charger linebacker, tackled her around the waist. They fell to the floor, the woman kicking and struggling while Grace fought to get control. The woman managed the beginning of a cry for help that died in her throat when she saw the man was holding the gun only inches from her face.

"Not a peep out of you," Towner ordered in as gruff a voice as he could muster. "One more sound, and you won't live to make a second one!"

The woman fell back, thoroughly cowed.

"Are you the only two in here?" Towner demanded.

She hesitated, then nodded.

"Hold this on her," Towner ordered, giving the gun to Grace. "I'll look around just to be sure."

The two women stared at each other. Grace saw that the initial surprise-turned-fear in the face of the Asian woman—Chinese, was Grace's guess—had already been replaced by a smoldering rage. The woman's small, wiry stature seemed even smaller now, coiled and

443

ready to attack. Grace wanted to reach out and help her to her feet, tell her that everything was going to be all right and assure her that nobody was going to be killed. She knew the woman had seen the gun waver. She moved her other hand around to help steady the barrel and keep it trained on her.

Then Towner was back.

"No one else here," he said, taking the gun away from Grace. "See if you can find something to tie these two up with. Some rope or wire or tape or whatever. And hurry."

As Grace darted to the kitchen, the other woman stirred, letting out a low moan.

"Quickly. Over there with your friend."

The woman struggled to get up.

"Hurry," Towner ordered. "Move it."

Crawling on her hands and knees across the tile floor, she reached her companion who took that moment to utter another groan, this one louder than the first. Towner moved around them to set the bolt lock on the landing door. Then, Grace reappeared carrying some appliance cords, masking tape, two washcloths, and a knife.

"There wasn't any rope or tape. Nothing but this. So, I cut these off a toaster and a blender. And I see an extension cord over there, attached to that lamp. Will these do?"

"Perfect. Here, take the gun and give me that stuff. And listen up, ladies, my partner here gets very mean when she's upset. And trust me, she's upset right now. She will put a bullet between your eyes quicker than I would, so don't do anything crazy. Cooperate, and you'll come through this little interruption of an otherwise lovely evening just fine."

Grace knew that Towner was bluffing. At the same time, she hoped the two women believed she would do it. As he twisted the cords tightly around their hands and feet, feelings of guilt over what they were doing to these two defenseless human beings upset her. This was all so terrible. Still, what other options were there? They *had* to find Brad and the children!

Towner stood and looked down at the two women on the floor. "Okay, I want you both to listen and answer me straight. The woman with the gun belongs with a man named Brad Weston."

Grace watched for any sign of recognition. Nothing.

"He was kidnapped by your boss, Mr. Brandenbury," Towner continued. "We've come to take him back. Tell us where he is." Her eyelids flickered. He glanced at the other woman. She looked befuddled. Was it fright? Or was she trying to decide whether or not to cooperate?

"Well? We're waiting, but not for long. It's best for you to understand that you have no choice in this matter. We have friends outside, and we're in complete control of this compound." Grace decided Towner was a convincing liar. "Don't forget for a minute that your lives are in our hands, so tell us what you know if you want to see the sun rise tomorrow."

The Chinese woman spoke up first. "I know nothing of any kidnapping. Mr. Brandenbury is an honorable man ... "

"That, lady, is a laugh!" Towner sneered, glaring at her. "Mr. Brandenbury doesn't have an honorable bone in his body. And I know you know something, so tell us all about it."

The plump lady spoke up.

"There's a guest who has been staying here. He arrived early in the morning on Tuesday. It was around four o'clock. The helicopter awakened both of us when it landed." She looked at her companion whose face had abruptly turned sullen. "Mr. Brandenbury said that his guest was an old friend who nearly died of a drug overdose. He wanted to help him, so he brought him here."

"Are there two children here?"

Both women looked puzzled at that.

"Did they bring two children here together with the man?" Grace persisted.

"There are no children here," the Chinese woman declared.

"Where is this man?" asked Towner. The plump woman glanced over at her roommate again. Her face was an inscrutable mask.

"We don't know," she continued. "Neither of us has ever seen him."

"What do you mean? Surely you've served him something to eat."

"Yes, we've prepared food for him—it's been mostly broth and bread. Some juice and water. We take it down the hall, knock on the door, and give it to the man."

"What man?" asked Grace.

"Whoever is there," the Chinese woman interrupted. "The men take turns staying in the room with Mr. Brandenbury's friend. Sometimes it's Cavanaugh—he works with the horses. I've seen Mr. Larson go in there, too." She hesitated, and then went on, "And, sometimes it's Harold."

"Harold? You mean Harold Jones?"

"Yes. The driver."

Grace cast a worried look at Towner as the woman continued.

"They tell us Mr. Brandenbury's friend gets very sick and sometimes he's violent while he's detoxing, so they don't let us in."

Grace's gaze returned to the women.

"Where do they keep this man? Where is his room?"

"Across from Mr. Brandenbury's office."

"Where is that exactly?"

The women looked at each other but said nothing.

"Never mind. We'll find it ourselves. I've already found the inside door leading out of here."

"Are you sure?" asked Grace, surprised at this bit of news.

"It's the only one with a bolt lock besides this one."

"It won't do you any good." It was the plump woman who spoke up again.

"What do you mean?"

"He's gone."

"Who's gone?" asked Towner.

"Mr. Brandenbury's friend."

"What are you saying?" asked Grace, fighting back the sudden churning in her stomach at this unexpected revelation.

"Mr. Brandenbury's helicopter. It came about an hour ago."

"They took Brad away?" Grace questioned in disbelief.

"They took away Mr. Brandenbury's friend. I was in the kitchen. I saw them through the window."

"Was he all right?"

"They were—"

"They? Are you sure there were no children here?"

"Sarah!" The Chinese woman spoke up sharply. "Enough. Don't say another word!"

The woman's plump coworker cowered at her reproving tone.

Grace and Towner waited for a moment for more, but it was clear that nothing further would be gained from these two.

"Very well," Towner said at last. "Thank you, ladies, for your cooperation. I do apologize for the way we've dropped in on you like this without calling first. But you know how it is."

By this time, the Chinese woman's mute stare had turned from anger to distrust and contempt, though both of them submitted without resistance as Towner stuffed a washcloth in each of their mouths, keeping it in place by several quick wraps around their heads with the masking tape. Their faces reflected no small amount of relief as they interpreted the gag to mean their lives really were going to be spared.

Grace helped carry them into separate bedrooms, dropped them on the bed and closed the doors. Towner twisted the last of the tape in a rope-like fashion. There wasn't enough to work both doors. Tying one end to the doorknob of the room in which the defiant woman had been taken and the other to a storage closet door across the hall, he stood back and eyed his work critically. Satisfied that it was the best he could do, he led the way to the kitchen.

"What did you make of that?"

"Do you think she's telling the truth?" Grace's tone betrayed the ache she felt inside—and the sense of impending failure. "We can't have gotten this close and then ... "

Towner stopped and bent down to examine the locked door.

"Is this it?" she asked. "The way into the hall?"

"It has to be. See the bolt lock? This goes out somewhere. My guess is that it leads out of here and down the hall to Brandenbury's office ... and to the room where they've been keeping your fiance." He paused. "Of course, on the other hand, this might open up into the big man's bedroom."

"And if Brad's not here? And the kids? If we've missed them ... oh, God, please don't let it be so."

"Nothing is for sure here," Towner mused as he turned to look at Grace. "I don't trust the oriental gal. She's tough, that one. Meanwhile, we can't stand around. We need to move fast and get out of here!"

Grace nodded, mustering up a weak half-smile. "I'm not used to this. It's not my style."

"Listen, you go back and get the others together."

"If I go you're coming with me."

"I can't. Not until I know for sure that they're not here. If something happens to me in the meantime, get out of here."

As Towner reached for the lock, Grace put her hand over his. "Wait. You've done stuff like this before, right? Like when you were in the military or something?"

"What do you think?" Towner handed the gun to Grace. "Do you know how to use this thing?"

Grace looked at the gun in her hand. It was shaking. "Are you sure you want to know?"

Towner nodded.

"The truth is I've shot a handgun only once in my entire life. My dad and I were at a target range years ago. He had a great time. I didn't. I hate guns."

Towner forced a grin. "Then what in the world are you doing here?"

"I'm here because of Brad and the children. And Maggie, pure and simple. She's been like a second mom in my life."

"When John told me she'd actually dropped someone with a frying pan to keep you from getting killed—well, I couldn't resist. I liked her before I met her. That is impressive."

Grace nodded her understanding.

"Besides," added Towner, "if even half what you have told me turns out to be true, Paul and Maggie have got the story of a lifetime here. Couldn't resist that either, now could we?"

Grace removed her hand from his. "Okay then, so let's find them and get out of here!"

Towner slowly twisted the deadbolt lock. Grace heard it click and her throat went dry. Towner gripped the handgun after checking again to make certain the safety was off. Then he cracked the door open and peered out into the hallway.

73

The hallway was wide, well lit—and empty.

It looked as though it ran the length of the house. There were doors on either side, some open, others closed. The staircase leading down to the first floor could be seen ahead on the left. Towner put a finger to his lips signaling silence as he motioned Grace to follow.

They had gone a half dozen meters when Towner halted so abruptly that Grace bumped into him. Then she heard them, too.

Someone was coming up the staircase. For an instant they stood frozen. Then Towner sprinted through the nearest open doorway, pulling Grace after him. They were barely inside when two men emerged at the top of the stairs.

Towner crouched down in the room's semi-darkness, gun held ready. Grace peered over his shoulder through the doorway's narrow opening, watching the men as they strode down the hall in the opposite direction. She was shaking with fright and excitement at the same time as they waited, listening.

"Harold's going to meet him then?"

"At eleven. That's when his plane gets in. He'll take him the rest of the way in the limo."

"Why didn't he just stick around when he was here this morning?"

"Had a meeting with a big donor just in from Hong Kong. Had

to go to Charlotte."

"How's he going to handle money like that?"

"You mean the foreign connection?"

"Yeah. After the fiasco with that Indonesian guy ... I mean, is Parker hurting for money that badly?"

The other man laughed hoarsely. "I think Parker will do the same thing as any presidential candidate. Take the money, then duck and delay any criticism after he's in the White House. Joe Voter doesn't really care about this kind of thing anyhow. It's expected. The price of democracy these days."

They laughed at that as one of them opened a door near the far end of the hall.

"I thought the boss intended to finish everything here."

"That was the plan until Reynolds ... " The door closed behind them as they disappeared from view into a room on the right, near the end of the hall.

Towner let out a sigh of relief. "That was close. I really think it's time for us to get out of here."

"No!" Grace whispered heatedly. The look she gave Towner was resolute. "I've got to know for sure."

"You heard what the woman said. He's gone. They've taken him God only knows where."

"They're lying."

"What?"

"Those two are lying."

"How do you know that?"

"Women's intuition."

"Oh, great."

"I watched their eyes, Towner. The way they looked at one another."

"What about Harold?" Towner demanded. "He told us he'd never

451

seen your husband."

"And later, he told us about two men helping a third one out of the helicopter and into the house. I think he was telling the truth."

"Those two back there said he went into the room, Grace. They claim he was in there, taking his turn as a guard."

"But the first one mentioned two other names—Cavanaugh and Larson. Remember how she hesitated for a second? It was as though she was searching for a specific response. For us to act like we knew one of them. Then she went on to say that Harold was in with him, too. And we reacted. She was fishing, trying to figure out who helped us get past all the security on this hill. And we told her everything she needed to know without saying a word."

"Maybe *you're* the one who's fishing. Harold could be smelling a major bonus or something even bigger. Maybe he likes the idea of driving the VP around Washington. What if he's the cheese in the trap? If Harold gets back to the others before we do ... "

"No. I'm right, Towner. Those two are in on this. At least the Chinese woman is for sure. I'm positive."

"And if you're wrong?"

"Look, we're wasting time arguing."

"Then let's think about getting out of here so we can tell your story to the rest of the world," urged Towner as he cast a nervous glance down the hall.

"Not without checking first!" She started for the door.

"What are you doing?"

"I'm going to check that room across from Brandenbury's office. Where they said he was being held. David and Nancy may have been there, too. I have to see!"

"Wait. You have no idea what you're doing!"

"Stay here. Cover me. It would be stupid for us both to be caught together now. I'll be right back."

"No. You wait here. I'll go."

"Towner. I have to do this. For my own sake."

Before he could protest further, Grace was out in the hall and headed in the same direction the two men had gone just moments before. She moved swiftly, slowing only as she passed the door the men had closed behind them. A low murmur of voices was all she could make out. Nothing more. Continuing on, she paused again in front of the next room on the right. Through the glass door, she glimpsed the outline of a lavishly furnished room. This had to be it. Brandenbury's office.

She turned away and tried the opposite door. To her relief, it was unlocked. Opening it, she stepped into the darkness and closed it behind her. She felt along the wall for a light switch.

A bright ceiling light illuminated the room. She was standing in a bedroom. She glanced about, taking in her surroundings. An open door into a small bathroom to her left. A window across from her and another to her right. It was a corner room. Her heart sank. The bed was made and there was no sign that anyone had used it.

As she turned to leave, her eye caught something in the half-open closet. Her heart skipped a beat. Walking across the room, she pushed the sliding door all the way back. Brad's jacket on a hanger! The one he'd been wearing on Monday when he left the house for Burbank. She slipped it off the hanger and folded it over her arm.

Brad was here! Oh, God, where have they taken him? And where are Nancy and David? Lord, why did you let me get so close and then take them from me again?

Quietly, she stepped back into the hall, careful to pull the door shut behind her just as she had found it. All at once, gunfire erupted somewhere outside the house. One, two, three rapid shots. A split-

453

second pause. Then two more, much closer! The door across the hall next to Brandenbury's office opened suddenly and the two they had observed earlier came running out, then halted in surprise.

"What the … Who are you?"

For one brief instant, Grace froze.

The men were blocking her escape. There was no way to get past them. Instinctively she opened the door she'd just closed and darted back inside. Slamming it shut, she twisted the lock she'd felt earlier on the handle. A moment later they were pounding on the door.

"Hey. Come out of there!"

Grace dropped Brad's jacket on the bed and ran to the windows. Desperate, she peered out into the darkness. She could see the garage from the window. The door was still open and the limousine still parked inside. But there was no one around. There was cursing and shouting outside the door as the pounding got more intense. Then there was a thud as one of the men threw his shoulder against the door. The lock held, but just barely. She looked around for something … anything to fight back with. Grabbing a ceramic lamp from the reading table next to the bed, she yanked it away from the wall plug, just as the door splintered, caving in under the force of a second blow.

The larger of the two men stumbled through the opening, momentarily losing his balance. Standing to one side, Grace swung the lamp with all the force she could muster, smashing it against the side of the man's head as he tried to right himself and reach for her. The blow drove him to his hands and knees. She kicked at his face, her foot hitting him squarely in the nose. Rolling over, he covered his head as she drew back, dropping the remains of the shattered lamp on the floor.

And then the man's companion was in the doorway, with a gun leveled at Grace. She flinched at the sound of the shot, shutting her eyes against the inevitable, then opening them in time to see the gunman stumble to one side and disappear from view.

"Grace!"

It was Towner's voice, calling to her.

Grace rushed for the open door. The big man rolled and grasped her ankle as she passed, causing her to pitch forward through the opening and into the hall, landing on her hands and knees. Scrambling to her feet, she ran toward Towner who stood halfway down the hall, on the near side of the staircase landing, gun in hand. She ran right into him, holding on for dear life. The man who had broken down the door came bursting back into the hall, brandishing a gun and cursing at the top of his lungs. Towner pushed Grace toward the stairs.

"Go!" he shouted.

Grace heard a gunshot as she stumbled down the steps. Then another. She looked back to see Towner, taking two steps at a time, coming down the staircase after her. She hesitated, unsure of what to do next.

"Keep going!"

Grace hurried down the remaining steps to a landing. There she glanced up in time to see the man who'd been shot in the hallway now sprawled at the top of the staircase. He was aiming a gun. Throwing herself against Towner, they both stumbled back into the banister and wall on the left just as the man fired—once, twice, three times!

Grace fell onto the staircase, Towner on top of her, their arms wrapped around each other, the force of his weight pushing the wind from her lungs as they bounced and tumbled down the remaining steps, fear clutching at her throat as she wondered if the volley of shots had hit either of them. That's when she saw she had inadvertently knocked Towner's gun out of his hand. It was on the floor in front of the staircase, just beyond her reach. Pushing him to one side, she lunged forward to grab it. A bullet buried itself in the hardwood floor, inches from her hand. Quickly, she drew back. Towner grabbed her by the arm and yanked her back against him. All the while, his eyes were on the shooter.

What seemed like an eternity had in reality been only seconds of pandemonium and panic. Now it was silent. The only sound that of her heart pounding in her breast. Why didn't the man shoot them? How could he miss? Then she heard a noise and looked up.

The front door had been thrown open and a man was standing in the doorway. It was impossible to read the look on his face, but there was no doubting whose face it was.

The man looking at her straight in the eyes was Harold Justiss Jones. And he was pointing a gun.

74

2400 local time

Maggie was sitting in a waiting room chair, cellular phone in hand, when two uniformed police officers entered Emergency. She'd made her 911 call, without giving up her identity, as they were approaching Asheville's city limits, just as the three of them had agreed. Then she followed up with a call to Paul's wife, Melody, explaining the situation and encouraging her to come right away.

A few minutes after Towner and Grace had disappeared around the corner of the house, John and Paul went to check on them. John recounted on the way to the hospital that they had seen the outdoor steps leading up to the second floor and decided Towner and Grace must be inside. They had paused for a moment, assessing their situation, when from out of nowhere, someone yelled and opened fire.

Meanwhile, Harold had returned from the house and was inside the garage with Maggie. That's when Maggie heard a shout, followed by a *pop pop pop*. Then a second burst followed the first. Harold raced to the car and retrieved the .45 from the glove box. Maggie was peering around the corner when he ran past her and out into the open. She watched as John and Paul lay flat on the ground a short distance from the corner of the house. A man standing between the house and

457

the helicopter-landing pad was firing an automatic weapon. Harold stopped, drew down, and fired a single shot. The man fell.

Harold checked to make sure he was dead while Maggie ran toward the others. Before she got to them, John was up and kneeling beside Paul, who was bleeding from having taken two hits, one in the arm and another in the chest. It was then that they heard shooting erupt inside the house. John and Maggie tore strips of John's shirt into pieces for a makeshift tourniquet to stop the blood loss in Paul's arm and to act as a press on his chest wound. Harold then ran for the house, threw open the door, and saw Grace and Towner huddled together at the bottom of the staircase. Glancing up the stairs, he saw George Turner, one of Brandenbury's right-hand men, pitched forward, a gun dangling from his hand. He wasn't moving.

Harold helped Grace to her feet as Towner released his hold on her. No bones were broken, and bruises would be tended to later. It was time to move fast. Harold pointed them to where John was tending to Paul. He ran for the car. Moments later, they were racing down the drive, past a surprised and sleepy gate guard and onto the deserted, but windy road leading to the Interstate. Harold was an excellent driver and broke all North Carolina speed laws until arriving at Biltmore Avenue and the Mission Hospital Emergency Center.

On the way, Grace had huddled silently in the backseat, staring out the side window at the dark shapes flashing by. Maggie had wondered what she must be thinking, how she was coping with the disappointment of knowing they had missed Brad and possibly the children by a matter of hours. And then, still gazing out the window, Maggie heard her half whisper, "I know."

"What?"

"I know where they are."

Paul had been in the operating room for almost thirty minutes with no word on his condition. Maggie took what little comfort she could in the thought that no news was probably good news. At least it meant he must still be alive.

She watched as the policemen conferred with the admittance nurse. The nurse nodded, pointing in her direction. The officers turned to check her out. Maggie half-smiled to herself in spite of the gravity of the situation, imagining what they might be thinking. *What's a nice little old lady like you doing in a place like this?And at this hour?*The officers headed toward her.

Fumbling in her purse for something that would identify her, she mentally rehearsed the story she intended to tell. It had to be the truth. They had left two men wounded, one critical, a pair of trussed-up women in their apartment, and a dead man in the driveway at Charles Brandenbury's Arabian Horse Farm. For a few incredible minutes it had been a war zone!

Though Maggie felt little compassion for any of them, they agreed on the way to Asheville that she should call 911 and ask for police and medical assistance at the Farm. Harold had even provided her with specific directions to give to the operator. She hadn't bothered to mention the women tied up in the bedroom of their apartment. The police would find them soon enough.

There was another problem, however. Maggie knew there usually was when things became as complicated and extraordinary as they were tonight. Grace and the others needed time and somehow she had to buy them as much as possible. If the highway patrol caught up with them, it would be impossible to untangle everything.

"Hello, ma'am." The officers stood looking down at her. One was a young woman. A twenty-something. The man she guessed to be in his late forties.

"Yes?"

"You brought in a ... " the older man paused to look at his notes,

"Mr. Paul Jacobsen. He has a gunshot wound?"

"Yes, Officer ... "

"Carrington. And this is Officer Tarcher."

"How do you do, ma'am?" The young woman offered up a disarming smile.

Maggie made a mental note. *Good cop.* "Hello, Officers. I'm very pleased to meet you. It's kind of you to come out so late at night like this."

They looked at her curiously. "It's what we do, ma'am," said Officer Carrington. His voice was gravelly. He assumed a kind of official, matter-of-fact approach, words forming at an unhurried pace and with an accent that betrayed his homegrown roots. But from the look in his eyes, she made another mental note. *Bad cop.* "Can you tell us what happened to your friend?"

"Well, not exactly, Officer. I didn't see everything." Maggie felt their steady gaze boring in, trying to pry open her mind and sort through whatever secrets they found inside. "I followed Harold into the house and ... "

"Harold? Who's Harold, ma'am?"

"Oh, why he's the man who drove us to the house. Harold Justiss Jones. He works for Mr. Brandenbury."

The officers exchanged looks at the mention of Brandenbury's name.

"You were at Charles Brandenbury's home?"

"Yes, I was."

"Here in town." It was a question, but the spokesman for the two officers had offered it as a matter of fact. He waited for her to confirm his statement.

"No," she said, pausing as though deciding what to say next. "It was at his farm. You know, the Brandenbury Horse Farm out north of town?"

"And what were you doing at Mr. Brandenbury's farm, Ms ... "

"Hinegardner. Mary Magdalene Hinegardner."

An amused look crinkled Carrington's face for an instant, then it was gone. Maggie was used to that kind of response. She thought her name was rather funny herself and was never offended by people's reactions. Besides, this all took time and time was what she was after at the moment.

"You want to spell that for me? Your last name, I mean."

"Certainly, Officer. I'd be happy to." Maggie did so, speaking out each letter with painful slowness as the officer wrote them down.

"What was I doing there?" she repeated thoughtfully. "Why, Mr. Jacobsen and I were waiting for Mr. Brandenbury to return."

"And where was he?"

"Mr. Brandenbury? I'm not certain, Officer, he was not at the farm."

"You the one who called 911 and asked for medical assistance out there?" Tarcher asked.

Maggie wavered. She had hoped these two would not be aware of the 911 call. At least not so soon. *Oh well* ... "Yes. Yes I am."

"Were you calling about your friend here?"

"No, I think someone else was hurt also, but I'm not sure because I didn't see him."

"Then what makes you think someone else was hurt?"

"That's what Harold said."

"Harold—the driver?"

"Yes. That's correct."

Officer Tarcher moved behind Carrington and crossed to the other side. Maggie sensed them trying to add up what they were hearing ... or not hearing.

"Did this Harold fellow see someone hurt?"

"I don't think so."

461

"Then how did he jump to that conclusion?"

"Perhaps Mr. Jacobsen told him before he fell unconscious. I'm not sure. You see, I was outside with Harold. Paul and John had gone over to the corner of the house when I heard someone shout out. We started in their direction but I only went a step or two when we heard shots fired. That's when Paul was shot. You must understand how frightened I was, to say the very least. I'm just not used to this sort of thing. Not used to it at all."

Maggie reached for a tissue from a packet next to the telephone and dabbed at her cheeks.

"Mr. Jacobsen?"

"Yes."

"The one here in the hospital now?"

"Yes."

"You mentioned someone named John?"

"Oh, yes. John Cain. He is our pastor."

She glanced back and forth between them as the officers stared back at her.

"Why were you and Mr. Jacobsen and this Cain fellow you say is your pastor waiting for Mr. Brandenbury?"

"We're reporters, Officer Tarcher. That is, Paul and I are reporters."

The officers glanced at each other again, this time in surprise.

"You're reporters? Newspaper reporters? Do you have some ID that we can see?"

Maggie handed Carrington her press card identifying her as a reporter with the *Desert Sun*.

"This says you're from all the way out in Palm Springs, California."

"That's correct."

"And Mr. Jacobsen? Is he from there, too?"

"Mr. Jacobsen is with the *Washington Post*."

"And?"

"And we wanted to talk with Mr. Brandenbury regarding certain allegations that have come to our attention in recent days."

"What sort of allegations, ma'am?" asked Tarcher.

"Oh, I'm afraid I couldn't divulge that, Officer Carrington. First Amendment rights and all, you know. It's confidential."

At that moment, Maggie heard the radio attached to Carrington's waist belt make a noisy squawk followed by the scratchy sound of a female dispatcher's voice. Carrington turned and walked away from Maggie as he responded to the call. Moments later he was back, facing her, his countenance solemn.

"Ms. Hinegardner, it looks like we're going to have to escort you downtown."

"Downtown? I don't understand."

Carrington turned to Tarcher. "Give Ms. Hinegardner her rights while I check with the nurse."

Tarcher gave him a surprised look. "Is she under arrest?"

"Maybe." He started for the desk, then stopped and turned back to Maggie. "By the way, where is this Harold fellow and this pastor person you've been telling us about?"

Maggie smiled sweetly. "I guess if you're taking me 'downtown,' I'd best not say anything more, Officer Carrington. At least not until I have an attorney present. And don't I get to make a phone call or something? I'm new at this sort of thing, so I apologize. You'll have to help me. No one's ever read me my Miranda rights before."

Both officers stared dubiously at their unlikely suspect.

75

By the time they reached the outskirts of Columbia, South Carolina, turned off Interstate 77, and headed south on the comparatively deserted State Highway 321, Harold mentioned that Maggie had probably managed to keep the police busy about as long as possible. He reminded Grace and the others that there could be a BOLO out for the limousine and its occupants.

Another BOLO.

Grace let out a sigh of resignation.

Last week I didn't know what a BOLO was, and now I'm the subject of one on both coasts. She visualized her picture hanging on bulletin boards in post offices across the country. Be On The Lookout … extremely dangerous …

Earlier, on the freeway east out of Asheville, they had discussed leaving the limo behind and renting a smaller, less visible car for the rest of the journey. Towner nixed the idea, deciding that it was too iffy for them to show up at an airport and try to rent something at this hour. They would also leave behind a paper trail for the authorities to follow. Better to get off the freeway and use the less-traveled roads

464

that threaded their way through small Carolina towns like Woodford and Ulmer and Garnett.

At four in the morning, while it was still dark, they crossed over the Savannah River into Georgia and stopped beside a telephone booth near a small gas station on the outskirts of Springfield. Harold, John, and Towner got out and looked around. When John was satisfied that there was no one about at this early hour, he came around and opened the door. Grace got out and braced herself against the car, stretching her arms and legs, fighting off the accumulated tension and weariness of these past few days. Towner had cautioned her to remove the battery and not use her cell phone. By now it was probably on a hot list and would be too easy to trace. So she stepped into the phone booth and dialed information.

"What city, please?"

"Savannah, Georgia."

"The person you're calling?"

"Fitzgerald. Ellie Fitzgerald."

"One moment."

A brief pause and then a recorded voice declared, "The number is 912 ... " Hurriedly Grace scribbled down the information. When she had finished, she nodded and gave a half wave to the men who waited by the car, stretching and bending, working at loosening up achy muscles resulting from the earlier mayhem and their all-night journey. She punched in the numbers she'd just been given.

One ring. Two. Three.

Is she home?

Grace glanced at her watch.

Four rings.

"Hello."

Grace's heart skipped a beat. It was a voice she'd not heard in seven years, but one she would never forget as long as she lived.

"Ellie?"

[Pause].

"Yes? Who is this?"

"It's Grace."

"I think you gots the wrong numbah. It's ... why it's fo in the mornin'. Who'd you say this is?"

"You picked me up one day seven years ago, Ellie, on your way back from shrimping. You took me to your house and cleaned me up and we ate shrimp that evening before I went away ... "

Grace heard a gasp of surprise.

"Grace?" Ellie's voice had taken on a note of incredulity. "Is that you, girl? Is it really you?"

"Yes, Ellie, it's really me ... and I'm sorry to tell you that I'm still in trouble. I need your help."

[Pause].

"Where you callin' from?"

"Not far away. I'm not exactly sure how close, but not far. My friends and I are in a car that we think the police may be looking for by now. Ellie, I hate to ask, but could you come get us?"

[Sounds of movement].

Grace pictured in her mind Ellie's room with its queen-size bed and the closet without doors, the dresser and cracked mirror, the picture of her late husband and little Sammy—and the Bible on the nightstand. It all seemed so long ago.

She could hear Ellie Fitzgerald heaving her bulk out from under the covers. Then she heard a deep chuckle. "I reckon some of us go through life rescuin' an' others of us needin' to be rescued. Where, hon? Do you know where you is?"

"I'm going to let you talk to my friend," said Grace, motioning

466

for Harold to come around to the phone. "He's driving. His name is Harold. There are four of us."

She handed Harold the receiver. "Her name is Ellie. Figure out a place where we can meet. She'll come pick us up."

"Miz Ellie? I'm drivin' our friend here an' we sure would appreciate you comin' this way to meet us, if you could. I been lookin' 'round a bit while y'all been talkin' an' I think I got just the spot picked out."

Grace looked at him, curious. He continued talking to Ellie, at the same time pointing through the gathering dawn toward an open field. Just beyond a pair of horses standing at the far side of the field was an old barn leaning precariously to the right, looking about as tired and lonely as she felt right now. She listened as Harold gave directions, shaking her head when he held the receiver out to her again. She didn't have anything else to say. All at once, Grace Grafton-Taylor Carroll felt drained. Totally and completely empty. She knew she couldn't drag this life nor the one she'd left behind seven years ago another mile.

Harold said something else into the phone that she didn't catch, then hung up.

"You okay?" he asked as he walked around to where she was standing with John and Towner.

"I'm wiped out. The last few days—actually, I guess, the last few years—have finally caught up. I'm exhausted. Everything set? She's on her way?"

"Yep. Say, you didn't tell me you had another black friend."

"I didn't used to have any, Harold. Oh, I knew a few black kids when I was younger, but no one I could honestly call a friend. My mother was a good woman, but when it came to race, she was all white, if you know what I mean. By the time I got to college, you all were 'African Americans.' We spoke to one another but I just never

467

had any close African American friends. Then one day God brought Ellie into my life. Or maybe it was the other way around.

"I was a total stranger—a lily white one at that—and I looked like I'd just dropped in from hell, which in reality was exactly where I'd been. She took me in. Cleaned me up. Fed me. Helped me get out of town to start a new life. I wouldn't have survived without her and a few other people who aren't exactly white either. And I learned a valuable lesson. A person's skin color is not important. It's the heart. People with a heart. Like yours. Like all of you. That's what I've been learning on my way to growing up. It's as simple as that." She leaned back against the car and closed her eyes.

"You really been through it, ain't you?" Harold muttered, a mixture of sympathy and admiration in his voice. "Come on, get in, and let's ditch this monster. I tol' her we'd be hangin' 'round that open field beyond the gas station when she got here. But we're gonna have to be careful. It's gettin' near daylight an' while you say color don' mean nothin' to you no more, a black dude like me on foot this early in the mornin' keepin' company with a woman white as you is bound to attract some memorable attention in these parts."

"I could use a cup of coffee," said John, brushing sleep away with the back of his hand. "Suppose there is a Starbuck's nearby?"

"Dreamer," muttered Harold. "Tell you what. Grace, you sack out for a while in the backseat. John, you and Towner go for a walk. Stretch your legs. I'll keep an eye out."

"But you're tired, too ... " Grace protested.

"How long has it been since you got any shuteye?"

She thought back on short Sunday and restless Monday nights in Palm Springs, the day this nightmare had resurfaced. It felt as though that had been light years ago—another life other than the one she was in now. Nothing on Tuesday, and an all night "red-eye" from West to East Coast early Wednesday morning. Now, here it was Thursday morning already.

"I guess it's been awhile," she admitted. "Maybe I will lie down for a few minutes. If I fall asleep, though, you may never get me up again."

"Don' worry none," said Harold reassuringly. "When your friend gets here, I'll make sure you don' miss our ride."

It was five-thirty when Ellie arrived, and though the temperature was cool, it was pleasant at this hour. Harold knew it was going to be a hot and humid Georgia day before they were done. He recognized the rattletrap pickup truck and the license plate number that had been described to him over the phone. He was standing by the road, alone, about fifty meters or so beyond the old station. No one had shown up for work there yet.

He waved as she slowed and came to a stop on the opposite side of the road. "Miz Ellie?"

A heavyset woman smiled out the open window. "Tha's me," she replied. "Where's our little frien'?"

"Over there where the others standin'," he replied, pointing across the field. "Sleepin' in the car."

"That girl an' I got to stop meetin' like this," said Ellic, shaking her head. "Hop in. Let's go get her an' take y'all home."

It was nearly seven-thirty when the young lad from the house across the road arrived at the fence. He pushed his way between the top and middle strands of barbed wire surrounding the field at exactly the same spot he did every day and walked toward the pair of horses. They looked up, waiting expectantly as their meal ticket approached.

He stopped at the first horse, running his hand over her nose and

469

along the mane. Then he moved around to the other, patting flanks, all the while talking to them in low, soothing tones. Appreciative of the boy's attention, the horses nuzzled his hand and neck in return. He patted the older sorrel's flank once more and headed for the barn to scoop out some oats, the horses attentive as they followed, sensing breakfast was near at hand.

This morning, however, breakfast would have to wait, though the horses would never understand why. As the boy entered the barn, he stopped, dumbstruck. He stared at the sleek, black limousine parked in what had forever been an animal walkway leading to the milking stalls and mangers. Forever that is, until now. He circled it once completely, his hand now and then brushing across the smooth metal surface. It was a car like no other he'd ever seen. He tried opening the driver's door, but it was locked. So were the others.

Morning chores were forgotten in the excitement of his discovery as the boy ran back outside, racing across the field toward the house. Meanwhile, the old sorrel snorted her displeasure at being put off like this while the younger horse stood by, head up, eyes following the young lad, puzzled at having been precluded from his customary ration of oats.

76

Thursday 0825 local time

Savannah, Georgia

"Come on, chil', you gots to eat more than that." Ellie came away from the stove with three more pancakes piled on a spatula. "Don' want you passin' out on me again like the las' time you was heah."

Grace smiled demurely, lifting her hands in protest. "Give them to Harold."

"No, ma'am, as wonderful as they are, even I've had enough," declared Harold, pushing back a plate still covered with swirls of maple and blueberry syrup where the last round of pancakes had been eagerly attacked and destroyed.

"You sho?" asked Ellie, a look of disbelief on her face that implied amazement over anyone being full while there was still batter left in the bowl. "How 'bout the rest o' you boys? Y'all had enough?"

"Positive, Ellie," replied John. "Those must be intended for the cook. Come and sit down."

Ellie's dark eyes held her unexpected guests a moment longer before returning her attention to the pancakes. "Well, my mother always said that food is so precious a gift from the Lord that we cain't

471

let it go to waste."

Ellie flipped the cakes onto her still unused plate and proceeded to stuff herself into one of the remaining chairs, patting her ample stomach as soon as she was situated. "But she didn' say nothin' 'bout *this* waist!"

Grace surprised herself by laughing. It was the first time she'd felt laughter emanating from within for—how long? She couldn't remember. Anyway, it felt good. Maybe it was the familiarity of this house that, for a few brief hours seven years before, had served as a refuge for a troubled and broken young woman. A quick glance around the old house when first they arrived had confirmed Grace's belief that some places are simply frozen in time. They never change. Nor should they. This was one of those places.

"Ellie," said John, leaning back in his chair, "you're not only a wonder for the body, what with all this food you've prepared, you're good for the soul, too."

Ellie's eyes twinkled, her mouth too full to say anything right away in response. They waited as she wiped a paper napkin across her mouth and said, "All right, now. I heard why you is heah. Now tell me what you got hidden up them sleeves o' yours. What y'all plannin' to do about it?"

"'Planning' may not exactly be the right word." Grace frowned at her own reminder of the fact that this was too critical a situation for them to be operating in such an impulsive, unpremeditated manner. But what other choice did they have? "We've been praying for wisdom and making this up as we go, Ellie. Up to now, we've mostly been reacting instead of acting.

"That's got to change though," said Harold, "before we can go on an' do this thing."

Ellie looked up at Grace. "You still believe the police might be bought off by Brandenbury?"

"It was two men in highway patrol uniforms who kidnapped Brad in California. I don't think we can take the chance," Grace replied. "Especially now that we're in his home territory. And I know he's here. I can feel him. He's waiting for me!"

The others looked at her, their eyes reflecting the pain from her own.

"Even if we went to the authorities and the ones we talked to were trustworthy, I'm afraid there are enough dishonest ones that word would get back to Brandenbury. He's got deep, deep pockets, Ellie. There doesn't seem to be anything or anyone that he can't buy."

"I know one person he ain't gonna buy," she said softly, putting down her fork. "Not in a million years."

They waited.

"I guess I don't understand what you mean," Grace said at last.

"Sammy."

"Sammy? Your son! What with all that's been happening, I forgot to ask about him. How is he? Where is he? Did he and Sandra ... "

Ellie grinned and pushed herself back from the table. "Sammy's fine. Since you saw him last he jus' got himself bigger and stronger, tha's all."

"That's hard to believe," Grace smiled, her mind flashing back to the day he'd carried her from the street into the house, remembering his strength and the gentle ease with which he had handled her.

"Two years in the Army an' he filled out real good," Ellie said proudly, folding her hands over her belly. "An' when he got out, he came straight home an' let the gov'ment help pay fo' his college. Which, besides servin' the country, was the real reason he joined up in the first place."

"College? Oh, I'm glad to hear that. What's he doing now?"

"Patience, chil', patience. I'm gettin' to it."

"Did he and Sandra get together when he came back?"

"Honey, them two ain't never been apart an' they ain't never gonna be apart. God brought 'em together in elementary school days an' on into high school like two stars in the heavens an' they been theah for each other ever since. They was married right after he got back home from the Army. Live 'bout five blocks from heah an' already made me a granddaughter to play with!"

"Congratulations, Ellie. Oh, you must be so proud."

Ellie beamed.

"How old is she?"

"Six an' a half months."

"What's her name?"

Ellie waited a moment before answering. Her words came soft and tender. "They named her Grace."

Grace sat speechless, then tears welled up in her eyes.

"We ain't never forgot you, chil'," said Ellie.

Grace, all at once self-conscious and overwhelmed, wiped at the tears spilling onto her checks.

Ellie continued. "In the Book—Jesus—he say, 'When I was thirsty you gave me somethin' to drink, an when I was a stranger you took me in, an' when I needed clothes, why you up an' gave me some.' So we come along an' say, 'I don' remember doin' all that. When did that happen, Lord?' An' he say, 'Whatever you did for the least of these heah chillen o' mine, you did fo' me.' Well, I reckon seven years ago, chil', you was about as 'least' as anyone ever gits. An' God—well, he honored us by sendin' one o' his neediest our way. I tol' you I'd pray fo you ever' day, chil'. I ain't missed a one. An' now, look at you. Up an' gonna be a preacher's wife. Can you believe it? Does that God of ours answer prayers or what?"

"Wendal and Tara said that very same thing to me seven years ago, Ellie. I think they learned it from you. Yes, I want to be the preacher's wife all right," said Grace, "but after all this, he may want to rethink his proposal. I'm still causing more trouble than good."

"Hush 'bout that. You jus' feelin' sorry fo yoself right now. An' you gots to move beyon' 'sorry' an' get on with gettin' on. Those people that belongs to you—the ones you think is out there on that island. That man and those precious little ones, they gots to be brought back safe, that's all."

"That's the problem, Ellie. I've gotten this far by putting people like Harold here and Pastor John and Towner … and Paul and Maggie back in Asheville in grave danger. What if Paul dies? He lost so much blood by the time we got him to the hospital. Then we just left him and kept on going. And we don't have any real plan from here. I just know that Brandenbury has Brad and the children out there on Daufuskie. I'm sure of it. He's out there all right, and he's waiting for me to come to him."

"I understand. But you interrupted me jus' 'bout the time I was leadin' up to somethin'. We was talkin' 'bout that sweet little namesake that Sandra and Sammy done brought into this world. Remember?"

Grace nodded.

"Well, ever' time they look into that chil's beautiful eyes, they think about you. They pray fo' you, too, jus' like me," she said triumphantly. "You see? You is very special to all of us!"

"I can't even begin to understand that, Ellie. Not at all. I feel like anything but special right now. I may be the preacher's wannabe wife, but you and I have got to sit down sometime long enough for you to teach me something more about true faith and redemption. You've certainly got it figured out a whole lot more than I do!"

Ellie shrugged and went on. "Anyway, you'll be mighty interested

475

in findin' out where Sammy's workin' these days."

Grace waited as Ellie set about rearranging herself on the chair that appeared hardly up to its task.

"He's a police officer."

Grace leaned back from the table. She had not expected that. "A police officer?"

"Here in Savannah?" asked Towner, who with John and Harold had been listening with interest as the two women conversed.

Ellie nodded. "An' he's one policeman that ol' Brandenbury ain't gonna own, no matter how hard he tries."

Grace thought back to the young teenager. The first teenager she had ever heard say a prayer.

Good Sammy.

That's the way she thought of him. Like the man in the Bible. A police officer!

"Will he help us?" she asked.

"We can ask. I got a feelin', though, that I already knows what his answer is gonna be," she said, frowning as she spoke, her voice suddenly trailing off as she pushed back from the table and stood up.

"What is it, Ellie?"

Ellie's brow furrowed, her eyes filled with a concern that belied her words. "Nothin, hon. I got a feelin' jus' then, tha's all."

"Something's wrong?"

"No, never mind."

"Tell me, Ellie. What's bothering you? Does it have to do with me?"

"I jus' got this feelin' that what we's about to do heah is gonna be real dangerous an' … an' tha's all." Ellie turned away and began running water over dishes in the sink.

476

77

Sammy and Sandra joined the huddle as soon as he came off duty as a night patrolman in Savannah's downtown historic section. Harold sat quietly next to Ellie on one side and Grace on the other, then Sandra and Sammy. John and Towner sat across from them. Grace cuddled Ellie's sleeping granddaughter in her arms. She had just finished reciting the critical details of her story once more, this time primarily for Sammy's benefit, though Sandra listened just as intently, with a look of concern on her face. Grace was certain she knew what Sandra must be thinking.

Isn't it enough that I send my husband and lover and the father of our daughter out into the streets at night to protect the citizens of Savannah from God knows what? Do I now have to offer him up for a woman we only briefly met seven years ago and who, for some mysterious reason, has become our firstborn's namesake?

So when Sandra reached over to touch Sammy's hand and asked softly, "What do you think, sweet? Are we going to help Grace get her family back?"

Grace was dumbfounded.

477

"I'm thinking about Jason Mack," replied Sammy. "Remember him?"

"You mean that Coast Guard dude with the cute blond wife? The one that was talking to you about joining the force once his tour is up?"

"That's him."

"You think he'll help?"

Sammy shrugged. "He knows the waters around here. Been working with rescue teams his whole time in. The two of us could go in underwater."

"Hold it!" It was Grace who spoke up, leaning forward in her chair, careful not to hit the baby's head against the table. "No one is going in without me!"

"And don't forget about us, Sammy," said John with a smile. "I guess I still have another invasion or two left in me." Towner smiled grimly and nodded, remembering the time he and John and gone after John's daughter who was being held by terrorists in Iran.

"Look," Sammy argued, "we aren't planning to launch another world war here. How many do you think he's got with him on the island?"

"There were only three or four the night I was there," said Grace.

"I don't think he'll have an army there now," Towner interrupted, tracing his finger over a map of the area spread out between them. "He's probably sporting a small hardcore team of bodyguards. Too many, and he can't keep who or what he's doing a secret. Three or four sounds about right. Six or eight tops. So we won't take on the whole 7th Cav. This has to be silent, quick, and clean. Grace here thinks Brandenbury is sitting out there waiting for her to come knocking. He'll be looking for her, not us. That's our ticket. We go in, grab the hostages and barrel out again."

"Yes!" Grace exclaimed, jumping to her feet. She handed little Grace back to her mother. "That's what we've got to do."

The others looked at her with surprise.

"You mean grab the hostages and run?"

"Yes—no. I mean, he'll be looking for me. Right? Then that's who he gets."

"What nonsense you talkin' now, girl?" exclaimed Ellie.

"First thing we've got to do is find a boat. Where do we go to rent one, and how much will it cost? No matter, I can use my credit card."

"No, you can't," cautioned Harold. "You'll tip off the police an' lead 'em right here to us."

"The boat ain't no problem."

Everyone turned to look at Ellie.

"I got the boat."

"You have a boat?" asked John, surprised.

"Sho. It's an ol' shrimper that tries hard to keep afloat, but it's a boat." Ellie chuckled. "I call 'er a hole in the water, sometimes, 'cause she sho ain't nothin' to count on fo' much other than shrimp. An' she's in bad shape. I been tryin' to sell 'er but ain't nobody fool enough to take 'er on, I guess. They say she'll cost too much to bring 'er up to snuff, an they're prob'ly right. So mostly, she just sits theah makin' a hole in the water."

"Is she in running condition?" asked Towner. "Will she get us there and back?"

"Sho she runs, but mostly she jus' runs me."

There was a murmuring of amused agreement from Sammy and Sandra.

"No, wait, hear me out. Your boat may be the answer, Ellie. At least part of the answer. This might just be the only way we can do it."

The others listened intently for the next hour, occasionally shaking

479

heads, butting in with alternate ideas, arguing, even raising their voices until, at one point, little Grace woke up and began to cry. Sandra went to the other room to feed her.

Finally, everyone appeared to be in agreement. And then Ellie led them in a simple, heartfelt prayer.

When it was over, they shook hands and slapped shoulders. Each of them gave Grace a hug. Sandra kissed Sammy on the cheek and smiled reassuringly at Grace, hugging her tightly. She tried very hard to hide it, but Grace could see the concern that filled her beautiful, dark eyes.

78

Charles Brandenbury smiled as he watched the launch come alongside the dock below the house. Noah Parker threw a small suitcase up to Dempsey Valbrick, who did double duty as a waiter and as one of Brandenbury's bodyguards. Valbrick was also in charge of engine maintenance for Brandenbury's small speedboats and the yacht. And he was also a qualified pilot and aviation mechanic, especially when it came to small airplanes like the one Senator Burton used to fly.

Brandenbury checked his watch as he stepped outside to greet the Senator. Still more than an hour until noon.

"You're late," he said as Parker came up the path.

"That's because I waited around for your driver for more than an hour before I rented a car and drove down."

"He didn't show up? Was your plane on time?"

"Right on the button. But your man didn't show."

"That's not like him. He went out to gas up the car yesterday and wasn't back by the time I left with our guests." Brandenbury frowned. "I'll have Ho San check on him. Come on in."

"I heard she's married. You have her husband here?"

"She's not married, but she's in love with the guy. A preacher, no less. He's here all right, in living color. And his kids, too."

"Kids?" Parker repeated incredulously. Face livid, he stepped closer

481

to Brandenbury. "You've got kids here, too?"

"They're not hers. They are his. Two of them. By his first wife, who died of cancer. The good Reverend has been seeing our runaway over a year now. Seems she just walked into his church, and they fell in love. Now the word is that he's proposed. They're getting married. Isn't that precious?"

"How did you find that out?"

"The kids. They overheard their dad ask her to marry him last Sunday night."

"Why did you have his kids picked up anyway?" Parker swore as he turned away to look out the window. "That's kidnapping!" He swore again.

"And taking her lover boy out of circulation isn't? Get a grip on reality, *Mr. President.* We have to take good care of Ms. Grafton this time—along with anyone else she may have let in on our little secret. And that includes the preacher's kids."

"How many are there?"

"Two."

"How old?"

"The oldest is ten. A boy. The girl is seven or eight, I think."

"You think. You don't seem to be thinking at all. How can you possibly be thinking and do something so stupid as taking a couple of kids? Taking the preacher is bad enough."

"Watch who you're calling stupid, *Mr. President.*"

"And stop with the 'Mr. President,'" Parker retorted.

"Back off, Noah. Don't forget what has brought you this far. It wasn't your brain, that's for sure. And your good looks never got you any farther than the nearest bedroom. If that woman spills her guts, then we've got a whole lot of backpedaling to do. And you can kiss your ticket to the White House goodbye. It could be the 'Big House' instead!"

Parker swallowed nervously at that. "So what's next?"

"The police have Reynolds. He's in a hospital out in California."

"What?"

"You heard me."

"How ... what happened? What's going on, Charlie?"

"They found him in a church in Palm Springs with the back of his head bashed in. Compliments of you-know-who."

Parker swallowed. "Was it ... "

"He went to meet with our missing friend. She goes by the name Taylor Carroll now. She must have surprised the stupid jerk. The report is they found his gun on the floor. One bullet fired. Into a wall. Apparently too slow on the draw. Anyway, he had orders to bring her to the Farm, and he obviously blew his assignment. But it's being taken care of."

Parker eyed Brandenbury. "What do you mean?"

"I mean what I said. 'Taken care of.' Sim is out there now to offer Terry our condolences."

"Charlie, he's been your right hand man for ... "

"Nobody fails and stays on my team," roared Brandenbury. "He was supposed to bring her back here. A simple assignment with four men out there to pick up one solitary woman masquerading as a preacher's girlfriend." Brandenbury suddenly broke into peals of laughter. "Isn't that great? A church lady. No wonder it took so long to find her."

"So what are we doing here?" Parker asked in exasperation.

"Waiting."

"For what?"

"For the preacher's girl friend to show up."

"What makes you think she'll come here?"

"Because the woman is clever, that's why. The way her mind works is impressive. Very impressive, as opposed to some minds we're both acquainted with around here. As soon as I heard about Reynolds, I knew we had to come to the island. She probably doesn't know the Farm exists. And, even if she does, she could never get past my security. But, it's different here. And this is a place she knows about. She'll think this through and realize that her dear husband-to-be and the brats are here—on Daufuskie—where it all started seven years ago. Rather poetic, don't you think?"

"You really think she's that smart?"

"Trust me, Noah. Our little fish is swimming upstream right now."

"What do you intend to do?"

"What I should have done back then. But, first, I want to know how she managed to escape that night and how she's been able to stay hidden all these years, in spite of all the money I've poured into finding her. It should be quite a story."

"You think she'll tell you?"

"Tell me? She was your escort for the evening, remember? You can ask her yourself. I'm sure she'd much rather talk with you than to me." Brandenbury laughed. "Come on. Let me introduce you to the soon-to-be-late Brad Weston. You'll like him. He's really quite a nice fellow. His son is a flippant smart aleck, but the girl is cute. Pretty, actually. Very pretty."

Noah Parker shuddered as Brandenbury's hand fell on his shoulder. *How did I ever get involved with this maniac?*

79

At ten-thirty, Grace had helped to cast off the dock lines as they got under way on the Savannah. Now, three hours later, Grace decided Ellie's assessment of her shrimper had been right. The boat was indeed little more than a "hole in the water." According to Ellie, the old wooden boat had been Jeffy's before he died. Back then he'd managed to keep her in pretty good shape. And she was paid for.

Now the aging vessel was mostly peeling paint and soggy timbers. She wasn't as big as most commercial shrimpers, but Ellie went ahead and worked the boat anyway, whenever she could, just because she loved the salt and the sea. And because she still loved Jeffy.

He had been so proud of the *Ellie I* and had worked hard to pay it off before he died. Now, sad to say, it was hard to keep up—and expensive, too. But, somehow she had managed, even if it was by the smallest of margins. This was an entirely different side of Ellie than Grace had known before. But it fit her persona in every respect.

Jeffy had loved shrimping, in spite of the fact that it meant working twelve to fourteen hour days, six days a week, from June to December. When it wasn't shrimping season in these waters, he would sometimes take the boat into the Gulf of Mexico or south of Key West.

Ellie had been his "First Mate" on those long trips. In later years, when his health began to fail, he chose to stay closer to home and trawl for crabs and conchs during the winter and spring. These were times when they had been the closest—living, loving, laughing— wishing for more time as the sand in Jeffy's hour glass slipped away too swiftly. And then he was gone.

Now, any day she could be out here with Jeffy's boat, well, that was a good day, that's all there was to say. It hadn't been easy, but between what little they had managed to save up, her dead husband's social security check and her part time job with Clean Well Janitorial Services, she made out just fine. Most of the time.

The boat smelled like dead fish and shrimp, and it wobbled as it plowed along through the Intracoastal Waterway. Though old and decrepit, it was pretty much like any other vessel of its kind. Shorter than most shrimp boats, the *Ellie I* measured about twenty meters in length. The engine room was located below the deck and the cabin above.

In the cabin was a small galley with a sink, stove, table, and even an old television set. There were two tiny bedrooms and a bathroom that Ellie referred to decorously as "the head" located in between. At the front of the cabin was the wheelhouse where Ellie was busy, at the moment, steering toward their destination.

The deck itself was littered with winches, cables, chains, lines, and nets. There was also a homing device attached to the outside of the cabin. In case the boat sank, Ellie told her, it would send a signal to a satellite with the boat's identity and last location. That way, Coast Guard rescuers might be able to rescue whoever had been on board. *Small comfort, that.*

When Grace asked how she could possibly handle all these lines and nets, Ellie said that in the days when she used to engage in some "serious shrimpin'," she would hire one or two crew members—strikers—who did most of the really hard work in return for a percentage of the day's catch for their wages.

The sun continued its slow decent in the west as Grace's thoughts returned to the last time she'd been on these waters. On that occasion, the yacht had been sleek, trim, and expensive. The wine and the company had been heady. She'd been young, adventurous, and alive.

Alive. And, before the night was over, desperate to stay that way.

The late afternoon breeze felt sultry and damp as she leaned against the side, watching the old shrimp boat carve a crude and artless path through the river, a path that tended to disappear as soon as it was formed.

Stroke ... stroke ... stroke ... Stay in the lane, Grace ... don't drift ... Grace!

She felt herself again clinging desperately to the line and the rubber fender ... being dragged through the waves until her arms lost their feeling ...

"Someone's broken in here!"

Another boat ... a stolen shower ... some crackers and a few clothes.

It's funny. I've wished so often that I knew their names—who they were—so that I could apologize for invading their space ... stealing their belongings ... maybe even repay them ...

It was all so long ago ... and she had been so desperate to survive ... to stay alive just a little longer. *Alive.* Seven years later that was about all she could say for herself. She was still alive.

Just then the boat shifted under her feet. She adjusted her stance and stared out across the steamy swamplands. How much longer she would be alive, she could only guess. Her body ached from lack of rest. All at once, she felt old and exhausted. Uneasy.

Her last time out here on this river had begun as a lark. It had ended in unspeakable tragedy. This time was no lark. It was life and death. But how would it end? The mission was clear and simple in her mind. Rescue Brad and the children. Bring them home safely. Or die in the attempt.

The air.

The smells.

The humidity.

It was all so familiar.

It felt as though no time had passed at all, that everything was still the same. The same and yet different, too. Seven years ago, Grace had been ready for what life was all about. Excited. Full of dreams. Ready to take all she had worked and studied for and find her place in the world. Ready to make a life.

Today, it was no longer about making a life. It was about clinging to life, to something so fundamentally basic as physical survival. Today, she felt grim. Beaten. Bone-tired. There was no excitement left inside. No thrill. Just emptiness. The dreams had been ripped from her soul in this place—in these very waters, and in the swamp that lay sweltering all around her. Mocking her still. She had vowed in her heart never to return to this place ... and now her heart had brought her here again. One last time.

Wiping the back of her hand across her forehead, she wished again that she had not acquiesced to the group's insistence that she not try to confront Brandenbury, but instead stay behind with the boat. If only hindsight would offer chances to right bad choices and terrible consequences. But it didn't. This was her mess. She had to clean it up.

Her gaze turned upriver.

Nothing had changed. And yet everything had changed. She felt it in her weariness. This time on the river she was ... old.

She glanced at the others. Pastor John and Sammy had driven to Hilton Head and were renting a boat to cross over to Daufuskie. Sammy was confident they could find the trail Grace had described to them on which she had escaped from Brandenbury and Parker and the one John was convinced had to have been Marwan Dosha. Once there, they would coordinate by cell phone with the others.

Towner and Jason Mack were busy sorting through the scuba gear spread out on the wooden deck. She looked again at the spare tank lying off to one side and wished that she'd insisted on going in with them.

Jason Mack had turned out to be Jason MacKinsey, news even to his good friend, Sammy. He hailed from a small town on the Cape, not far from Hyannis Port. He loved the sea, couldn't imagine living anywhere else than in a coastal town, but had come to prefer the warmer clime in Georgia to the harshness of Massachusetts's winters. When Sammy had invited him over to the house to explain the situation and the plan, Jason had nodded his acceptance of the challenge without hesitation.

Towner hadn't said much, but catching Grace's eye, he motioned toward Jason and gave nod of approval—a clear indication he liked the young man. They had been chosen for this role in their private little hit and grab exercise because of their skills as scuba divers. While Jason wasn't a SEAL, Towner was at least giving him credit for the appearance of being competent. Grace just hoped if things got out of hand that Jason was up to the task.

"If this happened to one of my little sisters," Jason stated flatly, "I'd make sure the guy was buried in a landfill somewhere like the garbage he is!"

Early on, Harold had stood in the wheelhouse talking to Ellie.

Now he was sitting to one side in the stern staring at the shoreline. Grace decided that if ever a black man could look pale, Harold was that man. He shifted around on the seat and glanced over at Grace. It was in his eyes. The river and open waters were not that rough and the swells hardly noticeable, but no matter. The man was seasick. He managed to give her a weak grin. "Now you know why I joined the Army. This is for fish, not humans!"

Grace patted him on the arm. "Hang in there, soldier. The enemy's not far away now." She felt her pulse quickening and the adrenaline kicking in, even though she knew she was running empty on empty. When she looked at herself in Ellie's bathroom mirror, she'd been shocked by the haggard lines at the edges of her eyes and mouth. They had appeared mysteriously, as though part of a black magic curse. And her eyes were rimmed with redness from lack of sleep. She wondered what Maggie was doing right now.

Dear, blessed Maggie. And Paul. Oh, please, God, let him be all right ...

As the boat rounded the point, Grace stepped up into the wheelhouse and tapped Ellie's arm, pointing off to the right at one o'clock. "That's it. That's Brandenbury's dock up ahead."

"All right, hon. Boys, git yoselves ready." Ellie glanced over her shoulder and called out to the others. "It's comin' up now. We'll be theah in a few minutes. Be careful, Mr. Towner. You, too, Jason. God go with you."

Jason smiled and nodded.

"About sixteen feet," she said.

"Meters, ma'am," Jason called out. "It's meters, now."

"Meters, shmeters," Ellie muttered, turning her attention back to the wheel. "It's 'feet' what's got me this far without drownin' an' 'feet' will git me home."

Grace could not resist smiling.

Jason came forward and gave Ellie a one-armed hug, kissing her pudgy cheek. "We'll be back before you know it, ma'am, with Sammy and Reverend Cain and the others," he assured her. "Be careful yourself. Keep this leaky old tub afloat so we can all ride home and not have to swim the whole way, okay?" He turned to Harold. "You going to be okay, man?"

Harold waved weakly.

"Oh ... oh ... look!" It was Grace who cried out. She was standing beside Ellie, peering through a set of binoculars.

Every one turned their gaze forward. Even Harold leaned over the side to get a better view.

"It's David and Nancy!" she exclaimed. "They're out there on the dock. There's a man with them."

"And in a couple of minutes we'll be close enough to be seen," Ellie declared, "so everbody, get down!"

Grace sat down and stared across at Harold and the others. She closed her eyes for a moment, breathing a prayer of thanks, and then opened them again. Her heart was pounding.

They're alive. And, they're here. They're really here!

"Towner. I'm going with you."

"No, you're not."

"David and Nancy are out there in the open," she insisted. "We can get them and bring them back to the boat."

Towner lifted his head in order to see the dock. "Jason and I will do this."

"No. They won't know you. They're afraid, Towner. They have to be frightened to death by now. They'll need to hear a familiar voice. And if they resist out of fear and an alarm is sounded before you can get to Brad ... "

Towner gave her a hard look. "You're a good swimmer, right?"

491

"Yes," she answered. "I need to go."

"I'm not going to argue with you. So are you ready, Grace?"

Grace blinked, still mounting a mental argument as to why she should be permitted to go with them. Towner was looking at her, addressing her by the name she had long ago abandoned because of what had happened on these waters. The name of Sammy's little girl.

"What?"

"I said, are you ready?"

She nodded, afraid that her voice would betray the way she was breaking up inside.

Towner, Jason, Harold, and Grace huddled together; listening as Towner went over their revised plan of attack. He reached out and put his hand on her shoulder. His gaze remained hard. Uncompromising. She remembered the same look from the Farm the night before in North Carolina.

"Okay, Grace. You do this, and we're going to be counting on you. You'll be the key. You mess up, and it's over. You sure you can do this?"

She nodded again and swallowed. "I'll be all right. Seeing the kids there ... it just hit me for a second."

"I know." Towner's voice was reassuring. He placed both hands on her face. "Listen. You've got to understand something. Those children are there. Right out in the open. Think about it. Why are they there? We can see 'em from here. They could be decoys. The kids don't know it but that could be why they're out there in the open like that. So they can be seen. They aren't just getting fresh air. They're part of this Brandenbury dude's scheme. If he thinks you are coming, he knows it will be by water. So put some more bait out. Reel her in. Just keep on remembering, those are some very bad dudes over there that are determined to come between those kids and us. This is war.

All right? No holds barred war. You got that?"

Grace stared back at Towner. "Yes," she replied finally, pressing her inner fears and uncertainties into a dark box to be sorted through later. She swallowed again. *Okay, Jesus, this is it. It's now or never. Help me to do this.*

And a gradual calm of sorts returned. Jason held up the spare tank and she slipped it onto her back, testing to make sure it was working.

"All right, people." It was Ellie who spoke up, her voice low, but commanding. "This ol' motor o' mine is about to give me a problem. In two minutes, it's gonna be runnin' out o' pushin' power. Looks like if I don' git it started up real quick, I'll drift right past that dock up ahead. The one with them kids standin' theah. I'll need to work on it a little while, so git yoself ready to do what you come to do."

80

Dempsey Valbrick had been watching the old boat wallow through the water like a pregnant walrus ever since it had cleared the point. At least it was something else to watch. He hated kids. And here he was, stuck with baby-sitting the two brats. Why Mr. Brandenbury wanted them out here, he wasn't sure. To get them out from under foot, most likely. He noticed the boat had their attention, too. They had halted their irritating whispering and were standing off to one side, watching.

As the boat came closer, he brought his binoculars up and peered out across the New River. A solitary, very rotund, black woman with graying hair was at the wheel. There did not appear to be anyone else aboard, though he couldn't see past the woman into the small wooden structure that served as a cabin. Dempsey shook his head as he lowered the glasses.

What's that old bat doing out there in that scow? It looks like it could sink any minute.

No sooner had the thought passed through his mind than he heard the rhythmic beat of the engine sputter, resume its pulsating chug-chugging, and sputter once more, before finally dying altogether. He looked through his binoculars again. The old woman was down on her knees now. Apparently she was checking the engine. Or maybe

494

she was praying. That old tub looked like it could use a little divine intervention. Or maybe better, last rites.

The boat continued drifting slowly, inching closer toward the dock, although it looked as though she would easily pass by, even if she didn't get the engine started up again.

"What's going on?" he shouted as the boat drifted closer.

"Got me an engine problem, I guess," the woman called back as she looked up from the open hatch. "Ain't no big deal though. It's happened befo. I jus' gotta blow the carb out a little an' I think it'll start right up."

If it doesn't, maybe you'll drift on out to sea. Make it back to where your ancestors came from and stop taking up space here.

He chuckled at the thought as the woman stood up and disappeared into the cabin.

Valbrick resented how the Asian population had invaded America in recent years. Who did they think they were anyway, taking all the good jobs? He had no use for these "foreigners" who were moving in from the four corners of the world. That included the Mexicans and Puerto Ricans, too. But the people he hated most were blacks. Hands down. He wasn't sure exactly why. He just did, that's all. Always had. It would be fun to put one more down. He'd done it before. He fingered the weapon strapped to his waist and wondered if he could hit her from this distance with a handgun. No problem. If she drifts much closer, this one would be easy. He released the strap, lifted his gun from its holster and sited in on the old woman.

How could you miss a target that big?

Suddenly, a small round hole appeared in his forehead, two inches above his nose. Valbrick crumpled to his knees and pitched forward face down, his gun clattering onto the wooden decking.

David and Nancy turned to stare at the fallen man, surprise written on their faces.

Seasick or not, from his position low and just outside the cabin hatch, Harold Justiss Jones grunted his satisfaction. The once-upon-a-time Army sniper had scored a direct hit. Target down! Where Towner had come up with this MSG90 and its sound suppressor in such short order, he could only imagine. He knew this weapon. It was a favorite among SWAT equivalent German *Spezialeinsatzkommando* units. The man obviously had connections. In any event he had no regrets for having taken out this evil child abductor and traitor to all he had stood for in his years of defending the country.

Seconds later, he and Ellie watched as a solitary head broke the river's surface on the near side of the dock. Then another bobbed up beside the first.

81

"David. Nancy!"

The children were still staring at the man who had been guarding them, now laying face down on the dock. He wasn't moving. But they could hear him still—calling their names! David threw his arms around Nancy.

"David. Nancy! Come over to the side of the dock. Quickly. My name is Jason. I'm with the Coast Guard. We're here for you. Hurry."

It wasn't the man with the gun after all!

What had the voice said? We're here for you?

David took Nancy's hand. They ran to the dock's edge and looked down. Two swimmers were in the water and one was …

Taylor!

"Jump into the water, guys." Taylor's voice was soft, but urgent. "We're here to take you home!"

David stifled a cry of relief. He gripped Nancy's hand tightly. "It's Taylor! She's come to get us."

"No, David. I can't," Nancy whispered, tearing her gaze away from the surprising sight of Taylor's familiar face to look at her brother. She started to cry. Relief. Fear. "It's too far. I can't jump. I can't swim."

"You don't have to, Sis," David pushed her closer to the edge. "We'll hold hands and jump together. Look. It's Taylor!"

"What about Daddy?" Nancy whimpered, looking into David's eyes.

"We'll get help and come back," David lied, sensing that they would not be returning, yet anxious to at least save his little sister. He'd promised himself that much when this ordeal had begun. "Hold your nose."

"I can't, David," she cried softly. "You go."

"Hurry!" It was Taylor calling to them again.

Suddenly David threw his arms around Nancy's waist and, holding her tight against his body, leaped off the dock. They sailed through the air and into the water with a splash. Beneath the surface, David turned Nancy loose and pushed her upward, flailing the water as best he could, struggling to hold his breath. Then, from out of the greenish darkness someone was beside him, wrapping an arm around his waist, lifting him to the surface. He broke free of the water, gasping for breath. It was Taylor. Taylor was holding him in her arms!

"Where's my sister?"

"Jason's got her. She's all right, David, thanks to you."

"How did you?"

"Later. Right now, I want you to go with Jason."

"But what about ... "

"I'm going to get your dad."

David stared deep into Taylor's eyes. "He's in the house, Taylor. Upstairs. They have him tied up. I think they gave him drugs or something."

"How many are there?"

"I don't know. I've seen four different men. I'm not sure. I think there are others."

"Okay. It's all right. You help Jason with Nancy."

"They have guns, Taylor."

"I know," Taylor replied as she reached over and hugged Nancy reassuringly. "Now both of you. Go with Jason."

"Have you ever gone scuba diving?" Jason asked the children.

"Once in a swimming pool with my dad," David answered.

Nancy shook her head, still crying softly. As she clung to Jason, it was obvious that just the thought paralyzed her with fear.

"Okay, guys, here's what we're going to do. You swim pretty good, David?"

"I'm okay."

"You'll be great. The hard part is already over. Nancy, this tank is light. It's filled with air. I'm going to slip your arms into the straps and tighten them. See? Now, put the mouthpiece in your mouth and breathe. Try it."

Nancy put it in her mouth and closed her eyes. She took a deep breath, and her eyes opened in surprise.

"See? That's perfect, Nancy," Jason encouraged. "You get all your air through that. All right?"

Nancy nodded, her eyes still showing fear as she clung to Jason's neck.

"Don't breathe through your nose any more until we surface, okay? Just keep this in your mouth, and you'll have plenty of air. Understand?"

"Yes," she said, looking up into this stranger's eyes, wanting desperately to be sure she could trust him.

"David, you and I will share this other one. I'll take a breath, and then you get one. We'll pass it back and forth. Just hang onto my suit with one hand and relax. Close your eyes or keep them open. I don't care. I'll do the swimming. All right?"

David nodded hesitantly, bucking up his courage.

"I'll keep hold on Nancy, David. You hang on to my belt, and

499

don't let go. What we have to do is stay under water, so we can't be seen. Okay?"

"Where are we going?"

"To that boat right out there."

David looked between the timbers of the dock and saw the boat he'd noticed earlier.

"Okay."

"I love you, kids," Taylor whispered as David and Nancy stared longingly at her.

"Come with us, Taylor," Nancy pleaded.

"Can't," she answered, her voice choking.

"All right, David. Ready, Nancy?" asked Jason. "Let's go."

Jason dove, taking the two children with him.

Grace stared for a moment at the ripples that marked where they had been. Then she looked up. Her part of the rescue had just begun. She pulled herself out of the water until she could stand on one of the cross beams that supported the dock platform. Crouching, she balanced on the narrow timber, listening for any sounds of people running toward her, letting her know that they had been seen. Thankfully, all was quiet. For all intents and purposes, serene.

She pulled herself up and peered over the edge of the deck, stifling a cry. A face. A face, strangely familiar and only inches from her own, eyes open but unseeing.

The waiter? This was the man who had served them dinner that night!

Quickly recovering from her surprise, she heaved herself onto the dock and moved swiftly, dragging the man's heavy body into the gazebo while thoughts of the two women servants back in North Carolina went through her mind. She felt for a pulse. Grace pushed back the feeling she was going to throw up over the realization that they had just killed a man. Unlike the two women, this one did not need to be tied up. And he wasn't getting away. Ever. She pushed him under one of the benches, out of sight.

Breathless from exertion, she sat down on the gazebo bench and leaned back, her heart pounding. She narrowed her eyes, peering into the sun across the water toward the boat trying to see some sign of the children. Nothing. *They're okay. They've got to be okay. Jason will take care of them.* Over and over. Reassuring herself. At last she turned and looked toward the house in the woods that lay beyond the land's end of the long dock. She was amazed at how well things had gone so far. It did not appear that anyone had noticed the flurry of activity on the dock.

Thank you, God!

It had been an unbelievable, last minute bonus to find the children outside, accessible to their rescue efforts. *Brandenbury knows what to use for bait, all right, but sometimes the fish manages to slip the bait off the hook before being reeled in.*

Grace decided this had better be one of those times.

She was beginning to breathe more easily, letting the tension and urgency inside her reshape itself into something useful instead of debilitating. She glanced at her watch. Twenty past. *Ten more minutes. Maybe this is going to work, after all! In ten more minutes, Pastor John and Sammy should be in place near the house.*

Their agreed upon timing was off a bit now, but they still should have had the time needed to come in from the north. Their last cell phone contact said they had reached the island. Their task consisted of overcoming whatever guards might be in that direction, clearing an escape route for their exit once they recovered Brad. All the while avoiding setting off any security alarms on the way.

So Pastor John was with Sammy, and Jason was back on the boat with the children, and Towner … well, Grace was not sure where he was. He had decided to approach the island from the south on his own. Everything had changed at the last minute when Grace had become part of the rescue mission. Once again Grace had the feeling of tumbling down a water slide on which she had no real control. Their plan had shifted dramatically. They were operating by the seat of their pants again. But so far, so good.

Next was the riskiest gamble of all. In ten minutes, Grace was to walk across the dock and up the path to the house, calling Brandenbury outside.

Would he come?

She believed he would, basing her conviction on the fact that his ego could not resist such a confrontation. Besides, he held all the cards. At least so he thought. Pastor John and Sammy would be waiting to take him by surprise. Towner would come in from the opposite direction. At least, that's what she thought. It all felt different now that she was right here, on the dock. They would then free Brad and run for it. Not complicated, but was their plan too simple? Were they walking into a trap? It was the best plan they had been able to come up with in the short time available. And now at least the children were safe. Already an added bonus.

At the sound, she looked up. Someone was coming down the path from the house.

Oh, great! She wished that when Towner had let her feel his service revolver in her hand back on the boat she had held on to it.

"It's simple enough," he had said. "Release the safety, get as close as you can, point the gun and shoot."

Her answer should have been, "Okay."

But it wasn't. Instead, she had handed it back to Towner saying, "I can't. I'm not sure I'd be able to do it." Three times he had urged her to take it, and three times she had refused. Now, second thoughts, heightened by her extreme vulnerability, flooded her mind.

As the man stepped from the path onto the land's end of the dock, Grace recognized him. He was wearing a short-sleeve shirt, no tie, slacks, and tennis shoes. With both hands stuffed in his pockets he ambled forward, pausing for a moment to take in the beauty of the surrounding scenery, his attention drawn to the old, worn-out wooden shrimp boat that drifted a hundred meters or so off shore.

He started toward her again, then slowed his pace. She knew when he'd caught sight of her in the gazebo's shadowy interior, though it was in a direct line with the sun and difficult to see clearly. She sensed him studying her while she remained as far back in the shadows as possible. *Maybe he thinks it's the guard.* She swallowed nervously. The plan she had started to believe in only a few moments ago had just fallen off the dock. Think. She resigned herself. Her only chance was a brazen bluff. Could she pull it off?

The man continued toward her, squinting as he drew closer.

Grace breathed a silent prayer, took a deep breath.

"Hello, Noah."

Parker stopped short, surprised at the sound of a woman's voice.

"Hello. I didn't know that Charles had any lady friends here today." Parker's voice took on an immediate tone of warmth and curiosity. Always the lady's man. He continued toward the gazebo.

"I think he's been expecting me, but maybe he doesn't know that his 'lady friend,' as you so delicately put it, has already arrived." Grace stepped out of the shadow and into the sunlight. "At least, not yet."

Parker's stunned look said it all. His step faltered, as if suddenly forgetting where to put his foot down, visibly shaken at the sight of her. Standing in water-soaked canvas shoes, shorts, and a blouse that clung to her body, hair damp and stringy, there was no mistaking this

503

man's recognition of her.

"Surprised to see me, Noah?" Grace folded her arms over her chest in an effort to appear confident instead of exposing the shaky nervousness that she felt. "It's been awhile."

As he moved toward her, she retreated back into the shadows.

"Easy, Noah. Not too close. As you can see, I've already put down one of your thugs. And the idea of doing the same to you has a certain appeal to me right now, if you know what I mean."

Parker hesitated as he took in the bloody streaks on the dock planks and then Valbrick's lifeless body stuffed beneath the gazebo bench. Grace was banking on this tweaking Parker's uncertainty. He would see that she did not appear to have a gun ... but now she had one hand behind her. How could she have done this without one?

"Grace. Let's talk about all this rationally."

"Okay, Senator, let's."

"What ... what do you think you can achieve by showing up here anyway? There are guards all over the place. And Charlie ... " Parker hesitated.

"And Charlie?" Grace repeated. "Oh, yes, what about Charlie? In fact, where *is* good old Charlie right now? I thought he'd be here to offer his love and greetings in person instead of sending you."

Parker didn't respond.

"Is he with my fiancé?"

Parker didn't answer.

"Is he?" Grace demanded, taking a step closer, one hand on her hip while keeping the other hidden behind her.

"Yes," Parker answered. Sweat, whether from the humidity or from apprehension, had formed a thin, moist line across his forehead.

"Thank you. And the children? David and Nancy? What about them?"

"They're around here somewhere. They're all right."

Good. He doesn't know.

Grace glanced at her watch, then back at Parker.

Three more minutes. The guys should be in place by now. But what should I do with Parker?

"Do you ever think much about BJ and Ilene, Noah? I think about them every day."

"Grace, you must believe me. I had no idea. I had nothing to do with that. He'd already killed her before we got up stairs. You know that."

"You mean Brandenbury murdered BJ by himself? And you had nothing at all to do with it?"

"Of course. But it was an accident. You were there!"

"But Ilene wasn't dead yet, was she? When I left to see about BJ, she was unconscious on the hallway floor. I left her with you, Noah. I told you to protect her. I left her with a United States senator. Servant of the people and all that. So what happened? Did you kill her yourself? Did you murder Ilene?"

"No, no. It was him. I mean ..." Noah seemed flustered. "It was Charlie. He ... broke her neck."

Grace flinched at that.

"It was ... it was ... " Parker stammered.

"It was cold-blooded murder. And you and Itana just stood there. You did nothing to stop him. You are both accomplices. By the way, where is Mr. Itana these days? Where is your international terrorist friend? Is he still masquerading as a Lebanese diplomat?

Parker's eyes flickered in surprise at the linking of Itana's name to international terrorism. He took a step back.

"Come on, Noah, don't tell me you are actually surprised at that. Itana turns out to be one of the most-wanted terrorists in the world.

505

Surely you of all people must have known that. The three of you conspired together to murder my best friends. But you didn't stop there, did you? Then you came looking for me. You went to my mother's home, and when you didn't find me, you murdered her! Right so far?"

"No … I mean … it wasn't like that. It was Charlie, believe me. It was Charlie all the way. "

"Sure it was. I saw you and Itana carry Ilene out of the house, Noah. I saw you! You put their bodies in a boat and then made their deaths look like a couple of pot-happy kids on a lark turned into a tragedy."

"Look, Grace." Parker opened his hands in surrender. "I know you're angry over this, and I don't blame you. But none of this was my fault. You've got to understand that. I had no idea what the man was up to that night. Itana and I just wanted to have a little fun. A summer night, a mansion on an island, some beautiful women—you know. It's all the pressures of my work—I just need some time out now and then. That's all it was. Then that young girl fell out of the window … "

"Fell out, Noah? *Fell* out?" Grace repeated angrily, her voice rising. "Your friend, Charlie, threw BJ out of the window. *Threw* her out. Do you understand? As if you didn't already know!"

Parker's next move caught Grace totally by surprise.

He moved fast, his hand flashing out, grasping her wrist. He was on her instantly, pinning her arms to her sides and throwing her back against the bench. As they struggled, she fell to the deck, Parker on top of her. Scratching and punching and clawing, she was no match for Parker's strength. He rolled her over onto her face, twisting her arm upward, behind her back in a vice-like grip. She stopped fighting and cried out.

His hold firm, Parker yanked her to her feet.

"You little witch," he snarled, his countenance flushed with hatred, "you're going to wish you'd never shown up here. I ought to kill you myself right now, but Charlie wants to see you first."

Grace winced as Parker twisted her arm behind her. "You're as evil as he is, aren't you Noah?"

"Shut up!" Parker gave her a vicious shove. Grace staggered forward, trying to stay on her feet, her arm throbbing. Parker stopped short to stare at the guard who lay beneath the bench. Then he shifted his gaze back to Grace, with a half-grin.

"Wait until ol' Charlie hears that you took out Dempsey. That'll stir him up a little. He thinks he's invincible."

"I know. He thinks he's God. But he's not."

Parker chuckled and put more pressure on her arm until she was standing on her tiptoes. She felt his hot breath on her neck as she twisted around to glare at him.

"You must have a weapon hidden somewhere. How else could you drop poor ol' Dempsey over there?" he asked, running his other hand over her body, then letting it linger, first on one leg, then the other.

He pushed her away. Stumbling backward, Grace caught herself before she fell. "No, I guess not. Well, it must be another one of our little 'Wonder Woman' mystery tricks. What do you say we go on up to the house and let Charlie know that his long anticipated guest has arrived. And then, who can tell. Maybe later you and I can take up where we left off the last time we were together. Would you like that? I've always been disappointed that we had to cut our evening short."

Humiliated and growing more anxious, Grace walked slowly, receiving an occasional jab from Parker urging her on.

Where is Towner? And Sammy and Pastor Cain? I blew it. They're not

507

going to know where I'm at until it's too ...

A sudden blur—out of the corner of her eye. Off to the left.

She caught only a glimpse as she stepped off the dock and onto the path.

A branch reached out from a tree ...

No. Not a branch. It was an arm.

Someone's arm!

A thud.

A groan.

What's happening?

Grace turned and stared in disbelief.

She was standing alone.

There was no one else there!

82

The face and shoulders of a man emerged from the bushes surrounding a magnolia tree to the left of the path.

"Towner!"

"Sorry I didn't get here sooner."

"How did you ... "

"I saw this joker coming down the path from the house and figured you might be in trouble, so I doubled back. You okay?"

"Yes, thank God—and thanks to you, I'm okay. But if you hadn't shown up I might not be. Do you know if the children are safe?"

"I saw Jason lift them up to Harold on the boat. They were like Navy Seals, both of them."

"Thank God!" she said again, heaving a sigh of relief.

"Our timing is shot all to—sorry—what I meant to say is we're off our scheduled meeting times. I'm going to see if I can find Sammy and John. We'll meet you back here and decide how to go about this from this point."

"They should be near the house."

"I know, but they've not contacted me. I need to find them for sure. You'd better stay back here and wait until we're able to regroup."

Grace hesitated, desperate to find Brad and get off the island. They were so close ...

"Okay," she said reluctantly, "but hurry, Towner, please?"

"Yes, ma'am. And you stay put until I come back for you."

Towner disappeared into the bushes.

Grace wondered what he would say if he knew that the "joker" he'd just put out of commission was a United States senator. She stood there for a moment, not knowing what to do next.

Should I go back to the gazebo? Or hide here?

She opted for "here." Going back to the gazebo was too much like retreating. She couldn't do that. She'd come too far to go back. Besides, she wasn't anxious to return to where Valbrick's dead body served as a reminder of what might be ahead. Towner was right. This really was a war. Glancing around for a suitable hiding place, she voted against being in those bushes with Parker for much the same reason.

Maybe over there, under that live oak ...

"Grace."

Grace froze. The voice came from the direction of the house. She looked up to see Charles Brandenbury waving from the front steps, looking and sounding for all purposes like an old friend greeting a long lost relative. He was smiling.

"I'm glad to see you made it. Come on up."

Grace hesitated, suddenly finding it impossible to swallow. Then she took a step forward, not knowing what else to do.

"Come on, don't be shy, Grace. I don't recall you being at all shy the last time you were here. My, my, how the years do fly."

He stood on the steps, watching as she approached. From this angle he looked even larger and more formidable than she remembered.

"I have people here you know who've been looking forward to seeing you, Grace. Mustn't keep them waiting."

A man with Asian features stepped through the front doorway and stood behind Brandenbury. The chef! The man had been the chef the night she and the others were here. Only this time he wasn't wearing a chef's apron. Her heart beat faster at the sight of the automatic weapon in his hand—what did they call them? AK-something-or-other? She'd never seen a real one before. Only in movies. But this one frightened her more than all the movies she'd ever seen put together.

"Ho San is going to relieve you of whatever weapons you may have brought along with you. Normally, my guests are polite enough not to carry, but you've always been a little testy, haven't you, Grace?"

Grace steeled herself as the beady-eyed cook came toward her. Once more she endured a stranger's hands on her body as he checked for anything concealed that could be dangerous to his master. In a matter of seconds, he stepped away, looked at Brandenbury and nodded.

"I'm not sure how you slipped in on us without being announced, but from the looks of things, you must have enjoyed a little swim. You do like to swim, don't you? Do you have a boat out there?" She saw Brandenbury glance beyond her to the channel and prayed that he couldn't see Ellie and the children. "Did you come alone or have others joined you?"

Grace didn't answer.

"Never mind. If there are any more trespassers found, they'll be shot on sight. No questions asked. This is private property. And these are dangerous times. So, if you brought a friend, I hope you said a fond farewell. A man in my position can't afford to put up with prowlers and interlopers. I'm sure you understand that. Besides, my dear, you are the only one I'm really interested in talking to. You have so much to tell me, I'm sure. In fact, I can hardly wait.

"Ho San, go get Valbrick and the brats. I thought they went down to the dock, but perhaps he took them to the north beach. Bring them back here. They've been *dying* to see their future stepmother. At least they soon will be." Brandenbury gave off an evil chuckle. "And I know

511

they'll want to hear all about the woman who is planning to marry their father. I'll bet I know some things they don't. Say, perhaps we could have a private little wedding ceremony right here. Would you like that, Grace?"

Ho San had already disappeared up the trail to the north.

How can a man look so normal and still be so crazy? He must be insane. Thank God, at least he doesn't know the kids are gone.

"I believe that's the same trail you left us on seven years ago, Grace—or do you prefer being called Taylor now? Which is it? They found pieces of your dress caught on tree limbs and bushes, so we decided to carve out a trail that goes all the way down to the beach. That was such a lovely dress you were wearing that night. Expensive, too. I saw the receipt. Anyway, this new path will be much easier on your clothes."

Brandenbury chuckled again at his attempt at humor.

"Noah!" he shouted. "Wherever you are, come back to the house. There's someone here to see you."

He turned his gaze back to Grace.

"You know, for years Noah has felt badly that you chose to leave us so early the last time we were together. But, all's well that ends well; isn't that right? Here you are again—ready to pick up right where you left off." He waved his hand in a sweeping manor toward the door. "Come. Please, come on in."

Grace concluded that the "great man" had already been drinking as she moved past. She remembered his having put away several glasses of wine the last time without it seeming to bother him. At least not outwardly. But there was something stronger on his breath this time. It leached through his laughter like a sunless mist.

His excessive gregariousness signaled he'd already done enough afternoon drinking to at least test his sobriety. Was this something common to him now or a more recent addition to his demented psyche? Would the alcohol slow his reflexes even fractionally? Or was he simply gearing up for the kill? What did it matter? She knew she was no match for a man of his size. There was only one thing of which she was certain. He did not have anything pleasant planned for her this evening.

Where is Towner? And where are Sammy and Cain?

Grace experienced a strange feeling of *déjà vu* as she crossed the patio and entered the Brandenbury island house. She flinched at the sound of rapid gunfire somewhere in the distance.

"Well, now, it seems we have the answer to my question. You did bring someone with you. However, it would appear that your friend or friends, whichever, have been duly dispatched by my men."

"Maybe my 'friend or *friends,*' have taken out your thugs," Grace countered, trying to lend more bravado to her voice than she felt.

"I doubt it very much, my dear," said Brandenbury as he took her by the arm and guided her toward the staircase. "The burst we just heard came from an AK-47. Did you know it fires at a cyclic rate of 300 to 400 rounds per minute? Its sound is quite distinctive, don't you think? And in anticipation of your coming, each one of my guards has one in his possession."

Grace bit her lip to hold back words forcing their way to the surface. Her fear of this man was steadily being matched by her anger. Anger at what he was capable of doing. Anger for permitting herself to be in his control, not just now, but for seven incredibly long years during which he had robbed her of so much of herself. And now here he was, about to do it again. Only this time, she was certain, he intended it to be the last.

At the top of the stairs they paused.

"This way, Grace," said Brandenbury, pulling her to the left and

513

pushing her forward. "You remember the room where last we met. It is the door to your left."

With each step, her mind filled once more with ghosts of BJ and Ilene. Ilene had lain right there in front of that doorway the last time she'd seen her alive. Eyes closed, hair strewn about, her new dress twisted awkwardly over her limp form—a dress for graduation that had become a death shroud instead.

"In there." Brandenbury's voice drew her back to the moment. They were there now, at the door to the room where BJ …

Brandenbury shoved her through the doorway. She stumbled, reaching out to regain her balance … and there he was.

"Brad!" His name exploded from her lips.

Brad was lying on a bed to the right of the room's only window, the window through which BJ had been thrown by this maniac. His hands and feet were bound and a rope around his neck was tied to the bedpost. His face looked pale and drawn. He stared at her, as though from some distant place, trying to discern who it was that had called out his name. His face was bruised, puffy around the left eye. Dried blood on his lip. He had obviously suffered beatings. She started toward him only to be yanked backward by Brandenbury's strong hand.

"Taylor?" Brad murmured. His eyes closed, then opened again as he struggled to form her name on lips that were swollen and disobliging. "Is that you?"

"Yes, darling. It's me. It's … Taylor." Grace whipped around on Brandenbury, her eyes blazing. "What have you done to him?"

"To your man of the cloth over there? For starters, it appears there may be the hint of an identity crisis going between the two of you. He knows you've lied to him. I made sure of that. But now you see he's not certain who you really are. After a few hours of, shall we say, persuasive dialogue, he convinced us that he knew nothing of ... well, you know, our little secret? Since then, we've kept him comfortably sedated. I'm actually quite surprised that you never said anything to your lover here. About us, I mean. After all, I understand you agreed to marry? Is that true? I thought happy couples shared everything with each other. Especially someone marrying a minister and all. Isn't that the idea? Tell me, when you go to confessional, is Bradley here on the other side of the curtain? Oh, wait, I almost forgot. You don't confess that way, do you? So what kind of 'Christian' are you anyway?"

"I've confessed," answered Grace, staring at Brad regretfully, "a long time ago. I confessed to Jesus and asked his forgiveness."

"Ah, yes. Jesus. And don't we sound like the pious little nun, now," sneered Brandenbury. "And I suppose that your teary nanoscale confession turned you into one of Jesus' sinless little saints? It's all a crock, Grace. Don't you get it? This God thing is just a sham scheme to suck in the gullible. "

Grace didn't dignify Brandenbury's taunting crudeness with a response. Instead, she watched as Brad's eyes made contact with hers. They never left her. He stared, expressionless. Grace couldn't tell whether it was an accusatory look or the result of whatever drugs they were using to keep him in a passive, lethargic state. Maybe it was both. Whatever, she felt hopeless guilt at the sight of him lying there.

"The kids ... " he mumbled, moving his tongue over his lips to moisten them.

Grace saw desperation in his eyes. Not for himself, she realized, but for the children. She wanted to announce that they were safe, that at least she'd been able to do that much. But she held back. They were not safe if Brandenbury discovered too soon that they were gone. Ellie was still somewhere off shore, close by, waiting. That was the plan. If Brandenbury sent his henchmen out after them in one of his speedboats, they'd be no match. Grace wished she'd told her to get out of the area just as soon as David and Nancy were safely on board. But it was too late for that now. One more loose end in danger of unraveling.

Just then, they heard footsteps on the staircase. A moment later, Noah Parker staggered into the room. Brandenbury's face registered shock at Parker's disheveled appearance.

"What happened to you?" he asked, tightening his grip on Grace's arm.

"Somebody jumped me after I found this one hiding in the gazebo," he said, pointing at Grace. "I was bringing her up to the house when someone came at me from out of nowhere. Knocked me out and dragged me off into the bushes."

"So you did bring someone with you," Brandenbury declared as he twisted Grace's arm. She winced in pain. "How many?"

"I don't know, Charlie."

"Don't lie to me."

"A hundred. Maybe more."

"She took out Valbrick, too," Parker added. "He's down at the gazebo."

"Why you little—," Brandenbury swore as he pulled her around to face him. "Valbrick had the brats with him."

"There was no one else when I got there," Parker declared. "Only her. But somebody hit me when we reached the land's end of the dock."

"Did you get a look at him?"

"No. Nothing. Did you hear gunfire a while ago?"

"Yes. Probably Ho San or Carl dispatching the one who knocked you out. Are you going to tell me how many you brought with you?" Brandenbury bullied her with a vicious twist of her arm. "Where are the brats?"

Tears filled her eyes. Grace grimaced in pain but said nothing. Brandenbury pushed her away. She fell forward onto the floor, coming to rest between him and the window, within reach of Brad whose hands were tied behind him. Scrambling to her knees, she reached for him— touched his face—but only for an instant before Brandenbury grabbed her by the hair and yanked her away, dragging her back across the floor.

He gripped the open collar of her blouse and slapped her across the mouth, flinging her away from the bed, sending her sprawling headfirst against an antique dresser. She lay stunned for a moment, her ears ringing from the blow. Then she struggled to her feet to face her nemesis. He was pointing the gun at Brad.

"No!" she shouted, rushing toward him, grabbing at his arm.

Brandenbury threw another vicious blow, his diamond-studded ring catching Grace full on the side of her face, driving her across the room. This time she rose slowly from the carpeted surface, blood running from a cut above her left eye. Brushing at it, she looked up.

Brandenbury leered at her with sadistic pleasure, a wild, dissolute look on his face. It was the most chilling look she had ever seen. Was this the last look BJ and Ilene had seen before … was this finally her own end come full circle? "How do you feel now, Grace? Are you ready to cooperate? Or do I need to impress you more?"

"What do you want?"

"Answers to my questions. Truthful answers, Grace. I'll know if you're lying. Anyway, a sweet little preacher's lover wouldn't lie, now would you? I'll ask you one last time. Where are the brats?"

"I don't know."

Brandenbury hit her hard across the face once again. "You're lying!"

83

Sammy and John ran their rented speedboat onto the beach in an island cove north of the Brandenbury estate. No one was visible along the bank. While still in open water, they had agreed that Sammy would take the lead. It was what he was trained for. John watched the man on Brandenbury's dock through borrowed field glasses. The man pulled a handgun and aimed in the direction of the shrimp boat that floated dead in the water. The scene did not look good at all. Then the man on the dock suddenly crumpled and disappeared from sight. Within seconds, Jason and Grace were treading water beneath its timbers.

John looked at Sammy and nodded grimly. "All right. Harold got the job done. So far so good."

Sammy took his service revolver from a waterproof pouch and slipped it into one of the pockets in his shorts. John checked his watch. Ducking into the trees and undergrowth, they began picking their way through the woods. Sammy, in hushed tones, spoke of days in the Army that he'd spent on maneuvers in woods and swampland just like this. He watched for trip wires, anything that suggested security cameras or alarms hidden in the brush or the trees near the estate. Suddenly, he stopped and motioned silently to John.

Just ahead, a trail cut diagonally through the woods. A few

meters to the right flowed the river from which they'd emerged moments before. To the left, up a gradual slope, the trail turned and disappeared. John waited as Sammy studied the trees for anything out of the ordinary. There was nothing. At least nothing he could see.

Satisfied that it was clear, he signaled John and started toward the path. He stopped short as a man appeared, rounding the corner to their left, headed toward the riverbank. He was dressed in a light-colored T-shirt, walking shorts, and hiking shoes. Thin, wiry physique. In another venue the guy could have been mistaken for a long-distance runner—except for the automatic weapon that hung by a strap over his shoulder. Obviously one of Brandenbury's guards. Sammy signaled John to stay back. Waiting, he crouched low and out of sight until the man was one ... two ... three strides past. Sammy leaped onto the trail, hitting the man hard with a chop to the base of his neck. A low moan escaped his lips as he fell. Sammy was on him, his gun pressed between the man's shoulder blades, but he didn't move.

Returning the gun to his pocket, he dragged the man over to the side of the trail. From his pouch, he withdrew a set of police cuffs, pulled the man's arms back around a small black gum tree, handcuffed his wrists, then covered his mouth and bound his legs together with more tape. By the time he was finished, the man was stirring. His eyes opened with a bewildered, glassy stare that quickly morphed into pinpoints of angry hatred. Sammy worked methodically to ensure that the man would not escape. The man squirmed and twisted on the ground, but his effort only confirmed the fact that he'd been rendered helpless. He mumbled something unintelligible.

Sammy grinned. "Have a nice day," he said, picking up the AK-47 and the two extra ammunition magazines he'd found while searching the man's pockets and nodded to John.

The two men crept back out on the trail and started up the slope, away from the river. Checking the weapon that he'd lifted from the guard, Sammy clucked his tongue against the roof of his mouth. Shaking his head, he pointed to the gun and grinned at John. It had been refitted and was *fully* automatic.

Figures. If you're going to break the law, might as well do it all the way.

Coming to a sharp bend in the trail, they moved forward slowly, cautious, listening for signs of another guard … anyone … somewhere. The path was empty, but just ahead he could see that it linked to yet another path. And this one headed in the direction of the house. It had to be the one Grace mentioned earlier. Glancing both ways along the new trail, they stepped out and began jogging in the direction of the house.

When Ho San rounded the bend, he stopped and stared, cursing as he did. Carl Gurling, one of Brandenbury's island guards, was lying on the trailside bound and gagged. Gurling nodded his head and eyes in the direction of the house. Ho San didn't stop long enough to set him free. He started jogging along the trail, slowing as he rounded a sharp turn. And there they were. Two of them.

"Hands up. Don't take another step!"

Sammy and John froze in mid-stride, grimacing with frustration as they glanced at one another.

Where did this guy come from?

"Either of you makes a move, you're both dead."

The voice was closer now. They could hear footsteps.

"Drop your weapon."

Sammy tossed the recently confiscated rifle to one side.

"And that one in your pocket. Reach back and pull out whatever you've got there, but do it real slow and easy, boy. Thumb and one finger only. Easy. That's it. Now, drop it on the ground."

Sammy did as he was told, letting the service revolver fall onto the path near his feet.

"Now, move ahead ... slowly ... a little further ... stop. Lay down. Hurry it up. Both of you, spread eagle!"

Face down in the dirt Sammy and John stretched arms and legs wide apart. They still had not seen the man's face but felt his hand running expertly over their shirts and shorts, looking for any other weapons.

"All right, get up," the man said, poking at them with the barrel of his gun. Sammy and John got to their feet and slowly turned around. This one was a big man—muscular, darkly tanned, wearing a sport shirt, shorts, and hiking boots. Another AK-47 was trained on them.

"Who are you?"

"I'm a police officer," Sammy answered.

"Huh!" the man snorted. "There's only one police officer on Daufuskie, boy. And he's as white as a winter's snow. Any islander knows that. Why are you here? You come to steal something or what?"

"I'm from Savannah PD."

"How'd you get here?"

Sammy didn't answer.

"And your friend? Another cop from Savannah?"

John shook his head, but said nothing.

"Well, no matter. The boss will decide what to do with you. If you guys really are Savannah cops, it doesn't mean a thing here. Whatever and whoever you are, you're out of your territory. And your league. Armed and dangerous even—trespassers, no less. Why I ought to shoot you right here and now. Can't you read the 'no trespassing' signs posted around this place, boy?"

Sammy waited, making no response.

"Maybe you *can't* read, boy ... or maybe ... maybe the two of you are just in the wrong place at the wrong time. But I doubt it. Yeah ... let's go." The guard motioned with his rifle. "Did you want to go up to the house? If so, you were headed in the right direction. Move. I'll take you there myself."

Sammy and John turned and began walking along the path.

"Come on." The man prodded again with the gun. "Move it."

Just then, there was a noise—off to the right of the trail. The man swung around as Towner charged into him with full force. Both men fell to the ground. Towner grabbed for the gun, but missed. The man was strong and wiry. As he rolled away from Towner, Sammy fell on top of him, wrestling for the weapon when it went off. A three round burst!

Towner swung with all his might as the man turned to face him. His fist glanced off the barrel and another burst of gunfire rattled next to his ear. His left hand brushed against Sammy's service revolver. The guard had stuffed it under his belt. Towner yanked it free, felt for the safety and pulled the trigger, firing a single round. The guard twisted away, crying out in pain as he let go of the rifle.

Gasping for breath, Towner rolled to the left and leaped to his feet, crouching warily, pointing Sammy's gun at the man who was clutching at his forearm, blood running down his hand. A wild, desperate shot, but it had been effective.

"You okay, John?" said Towner, at the same time keeping his gun trained on the big guard.

"I'm okay," said John as he looked to where he had last seen his young friend. His eyes widened with alarm.

"Sammy!"

84

"What is it that you want from me?" Grace repeated on her hands and knees, blood oozing from the cut near her hairline. She glanced over at Brad as he watched powerless, concern etched in lines on his face.

"My curiosity satisfied, for one thing," said Brandenbury. "How did you get away from here that night? A rare mistake in judgment on my part. I didn't think you had it in you."

"I swam."

"Across the New River? To the mainland side?"

"Yes."

"But how did you avoid being detected by one of our boats?"

Grace's lip had begun to swell. She licked it with her tongue. A tooth had cut into it with Brandenbury's last blow to her jaw. She could taste blood inside her mouth.

"I was better than your goons."

Brandenbury chuckled.

"Yes, I'll grant you that much. You were, weren't you? And then what?"

"And then I walked to Savannah."

Brandenbury gave her a look of surprise that turned to disbelief.

"You expect me to believe that? Someone must have picked you up in a boat. Who was it?"

"No boat," mumbled Grace, finding it difficult to form the words with her puffy lip. "No one picked me up. I walked, and I swam."

"I still don't believe you. There's no way you could have done that. But go on. What happened after you made it back to the city?" he asked, apparently willing to pass it off for the moment as a possibility, however remote.

"I got on a bus and went as far away as I could," she continued, careful to omit any reference to Ellie Fitzgerald or her son.

"Impossible!" Brandenbury roared, taking a step toward her. "I had the bus terminals covered in Savannah *and* Charleston. Trains and airports, too. You're lying, Grace. Somebody helped you. Who was it?"

"Not lying," said Grace, shaking her head. "You didn't cover Jacksonville's bus terminal."

"Jacksonville?" Brandenbury studied her face. Grace's eyes never left his. A slight smile formed on his face. "Well, now. Very clever, indeed. And how did you get to Jacksonville? You never went back to the car. We staked it out."

Grace's mind was swirling now, desperate to think of something, cluttered with jumbled details left over from that night, made even fresher now that she was actually here again.

As if anticipating her thoughts, Brandenbury added, "It was an easy check with DMV to find out which one of you owned a car. Process of license plate elimination. We located your friend's car by noon the next day and had it watched until the police retrieved it the day following. Our man even stayed around the garage for another forty-eight hours. You never showed up."

Incredible. The man owns the DMV, too. He got there before the police.

"Grace?"

"I hitchhiked."

"She's lying," declared Parker angrily.

"You didn't go by train or bus or airplane," said Brandenbury, "and we know you don't have any relatives in Savannah, so did you get a friend to drive you there?"

Is there anything he doesn't know about me?

"I told you. I hitchhiked when I got to Savannah. I didn't have any friends there. I put out my thumb and got there the hard way."

That's true—minus a few details.

Grace's conscience balked at lying ever again, even to this tragic excuse for a human being. But she was equally determined not to lead him to Ellie and the children, no matter what.

Brandenbury continued to question her about her journey to California. "Where did you get the money necessary for such a journey?"

"You," she replied. "You paid us each a thousand dollars. You financed my disappearance."

Brandenbury studied her for a long moment and then burst out in laughter at the irony of finding that it was he, himself, who had in an oblique way, financed her escape. What about friends there? What were their names? Where did she work and for whom? And over and over—*whom did you talk to about this?* His badgering her for information went on and on.

"There's one thing I've learned that you should know," she said finally.

"I'm waiting," he said, glancing at his watch and then at the door. *He's wondering where the children are.*

"Where are the kids?" Parker interrupted impatiently, almost as though he had read her thoughts. Then she saw the light go on. Hey. There was an old shrimp boat off shore. Was that your ride out here?

Maybe I should go check it out."

Brandenbury appeared to mull over that possibility. Then he nodded. Parker turned toward the door just as Brandenbury reached for Grace's arm and yanked her to her feet.

"Freeze! Don't anybody move!"

The voice came from behind them.

Brandenbury whirled, the gun that had been in his belt now in his hand. He wrapped his other arm in a vice-like grip around Grace's neck. Her head twisted at an upward angle so that she could see only the ceiling and the upper part of an empty doorway. Then out of the corner of her eye she saw him. He was on the floor—with only his head and shoulders visible—and he was pointing a gun.

"What are you doing here?" roared Brandenbury.

"Drop the gun!"

The next few seconds seemed like forever. Parker stood frozen, his mouth open in surprise, his countenance turning pale. Brandenbury instinctively backed away, dragging Grace with him as a shield, a move that placed Parker between him and the gunman. His backward steps moved him closer to the bed and, for a moment, he and Grace were outlined in the clear glass of the window. Her hands hung helplessly at her sides. Then she heard movement behind them.

Bound and still affected by the drugs they had used to keep him sedated, Brad was lying on the bed, fighting to clear his mind, bathed in sweat and tension as he watched what was going on in the room. He had listened as Brandenbury probed the past with Taylor, all the while pressing against his bonds for the thousandth time, still to no avail. And he had heard Taylor's amazing responses.

It was Taylor all right. It was her voice. Her face. But it was another woman's life they were talking about. Someone named Grace.

A woman he didn't know, from a different world. Was this the world that Taylor disappeared into on those evenings when he had felt her drifting away from him?

Then another voice, from someone he couldn't see. He saw Brandenbury, though, backing toward the window, a gun in his hand, dragging Taylor with him, using her as a protective shield. He was closer now, nearer the bed, his attention riveted on whoever it was that Brad could not see. Brad struggled sideways toward the edge of the bed. It all seemed to be happening so fast. Each move was in slow motion, his judgment foggy, his reflexes uncertain. But as Brandenbury moved past, he pushed off!

The rope burned against his neck, wrenching his head backward, choking him as, with every ounce of remaining strength, he lashed out. His timing was off. He missed Brandenbury altogether and fell choking, with the full weight of his body dangling on the rope. Then Brandenbury took another step back.

Grace felt Brandenbury stagger, and for a split second his hold on her loosened. Twisting away, she drove an elbow into his ribs as hard as she could, at the same time kicking at his shin with the heel of her bare foot. He grunted in pain, his hand tangled in her hair, jerking her toward him as he tried to regain his balance, refusing to turn loose. Changing her tactics, she stopped struggling, and with all her might she dug in, pushing backward instead, driving Brandenbury further off balance. The gun was only inches away from Grace's ear when he fired. And then she was free!

Stumbling to the floor, Grace glanced up in time to see the stunned look on Noah Parker's face, his hands lifting upward in a kind of awkward surrender.

Brandenbury fired again wildly, the next bullet slamming into the ceiling near the light fixture. No matter. The real damage had already been done. Clutching at his chest, Parker dropped forward onto the floor, his face inches from her own. Then a third gunshot rang out. This one from near the doorway. Grace was on her hands and knees now, scrambling to get out of the way of any more gunfire when she heard the shattering of glass.

Brandenbury teetered awkwardly in the window. Shards of glass were falling onto the flagstones two stories below. He continued pitching backward, unable to regain his balance. The gun dropped to the floor. A small red stain appeared near the shoulder area on his shirt. He reached in desperation for the sill with his good hand, the other fumbling crazily, like a windmill beating in the air.

Grace scrambled to her feet. Everything suddenly as focused for her as it had ever been in seven unbelievable years. It was Bonnie Jo falling backward through that window—flung to her death by the man who himself now teetered precariously at the window's edge.

She heard a guttural cry, felt its rage roiling up from deep within herself as she rushed at this killer-who-would-be-president, tasting the wild, seething fury over what he had done to Bonnie Jo. To Ilene. To her mother. To her. The door of unrequited memories had snapped open at last, erupting with a volcanic force.

Push him, Grace! Kill him!

"You kidnapped my family, you … you … " Grace's fury spilled over like molten lava, generating its own heat and energy, gushing across an emotional spillway.

"You killed my friends. You murdered my mother. God only knows how many others you're responsible for. You use and abuse everyone. You robbed me of my life. It was *my* life! Not yours! It belonged to *me,* and you stole it!"

Grace was screaming—tears coursing down her cheeks.

"You stole it!" she cried again. "You stole my life!"

She came closer. Their eyes locked on each other. The room for Grace became strangely silent, as though the two of them were alone and no others were present. No more words. Nothing left to say. She stared at the fingers of his hand, white from the strain of holding on. They couldn't hurt her anymore. She could pry them loose. Or just grab his foot and fling him outward. From his position, from the way in which he clung to the edge, dangling out the window, it would not be hard.

Not hard at all.

If she simply waited and did nothing, he might even plunge to his death of his own accord. Her face was wet with tears. The revulsion and abhorrence she felt for Charles Brandenbury had filled to the rim and now it was spilling over. There was nothing left to hold it back. The Wall was gone!

"Help me ... " Brandenbury's lips formed the word in a whisper, his eyes pleading.

Grace stood over him now, eyes cold; her face flushed with a fierce passion, rubbing her hands together as she took the last step toward him.

Brandenbury saw the look in her eyes.

He'd seen it before.

The tips of his fingers continued slipping ...

He grinned at the last. An evil, vile lecherous grin.

Still the victor in defeat.

And let go.

85

Deputy Sheriff Arthur Quigley was on duty when 911 operators contacted the Beaufort County Sheriff's Office in Bluffton, South Carolina.

"Sheriff, we received a call at two minutes past the hour—a male, identifying himself as Harold Justiss Jones. Said he was calling from the Charles Brandenbury estate on Daufuskie Island. He claims there's been a shooting with at least one dead and an undetermined number of others wounded or otherwise injured. The caller believes four or five. He identified the known dead as Senator Noah Parker ... that's right ... yes ... says there are others critical, too. I'll contact Memorial in Savannah. They're the closest in response time. Yes, Sheriff. Good-bye."

"Hello, Alice. Is George there? Yes, please ... thank you. Hey, George. Just got a 911 in here. May be something big going down. Dispatch says Noah Parker has been shot and killed ... that's right ... the Senator. An accident? Don't think so. Some others are supposedly wounded, as well. Sounds like they've started a war out there ... it's all happening on Daufuskie ... yeah ... at the Brandenbury place ... okay ... okay. I'll call Frank while you notify the FBI. See ya."

"FBI."

"Hello. This is Sheriff George Mapes calling from Bluffton. I need to speak with your SRA in Beaufort ... thank you ... yes, it's an emergency ... What? Looks to be Senator Parker. Report is he's been shot. Yeah, I'll wait."

"Hello ... is this Casey St. John? Casey, it's John Mapes over in Bluffton. How're you doin'? How's it feel to be the new SRA in Beaufort? Yeah, I knew Lovell pretty well. Good guy. How's he likin' it down in Savannah? Yeah? I hadn't heard that. Supervisory Senior Resident Agent. Well, now that's mighty nice. Good for him. Beefs up the pay check a little, I imagine.

"Say, the reason I'm callin' is we got word here that Senator Parker has been shot and killed out on Daufuskie. Still unconfirmed, but it doesn't sound good ... yep, the Brandenbury place ... yep ... I guess there's some others that're supposedly down as well ... yeah ... sounds like somebody declared war all right ... who knows? My boys and I are headin' out there right now ... no problem ... yeah, you're welcome. See you there."

"This is SRA Casey St. John in Beaufort. Patch me into the SAC, will you, please? Yes, I need to speak with him immediately ... okay ... sure, I'll wait, but this is top priority ... "

A half-minute went by before a deep, raspy voice filled the receiver. "Spencer, here."

The Special Agent in Charge of the FBI Field Office in Columbia, South Carolina, sounded as though he was battling a summer cold. Either that or his cigars had finally caught up to him.

"Sir, this is Casey St. John, in Beaufort. Sheriff Mapes from the Beaufort County SO just checked in. They received a 911 a short while ago from the home of Charles Brandenbury ... what's that? ... yes, the one and only. He's got that place of his out on Daufuskie

Island? Well, the caller indicated shots have been fired. We may have an AFO on our hands."

"Assault of a federal officer?" Charlie Spencer's voice exploded in St. John's ear. "On Daufuskie? Who?"

"It's Senator Noah Parker, sir. The caller said he's been shot and killed. It's all still unconfirmed, but I thought you should know."

Spencer swore into the telephone.

"Who've you got there with you now?"

"Agents Sanford and Patterson, sir. Both are in town tonight."

"Okay, the three of you get over there immediately. How long will it take you?"

"Thirty, maybe forty minutes by speedboat, sir. An hour tops. Maybe a little longer 'cause it's dark. Being the new kid on the block, I've never been out there. I know the drill though. We've got a boat here, and if it was daylight, I'd take it over myself. Patterson may be able to do it, but I'm thinking it's probably too easy to get lost at night, so I'll try rousting out the Coast Guard duty agent and have him take us over."

"Good idea. Check in when you get there. I'm giving you the ticket on this one."

"Yes sir."

"Meanwhile, I'll do some calling around myself and get you as much help as I can ASAP."

"Sir?"

"Yes?"

"How about John Lovell? He's close by in Savannah. He's the SSRA there now. He knows this area and the people in it a whole lot better than I do. He spent five years here in Beaufort."

"Good idea. May be some jurisdictional problems, but I'll take care of it. Now, go."

"I'm on my way. Goodnight, sir."

"Hi there, Linda. Sorry to bother you, but I need to speak to Dan, please ... yes, thanks, it's just a little cold, but thanks for asking ... Dan? Spencer here. Looks like we've got a mess developing over on Daufuskie Island. Early indication is that Noah Parker may have bought it ... yeah, word is he's been shot ... no, doesn't appear to have been an accident, but we're not exactly sure what. There are supposed to be some more wounded. They're calling for EMTs.

"So I want you to take all ten of your guys and get down there pronto. I'm calling Lovell in on this one, too. By rights, he'd be our boy if he was still in South Carolina. That's an out-of-the-way spot, but he knows the people and the area ... yeah ... sure ... okay, get going and be careful."

"Hey there, John. It's Charlie Spencer. How's Georgia treating you these days? You get unpacked yet? Yeah, it takes a while to settle in, doesn't it? Even though you didn't move all that far away from us ... yeah ... that's right. Naw, she's fine. And, Sally and the kids? Good. Glad to hear it. And congratulations on your promotion.

"Listen, John, we've got a problem. Out on Daufuskie. Word is that Noah Parker's been shot and killed ... yeah ... we don't know much more than that ... St. John and his boys are on the way. The Beaufort County SO took the call. They're headed out there, too. Dan Hahn is flying down from here with the Criminal Squad as soon as they can pull together ... no, I don't think an HRT is called for. Apparently, whatever happened is over. There's no report of hostages. Just be careful, that's all.

"You know everybody, and you're familiar with the island. I think some of this is going to wind up in your town anyhow ... What? Well, there's some additional wounded, I'm told. Don't know how many ...

just get on out there, John. I can ask for a plane from Atlanta, but ... okay ... you work it out. It may be faster for you to cop a chopper ride with the Coast Guard at Hunter ... Just get out there fast. I'll let the others know that we're doing some crossover here, jurisdiction-wise. So long, friend. Have fun and stay in touch.

Ten minutes later, Charlie Spencer, Columbia Field Office SAC, was dressed and back on the phone, explaining the situation to FBI Director Herb Crowley in Washington, DC.

"Okay, Charlie," said the Director at last, "stay on this one. We don't want any holes we can't fill in later on. You get your people in there and stay on top of it personally all the way ... No, I don't know St. John. But I know Lovell. We've met several times. Good man. I agree with what you're doing there. Good decision on your part ...

"Should I send Carmichael down? He just got back from New Orleans. At least he was supposed to come in earlier this evening. You know him? ... He was appointed the Criminal Division's Assistant Director a couple of weeks ago ... Okay, I'll hold off. If you want him there, he's yours. He may want in on this anyway, but we'll cross that bridge when we get to it. Take care now. Give me an update as soon as you sort things out."

86

Grace had no idea there were this many law enforcement people around that could suddenly converge on an out-of-the-way place like Daufuskie Island. They were everywhere, hovering over her, around her, suffocating her. Only after considerable time had passed was she informed that the Beaufort County SO had only one deputy stationed on Daufuskie. That's why it had taken the better part of an hour for a full response to Harold's 911 call.

The LifeStar 1 BK117 from Savannah Memorial Medical Center had been the first rescue helicopter to arrive on the island. Sammy had been deemed most critically wounded of all and thus had been the first to be evacuated out of the area. Pastor John, Jason, and FBI Agent Sanford had gone with him. She listened as a Coast Guard helicopter lifted off from somewhere behind the house with one of the wounded Brandenbury guards.

From where she was sitting, she could see Ho San's black hair and the side of his face as he lay on a stretcher awaiting the next helicopter. A female paramedic was kneeling beside him checking the dressing that she and her male counterpart had hastily applied to stem the flow of blood from his shoulder wound. Nothing he wouldn't get over, Harold had declared unsympathetically.

She heard more aircraft overhead and, for a brief moment,

glimpsed two more helicopters through the front window, hovering over the river, outlined in the orange colors of the setting sun. One was painted Army green. The other, a red and white Coast Guard unit that had been dispatched from Hunter Army Airfield near Savannah. Though it would be daylight for another hour, the estate was already well lit inside and out, ensuring visual access for pilots to land and take off as long as they were needed. The helicopters disappeared from view one at a time behind the house, then reappeared again, coming to rest on a large lawn that Grace had not even realized was there until now. The noise they created caused voices to be raised inside the house where the chaos of the last couple of hours was slowly but surely coming to some sort of resolve.

Three men, all handcuffed, sat stoically in the living room awaiting their removal while Towner stood a few feet away talking to two of the FBI agents who had arrived a short while before. The one man wore a light gray suit and tie, while the other looked out of place in jeans, a white shirt open at the collar, and a wide-brimmed cowboy hat that shaded his weathered-looking face, mustache, and glasses. Even though they were inside the house, he had not bothered to remove his hat. Grace wondered, absently, where he had come from. He looked more in keeping with someone from Phoenix or Grand Junction. What was he doing here on Daufuskie Island? For that matter, what were any of them doing here?

Her fingers idly moved through Brad's tousled hair, his head resting on her lap. His eyes were closed, and she wondered if he had fallen asleep. Whatever drugs he had been given were still very much in control. Though he had responded with a grateful smile at the news that David and Nancy were safe, he had asked nothing more of her in return—only locking his hand with hers once Harold had cut him free from his bonds. How many times, through tears, had she whispered,

"I'm so sorry, darling," while they waited for the paramedics to arrive?

According to what the paramedic in charge of evacuating the wounded had said a few minutes before, Brad was next to be airlifted to Savannah Memorial, where, she'd been told, he would undergo a complete physical examination and spend the night. The remaining helicopter was designated for Ho San, the AK47-wielding Asian chef, who also headed to Savannah Memorial.

Glancing at a clock across the room, she guessed that ninety minutes had passed since she'd grabbed hold of Brandenbury's leg, preventing him from falling to his death, holding on to him as he dangled out of the window until Harold could help pull him back inside the room.

Seconds before, she had been as shocked as anyone to hear Harold's voice commanding Brandenbury to drop his gun. Then she glimpsed his head and shoulders, low in the doorway, elbows on the carpet and a handgun cradled in his big, paw-like hands.

Brandenbury had pulled her around to act as a shield, backing away from Harold, dragging her with him as he did. Somehow, in his semi-drugged condition, Brad had managed to roll off the bed in an attempt to kick at his legs. He had missed, but Brandenbury had tripped over him anyway, losing his balance, firing once as he fell backward. Grace shuddered as she recalled the sound of the gun, still ringing in her ear. And then his grip on her throat had loosened as he tried to catch himself from falling.

A second gunshot. And still another came from a different location. Harold? She remembered scrambling on all fours, trying to get out of the line of fire, all the while knowing that this room had suddenly become way too small. There was no safe place. Then came the breaking of glass. She looked up to see that Brandenbury had stumbled and was falling backward through the window. The explosion of rage that swept through her had surprised her; its hidden power released at last still left her raw inside. She would not forget its incredible force, rising from the depths of her soul. Where had all this fury been stored? It was unimaginable. She had not wanted Brandenbury to fall accidentally. No. She shuddered again at the thought. She'd wanted to hit him, push him, watch him fall. The pent-up anger, hidden in the deepest part of her for so long, now loose like a sudden storm. Rage enough to kill!

And then as quickly as it had come, it was gone, leaving her soul vacant and blackened, like a burned-out forest. When she reached out her hand, it had not been to hurt him. It had been to bring him back. Life for death. Killing Brandenbury, no matter the vile person that he was, was not her right. Not when she had the power to save him. But the acceptance of that fact had left her passionless and remote, without any feeling toward him at all. Brandenbury's judgment belonged to someone else; some impartial, disinterested other. She could only hope that the legal system would be more effective against all his wealth and power than she thought it might.

Harold had helped pull the big man back through the window, kicking Brandenbury's weapon into the corner, out of reach. Brandenbury slumped back against the wall beneath the window, with Harold on top of him shouting to Grace that Brad needed help.

She was still staring at Brandenbury as her mind cleared, the sounds and sights of the room returning. Grace saw Brad dangling helplessly to one side of the bed, choking on the rope around his neck. She rushed to him and struggled to lift him back onto the bed, where her fingers tugged and pulled at the knotted rope making it impossible to breathe.

She stared in bewilderment at Harold as he tossed her a pocketknife. He read her unspoken questions. She turned to Brad and carefully cut through the stubborn noose. When the rope fell away, Brad took several deep breaths.

"It's that voice o' his," Harold said at last. "Carried all the way out to the boat. I didn't know where everyone else was, but I knew you was in trouble when he called your name, so I tol' Ellie to take the kids an' git out o' here. They're safe an' on their way back to Savannah."

Relief swept through her at that bit of news. Harold's water-soaked clothes and bare feet told her everything else.

She looked back at Brad. Their eyes met for the first time since she'd kissed him good-bye in their driveway on Monday morning. And she wondered. Are ours the eyes of lovers or strangers now?

She then had proceeded to cut the tape that bound his wrists and feet, looking again at the rope burn on his neck. It had left a harsh welt. She stared at it, then reached across, and touched it. Brad flinched. At the same time she felt her tears falling through her fingers, spilling onto the raw bruise. She kept her eyes averted from his.

Up to now, nothing had been said between them. Then, ever so gently, Brad's hand came up to her face and drew her to him until she lay across his chest, his arms around her, her face buried next to his. She trembled as the tension of past hours and days made its way through her body. She had lain like that for what seemed only a short time, her face moist with tears, when she heard him mumble, "I love you. It's all right now."

Over and over, she rehearsed those words in her mind. Was it all right now? Was it finally—totally and completely—all right?

Her eyes remained moist at the thought while her fingers caressed strands of his hair.

"Ms. Grafton?"

She looked up. A man in suit and tie was standing beside the cowboy and the female paramedic.

"I'm Special Agent St. John, FBI. This is Special Agent Lovell."

The woman stepped between them as two other paramedics followed with Brad's stretcher. "It's time," she said to Grace. "We're taking Reverend Weston out on this trip."

"Can I go with him?"

The paramedic looked at the agent with the cowboy hat.

"Ma'am," he said, his voice revealing what sounded to Grace like a west Texas or maybe an Oklahoma drawl, "we need you to stay with us for a while longer."

"But I want to go with him," Grace repeated, then added, "if there's room enough on the helicopter."

"It will have to be later, Ms. Grafton," Agent St. John said firmly.

"But why can't I ... "

"We need to talk. There are some questions that we'd like you to answer, if you don't mind."

"But, I do mind. I want to go with Brad!"

"There seems to be a disagreement about what went on here tonight," the agent continued, ignoring her demand. "Perhaps you can help shed a little light for us."

"Disagreement? I don't understand." She stepped back as the three paramedics lifted Brad onto a stretcher. Grace put her hand on his arm. "Brad?"

"Wait." Brad's voice was hoarse as he tried to rise up on one elbow. "Let me stay here with her." Then he fell back, surrounded by two uniformed officers and the medics who moved him out the door without another word.

"Brad!" Grace started after him.

The cowboy's hand came to rest firmly on her arm.

"Please, Ms. Grafton. Reverend Weston is going to be all right. And as soon as we can, we'll see that you are taken to him. In fact, from the looks of the bruises and cuts on your face, you'll need to head in for a checkup yourself. But right now, you can help us clear up a few things."

Grace glanced at the man's eyes. His face was stern. Hard. He reminded her of a Tommy Lee Jones movie character. All at once, her old fears surfaced once again. She looked across the room at Brandenbury. His face was sullen, defiant. He glared at her with unmasked hatred. Had she been right all along? Had he somehow been able to buy off all these law enforcement people after all? She'd always believed that was possible.

Harold.

She looked to where he'd been standing, moments earlier. He was gone.

"Where's Harold?" she demanded.

"You mean, Mr. Jones? He's in the next room, meeting with a couple of our agents."

Grace sank back onto the chair. All at once, she felt small, shriveled up, lost, alone.

Lord help me ... "

"Ms. Grafton?"

Grace blinked as she focused her eyes on the cowboy.

"Agent St. John has already mentioned that my name is John Lovell." He flashed a leather folder with a badge as verification, then closed it, and stuffed it back into his jeans. "I know you've been through a great deal, and I don't want to upset you further, but I need to read you your rights."

"My rights?" Grace repeated incredulously.

"Yes. You should know that you have the right to an attorney, and that anything you say from this point on may be used against you in a court of law."

Grace's mouth opened, then closed, in disbelief. This couldn't be happening. But it was.

"Do you understand what we told you?"

"Yes, I understand," she answered.

"First of all, Ms. Grafton, there seems to be some confusion as to your real name. Mr. Brandenbury, over there, says your name is Grace Grafton, but you apparently have also been living under the name of Taylor Carroll. He says that you're wanted for murder, and you've been stalking him for years. That today you invaded his estate with these other people, intent on assassinating him and Senator Parker. Do you have anything you'd like to say?"

Grace stared at the agent in disbelief. "He's lying!" she declared, her voice low but vehement, her fists doubled tightly in her lap. "That man killed my roommates and murdered my mother seven years ago!"

The agent glanced over at Brandenbury.

Brandenbury shrugged, shaking his head, still cradling his arm. Harold's one shot had hit its mark.

"Didn't I tell you that she's crazy?" declared Brandenbury. "She and her cohorts came onto my property and tried to kill me! She shot Noah Parker. Arrest her and get her out of here. And while you are at it, arrest that black schemer in the next room. She planted him. He's my chauffeur. I see it all now, and it's a wonder I'm still alive. Probably the only reason is that she wanted to do the job on me herself!"

"All right, Mr. Brandenbury, that's enough for now. I'm sure this has all been very upsetting, but we do want to get to the bottom of this, and we'll do it quicker without you two throwing stones at one another." Lovell turned to the man who appeared to be heading up the local police contingent. "When they take Mr. Brandenbury to the hospital, assign two of your men to go with him, will you? Just as a precaution? For his safety. He's to stay there under guard until I give further orders. No one in or out of his room but the hospital staff. Require ID from everyone. And keep the media hounds away."

The man nodded and turned to wave over one of his officers.

"Now, Ms. Grafton—or Ms. Carroll, whichever it is? Shall we continue?"

"Don't I get a phone call or something?" Her tone was acerbic, her spirit bitter as she glared at the cowboy.

"Yes, actually you're entitled to make a phone call, if you like."

Grace collected her thoughts for a moment and then nodded her head. "I would like."

The cowboy walked with her to a telephone that rested on a small table near one of the room's sofas. She picked it up, turned her back to the man, and began dialing the area code and number she had memorized from having used it so often before. It rang three times.

"Hello," the recording began. "This is Maggie at the *Desert Sun*. Sorry to have missed you. I'm either out of the office or on another line at the moment. At the beep, please leave your number and a brief message. I'll get back to you as soon as possible. If you need immediate assistance, press 'O' now."

Grace pressed "O," and listened as the phone rang.

"Hello, *Desert Sun*. How may I direct your call?"

"Yes, this is Grace Grafton. I'm trying to get in touch with Maggie Hinegardner. Has she called in? It's urgent that I speak with her."

There was a brief hesitation on the other end of the line.

"One moment, please," said the voice. Seconds later another voice, this one also female, with the telltale gravely tones of a heavy smoker.

"Hello. You're looking for Maggie?"

"Yes. My name is Grace Grafton. Actually, you may know me by the name Taylor Carroll. Who are you?"

"Jodi Sanderson, editor-in-chief. Unless I'm mistaken, you're connected with Maggie and the preacher that's missing. You and the preacher and his kids are all missing. Right?"

"I guess we are—at least we were," Grace admitted, anxious to get on with this conversation, noting out of the corner of her eye the impatient look on the cowboy's face. "I need to get in touch with Maggie. It's very important. Do you know how to reach her?"

"Yes, as a matter of fact, I do. I just bailed her out of jail in Asheville, North Carolina, a few hours ago. What's going on back there anyway? I'm not used to having to dig my religion editor out of jail—and clear across the country at that!"

"Later. Please. Just tell me how I can reach her. Better still, will you call her and tell her that Grace Grafton is being taken to—" She gave the cowboy a questioning glance.

"Savannah. FBI office."

"To the FBI office in Savannah. Tell her to come there as soon as she can—and ask her to bring a good attorney with her."

She heard the woman swear and imagined what she must be thinking.

"All right, Ms. Grafton, I'll get in touch with Maggie. But I guess you know this is going to cost you. I want whatever story you two have been hatching up back there. An exclusive!"

"Thank you," Grace answered, hearing the relief in her own voice. "I'm sure Maggie would like nothing better than to comply."

As she hung up the phone she felt a sudden calm, like a vaporous quiet between thunderclap and rain. Maybe it was because from where she was standing she couldn't see Brandenbury any longer. Maybe it was because she was going to be in touch with Maggie once again. Maybe it was because she knew that Brad and the children were safe. Maybe it was some unexplainable connection between her spiritual self and Jesus Christ in whom, through all that had happened the last few days, her faith had become firmly anchored at an entirely new level. Maybe she had found a whole other dimension of God's grace.

Maybe it was all of the above.

A lot *had* changed in the last seven years.

87

It was late by the time Maggie arrived at 220 Bryan Street in a Lexus that still smelled "new," driven by a tall woman with salt and pepper hair, dressed in a rumpled blue skirt and matching jacket.

"Here it is," the woman announced. They parked a block farther down beyond several cars that lined the one-way street and walked back toward an ordinary-looking, four-story, brick and stucco building.

"Did you see the sign where we parked?" Maggie said. "A white sign with bright red lettering: *Reserved for FBI?*"

"So maybe they'll arrest me. I know a good lawyer. Come on."

They continued along the dimly lit sidewalk.

"Would you call this downtown Savannah, Diane?" asked Maggie. "I've never been here before."

"It doesn't get any more downtown around here than this, except maybe on River Street on Friday and Saturday nights. Reynolds Square is just beyond where we parked. If you get a chance tomorrow, or any time before you leave, walk around some of the city's old squares. It's a great tour through history. Goes all the way, well back before the Civil War."

"Maybe later. Right now, we've got to find Grace and deal with this situation. You said 'River Street,' didn't you?"

"Yes."

"I've heard Grace talk about River Street. That's where this whole thing got started. Is it close by?"

"Not far. Over that way." She pointed in the direction of the river. "We're a short distance from the Hyatt. Hopefully, we can call from inside and get you a room there for the night. When is the last time you had any sleep, Maggie?"

"What year is it?"

The two women paused in front of the entrance. Above the door were the words: *Federal Bureau of Investigation*. To the left, in brass letters: *Savannah Resident Agency—Two-Twenty East Bryan Street;* and, to the right: *Information—Technology Center.*

"Here?" asked Maggie.

"This is it. In the old days, this was a Field Office, but one of the smaller ones in the country, so I'm told. Now, the first three floors are devoted to just what it says—information and technology. Lots of records and stuff, I guess. We want the fourth floor. That's where everyone will be."

"You've been here before?"

"Once. Defending a bank robber."

"Innocent or guilty."

"Guilty as sin."

"How much time did your client get?"

"No time. Mistrial."

Maggie looked at her companion curiously as they pushed open the door and entered a small alcove.

Diane shrugged. "The system. Who can fathom all its wonders? Well, isn't this cute? I remember now." She ran her finger down a directory mounted on the wall to the left of the door, near an intercom phone. Then she picked up the receiver, holding it away from her ear.

"Yeah?" A man's voice.

"Hello? Attorney Diane Hollister and Mary Hinegardner are here to see Agent Lovell and my client, Ms. Grace Grafton."

Voices in the background, then the man was back on the line. "Just a sec."

Maggie waited anxiously as the sound of an elevator announced that someone was coming to meet them.

"Evenin', ladies." A man smiled as the door opened. "Come on in and join the party."

Minutes later, they were ushered into a room where Grace, red-eyed and exhausted, was pacing back and forth on the far side of a rectangular wood table with straight-back chairs pushed in around it as well as another in the corner against the wall.

"Maggie!" Grace exclaimed as they embraced. "It's such a relief to see you. I've been so worried. How's Paul? Is he …"

Grace paused, unable to speak the fears that filled her mind.

"He's going to be all right," Maggie declared with a reassuring smile. "It was close—another few minutes or half an hour—maybe not. But he's young. Like you. And a fighter—again, like you. Melody got in this morning. I talked with her briefly on the phone. They're together at the hospital. She's a wonderful woman, Grace. I want you to meet her."

"I doubt very much that she wants to meet the woman who nearly got her husband killed."

"Don't be silly. And will you stop blaming yourself for everything?" Maggie stepped back. "If you don't mind my saying so, that looks like a real shiner coming on. And your lip. How many times have I told you to stop fighting with people bigger and stronger than you?"

Grace smiled ruefully as her fingers touched the most tender spot. "How did you get here so fast?" she asked.

"Tried the airport but no connections coming this way in the middle of the night, so I rented a car and drove. I figured that I'd find you somewhere down here. That's when Jodi called. Thank God for cell phones. This one's come through for us more than once during the last couple of days.

"Jodi had already been doing her long-distance thing, getting me released from custody. I'm not real sure yet how she did it. The Asheville police were not happy about turning 'Ma Barker' loose, as Harold would say. But she managed to cuss and snort and pull more strings with the local press than I ever imagined the woman had.

"After telling me you had called, Jodi contacted the *Savannah Morning News* editor and got the name of the local law firm that they use. No Spanish moss grows under their feet here either, I'll say that. Jodie got Diane here, and she was holding a card with my name on it by the time I dropped the rental at the Savannah/Hilton Head Airport. Diane Hollister, meet the former Taylor Carroll, née Grace Grafton."

"How do you do?" she said, her voice surprisingly soft and feminine, given the plain characteristics of her face and features. Grace returned her gaze through eyes that burned from lack of sleep and felt the lawyer checking her over. She was beginning to get used to it. She'd already been picked over, stared at, and examined like a dog in an animal shelter before deciding whether or not it had fleas or was safe to take home.

"I've had better weeks," Grace answered, "but never a longer one. They wanted to question me about what's happened. I told them I'd have to have an attorney present. Brandenbury has denied everything. He claims that I invaded his little island hideaway in an attempt to assassinate him. He says I killed Senator Parker, and I really think the police believe him. The FBI, too. Right now, I just feel incredibly angry and stupid. I've done a few things that are illegal in the past seven years. That has me concerned. What if he manages to con these guys, Maggie? What if ... "

"Easy, girl, easy." Maggie's voice was calm as she guided Grace toward a chair at the end of the table.

"Like what?" asked Hollister as she pulled one of the chairs back and sat down.

"What?" asked Grace, struggling to keep focused, fatigue having long since gained the upper hand in dulling both mind and vision.

"Like what have you done that you know is illegal?"

"Where do I start? Falsifying identity papers, for example. That was seven years ago, when this whole nightmare started. But I had a good reason if that counts."

"She knew she'd be killed if they ever found her," Maggie interjected.

"That's what you said on the way over," said Ms. Hollister, her gaze remaining on Grace as she spoke. Just then, the door opened and the cowboy re-entered the room, followed by an balding older man in a light tan suit.

"I see that your friends have arrived." Lovell did not smile as matter-of-fact introductions were made. He placed a small tape recorder in the center of the table. "Shall we proceed with our little Q and A time?"

"I'll sit here with you, Grace," said the lawyer, moving to a chair next to Grace and opposite Lovell. "Answer Mr. Lovell's questions, and I'll stop you if the need arises. Okay?"

Grace nodded, licking her lips and swallowing nervously. "May I have a glass of water?"

The older man stepped out into a larger open area that had been partitioned into various cubical offices. A moment later he was back and handed a plastic cup to Grace. Grace glanced through the open door and was surprised at the number of people and the level of activity for this late hour. She had the feeling that it may not have been the norm and, with a sickening trepidation, surmised that she and one dead public servant were probably the reasons most of them were here.

For the last few hours, it felt as though the government's entire law enforcement staff had been hovering over her, suffocating her with their oppressive presence. In truth, after the door was closed, only three others were present besides Grace and her attorney. Lovell and St. John and the balding fellow who did not sit with them, but remained standing near the door. His name was Franklin. Grace wasn't certain whether or not it was his first or last name. Just Franklin. Oh well, what difference did it make? She forced herself to concentrate on the tape machine and watched as Lovell reached across to push the record button.

Time passed quickly as the people in the room became absorbed with Grace's story, punctuated by the cowboy's occasional questions, always couched in a calm, somewhat detached tone. She was stopped only twice by her attorney, once when she got to the part about breaking into the boat at the marina and again regarding her forged identity documents.

The agent didn't seem all that concerned about either point and continued leading her through the recounting of events that had been locked inside her for so long they seemed almost brittle with age. One by one, she withdrew them, like an archaeologist bringing never-before-seen artifacts out of an ancient burial ground and into the public domain. Did she trust them to believe her? Did it matter anymore? Lovell stopped her once, but that was it. Everything was being recorded, she knew that. Was there a camera somewhere, too?

She wasn't sure. She didn't care anymore. These people were good at what they did. She just hoped and prayed that they were good people, period. And not in Brandenbury's pocketbook. It was bizarre actually. They were gathering up her statement for others to pass judgment upon later. Others whom she did not know and wondered if she would ever be able to trust.

When she had finished, Lovell ran his hand through his hair and leaned back, stretching the muscles in his arms and shoulders. Grace pushed away from the table, too, noticing for the first time that another man with graying hair and a tie knotted loosely over a white shirt, had entered the room and was standing near Franklin. How long had he been there? No sooner had she noticed him than the man turned and left.

"Well, Ms. Grafton, that is quite a story. Let me get a couple of things fresh in my mind one more time. You said that seven years ago, on June 5, you and your friends were staying here in Savannah?" Lovell asked again. "At the Hyatt?"

"We weren't staying there. We met this Reynolds fellow there— the one who tried to kill Maggie and me in Palm Springs. We were in the bar."

"Had you been drinking a lot?"

"No. We were just enjoying the afternoon. No one had more than one drink. In fact, BJ had a beer, Ilene had a glass of wine, and I had sweet tea that day."

"Are you certain of that?"

Grace started to answer when Diane Hollister interrupted.

"Mr. Lovell, my client is exhausted as I'm sure you can see. By her own admission, she's had virtually no rest at all since last Sunday. She's given you her statement. Unless she's under arrest, I believe it's time for you to excuse her and let her get some sleep. And to see her fiancé."

"Just a few more questions," said Lovell.

"But she has obviously been through hell," protested Hollister.

"Just a few more questions," Lovell repeated, motioning for Hollister to be silent. Then he looked across at Grace. "I thought I heard you say that you had a room in the Hyatt. Now you say you weren't staying there?"

"We went to a room there to change," Grace answered. "A suite that Reynolds rented for us. That's different than staying there. We were supposed to come back later and spend the night. That was part of the deal."

Franklin stepped forward and placed a file in front of Lovell.

"So what did you find?" asked Lovell as he opened the file and began thumbing through its numerous pages, looking for something.

"Terry pulled it up," Franklin answered. "Everything is pretty much there from the investigation. The car was in the garage, like she said. Hotel registrations in the surrounding area were checked at the time. No record of the ladies being registered anywhere. But Brandenbury did stay in the hotel that night. In the VIP suite."

"Reynolds handled our reservation," said Grace. "He went to the desk and got the room. He said it was all taken care of and that we'd return by boat after dinner. We went up to the room and changed and … "

"Do you remember what room it was?"

"*Mr.* Lovell—" Diane Hollister began again.

Lovell waved her off.

Grace frowned.

"Not the number. But I can take you to it. It's on the top floor. It was a suite with two adjoining bedrooms and individual baths. I remember exactly which one it was."

"And you were supposed to come back there that night?"

553

Grace nodded, noticing as she did the glance that Lovell gave to the other men.

He doesn't believe me.

Her heart sank. Then, suddenly she thought of something.

"Listen, Mr. Lovell. Take me to the hotel. I'll show you the room."

"Grace," Hollister placed her hand over Grace's. "I think we'd better ... "

"No! Take me to the hotel. I just remembered something. Maybe it's still there."

"What's still there?" asked Lovell.

"Are you going to take me or not?" asked Grace.

"Mr. Lovell, I must insist that my client's injuries be checked by a doctor," Hollister stated emphatically as she stood to her feet. "Ms. Grafton has obviously been through a great deal and I ... "

"No, wait," Grace put her hand on Hollister's arm. "The paramedics have checked me. No stitches required and there's nothing I can do about the bruises. I'll get over them. What do you say, Mr. Lovell?"

Lovell looked across at St. John and Franklin. St. John rolled his eyes. Lovell looked back at Grace.

"Okay," he said at last. "Are you going to tell Agent St. John and me what it is you hope to find in that room after seven years?"

"You have to take me there," she answered. Grace looked around, conscious of her burning eyes and wishing she had something to put in them. "Please?"

Lovell sighed and looked at St. John again. St. John nodded.

"Okay," said Lovell. "Let's go."

88

During the short drive to the hotel Grace sat in the back, between Hollister and Maggie, with Franklin and Lovell in front. St. John had stayed at the office to call Charlie Spencer with an update. There was little conversation, each person lost in thought, gazing out the window at passing lights or the occasional late-night pedestrian.

Suddenly, Grace leaned forward and tapped Lovell on the shoulder. "Mr. Lovell, I remember that we bought our dresses for the evening at a store near here. I know I can take us there when it's daylight."

"And you think the same clerk will be there after all these years, Grace?" asked Maggie.

Grace fell silent.

Though it had been dark for a while, the summer air was still sultry and sticky. Grace had earlier asked for, and received, a pair of jeans and a blouse, a size too large, sports socks and canvas slip-ons borrowed from a sympathetic female agent who had been working at a desk in the outer office when they arrived. Now, she was suddenly very conscious of her appearance—tangled hair and bruised face, very much the ragamuffin—as the entourage made their way through the front entrance into the hotel.

It was much as she had pictured it in her mind at least a thousand times before. The registration desk, the escalator, the rooms that opened onto indoor balconies. And across the way, MD's, the bar where it had all begun. It felt strange to be in this place again.

Lovell spoke with the desk clerk who in turn spoke with someone else by telephone. Lovell then reported to the others that the hotel manager had been notified and was on his way. Time to sit back and relax.

Grace was anything but relaxed, her eyes continuing to wander as a gradual uneasiness gripped her. Things were the same at first glance, but they were different, too. She was positive there had been a specialty store—right over there. It was gone. What did she expect? Seven years had come and gone.

Oh please, God ...

"Ms. Grafton?"

Grace blinked. She couldn't believe she had dozed off. A man in a brown shirt, open-collared, tan slacks, and sandals with no socks was bending over her. Not smiling.

"My name is Brent Carlson. I'm the hotel manager. Mr. Lovell here has briefed me regarding your situation."

Grace took note from his voice that this man was from somewhere other than Savannah. Up north perhaps. Or the Midwest. She wasn't sure, but there was no southern accent.

"I understand you don't remember the room number that is in question?"

"I'm sorry, no," she replied, getting to her feet. "Just that it was on the top floor. A suite with two adjoining bedrooms, each with its own bath. It was well appointed, and it had a wet bar. And mirrors surrounded the bar. The furniture was done in flower prints as I recall.

And the room looked out over the river. I remember that. When we got out of the elevator, we turned right and walked to the end of the hall. Then we turned right again. It was about half way down, on the left."

The man looked at her for a moment, then turned to Lovell. "Follow me. Let's see if we can find it. If it's the one I think she's remembering, it is not occupied this evening. Shall we?"

They followed Carlson across the lobby to the elevators. Grace walked next to Lovell. Franklin, Hollister, and Maggie trailed along behind. They crowded into the elevator and fell silent again as it carried them upward.

When the door opened on the seventh floor, they stepped out and continued after Carlson as he made his way down the hall. Grace glanced around as they walked, remembering that there had been pictures along the walls. They were still there. Now Carlson stopped in front of a door.

"Yes! This is the right one. 722. I remember now."

Lovell looked at her dubiously. A moment later, the door was opened and they walked inside. Grace pushed passed Lovell and Carlson and then stopped suddenly.

No!

"Is this the room you were in that night?" asked Lovell, scrutinizing Grace's reaction to her surroundings.

She nodded.

"Yes, this is the room. But it's different. It's not the same as it was."

"Our VIP suite was completely renovated approximately six months ago," Carlson concurred. "It had been several years since it had last been refurbished."

"Then everything in here has been remodeled?" Lovell queried.

"Well, no walls changed or anything, but, yes. New furnishings, carpet, wall coverings—the works. It's very attractive, don't you think?"

"The bathroom."

Everyone looked at Grace.

"Did you refurbish the bathroom, too?"

"What's that got to do with anything?" asked Lovell.

"Did you refurbish the bathroom?" Grace persisted, staring at the hotel manager.

Carlson walked over to the bathroom door and motioned for her to take a look. As she did, her heart sank. She stared at a sparkling, newly-tiled floor. And with it, her hopes of finding any evidence corroborating her story were eclipsed. After a long moment, she turned away.

"What was it you were looking for?" asked Carlson.

"Ilene's money," Grace answered, her voice flat with disappointment. "I knew it was a long shot, but I had to try. It was probably long gone anyway."

"You thought she left some money here?" The hotel manager's tone sounded disbelieving to Grace. "If your friend had left any cash money here, don't you think the next guests would have taken it?"

"It was hidden," said Grace disconsolately. "BJ had left the money Reynolds gave us in her clothes in the bedroom where she and I changed. That one, over there. But as we were leaving the hotel, Ilene told us that she'd hidden her money in this bathroom behind the bathroom stool, under a loose tile."

"How much was there?" asked Carlson, curious now.

"A thousand dollars. Ten one hundred dollar bills. That's what each of us was given."

The hotel manager stared at Grace for a moment, then turned to Lovell and Franklin. "She's telling the truth, gentlemen."

"What?" asked Lovell, unable to mask his surprise.

"She's telling the truth. My brother is the best tile man in Savannah. Married a girl from near here while he was still in the Army, stationed out at Fort Stewart. He liked the area, and she liked being close to her parents, so they settled here. In fact, he's the reason I took the transfer to this hotel when the opportunity came. We just wanted to live near one another again. Have some family around. We're originally from Illinois."

"And he found the money like Ms. Grafton here says?" asked Franklin.

"Just like it," declared Carlson. "Jim got the bid on this job and when he was cleaning out this room, he found ten one hundred dollar bills stuffed underneath a loose tile in back of the stool, exactly the way this lady described."

Voices were buzzing excitedly around her now as the agents bent down near the stool to examine the spot where the money had been found, imagining for themselves how it must have looked to the young woman who had hidden it there seven years before.

A mixture of overwhelming relief and deep sadness fell like a coat of many colors over Grace. Relief at being believed at last. Sadness as her spirit wavered, then cracked to uncover a flood of grief. Tears trickled down her cheeks, and she turned away from the others as she recalled the three of them standing here, in this very room, getting ready for a night filled with fun and adventure. They had laughed together in this room. A celebration of personal accomplishment now crowned with much-needed money and an evening others only dreamed about—stories to tell their children someday about the night they kept company with the rich and powerful. Maggie, sensing her extreme vulnerability, stepped up and put an arm around her.

"You wouldn't happen to have any of those bills still around,

559

would you?" asked Lovell.

Carlson shook his head.

"We did report the money being found, though. There's a record of that. My boss was feeling generous, I guess. He gave me the money—my brother and I split it. We took our families to Hilton Head for a long weekend."

"Well, Ms. Grafton," said Lovell, turning his attention back to Grace with a thoughtful look, "Mr. Carlson's story seems to corroborate your own, I'll say that. At least about you being here in this room that night. Is there anything else you recall that might help us?"

"I thought perhaps the woman who worked in the store might remember me. If she still lives here. You know, three college girls spending like we had all the money in the world."

"You mentioned that coming over. What was the store's name?"

Grace struggled to remember, her mind overcome with exhaustion.

"I don't know," she admitted finally, "but, if it's still there, I can take you to it tomorrow. I think it's on Liberty Street or something like that. I do remember that it faced out on a corner. There was a small cafe next door, I believe. I know I'll recognize it, if it's still there."

"Okay," said Lovell, "we'll check that out tomorrow."

Franklin nodded his agreement.

"There was a female clerk who was interviewed during this case," said Franklin. "She reportedly sold some expensive outfits to three GSU students—two of which were found in Brandenbury's speedboat the next day on the bodies of the deceased. She came forward with descriptions of the clothing and confirming sales tags as a result of seeing their pictures in the paper. Her description matched what your two friends were wearing."

Lovell looked at Grace. "Franklin was here seven years ago. This was his case."

Grace stared at Franklin through eyes burning from lack of sleep. *So that's why he's here. He was looking for me then. And he's not ... he's not Brandenbury's lackey after all. There were some people Brandenbury didn't own ... if only I had known ... hadn't been so frightened ...*

"Can we go now?" All at once, Grace's voice sounded frail and thin.

"Yes, Mr. Lovell," said Hollister, "I think this should be proof enough that my client is not lying. She's the victim here."

"It's certainly beginning to look that way. What do you say, let's call it a night?" said Lovell. "I'll need to have somebody come by in the morning and get your statement, Mr. Carlson. And a copy of that record you mentioned regarding the money. Is that all right with you?"

"Certainly. No problem at all. Glad to be of help."

Carlson was clearly enjoying his "fifteen minutes." They left the hotel suite together and retraced their steps back to the main lobby. As they walked toward the exit, Grace stopped so abruptly that the others slowed and then paused.

"What's the matter?" asked Maggie.

"Mr. Carlson, is there, by any chance, a man on River Street that plays a trumpet?"

"You mean old Malachi? Sure, he's out there 'most every night. Been there for years, so I'm told. Why do you ask?"

"Mr. Lovell, may we go downstairs?" she asked.

"Downstairs? What for?" asked Lovell.

"It's late enough now that he might not be there, if you're looking for Malachi. He usually knocks off about this time of night, I think," said Carlson.

561

"Come on," Grace urged the others.

She hurried across to the elevator that went from the lobby to the River Street exit, the others following after her. They descended, and once out of the elevator, Grace led the way through the exit door and—

Yes! There he is!

For a moment, Grace hesitated then stepped forward and stopped in front of a man who was bending over an open trumpet case, counting a handful of crumpled bills. A variety of coins lay scattered on faded red velvet lining.

When the hotel door first opened, the man had paid no attention. Now, as the group came outside and surrounded him, he looked up, curious at first, then apprehensive. Finally, seeing the hotel manager standing among the others, he smiled.

"Hello, Mr. Carlson. To what do I owe the honor of this visit?"

No one spoke and, for a moment, there followed an awkward silence. Then Grace stepped forward.

"Do you remember me?"

89

The pain in his arthritic knees forced Malachi to get up slowly. It was a daily thing now. He was beginning to feel it in his fingers, too. Time and life on the street had not been kind to the old man.

However, there was a kind of earthy dignity that he assumed as he stood before them, the practiced art of a man who lives by his wits. It was unusual for someone to talk to him. Mr. Carlson was always pleasant enough whenever he happened by, but to stop and talk? Ask a question? Have a conversation? Maybe he would make a comment about Malachi's playing while dropping a dollar bill or some change in his case, but that was it. Anyway, people who talk generally want something. Even from street people.

So what do these people want?

Most often, they just came through the hotel doorway, talking to each other or laughing and jostling one another playfully as they strolled on by without a word, leaving Malachi alone with his tunes. Even if they wanted to, what would they talk about with a black man making his pitiful living on the street with a horn, when they had just spent more money on a room for the night than he would make in a week down here? Whatever would they have in common?

Back in the 70s they use to stop, though.

To talk by the bandstand.

Request a favorite song.

Ask for an autograph.

Back in the 70s when Malachi Samuel Woodling, the avant-garde trumpeter, had played with the Big Band!

But that was long ago.

Times had been good then as a young disciple, baptized in the music of Muhal Richard Abrams, Henry Threadgill, and Lester Bowie. Malachi had toured the country with these older musicians folding him under their wings, guiding him toward the jazz trumpet as an art form.

In the 80s, he'd begun developing and leading his own bands and had gone on to perform in fourteen different countries around the world. For a while, he even lived in Vienna, Austria. It was in this grand old city that his life forever changed.

It happened while walking across the Stephensplatz on a warm summer evening on his way to one of the nearby cafes. Rounding the side of the darkened St. Stephen's Cathedral, he literally ran into an African-American named Angie Turlman. He held onto her for an instant, to keep her from falling, offering profuse apologies for not paying more attention to where he was going.

He'd been surprised when she introduced herself by name—even more so when he realized she knew his name. When he asked how it was that she recognized him, Angie laughed and told him that she had been in the audience two nights earlier at his concert. And that night, standing next to the old, steep-roofed cathedral, he fell in love with the voice and the laughter of Angie Turlman. Six unbelievable months later, Malachi and Angie were married. For the first time in his life, Malachi knew happiness and a love even greater than that of making music.

And then in three short years, Angie was gone. Just like that. Her laughter forever silenced, the bloom of her life snuffed out, destroyed by a harsh, unrelenting cancer that had devastated her body.

Overwhelmed by despair and loneliness, shattered by the weight of his loss, Malachi began a long and steady slide that finally ended on the backstreets of his hometown, Savannah. After several perilous years, more often than not eating out of garbage cans and sleeping in doorways, he had been able to dry out through the help of the brothers and sisters in Alcoholics Anonymous.

But the song that had entered his life through the sweet love of Angie Turlman was gone.

And with it his desire to succeed in the music world had gone as well. Floating away on the last sad note of Angie's young life. Now he played for a few dollars. That was all. Enough for food and a small room on the second floor of a rundown tenement. This spot, near the Hyatt Hotel's River Street entrance, had been his for more than eight years now, the place where he played mostly sad songs for people who drifted past on the arms of a happiness he, too, had once known.

No one knew Malachi Samuel Woodling anymore. Not really. To passersby, he was just another poor soul, part of the torn fabric that went with living off the street in this part of the city. So, who were these people with Mr. Carlson, and what did they want? Everybody wants something. He looked first at one, then another. They were staring at him with faces clearly intent upon his answer. Then he let his attention settle in on the woman who had asked the question—

Do you remember me?

"It's been a long time," the woman said, breaking the silence between them. "Seven years."

Seven years.

Malachi let a slow grin form on his face as he bent to place the worn trumpet in its case.

565

"Why should I? Did we have a drink together or somethin'?"

He chuckled at the irony of his little joke. The white woman standing in front of him looked disheveled and tense, but he saw her for what she was. In spite of the fact that she appeared to have had a very hard night, her eyes, the shape of her face, they all said this lady was still in a class by herself. He was confident he'd never spent the night drinking cheap wine with her in some forgotten Savannah alleyway. No way.

The woman reached out and touched his wrist with her fingers. Long lovely fingers. Tan. White.

"Please. Look at me and think back. I remember you. You were here that afternoon when my friends and I left the hotel. You were playing *Amazing Grace.*"

"Lady, I play *Amazin' Grace* ever' night o' the year. It's the greatest tune theah is, 'cept maybe for 'Nubian Call.' An' lots o' folk go in an' out o' them doors theah. I jus' stan' heah an' play. Tha's all."

Malachi saw the woman's shoulders drop. She was obviously disappointed. Turning away, she glanced at one of the men standing next to her. He stepped forward.

"What's your name?" asked the strange looking dude with the cowboy hat and shiny boots.

"Malachi."

"My name is Lovell. FBI."

Lovell handed Malachi a card.

The street performer's eyes widened as he examined it, turning it over in his hand. Then he looked up, squaring his shoulders.

"The name is Malachi Samuel Woodling."

"Well, Malachi, this lady was thinking you might have remembered her from the afternoon she and her friends were here."

"Why? Was theah somethin' special 'bout them bein' heah? It'd have to be if I was goin' to remember 'em after seven years. Your frien' in some sort o' trouble?"

"You could say that. You sure you don't remember seeing her? There were two other women with her as well."

"And a man," the woman added. "Terry Reynolds was with us, too."

Malachi blinked.

"Mr. Reynolds was with you?" he repeated. Then he leaned forward to look at her more closely. "You don' look like the type. No offense, ma'am."

"What type?" asked Lovell. Then he repeated, "By the way, my name is Lovell. FBI."

Malachi blinked again.

"You know this Reynolds fellow?" Lovell persisted.

"Sho, I know Mr. Reynolds. He always drops a five or ten in fo 'Angie' heah, when he comes by."

"'Angie?'"

"Someone I used to know. I call my horn, 'Angie'."

"What do you know about this man, Reynolds?"

"He in trouble or somethin'?" Malachi asked, at once wary and suspicious of what he might be getting into. He was acquainted with Mr. Carlson, the hotel manager, standing behind the FBI agent. Nice man. Real friendly. But the rest were all strangers—though there *was* something about the woman …

"He's in a hospital," said Lovell. "He may be in a lot of trouble when he gets out."

Malachi didn't respond. He understood trouble. He just didn't like to talk about it. His eyes moved back and forth between the woman and the agent.

What do you suppose is goin' down?

He closed the trumpet case and locked the lid clasp, picking up the instrument as though preparing to leave.

"Sorry to hear it. The man was a good tipper, though I didn' much care fo what he done, y'understan'."

"What do you mean?" asked Lovell.

Malachi wished he hadn't said anything. He bit his lip and started to shuffle off.

"Wait." Lovell's hand was on his shoulder. "What did you mean by 'not liking' what Reynolds did? It's important."

Malachi looked down at the sidewalk for a long moment. Then, glancing at the woman, he slowly turned his dark eyes toward the agent. "He's Mr. Brandenbury's gofer. Tha's all."

He started to walk away once more.

"Brandenbury's gofer? What's that mean?"

Malachi stopped and stood in front of the woman. His eyes looked straight into hers. "He collects girls. You know, women for Mr. Brandenbury an' his friends. He's like Mr. Brandenbury's pimp."

"Are you certain about that?" asked Lovell.

"Huh," Malachi retorted, "as certain as you an' me are to be standin' here. In my neighborhood, we call guys that do what he does by theah right name, though. Reynolds—he pimps fo that rich Brandenbury fella. He gathers up girls maybe fo, five, six times a year. Been doin' it fo as long as I kin remember. This is his favorite place. Now an' then they stay inside—you know, like in the hotel theah. But, mos' times, he loads 'em up on his boat over theah ... "

Malachi pointed toward the dock and the darkness beyond it that was the Savannah River. Then he stopped and stared at the woman again. Slowly he brought his hand up until it was pointing at her.

"You!" he declared emphatically. "You was one of 'em, wasn't you?"

Grace diverted her eyes away, embarrassed to be numbered among a host of loose women—no, not just loose women—*prostitutes*. Women who sold their bodies and souls for money or, at the very least, for the thrill of spending a night with the rich and powerful. Though seven years ago she'd had no intention of fulfilling either role, the woman standing here tonight, in love with a man who lay in a hospital bed across town recovering from an ordeal she was confident he still did not fully understand, would surely be viewed by these people as nothing more than a glorified hooker. And in some way, perhaps, that is what she had been that night. That had not been on her mind at the time. She would have cringed at the idea. But she didn't care anymore. The only thing she wanted was for her long nightmare to finally be over.

"Theah was three o' y'all that evenin'," Malachi declared, rubbing his chin with his hand. "One o' the others looked like a female tiger. I 'member now. Hard to forget a looker like that one. An' you—you was the nicest lookin' of all. I think you had on a black dress or somethin'. I 'member you was laughin' an' looked real happy an' all. Y'all was different from most o' them girls that Mr. Reynolds managed to dig out o' the upstairs bar or from along the street down heah. He gets some young-uns, too, ain't goin' to git into the bar, if y'know what I mean. Always hated to see it. Ever'body thinkin' how won'erful an' rich this Brandenbury guy is an' all. Well, they don' see 'im the way this ol' street boy sees 'im."

"How can you be sure this was the same woman you saw that night?" asked Lovell.

"Oh, I 'members her now all right. 'Cause I saw the three of 'em with their pitchers in the paper a couple o' days after, thas' how," Malachi said confidently. He looked at Grace. "Y'all was supposed to be dead. I 'member sayin' to somebody that I saw them three goin' out to Mr. Brandenbury's boat."

"You actually saw them walking toward his yacht?"

It was Franklin who spoke up this time, busy jotting notes in a small pad, clearly wondering how he had missed talking to this character seven years ago.

"Yessir, I watched 'em get *on* that boat," declared Malachi. "I could see all three o' them girls right up 'til they went inside the cabin."

"Would you be willing to swear to that in a formal statement?"

Malachi let his eyes roam over the little group huddled in conversation around him. His gaze settled once more on Grace. He saw the hopeful look in her eyes. He nodded. "Yep. I ain't quite sure o' who it is I'm helpin' but, yes, I'll swear to it. Thas' what I saw. I saw them girls git on the man's boat. The man was out theah himself, wavin' an' invitin' them girls on board. Then Reynolds, he come back to the hotel an' went inside."

The old jazz man paused as he reached out a hand to Grace.

"Them other two—the girls you was with? They really did die that night, right?"

Grace took his hand and covered it with hers. There was a tenderness in this old man. She could feel it. A tear fell onto her cheek as she pursed her lips, holding back her emotions.

"I thought so," he said, when she didn't answer. "I'm real sorry. Real, real sorry, Miss. It's hard losin' someone like that—someone you's real close to an' all."

No one said anything for a long moment.

Then, Grace leaned forward and kissed Malachi's cheek.

"Thank you," she whispered.

He looked surprised, embarrassed, then his face broke into a sympathetic smile. He patted her hand.

"I don' know what kind o' trouble you is in, but it's gonna be all right. You'll see."

"I know," Grace answered, stepping back.

"You jus' gotta believe, tha's all. The Man is still up theah lookin' down on us, y'know." Malachi rolled his eyes upward.

They looked at each other again and smiled.

"Yes, you're right," she said softly. "He is still up there."

"Mr. Lovell." It was Diane Hollister who spoke up. "I think we've heard more than enough to exonerate my client. And it's obvious that she's near total exhaustion. Let her go and get some rest."

"We'll be happy to give you a room for the night in the hotel," offered Carlson. "Compliments of the Hyatt."

Lovell nodded and turned to Franklin. "I think we'd better pick up Agent St. John and pay Mr. Brandenbury a visit over at Memorial."

"I want to go, too."

Lovell looked at her quizzically.

"To see Brad."

"Honey, don't you think you'd better accept Mr. Carlson's offer and get some rest first?" asked Maggie.

"I'd appreciate the room," Grace answered. "If you could give us one with two beds, Maggie and I could stay together."

"That's no problem," Carlson answered. "Consider it done—and for as long as you need it. From the sound of things, you may be with us for a few days. Consider yourselves our guests until you are ready to go home."

"That's more than generous, but first I need to check on David and Nancy. Then I want to see Brad. I need to ... " her voice broke as the enormity of what was coming hit her.

Maggie wrapped her arms around Grace as she started to cry, in part from sheer exhaustion, and in part from the awesome feeling of relief. In part from having to face Brad and what could well be the end of their relationship. Blinking away her tears, she stared out into the darkness toward the river.

571

90

Ellie's embrace reminded her of her mother ... and also the day the two of them had met along the roadway ... of the smell of shrimp and the story of Good Sam. A kaleidoscope of memories came tumbling in random shapes and places in her mind, bringing still more tears to her eyes. "I keep crying and I don't know why. I wish for everyone's sake I could stop. I never cry like this. Ever."

"Seven long years."

"What?"

"That's yo reason, hon. Seven long years you been hidin' out. Thas' a long time holdin' back all them tears."

Grace nodded and smiled, accepting a tissue as she introduced Ellie to Maggie and Diane Hollister, who earlier had volunteered to stay with them. She told them, "My night is already pretty well used up, and I don't have anything better to do." Her husband was out of town on business, and their youngest son was away at Miami University.

"How are David and Nancy?" Grace asked anxiously.

"They be fine, hon, jus' fine," said Ellie. "They went to sleep 'bout an hour ago. I tol' 'em you were safe an' fine an' their daddy was safe an' fine, an' they ate a little sumpthin' an' that was that."

"And Sammy? How's Sammy? Have you heard?"

"They say he's holdin' his own. He lost a lot o' blood. Sandra's with him at the hospital. She called jus' before I put the little ones down."

"I'm so sorry that Sammy was hurt. I feel terrible. There's been so much death and dying in everything that has happened. Do you want to go to the hospital with us? I'm going to see Brad. And I'll check in with Sandra and Sammy, too."

"I heard 'em callin' in on the radio when we was comin' back on the river. Jason tol' me we had to git them kids outta theah. We heard that there fella call out yo name and knew you was in trouble. Harold, he say it was his turn to help y'all, an' Jason and I was to make sure the kids were safe, so we did. As soon as we got in, I got the word and hustled over to the hospital. I already seen Sammy an' Sandra. He had jus' been brought in an' was unconscious, but, like I say, he's gonna make it. Tha's what the doctors are sayin' an' tha's what the Man is tellin' me, too." She pointed at the ceiling. "So, go on an' do what's you gotta do, darlin'. I'll stay with these young-uns. They be fine heah tonight. Y'all are welcome to come back, too, if you wants."

"Thanks. The hotel offered Maggie and me a room, so, we'll be all right. I'll come and get the children tomorrow, once I know for sure that I'm a free woman. I just wish that Sammy hadn't ... "

"He was doin' what he wanted to do. What he had to do, hon. We all knew it was important, his bein' theah with yo."

"But Sandra ... "

"Don' you worry none 'bout Sandra. She knew it was dangerous goin' in theah, but it's like that ever' night he goes off to work, so tha's jus' the way life is."

"I want to see them."

"The kids? They's in my bed."

Grace tiptoed into Ellie's bedroom and stared at the sleeping faces of her two young charges.

Your mother would be so proud of you two.

Their shoes were by the side of the bed, and Ellie had managed to find some clean clothes for them to wear.

How did she do that? Probably some neighbors.

Grace tucked the sheet around them. Behind her, Ellie was adjusting the fan. Maggie watched from the doorway.

As Grace turned away from the bed, she heard movement under the sheet.

"Mom? Is that you?"

Grace came back to David who was propped up on one elbow, squinting into the light from the open doorway.

Kneeling, she folded her arms around David.

"Yes, it's me, sweetheart. It's Taylor. Only I'm not Taylor anymore. I'm Grace now."

"Are you okay? You changed your name?"

"I'm fine. We'll talk later."

"And, Dad?"

"He's still in the hospital, but he's going to be fine, too."

"Have you seen him?"

"Not since he left the island, but, yes, I was with him there. I'm going to go see him now."

"Can I go with you?"

"No, darling, I need you to stay with Nancy and get some rest. You've taken such good care of her through all of this. I'm so very proud of you."

"Ellie is nice, isn't she?"

"Yes, she is."

"Is that Mrs. Hinegardner?"

"Hi, David," Maggie waved from the doorway.

"Hi. Are you okay?"

"Yes. I'm fine."

"Those were bad dudes, weren't they?"

"Yes, they were, David. Very *bad dudes*," she agreed with a smile.

"I can describe them. I memorized what they looked like."

"Good for you," said Grace, "maybe you can tell Mr. Lovell tomorrow."

"Who's he?"

"He's with the FBI."

"Wow! An FBI man? Do I get to see him?"

"I promise."

"I was scared."

"So was I."

David lay back on the pillow. His eyes closed and his hand squeezed Grace's. "I love you."

"I love you, too, sweetheart. More than you'll ever know."

Grace rose and followed the others out, closing the door behind her until just a crack of light entered the darkened room.

"Did you hear that, Maggie?" asked Grace, still basking in the wonder of it.

Maggie nodded.

Grace hugged herself and grinned. "He actually called me 'Mom.'"

With Grace beside her and Maggie in the back seat, Diane drove to the Delesseps Avenue exit off Harry S. Truman Parkway and followed it for a short distance, turning left onto Metts Drive, running adjacent to the Casey Canal. Memorial Medical Center's several massive structures loomed tall in the darkness, lights from windows and doorways ever the reminder that this "city of healing" never slept.

"There's one of the helicopters that was on Daufuskie," Grace observed, pointing to the right. In an area surrounded by a fence and illuminated by low lights was the orange and white helicopter—LifeStar 1 BK117.

"See that row of ambulances?" Diane pointed toward a line of eight or ten vehicles parked nearby. "The drivers and the pilots hang out over there in those portables. I've seen them do this before. When the helicopter brought your fiance in, they landed here and then off-loaded him into one of those ambulances. They drove him around to—over there. See? That area marked, *Ambulance Entrance/Trauma Center One*. You said there were at least three helicopters out there?"

Grace nodded, her eyes on the entrance to the Trauma Center.

"This must have been one busy place for a little while," Diane mused. "We'll park here and go in that door. We should be able to find Brad from there."

"Jason!"

Grace saw the young Coast Guardsman sitting by himself in the waiting area, thumbing through a *New Yorker*. She wondered, in passing, if hospitals and doctors' offices were the only places people actually read that magazine. He acknowledged them and stood as the three women approached.

"Sammy's in ICU, but he's going to make it."

"Thank God!" Grace exclaimed fervently. "If something would have ... if Sammy ... I don't think I could bear it."

"I know," Jason reassured her. "They got the bullets out about an hour ago. One in his upper thigh and the other missed his heart by a couple of inches. Collapsed a lung. He's listed as 'serious,' but 'stable.' They let Sandra in to see him a little while ago—wait—here she comes now."

Sandra walked down the hall toward them. Grace went to meet her. They hugged each other.

"How is he?"

"He's still not out from under the anesthetic. He lost a lost of blood before he got here, but the doctor says he's going to be fine. A hundred percent recovery."

"I am so thankful. That's wonderful news!" Grace breathed a sigh of relief.

"Yes, it is," Sandra agreed as they hugged each other again. "And you? Are you okay?"

"Yes. Thanks to you letting your man help mine. You two haven't even met him, and yet you risked everything for us!"

"You'd have done the same."

"I know, but ... "

Sandra patted her arm. "I've never had a sister, Grace. Sammy hasn't either. But we're officially adopting you as of tonight."

"I'm an only kid myself. And I accept!"

They hugged again, sharing the laughter that comes with relief in the knowledge that a terrible crisis has been met, and the worst is over.

"Now, go see your man."

Maggie walked back from the nurse's station. "He's in 424. They said to take the elevator over there."

Grace smiled, but said nothing, swallowing the queasiness in her stomach. Maggie understood immediately, and put her arm around her. "It's going to be okay," she said with quiet reassurance. "Do you want me to go with you?"

Grace shook her head and looked away.

"Wait for me here, okay?"

Three policemen were standing in the hall as Grace stepped from the elevator.

"Ma'am?" It was the one nearest who spoke as she approached. The others were quiet, but observant.

"I'm Grace Grafton. My fiancé is in 424. Brad Weston?"

The officer eyed her suspiciously.

"Do you have some identification? This is a secured area."

Grace shook her head.

"It's all at the house where my children are staying."

"It's okay, Officer." Harold Justiss Jones strolled out of the room behind where Grace was standing. "She may not look like much, but this is one courageous woman—and she is the Rev's fiancé. I can vouch for that."

"Are you all right, Harold?" asked Grace, wrapping her arms around his huge, muscular frame.

"I'm fine," he responded. "One of Brandenbury's wild-eyed shots chipped a chunk o' marble off the lamp in that room out there. Drove it into my side. Nothin' really. My real problem was twistin' my bad leg when I was hurryin' from the riverbank up to the house. They want to look it over again in the mornin' so they're puttin' me up for the night."

"I didn't even know you were hurt," Grace apologized. "I'm so sorry. Wow. I guess I'm saying those words to a lot of people tonight."

"Nuthin' to be sorry 'bout. Hey, I've not had this much action since Afghanistan. Ever since we met, you have been a pain in my side, Grace—in the very best sense of the word, of course."

"Of course," said Grace. They laughed, and Grace hugged Harold again, careful this time to avoid his injury.

"They got the man across over there in 447," Harold indicated.

The door was closed. Grace stared at it and the officer seated in a chair close by.

"I guess word came up a few minutes ago that they was s'posed to keep him on tap for awhile. I think they plan on pressin' some charges, once everythin' gits sorted out. Least tha's what I hear through my door there. He's already been visited by some of his lawyer fellas."

"Have you seen Towner or Pastor John?"

"No. I think they're still with the FBI boys, sorting things out. Lots o' questions. Lots to talk about. I imagine you've found that out pretty much already."

Grace sighed. The heaviness had returned.

"Excuse me, Harold, I need to see Brad." She kissed his cheek. "Thank you, Mr. Jones. You are one incredible guy!"

Harold grinned and patted her shoulder.

"Like I tol' you before, there's one thing I got goin' for me. I'm a pretty good judge o' character."

91

The room was dark except for light emanating from the bathroom's half-open door.

Grace stepped in, shut the door behind her, and tiptoed softly to the room's solitary bed. She stood for a moment, hesitant, her heart pounding, taking in the dim outline of his form, wondering if he was asleep or awake. As if to answer her unspoken question, he stirred and opened his eyes.

"Hi," he mumbled, a half-smile crossing his face. "They finally turn you loose?"

"Yep," she answered, taking his hand in hers. "They did for a fact."

"I didn't realize you were such a desperado, lady." Brad paused, as if gathering strength, closing, then opening his eyes again. "I'd have worn my six-guns and spurs, if I had only known."

"Oh, Brad," Grace began, "I'm so incredibly ashamed and so sorry. I don't even know where to begin."

Brad raised his other hand toward her and drew her down to himself. They clung to each other, in silence. Then Grace began to cry.

Will I ever stop crying?

She wept softly for a long while. Brad said nothing, perhaps sensing her need to let it spill over; the cleansing of a deep wound. Finally he spoke.

"It's over now, sweetheart. At least the worst of it."

Grace drew back, wiping her eyes with a tissue from off the bedside table.

"Come here." Brad motioned to the bed. "Lay down beside me."

Grace hesitated, feeling very self-conscious. She looked at the door.

"Come," he said again, his voice gentle, inviting her.

Grace stepped up on the bed and came into his arms again, lying on the sheet that covered Brad's hospital-gowned body. He drew her to himself, his embrace strong and warm.

"Your accomplice out there—the big guy—the one named Harold? He filled me in on a lot of what happened. As much as he could anyway. But, I guess there are probably a few things he doesn't know yet. I imagine that's true where you and I are concerned as well. When I sleep off these drugs, or whatever they've stuffed me with, we can talk about it."

Grace lifted her face and looked at Brad.

"There are quite a few things, actually. I've wanted so badly to tell you a thousand times, but ... I was afraid."

"Afraid? Of what?"

She hesitated before exposing her darkest fear of all.

"Afraid of losing you."

Brad ran his hand through her hair and lowered her face to his. Looking into her eyes and in a voice husky with emotion, he said. "You are never going to get rid of me. Do you hear me? Never. Whenever you are ready to tell me about all this, I know you'll share in time. But it will make no difference. I love you, Taylor ... I mean, Grace. It is going to take a day or two to get used to the fact that I'm in love with a woman named Grace instead of Taylor."

"I know. Crazy, huh?"

"Yeah, kind of crazy. But I'll get used to it. Grace is a good word and a great name for you. I loved Taylor before this all went down, and I love Grace even more now. And after all you've been through this week—and the past several years, so I'm told—I can't tell you how much I admire your courage!"

"Courage? Oh, no, Brad, I've been such a coward ... "

"Shh," Brad held her close until her head was snuggled in on the curve of his neck and shoulder. "Tell me more later, darling. I know the children are safe—thanks to you and your friends out there. And we're safe, too. That's enough for now."

"I'd better go and let you get some rest."

"Stay here with me."

"Maggie and I have a room at the hotel. She's waiting downstairs."

"Stay here—please?"

"But, Maggie ... "

"Use the phone."

Grace looked down at Brad's face. His eyes were closed.

"Are you sure? I mean we've never—you know."

"Know what?"

"Been in bed together."

"Stay," he mumbled. "I promise we won't do anything we'd have to confess later. I just need you to stay close right now. Safe here in my arms."

Smiling with a mixture of resignation and relief, she reached for the phone.

At two o'clock, the nurse, making her rounds, opened the door and started to enter. To her surprise, she saw a woman lying on the bed next to the only listed patient, Bradley Weston, one of several brought in earlier from Daufuskie Island.

The woman's arm was draped over the patient's chest.

Both were sound asleep.

The nurse stepped back with a questioning look at the policeman guarding the door.

He grinned and shrugged. "I think it's what the doctor ordered."

Her hand remained on the door, as if trying to decide what to do next.

"Medicine is a wonderful thing, isn't it?" she said at last.

Then she smiled back at the policeman, closed the door, and continued down the hallway.

92

"Are you ready for dinner?" Brad called out, opening the door to the adjoining room—a room that had been provided them following his release from the hospital, once again compliments of the hotel management. The girls slept in two queens in one room, the guys in the other. Grace and Brad and their role in what within hours had become an overnight media blockbuster, along with the presence of their two children, had more than adequately offset the write-off expense of their stay.

"I will be if Nancy ever gets out of the bathroom."

"There is another bathroom, David. Use it."

"My toothbrush is in this one," David explained to his father, who wondered how it had gotten over there instead of the room they were staying in. David turned back to the door. "Come on, Nancy. Hurry up."

Brad turned to Grace, shaking his head. "Some things will never change."

"And some things will be changing forever," she added.

"You're right about that," he said, glancing at the newspapers strewn about on the sofa and the coffee table. A headline stood out on the front page of *USA Today*, one he'd read a dozen times already: PARKER FAMILY SAYS GOOD-BYE.

He found himself unable to withhold sympathy from the Senator's grieving family, even after all that Parker and the others had put him and his own family and, in fact, the entire nation through. Hate was such a debilitating thing, and as much as he despised what they had done, he could not help but sense the shame and loss that Parker's wife, children, and the man's elderly parents were going through.

His own feelings of loss from when Helen died had re-surfaced while watching the Parkers' sorrow spill across the television screen. But with Helen, there had been sadness over the loss, not remorse over the life. That was huge, he thought on reflection. The humiliation of Parker's checkered past, made public in the last few days, together with the embarrassing revelations of his unconscionable grasping for power, was not something that Brad had needed to deal with in the aftermath of Helen's death. For him and his children there was only love and pride when Helen came to mind—pride in a life that had been well-lived, albeit, too swift in its passing.

The *CBS Evening News* had devoted more than half of its regular airtime to the *Parker-Brandenbury Story: A Nation At The Edge*. ABC, NBC, CNN, PBNC, Fox, and a host of cable networks were each offering competing coverage of events that had suddenly turned a nation and the world upside down. Numerous television specials and hundreds of articles and editorials on this stunning series of events riveted a nation moving inexorably toward another presidential election. An election that was not only about what was going to be, but even more so, about what might have been.

Parker's public persona had brought him so close to that great

White House on Pennsylvania Avenue. Close enough for him to believe that he could actually live there. But the Devil was in the plans. Truly. His lack of character in private life and faulty judgment in selecting power partners had proven to be his folly. And, today, it was Parker's family who mourned at a graveside in Charleston, without even a shred of the loving pride that Brad had known with Helen. Brad sensed there was something awesomely divine in what had transpired these last several days. Indeed, during the last seven years, unbeknownst to anyone until now.

According to CNN's latest news update, Charles Brandenbury was facing indictments on at least three murder charges. It was rumored that there might be others. His present wife, Claudia, remained in seclusion at a friend's home in Asheville, unavailable for comment.

Search warrants had been issued late the day following Daufuskie, enabling the FBI to enter Parker's residence in Washington, D.C., his office, and all three of Brandenbury's residences, including the Farm. His personal records had been removed. The FBI had also entered CB Enterprises' corporate headquarters in Asheville under the authority of yet another search warrant.

Brandenbury's lawyers had, so far, moved heaven and earth to keep the South's best-known business tycoon from being placed in custody, but formal charges were believed imminent, possibly as early as Monday according to Charles Spencer, the FBI's Special Agent in Charge of the Columbia, South Carolina, Field Office. Meanwhile, Brandenbury had returned to Asheville and he, too, remained in seclusion while under house arrest, unavailable for comment.

Since the story had broken, it had been on the front pages of every newspaper and the lead story on every network and cable newscast. And new pieces to this bold reach for political omnipotence continued to be uncovered almost daily.

The *Washington Post* set off yet another political explosion when they ran a story declaring that the alleged UN diplomat, Talal Itana, whose name had surfaced as a co-conspirator with Parker and Brandenbury in the murders of Bonnie Jo Senter and Ilene Hunter, was alleged to be the notorious Marwan Dosha, one of the world's most sought after terrorists.

Terry Reynolds was in the custody of local and federal authorities in Palm Springs following a thwarted attempt on his life by a man posing as a hospital intern. Authorities were optimistic about what they were learning from him as a result of this amazing turn of events.

A citizenry, grown casual in its callousness toward business and political leaders using and abusing their power base to further their own self-interests and appetites, was awakening to this latest, and perhaps, most outrageous political debacle of all.

Lora Hardin's special hour-long feature headlined *"How the Mighty are Fallen!"* seemed to encapsulate the questions and the feelings of people throughout the world: How could this happen in America? For many, the last few days had become a time of deep soul-searching. And, according to Hardin, also a time during which political insiders were scrambling either for cover or for the camera, depending on whether they had been friends or foes of the late Noah Parker. Their colleague's meteoric career had gone up in smoke.

"Once the ashes have settled into the dust of a nation's short memory, will the elected leaders revert back to 'business as usual' in the nation's capital? One would wonder," mused Sandra Cole on PBNC's evening news.

Grace came through the room and reached for the off-button just as Diane Hollister's face filled the screen. A moment later she saw images of herself standing close to Brad, during their first and only media interview, given to assuage America's incurably curious public.

She felt uncomfortable at seeing her image flickering across the tube. Absolute secrecy had been her only protection for so long. The one time she had slipped, by allowing her picture to appear in the *LA Times*, her life had come tumbling down like a house of cards. It was hard to accept that the danger was really over.

Now Diane was explaining how she and her family had been working to assist her client with the "legalities of Ms. Grafton's situation, including the falsification of legal documents and her failure to come forward with information at an earlier time." She confirmed that there did not appear to be any insurmountable hurdles in this regard, and that Ms. Grafton was cooperating fully with state and federal authorities. Diane had started to respond to another question when Grace switched it off. She hated the way she had looked during their interview and was grateful when the screen went dark.

"Where are we eating tonight?" asked Nancy, emerging at last from the bathroom.

"Downstairs for a change," promised Grace. "No room service tonight."

Since the story had first broken in the media, all their meals had been taken in their room. Tonight was to be their first night out together in the old Southern city.

"Will there be reporters and stuff?" David asked hopefully, his eyes bright with adventure and the excitement of getting out of the room.

"Probably," said Brad, "but, Mrs. Hollister is meeting us in the lobby and has promised to deal with them, so we can have some privacy."

David responded with a disappointed "whatever" expression at his father's announcement, but quickly recovered.

"I wish Maggie were here," he said.

"Actually, she will be. She flew to Asheville this morning to spend some time with Mr. Jacobson, the reporter from Washington. They're going to collaborate on a series of articles about all this once he is released."

"What's 'collaborate'?" asked David.

"It means that Maggie and Mr. Jacobson are going to work together on a writing project. But she flew back this afternoon to be with us."

"Ellie and Sandra are joining us for dinner as well," said Grace. "Along with Jason MacKinsey and Harold. Towner has gone back to Seattle, but Pastor Cain is here with Mrs. Cain. It's going to bring us all together—except for Paul and Sammy—so we can say 'thank you' to the people who helped rescue us."

"All right!" David responded, eyes alight with excitement.

He had been overawed at his earlier introduction to the American warrior who had been instrumental in helping save his parents. Never mind that he was also the man who had served as chauffeur to the mastermind of his own kidnapping and that of the rest of his family. In the marvelous way that children have of handling incongruent realities, David's imagination focused instead on the visible mark of heroism that had left this former soldier with a permanent falter in his step.

"But what about Sammy? When do we get to tell him 'thank you'?"

"Tomorrow. We'll visit him at the hospital."

"When does he get to go home?" asked Nancy.

"Sandra says maybe in a day or two."

"I understand Ellie and Harold were on the *Ellie I* this morning," Brad commented, while adjusting David's shirt collar. "Took it out for a little run on the river."

"Really?" said Grace. "Well, now, wouldn't they make a pair, sailing out there on the Savannah? They are kind of cute together."

"You think?"

"I do. Apparently Harold must feel the same way."

"Why do you say that?"

"Because he gets deathly seasick when he even gets close to open water. He wouldn't be out there just for the fun of it, trust me on that. He wasn't having a very good time when we came out to get you all."

"Y'all?" Brad chuckled as he opened the door. "You're reverting back to your Southern ways rather quickly, darling."

The children ran on ahead to the elevator while Brad and Grace followed behind. As they descended into the lobby, Grace saw Diane Hollister still surrounded by a cluster of reporters and CNN, ABC, and Fox camera crews, whom she recognized from their earlier interview. All were busy recording her responses to their questions. An elderly couple and a few others whose curiosity had been piqued, and whom Grace assumed must be out-of-towners staying in the hotel, lingered nearby, watching history unfold.

Because of the way the elevators were located, when the door opened and they filed out onto the main floor, they were still hidden from the reporters.

"If we hurry, I think we can make it to the dining room before they see us," Brad said hopefully.

"Wait a minute." Grace turned instead to the left.

"Where are you going?"

"Come on," she said, motioning to the others, "there's someone downstairs I want to see."

"Who is it, Mom?"

Brad raised his eyebrows at David in surprise, while Grace kept her eyes averted, though unable to resist the smile that lit up her countenance at this ten-year-old's fresh confirmation of her new place in his heart.

"Wait and see, David."

Intrigued, the others followed as Grace pressed the River Street elevator button.

Moments later, they emerged from the hotel onto the lower street level. A few feet away, Grace caught sight of the person she had hoped would be here.

"Malachi!"

The old musician was removing his trumpet from its case. He turned at the sound of her voice, and when he saw who it was, a broad smile lit up his stubbly face.

"Why, hello theah, Miz Grace. Say, now, it's mighty nice to see you—an' lookin' so well, too. I reckon this mus' be yo family."

Grace introduced Brad and the children, and Malachi shook each hand warmly, taking extra time to greet the children.

"Malachi," Grace said finally, "we want you to join us for dinner this evening. Upstairs, in the hotel."

Malachi stammered and politely began excusing himself, surprised and flustered by the unexpected invitation.

"I understand that you'll miss some work if you come, but we—"

"Oh, no, Miz Grace, it ain't that. I ... well, I ain't dressed fo such a fine place as upstairs ... fact is, I only been through the lobby once or twice. I ain't never been inside the dinin' room. I thank you, but—"

"You're dressed just fine, Malachi. And I think that it's time you had dinner in the hotel. In fact, it's long past time. Our treat. Please come."

"But ... my horn ... "

"Bring it with you. Please say yes."

Nancy reached across and took hold of his hand, looking up into his face. "You can sit next to me, Mr. Malachi."

591

Malachi looked down at her, then at the others. He shook his head in surrender as he bent down and hugged her. "Now, how can I turn down an invitation like that?" he asked.

Everyone laughed.

"We're honored, Malachi," said Brad. "Grace says you are very good, and I'd like to hear you play, but that's not why we're asking you to join us. Tonight, we'd just like to have some friends help us celebrate the fact that we're safe and all together again."

Malachi gestured helplessly and picked up his instrument case. "Well, sir, I'd be delighted. But they sho is gonna be surprised to see ol' Malachi upstairs tonight!"

Nancy, with Malachi firmly in tow, led the way as the family moved back inside the hotel.

They were halfway across the lobby when one of the reporters glanced up. Diane Hollister's audience evaporated as quickly as mist on a sunny meadow. The media entourage rushed to encircle them. Questions were shouted out as they jostled one another in the rude, but not unusual manner of the press.

"Okay ... please ... *please* ... " Brad lifted his hands signaling a surrender of sorts. "If you'll be quiet for a moment, I'd like to say something. Something very important that you will all want to hear."

The din of voices fell silent as Brad stepped forward. Grace kept her arms around the children, spying as she did, Ellie and Sandra, along with Harold, standing by the entrance to Windows. And out of the corner of her eye she saw Maggie and the Cains walking toward them along the perimeter of the lobby.

"At least, it's important to us," Brad continued, "though I doubt that it will do anything for your storylines tonight. As you can well imagine, it's been a very long week for our family. We've already shared that with you earlier today. At that time, I mentioned that someone is filling in for me again at our church on Sunday. We're taking a few days to rest and get reacquainted as a family before returning home. And that's really all I have to tell you.

"The only other thing is: This coming Wednesday, Grace is going back to Georgia State University. We've been in touch with the Dean today, and I'm proud to say that Grace will be joining the other graduates to receive her Master's degree; one that was earned with high honors, seven years ago."

The company of reporters paused in their scribbling, looking up at Grace to see her face flushed with pleased embarrassment. There was a chorus of "All right," "Congratulations, Grace," and "Way to go!"

"We're pleased that the University will also confer degrees posthumously on Ilene Hunter and Bonnie Jo Senter, my fiancé's former roommates at GSU. Grace has recently spoken to each of their families, and they will be present for this long overdue occasion."

The group of reporters received this announcement without comment. What more could be added that would ameliorate the tragedy that had been carried so long in the hearts of parents deprived of sharing in the real successes of their children, obliterated forever by one brutal act.

"After that," Brad said, "we're going to Atlanta to pay our respects to Grace's mother, who is buried there. Due to circumstances forced upon her by others, Grace has never been able to visit her mother's resting place until now. And, best of all, in September, Grace and I are going to be married. You're all so tenacious, I'm telling you this because I know that somehow you'll find out anyway."

Laughter rippled through the press corps. They liked this handsome, amiable preacher whose candor and personality had proven throughout the day to be refreshingly open and forthright.

"So, if you'll excuse us, we're going to have dinner right over there," Brad said, pointing toward the hotel restaurant, *Windows.* "We want to spend a quiet evening with our friends—including Malachi, here. Some of you may know that you can often find Malachi playing downstairs on River Street. Grace tells me that he's a fine musician, and I do love a good horn.

"Maybe later we'll talk Malachi into playing for us. I saw a piano while passing by the bar this morning. You're welcome to join us there later, if you'd like. We're not a drinking family, but I think they'll work something out so that David and Nancy can come in—maybe if we sit next to the entrance and promise not to get liquored up."

More laughter.

"That's it. We're not answering any more questions or giving any interviews. None at all. So, file your stories now and join us later, if you wish—but if you do, come as friends. Leave your cameras and pencils in your rooms. Thank you, all."

They passed through the group to where Ellie, Sandra, Maggie, the Cains, Diane, and Harold stood waiting. There were welcome hugs, and Ellie, Harold, and the Cains were introduced to Malachi. Then the Windows' restaurant hostess led them to tables that had been drawn together in the far corner next to windows that looked out onto the Savannah River.

93

When dinner was over, they walked next door to MD's and gathered around the piano. A couple of the reporters sat on bar stools a few meters away, nursing their drinks and taking in the proceedings. They were joined by several of MD's curious customers. Grace watched as Malachi, dressed in second-hand clothes, his face stubbly, and with more streaks of gray than black in his hair, stood next to the piano fingering his trumpet.

He nodded to the man who had earlier been entertaining MD's customers at the keyboard, then smiled at Grace and the rest of his impromptu audience. Grace stood with Brad on one side and Maggie on the other. Her hands rested lightly on Nancy's shoulders. David had managed to squeeze in between his father and Harold. Both youngsters were watching with wide-eyed anticipation. This was a new experience.

Malachi lifted the instrument and began to play ... sweet ... smooth ... the pianist improvising ... the notes and chords mingling in the manner loved by all true jazz and blues aficionados.

The small crowd looked on with growing admiration, nudging one another, nodding their approval at the sound of the old man's trumpet ringing clear and clean.

Grace leaned over to Brad.

"Have you ever heard anything more pure … more beautiful than that?"

The old man continued to make musical poetry with his horn. He had been good on the street, but somehow Grace thought him even better here. It was as though he had been lifted to a higher plane, a new level of musical existence. Perhaps one that he'd known somewhere before. She made a mental note to ask him more about his past. A warm, contented feeling seemed to wrap around all those who had gathered to listen.

Grace looked around her, smiling at John and Esther Cain, two among all those gathered who truly understood what she was feeling, what she'd been through. They had stayed over in Savannah in order to spend time with Brad and Grace, to counsel and confide and encourage them from their own life experience. They looked at Scripture together. They spent hours discussing what had interrupted Grace's life so tragically, and how it had transformed them all as a result.

How different it all seems from the last time I was here … in this room … Her eyes moistened with mental images of three young women standing near the window overlooking the river while the old man climbed a musical scale to touch the pinnacle of his song, a haunting refrain, like a summer's rain falling lightly over her soul.

She drew Nancy close and glanced over at Maggie.

Maggie nodded, a knowing smile on her face.

Then she turned her attention back to the song. Grace wanted to remember this always. It was too precious a memory—an almost sacred moment—as Malachi Samuel Woodling and his song were reborn in their presence.

He lingered on the last note as MD's patrons broke out in spontaneous applause. They moved in closer to the others.

"That was wonderful!" someone shouted. "Give us another."

"What's your name again?" a reporter asked. "Malachi?"

"Say, aren't you the guy that plays down on River Street? How come you're not up here every night?"

Grace waved her hands, signaling for silence.

"This is our friend, Malachi Samuel Woodling, and yes, he does play downstairs on River Street almost every evening."

"Well, with that kind of talent, you should be up here, Malachi," another one of MD's customers called out. "You're the best kept secret in Savannah!"

There was a chorus of agreement from the rest of the group.

"Not any more," declared Grace. "You all have heard him now. Malachi is no longer Savannah's best kept secret." Turning to Brad, she took his hand and smiled at their children, friends, and the strangers standing nearby.

"And neither am I," she said softly, yet clear enough for everyone to hear. "Neither am I."

Made in the USA
Charleston, SC
15 April 2013